Novelist, broadcaster, [...] was born in Ireland. [...] James Joyce, John Betje[...] European Middle Ages [...] has lived in Britain for [...] where he broadcasts frequently on BBC Radio and Television and on the Sky networks. *Desire and Pursuit* is his fifth full-length novel.

'Two first-person narratives twisted together into a fat plait of a story. I kept turning the pages.' *Independent*

'Powerfully realized ... telling parallels between marital cruelty and sectarian violence.' *The Times*

'Full of big, fat ideas, astute observations on Irish snobbery and searing descriptions of Ireland in the 1970s, all underscored with sharp psychological touches. The ideas and characters seem to hang around the brain a lot longer than you might expect.' *Sunday Times*

'A fast-moving story, embellished with such incident that it seems unimaginable that the next page could yield even more shocks.' *Irish Independent*

'Complex, sharply observed. There is a magnificent twist in the tail, which brings the story rushing to a satisfying ending.' *Irish Times*

'Has the poet's eye for an arresting image, as well as a clear understanding of the psychology of loneliness, of fear, of jealousy.' *Magill Magazine*

FRANK DELANEY

Desire and Pursuit

HarperCollins*Publishers*

HarperCollins*Publishers*
77–85 Fulham Palace Road,
Hammersmith, London W6 8JB

Special overseas edition 1999
1 3 5 7 9 8 6 4 2

First published in Great Britain by
HarperCollins*Publishers* 1998

This novel is entirely a work of fiction. The names,
characters and incidents portrayed in it are the work of the
author's imagination. Any resemblance to actual persons,
living or dead, events or localities is entirely coincidental.

ISBN 0 00 651346 8

Typeset in Sabon by
Palimpsest Book Production Limited,
Polmont, Stirlingshire

Printed and bound in Great Britain by
Caledonian International Book Manufacturing Ltd, Glasgow

For Patricia Parkin

What they undertook to do
They brought to pass;
All things hang like a drop of dew
Upon a blade of grass.

WILLIAM BUTLER YEATS 1865–1939

Part One

1

The woman I crave, as the earth needs the sun, does not know I exist. But I need and want her. I saw her for the first and only time a week ago, on the day she married another man, and I mean to love her, sickness and health, richer, poorer, to have and to hold. She does not know this; she has never met me, may not even have observed me staring at her as she gazed out on the mountains.

I hope not to be rendered distraught by this longing for her; I hope not to mope, nor lose sleep. My work will proceed, I will continue to eat well and I hope to experience long periods of calm, but beneath my surface this passion for her has reared and bucked since the moment I looked at her lovely, grave face.

We know that far beneath the earth there are rivers roaring torrentially, rivers fiercer than anything we have seen above ground; if they ever surface, they will inundate us; the Amazon, the Ganges will be as streams. For most of the past week I have managed to keep my – exceptional – feelings underground. I must control them, I must, because if they break the surface my life will drown; I, and I alone, know this. Indeed, they have already threatened to submerge me; twice this week I have been unable to work, able only to walk – for miles and miles and miles. People found a taxi to take me back here to my hotel, exhausted, where the hall porter was kind enough to escort me in the lift to my room and ask if I were all right. Whatever their violent drawbacks, the people of this country have a natural kindness.

Has my passion taken all its thrust from my first glimpse of her; or from the turbulence of the events I have just been through? January snarled, a terrible month of killings and injustice, and it continues; last Wednesday, the day I saw her, was February the ninth, a day of arms finds and robberies; and yesterday we had bombs again.

Today it rains, but she was a sunshine bride; her wedding day was what they call in Ireland a 'pet day', meaning that the sun shone unseasonably warm, more like May. I have never kept a journal before, but now I need to; I have no other means of holding her image to me, until such time as I hold her in my arms, lie with her by my side.

2

My name is Ann Martin. That is the name I think of as mine. That is the name Life affixed to me. And it is the name I was crucified on. Born Ann Elizabeth Halpin. Ann was the name of my father's mother, Elizabeth was my mother's mother. That is the custom. My mother, as the oldest child, has her grandmother's name. My father has his grandfather's.

I suppose their parents were named in the same way, and their grandparents – so that my great-great-grandmother bears the first name of my great-great-great-great-grandmother and the second name of my great-grandfather's mother, and my great-great-great-great-grandfather bears the first name of my great-great-great-great . . .Well, so it goes . . .

February 1972, sun shining, me in a cream dress, tears inside me. Looking out on the mountains and wondering how in the name of God am I going to get myself out of this. Married, not wanting to be. A man surnamed Martin and I took his name, Ann Martin. Because that is the custom, too, you take your husband's name, it doesn't matter what kind of man. He was – is – called Joey but I gave him several other names, private names, names he never heard and would not like. So downcast that day I did not buy one scrap of new underwear. Only the dress was new. And the hat. I actually wore my

13

oldest knickers. Rebellion, I suppose, although I don't remember having that thought at the time.

That day often comes back to me. Lovely mountains, heavy heart. The thing we know least in life is what we do to ourselves.

Joey Martin worked for my father. Joss Halpin was a very successful on-course bookmaker – *Halpin's: We're the Best Bet!*

'Ah, you're Joss's daughter, are you?' That's what I grew up hearing. 'Jaysus, he's after gettin' enough of my money!' Smile at the joke, I'd say to myself, if joke it was.

One flat-racing season when I was three, we became very rich and we moved a few miles to Grennanstown House. I had fields and an old graveyard to roam in and the top landing of the house all to myself. Now I know that was the moment we joined the nouveaux riches. 'Nooves' they're called in Ireland and many people hate them.

The 'Nooves' flaunt their money. Use it to buy what they are not born to, nor inherit. They often try to give the way they speak the same flash they give their clothes and they sound droll. And they're desperate to learn what they can about the world into which they wish they were born. I longed for the day when Lucy O'Connor might come and announce to my mother with her well-known look of triumph, 'Moya, you'll never guess! I bought fourteen great pictures, Moya, all oil paintings' – and they would turn out to be the Stations of the Cross!

I was an only child. What was I like? Anxious. A bit talkative. Touchy. And I was a leggy child. But something worried me from very early. I felt we were something that I did not like. My feelings rule my life. Some bad kind of air hung around us, and it made me uncomfortable.

14

I think a lot of it rose from the way Mother hid behind herself. She pretended to be what she wanted to be, not what she was. So although she was as much on the make as he was, she looked down on my father. He irritated her decorum. Each morning, my father came to the kitchen, took a teacup off a hook, filled it with hot water and used it for his shaving mug. She hated that. My heart used to worry for him. No matter how many shaving mugs and leather toiletry cases Mother bought him, that's what he did at home every morning of his life. A teacup full of hot water. If Mother was out of the kitchen I'd pour it for him.

He was six feet four and a half inches tall. He's slightly stooped now, but he's still as thin as a cigarette. She never trained him to wear a dressing-gown. He still arrived for breakfast in his vest and trousers and braces.

Always that gap, between what he came from and where she wanted to be. When they travelled anywhere, she forced meekness on him, and manners. I often watched his confusion. I wish I had spoken up for him. Was I afraid of falling into that gap too? She bought all his clothes. In restaurants she ordered food for him that he did not have to cut with a knife and fork. But he was a steak-and-onions man, a bacon-and-cabbage man.

He told me once, he couldn't drink a cup of tea near her without being afraid he'd spill it. At home he drank out of a mug, with both hands.

Which of them am I like? Oh, God, I don't know. I ask myself that every day. I've no answer. Or I'm afraid of the answer.

I'm not as hard as she was. Not hail-fellow-well-met de luxe as my father was in those days. He had an easy word for everyone, probably because she made him feel so uncomfortable. As a little girl by his side I often

15

squirmed a bit while he moved from person to person. He had a patter made up of homilies, observations and devices. 'There you have it. As round as a hoop,' he would summarize. Or, 'Ah, what's meant for you never goes past you.'

Too many things to too many men. Blather and laughs. There's a tawny dog outside the window now, tearing round in circles like an innocent fool. My father had a bit of that in him.

He tried to buy things for Grennanstown – furniture, old silver, paintings – but he didn't know the first thing about them. 'Joss,' she'd say to him, 'an elephant's foot, even if it has a silver rim on it, is still an elephant's foot.' Her voice could slit you.

Children can do little when they're embarrassed. The worst thing was that I knew he was doing it to raise himself in her eyes. She stopped him doing it and did all the buying herself. If he did break out and bring home something like a pianola or a stuffed fish, she found out where he had bought it and sent it back. Awful, the hurt in his eyes looking at the empty space.

I know why she did it. She did it because the only thing Mother ever cared about was what people thought of her.

Her other method-of-life was to spend his money. She was a shopping machine. Boxes and bags and bags and boxes. Pink stripes, brown paper, blue cardboard, boxes with fancy writing. Maybe she did it to quell the feeling of discomfort he gave her. But I think her vulgarity was worse than his. When I try to remember all these things to write them down, some thoughts come as clear as day, and some kind of swim towards me.

I find it odd to reflect on her so calmly after all that has happened. One of the things I now think is that she

16

was slowly overpowered by having so much money. She lost herself.

A word I often dwell on in relation to Mother is the word 'price'. Whenever she paid a price, she exacted one. The price she paid came in people. She had to mix with men of red faces and flatulence, and women with accents as flat as a pancake. In other words my father's society. And she covered it well. She went with his friends to Aintree, and Cheltenham, to Fairyhouse for the Irish Grand National, and Epsom for the Derby, and Ascot for the Gold Cup.

The price she exacted came in those bags and boxes. For every common woman she had to travel with she got a Dior dress and for every beery man with bad breath she bought what she called 'a little bit of Chanel'. Mother quite simply believed that men were put on earth to pay for everything. She didn't realize that this revealed the very vulgarity she tried to conceal. I think that the common side of her had a wild power that burst out through her pores unstoppably. But to see her and hear her was to think her, at first glance anyway, something of a lady. As Richard would say, 'No way, Doll.' Because the loud women and belching men were no coarser than Mother's own soul.

Things didn't always work for her. One Sunday when I was about five, my father's father came on a visit to Grennanstown House. The afternoon was like a play on a stage. Gravel crunching. My patent shoes catching the sunlight. Leaves everywhere on the trees. My shoulder blades warm from the sun. Granddad's hard hand on my hair. Mother standing at the door looking very uncomfortable. I realize now that the old people in our family disregarded her control, which must be why we rarely saw them.

17

My father looked just like his father, same angles to his body. Granddad Halpin walked into every room on the ground floor and tapped all the walls and all the doors. I followed him, looking up, watching. The excitement of him! Nobody was going to tell him what not to do or say. Mother walked behind him anxious as a bat and my father laughed all the time.

'I s'pose,' said my grandfather, rapping the wall of the drawing-room, 'Early Mist paid for this.' He tapped everything he passed. 'Christ, aye. Early Mist. A great, strong shagger of a horse.'

Early Mist, trained a few miles away, the first of Vincent O'Brien's three-in-a-row Grand Nationals.

In the small drawing-room, Granddad stopped and laughed.

'Christ, Moya, Royal Tan did this, didn't he? Wasn't he shorter odds? Joss, he came in, what was he, fifteen to one?'

Even at that age I could tell what was coming. My father whispered to me, 'He's going for the treble.'

'Ha-Ha! Well, shite itself!' chuckled my grandfather in the dining-room, at the long mahogany table, the candelabra, the silver epergne. 'Quare Times, no doubt. Three-in-a-row. You must be prayin' to him – "St Vincent O'Brien"? Three-in-a-row! Ha, shite itself! Moya girl, you'll have to have his name carved into that table. "St Vincent O'Brien", Christ, aye! 'Tis Quare Times you'll have in here with some of the people who'll be eating and drinking here, I'd say.'

He and my father laughed and laughed. I joined in, a child does, and Mother shoved me from the room so hard that I was frightened. She so rarely showed anger towards me in those early days.

Sometimes now, when I remember Grennanstown

House without too much pain, I laugh at our three Grand-National-Winner rooms. My grandfather put anger and confusion into Mother's cold, clear eye. Of course, Nooves hate being reminded of whence they came. I got freckles on my arms that day and I loved them, never tried to rub them off. I got a moss stain on my white socks from sitting on the wall of the grave-yard. There was a song going round my head that people were singing, 'Chick-a-boom, chick-a-rack, chick-a-boom, chick-a-rack, chick-a-boom, chick-a-rack she's singing. Her shoes paddy-whack in the front and the back and her yellow pigtail swinging' . . . At least that's what I think the words were. The dog outside the window has stopped chasing his tail and he's asleep in the sun.

3

Two armed robberies happened in Dublin today; I should have kept a record of how many I have reported. Frost tonight; I can see the stars and they shine so brilliantly that the streetlights outside the hotel window do not mask them. If I objectify the story of how I saw her, perhaps I can begin to understand her impact upon me.

I have been asking myself why I turned my head at that precise moment. She was standing there, alone, directly by the door of the dining-room, gazing out at the mountains. Had she seemed a vain woman I would have suspected her of posing in front of me, because I had a perfect view of her face and her body as she stood in a pool of sunlight. Unlike the conventional bride one sees if one happens on a wedding, she did not carry flowers; she held her hands folded at her waist like a Madonna.

She turned to look at me, held my eyes for longer than perhaps a bride should, and frowned, but although I want to insist to myself that she saw me, I know that she did not register me; she was preoccupied, and nothing firm appeared in her eyes. The 'V' of her frown lifted her eyebrows; her fair hair had been built high on her head; she wore a long cream dress. As the days pass I become not merely persuaded but convinced that this is the most arresting woman I have ever seen.

Tonight, after these days of thought and desire, I attribute all kinds of benign chance to the fact that I saw her; after all I had never been in that hotel before, never in that countryside. I was passing through, returning to Dublin from an assignment in Cork, where overnight the police had found a cache of arms and ammunition – not an unusual occurrence, but the Editor wanted a think-piece to reinforce his view that deep beneath the surface of the South's culture lay a true and deep support for the IRA.

Caches of arms seem to have become my speciality; they are metaphors, these sacking-and-polythene mounds, little lethal tumuli; I have now been at two unwrappings. In this country where a find has traditionally been a beautiful penannular brooch or a chalice, they now unearth Armalite rifles, and decisive handguns, and boxes of bullets and shells.

This tidal wave of emotion: what shall I do about it? Nothing like it has confronted me before: I have never spent a week like the past one; I cannot concentrate.

At lunch time, still bleary from the four a.m. rise, I saw near the foot of some mountains the inviting sign, Kilnoran Lodge. I took a window table in the empty dining-room and asked for a sherry.

It was late for lunch, almost two o'clock, and in the foyer outside the dining-room door wedding revellers moved from the bar towards their private room. I glanced at them with no great interest, then returned to my bundle of newspapers and all fell quiet in the otherwise empty dining-room – and, as a song might say, suddenly I looked again and suddenly she was there.

My good manners vanished – I stared; and I turned further in her direction and continued to stare so intensely that I cannot believe she did not feel the heat radiating

21

from my eyes. I had an impression of great wistfulness in her; I know I did not imagine that wistfulness.

A man materialized and spoke to her; as she nodded she stepped a fraction away from him, became more self-contained, composed. I felt certain he was her husband – he took a proprietorial attitude with her; a big man with heavy shoulders, I didn't like that he had the quick walk of the highly intelligent. For a moment she seemed oblivious; then she walked with him towards the wedding-room, a person apart from her surroundings.

The waiter hiked a thumb towards the bridal couple.

'Heh, sir, I'd say there'll be nothing new there bar the breakfast.'

That, apparently, is an old and crude saying among country people to indicate that everyone knows the bride is pregnant, i.e., that the couple have already slept together, therefore the honeymoon will contain no novelty. Today, seventy years into the century, sex-before-marriage remains the great prurience of Ireland. The old have fears of the young's unbridlednesses. This is a morality more practical than spiritual: the old fear illegitimate children's claims upon farms and inheritances. But there is a revolution on the way, and as contraception becomes a fierce debate the younger women have grown freer.

'Oh, aye, sir. Nothing new. Bar the breakfast. Did yeh enjoy yer steak?'

The waiter walked away and I felt myself short of breath, as I have been many times this week.

Why has this passion struck at this time in my life? I will be forty this coming June. My age makes me melancholy, it divides me – not yet old enough, and yet a touch too old. I am too young, almost, to be taken seriously by the older sub-editors, far too old to be hailed as a young

22

tiger by the cub reporters. In addition, I do not look as I wish to: my face is not grizzled and lived-in – as it would be, I feel, had I covered Korea, Vietnam, some such fierce and concentrated theatre instead of this peacetime war.

I think I must be reaching for some sort of explanation to myself of my own life. Perhaps that is the purpose of this strange woman – to make me concentrate on the single, central effort in which I have failed, that is, to order my life. Internally, therefore, I have much food for thought – and externally I have much stimulation. I move among curious people, curious in both the original and colloquial senses – inquisitive and unusual. Every virtue here dances cheek-to-cheek with a corresponding vice. A hotel will show the warmest hospitality, and then jack up its prices if it thinks a company is paying your bill. A woman will kiss a man passionately in secret and then tell her husband to threaten him; one of my colleagues has had that happen to him twice. He also reports that as the women race into bed with him, they murmur that they will have to go to confession on Saturday.

The national warmth extends principally to strangers, and burns brilliantly – for a short time. A natural courtesy is offset by an inability to be thankful. They kill their fellow islanders in the name of peace and unity. A most hospitable people, they rip conviviality's memory apart. On my first trip to this country I stood speaking to some soldiers at an army checkpoint on the Border. Three yards away, the young Ulsterman who had conducted me there, a Northern Ireland Office PR man with whom I had got drunk the night before, was shot through the throat by a sniper and his life ended in a necklace of red bloody froth around his neck.

I have to keep reminding myself that this is a foreign country. They may speak the same language as us, they

23

may have social and cultural recognizabilities, but in mind and spirit the Irish might as well be Venusians. Now I have fallen blindly in love with one of their women.

Why, oh why? This is like being drawn into a local war. On several occasions this past few days I have felt the strange combination of elation and near-revulsion and fear that soldiers talk about.

I ask myself another question: has this passion come to my life because of – and has it taken fuel from – heightened awareness? In the last month, I have witnessed, tried to describe and make sense of atrocious events. A truck full of fertilizer and nitro-glycerine sucked the air from the sky one lunch time in Belfast; sixty people lay injured, some disfigured forever, and they shrieked and bled into the dust. The air compression that a car-bomb causes leaves behind an indescribable disquiet; my neck muscles froze.

On Belfast Lough three weeks ago, hilarity took over when seven men, some bearded, all passionate Republicans, escaped from a prison ship. They swam like cold-water sharks to the shore, hijacked a bus and drove home to their suburb – where a lavish reception party had already gathered, meaning that everybody in their neighbourhood knew when to expect them.

Two weeks ago, in the west of the province, marchers for civil rights and against internment without trial were beaten into the sea by the First Paratroop Regiment. Next day came Londonderry: another protest march, another paratroop regiment, thirteen people shot dead during what the Irish are now calling 'Bloody' Sunday – the army's running feet, the officers' shouted commands and the death-rattle of the soldiers opening fire; then came the crouching priest and his white handkerchief

24

which has become a symbol for all that takes place on this island where peace evades definition.

I was not there – but two days later I watched in silence as a marching, carnival protest first besieged and then burned to the ground our embassy in Dublin. Then came my journey to Cork, and six policemen hauled rocket launchers and self-loading rifles from the mire of a pigsty on a lovely farm by a lake. The Editor has suggested that I should keep a diary; will this do?

My disinterest breaks down too often for my liking. The 'war', if such it is, seems to be getting closer to me – or is it that everything becomes personal here? Last evening, I rang the doorbell of an IRA man recently released from jail to ask for an interview and his wife threw a pan of boiling water towards my face. She missed, then apologized, saying she thought I was someone else.

4

I never want to be like Mother. She never had a relationship that she did not control. Mother always wanted me for herself. Is that why I destroyed her? She nearly destroyed me. Those days, those young ambitions. I miss them. I don't have them now. They were never satisfied anyway. Mother stopped that. Am I a better human being because she did? Who knows? I didn't get what I wanted then, she stopped me. A habit of being stopped is hard to break.

Highly intelligent, that was what everybody said about me. So why merely to the local Mercy Convent Primary School, whose Secondary I moved to when I was ten? No exotic boarding school for me, no foreign travel during summer holidays.

I felt wistful when I met local girls who boarded. Haughty they were, from faraway, spicy boarding schools – Killiney, Rathnew. How I wanted to go to such schools. I would play lacrosse. And sit up late chatting by the light of a torch. At least I had comics from Falveys shop to tell me what their lives must be like. Midnight feasts and conspiracies. Nothing like that for me.

My father thought me a genius.

'Moya, we done great havin' her, didn't we?' he often said proudly. And to me, 'Wasn't it the great gooseberry bush you were foaled under?'

26

That's what I mean about confused. If you confuse your euphemisms you have no chance. But my hopeless father thought the stork had a sire and a dam. My dear father; I love him still.

I always came top of the class. This he loved.

'I'll have you working out cross-trebles any day soon,' he would say.

I winced. For him it was a great compliment. He most admired the prodigies who dangled odds-on each-way accumulators and ante-post cross-trebles in front of him daily. Jerry Hogan was his Einstein. Jerry Hogan could work out the likely payout on a five-way, each-way or place-only seven-to-four-on accumulator. Jerry Hogan smelt of urine. He had a coat that stood by itself when he took it off. If he ever did. Which we all doubted.

'He'll have to have a surgical operation', said my father, 'to diverge him outa that coat.'

I still find that endearing in my father, his misuse of words. My mother liked it less. She was once most embarrassed when, at a dinner-table in Grennanstown, my father wondered about these spies who were 'always defecating to the Russians'.

I see myself now in that house at that age. Watching everything. Fighting off embarrassment. Slipping from room to room. Washing myself often. I'm fond of that girl. She was sharp-eyed and awkward.

The schooldays just slid by. We wore royal blue and navy blue uniforms, with white stockings. We had hours of reciting, learning poems and history by rote. The teachers reminded us to pray for particular nuns on their feast-days. For confirmations or Reverend Mother's feast-day we wore white gloves. I still have mine.

It was all as ordinary as that. We were well drilled in the basics. The school had competent nuns and better lay teachers. Anyway, in a school of farmers' daughters and the children of small-town merchants what could you expect?

But I had daydreams. I wanted desperately to become respectable. We weren't respectable – I knew that. It was a most difficult feeling. None of Mother's fine possessions could ever make us respectable – I knew that also.

I hoped schooling would make me respectable. Music would do it, and Etiquette and French. At school what I got was Algebra and Book-keeping and Geography and Domestic Economy. With a little Elocution, some rudimentary Deportment and a heavy emphasis on being a nun or a wife. I think I knew then that I would have to become respectable all by myself. So I alerted myself to try and discover how respectable people lived.

In the earliest days, I loved going home from school. I ran to the house with excitement. Janey the housekeeper was safe and lovely to be with. She was mordant and affectionate.

'Janey, what is so-and-so like?' I would ask her of someone I had seen at Mass.

'Lovey-girl, they have to comb his own hair for him he's so lazy.'

Janey had cures. My father had a bad-tempered horse and Janey insisted he put 'lashings of parsley' in the feed. When the horse threw someone again, Janey said they gave him the parsley at the wrong time of the day. Mother declined Janey's cure for my whooping cough. It was based on what was left of a rabbit after a ferret had fed on it.

Janey made me small apple tarts for myself alone and in the summer something special – a blackcurrant tart from the lone little bush outside her own cottage door.

It took the bush's entire crop: 'They'll grow again next year, lovey-girl.'

It was Janey who said of Joey, 'He'd promise you an elephant and all you'd get is a mouse.' Then added darkly, 'Or in his case, a rat.' I loved Janey.

Above all I loved Mother. I loved to look at her. I touched her clothes. It delighted me to hear her speak. When she wasn't looking, I imitated her walk. Everywhere she moved around the house I followed her.

When she went out, I moved to the window an hour or two before she was due to return. I waited for her. I wanted to tell her how fond of her I was. Such fears I had then. I dreaded that she would never return, that she would die. If that happened, I would drown in my own tears like my friend *Alice in Wonderland*.

When I was six Janey showed me how to make tea. Mother loved tea. She also loved tinned pears, and she loved silk stockings. When I was seven I sent Janey down the town with money I had saved. She bought a large can of KP tinned pears and a pair of thirty-gauge fifteen-denier nylons by Kayser Bondor. It was Mother's birthday and she received my gifts so warmly I glowed for days.

There was a day we had together that I think of as 'Tramore'. I used to think it one of the best days of my life. My father went to the races, and Mother took me to the beach. We sat on the sand. I ran in the waves wearing only my knickers and although Mother did not join in, she laughed as I rarely saw her do again.

When I came out she dried me and we ate the sandwiches made by Janey. Mother began to tell me about her own childhood. I leaned against her and she talked on. Later, we walked to the ice-cream café with her arm around my shoulder. People smiled at us; they perceived our closeness. Sometimes now, especially if I have the glow of a drink or two on me, I remember that day.

Odd thing – Mother gave me some of the best conversations I have ever had in my life. I can remember settling into them as into a favourite chair. She told me about her grandparent Beresfords and her own parents. Mother knew how everybody's children got their names. She knew how some men died in wars, why certain marriages were formed.

I heard about her training. She had nursed rich patients. Some doctors had admired her. One hoped to marry her but, she said, he had a nervous tic that made her think he was always winking at her.

When she sat at her dressing-table, getting ready to go out, I studied her. I might have been watching a magician, or an actress in a dressing-room. First, the hair; she brushed and brushed. Then she arranged it with hidden clips so that it stayed tight to the sides of her head but never looked pinned.

Next, a damp handkerchief to her eyebrows; stroke after stroke after stroke. Powder followed, matted delicately from Arabian Nights boxes. She put on her lipstick last, always strong red.

Then she walked around the room while she finished dressing. Finally the ritual of scent; usually she used a bottle with a little bladder of gold mesh.

I remember my own skin from those moments. I remember the down at the nape of Mother's neck that I could only see when the hairbrush lifted the short tresses. I remember the corner of the handkerchief dampened at the top of a bottle of cologne.

And I remember the slightly bulging flesh at her shoulder where her straps bit. That was the sight that made me feel closest to her and it was also the sight that gave me the first real worry about her. One night I asked Mother if the straps left marks or if they hurt and she gave me the first really cold look that I recall. Cross looks weren't too bad, every child gets them. Cold, though – that was awful.

For all our closeness I never managed to mention my awkward feelings. About why she and my father were always buying things. I often walked in that big front door and saw Mother showing Mrs O'Connor some new thing. It might have been a picture or a dress or a piece of silver. Mother always ended by saying what the price was. I hated that. They bought everything for the price, not for the looks. My father probably thought Rembrandt was the name of a horse.

Then I felt guilty about these feelings. Especially because Mother was so nice to me. Seemed to need me. Seemed to welcome our talks. Seemed to get closer. That loving closeness, it still stabs me. Right up to the age of fifteen, I used to rush home in order to see Mother. I longed to talk to her and listen to her. Indeed, we often mentioned Tramore.

'D'you remember that day we went to Tramore,' she would say. 'Your father was at the races and we went down the strand. To the shore. You ran in the waves.' And we would smile at each other.

When she turned so suddenly and utterly against me, I did not quite grasp it to begin with. Then I became bewildered, lost. She just switched off me. Turned off the tap. No more chats. No more friendliness. No more smiles.

5

I have rarely worked so hard: two more armed robberies in central Dublin and a bombed break-out from the holding cells at the courthouse in Green Street; copy filed every day, sometimes twice, three times a day; police and political briefings; backgrounders and off-the-record meetings.

March is coming in like a lion; the wind on the streets yesterday was exhilarating and the days are full of occurrences; I find it interesting that people here look so bewildered; they seem unable to make their minds up about the incidents they see and hear. Their race memory of the 'old days', or what some call 'the real Troubles', remains vivid and they feel both admiring of, and uneasy about, this new breed of gunman.

But from moment to moment my mind lights with the image of that glorious bride. I think I dreamed last night of the wedding party. They made a great deal of noise for a group so small; I ate lunch trying to catch a voice that I might identify as hers; how easily I can reach back and touch every moment of that day. Pretending sun-dazzle, I moved my chair so that I could see clearly across the foyer through the ajar door of the wedding reception.

The bride's face I could not quite see, although occasionally her shoulder moved into view, and some of her hair and her neck, but I had a clear view of the bridegroom and of a woman I took from a general family resemblance to be the bride's mother. The bridegroom and bride's mother talked to each other unceasingly, and he made her laugh often; they obviously had known each other a long time. Around here, I expect, these are not so much weddings as marriage alliances. Unusually for such a small gathering (although not perhaps unusually for Ireland) many of the people seemed extremely drunk.

I returned to the newspapers, looking for my own by-line (nothing levels the mind like the sinking ache of seeing one's copy cut) but I found I kept glancing at the wedding-room. The excuses one makes to one-self! Briefly I tried to attribute this sudden interest in a strange wedding to my journalistic role, to persuade myself that weddings have possibilities. Cataclysm visits weddings – isn't that well known? People behave violently out of character; they leave their long-standing partners for the sake of a sudden joust in an upstairs room; or they insult irretrievably guests who have long been dear friends – weddings are occasions when chaos and mayhem rampage barely beneath the surface. However, I failed to persuade myself that such a private occasion could possibly hold any interest for an English broadsheet readership!

The vision of the bride, still and grave, rushes back into my eyes. She was remarkable. I thought I might get another glimpse of her so I crossed the reception area and went to the lavatory. Enter the bridegroom. He stood beside me at the urinal where he exhaled massively, in a whistle, and nodded downwards towards his member.

'Himself's under starter's orders,' he chuckled aside to me, a complete stranger to him, and he zipped his flies with a cough and a shrug.

The Irish have this frightful gift of intimacy, yet he

33

forced a half-smile from me; then I walked a little behind him as he left the lavatories and saw him greeted by the woman for whom I now hunger. Her dress billowed a little in the breeze from the open door. They looked a fine couple, she very tall, he taller, she much more elegant than him – or is that my wishful imagination?

'Havin' a brandy, sir? Sure, you might as well. Throw the handle after the hatchet.' The invasive waiter sucked his teeth between sentences. And I am left with that tall vision in a cream dress; I must sound like a clichéd hack!

I am exhausted – and too moved to write in my journal. Nor can I go down to dinner because I have no clothes – they are still drying in some airing cupboard in the hotel. Today I got rained upon more than I ever have in my life: East Anglia tipped her big skies on my head. Dinner has arrived, and shows no promise of being attractive, a steak-and-chips job, and the hotel has thoughtfully supplied some little plastic sachets of tomato ketchup and brown sauce. The television works on only one channel. Welcome to Aldeburgh!

A story broke last week from the IRA that the army was playing down the number of military casualties, that more soldiers' coffins went back across the Irish Sea than Stormont or Whitehall admitted. It was a clever piece of propaganda, because the story could never be checked, a fact the original piece in *Republican News* pointed out, saying families had been given large cash payments to pretend sons had moved away or, at worst, had died in road accidents. It was my idea to come here, to follow a military funeral back to the soldier's home town; these huge, renowned skies have never seemed so sad. I like the North Sea, but I suspect myself for liking it so; I suspect that it increments my melancholy.

The town carries posters of Benjamin Britten's face; he lives nearby. I said to my photographer that the names of Britten's operas, *Peter Grimes*, *Albert Herring*, *Billy Budd* and *Owen Wingrave* sound like a homosexual darts team; he grunted and said nothing. I am putting this bottle of whiskey on my expenses; I deserve it. My father still has my record of *Gloriana*.

Private Eric Kelletts died in a booby-trap explosion at the barracks gate in Castlereagh. He had been in the province thirty-six hours and went to greet what he thought was the milk float. It was, but the 'milkman' asked if he could leave the keys briefly with Private Kelletts while he ran back down the road to pick up a box of butter he had dropped – he even pointed to it. Private Kelletts, from his photographs, was large and young, with cowlicked straw-coloured hair and a big grin; he supported Queens Park Rangers and had the blue-and-white scarf draped above his billet. In the army just under a year, he had one expertise: somewhere in East Anglia, in some pub or bunch of friends, he became a first-rate dominoes player and for his birthday his mother had sent him a new set of dominoes. The chaplain told me he placed the box, still gift-wrapped, in the soldier's coffin – lonely and innocent grave goods for the young man to play with in the next world.

After long negotiation with the army, who involved the chaplain and the soldier's family, I took the train to Belfast last night and joined the funeral this morning at the military service in Castlereagh. The chaplain gave a strong, quite moving sermon about young life not yet knowing its own purpose. More negotiations with the army; their PR man took me aside and suggested that I not mix too closely with the family when the private funeral took over; they had taken exception to some of the newspaper reports criticizing the soldier for lack of intelligence: by all accounts Private Kelletts had been quite sensitive regarding the question of brain cell distribution, and had a bad time in the army as the butt of Einstein jokes.

I rejected the PR advice and after the service found Mrs Kelletts, a surprisingly young woman; her son's eyes came from his mother – same eyebrows, same shape. She greeted me more sensitively than the army led me to expect; when I introduced myself, her only remark was, 'I'm very tired.'

I hate these situations; I have never been good at going to the doorstep and asking, 'Well, Mrs Snodgrass, how do you feel now that your son has been blown to bits?' The only fit way to handle such moments involves going straight to the emotions and I said to Mrs Kelletts, 'You're going to miss him.' She looked at me and – perhaps thinking I was an officer – said, 'Oh, sir.' That was all she said, 'Oh, sir,' and she said it over and over. A brother appeared and was about to get heavy until he saw that his mother took my presence easily. I explained to him what I wanted to do and he called over the father, a quiet man with grey face, hair, suit and shoes.

'I was at Arnhem,' the father said to me. 'I was with the gliders. I'd have been proud to die there, that was a war, D-Day was. Not this cowardice.'

'People say he was a very nice young man,' I said to the father; I was in.

They gave Private Kelletts a military aircraft from Aldergrove to Norwich after which the family took over the funeral. Our photographer met me at the coffee bar in the minuscule terminal; I had worked with him in Lebanon and he knew his stuff. At Norwich he told the local press he was waiting for Rod Stewart who was coming in later.

This job rollercoasts me, and this afternoon proved it. The funeral itself was poignant in the extreme; suddenly, Mrs Kelletts began to weep ferociously, a deep, uncontrolled sobbing that made me want to go over and put my arms around her – such journalistic objectivity! They held a brief service in the nonconformist church, at which a trendy minister talked about 'Eric's passions', which included Queens Park Rangers. Sixty or seventy people from the extended family stuck together as if held by glue. A relative (his uncle, it transpired) rose and described the manner of death in the most graphic detail; he had obviously been given the information by some misguided military counsellor. Then he called for the bloodiest revenge on the killers, the 'murdering bastards', and nobody attempted to remind him that he was in a house of prayer. The women wept louder and I have to confess that I drew near to tears myself.

A photograph of the young man, enlarged and in colour, taken in uniform on his last leave home, was then raised to the prayer table. Finally the young soldier's NCO spoke the most moving eulogy; he may not have known that he was doing so, but no Greek warrior was ever praise-sung so sweetly. He talked of the boy's innocence, his generosity with cigarettes or small loans – a quality, the corporal admitted, that had been exploited; he talked of Eric's natural kindness and his bewilderment at the death of comrades, the first time, said the NCO, that Eric realized people actually did get killed in the army. Nobody mentioned the filching of the dead soldier's pay packet from his locker.

At the graveyard, which is completely flat, with no hiding places, it rained and rained; again I offered my condolences and tried not to pry into the dreadful grief of the parents. His mother placed something else on top of the coffin and to my shame as a reporter I turned away because if I knew what it was, I would have felt compelled to report it and I wanted to give them some privacy from me. Behind me an incident was developing; some of the young soldier's local friends took exception to my photographer and began to hurl stones at him – although I feel we were discreet, followed the funeral at a considerable distance and I made no notes, did nothing overt. The photographer lost his camera and the police outside the gates did nothing to help us. When we got to the car every window was broken, every tyre slashed.

Which explains why I am in this hotel tonight; Ireland, it seems, is a moveable feast and yet I felt obliged – for reasons I cannot quite fathom – to report the funeral of a young soldier killed by a people who should be our greatest friends, our most loved and loving neighbours, upon whom we too have perpetrated the most awful injustices.

How can I ever explain these paradoxes to her, the woman of whom I think and think and think? Shall I ever discuss them with her? She may, for all I know, be a natural, family-born Republican – as so many in the South are.

I have had a new thought. Perhaps my sudden obsession has a root in self-preservation; perhaps I have fallen in love with this unknown woman in order to address, cope with, eradicate, the loneliness which dogs my life, which threatens it. People romanticize loneliness. Wrong: loneliness has no flair, no good humour, no grin; loneliness has no style, no reward; it weighs and nags like a debt; it troubles in an unseen way, like a rough and unpleasant skin complaint beneath the clothes, and like an alcoholic one can only face it by saying to oneself, 'I. Am. Lonely.' – or at least that is what I would do if I had the courage.

With this thought of loneliness comes a new worry: why have I chosen as an antidote someone I have seen only once, do not know and with whom I became obsessed on the day of her life when surely she stands at her most unattainable?

I think of that big innocent soldier with his straw-coloured hair and his cowlick and his football shirt.

6

Looked at myself this morning in the long mirror. The hair might need a bit of something soon, highlights maybe. Lucky to have it this way so long. The body looks OK. 'Hallo,' I say to it in my mind, and I stroke it. A sin, the nuns would say, to rub my hands down along my whole skin.

Nobody would ever know my poor body had such a history. It has a little fat here, a few creases there. But, good shape by and large. It has recovered and it looks nice. I'm wearing all black this morning, a shirt with quite a severe collar, and black trousers.

To this day I do not know what cost me Mother's sweet affections. Was it because we were both snobs? But – different standards? She valued possessions and status. I wanted (I liked to think) more thoughtful matter.

Sometimes I believe that it was my body alone did the damage. It was nice then, but I got ashamed of it. Mother envied it, I'm sure she did. That must be why I keep no photographs of myself when young. I only realized that fact when Richard asked to see some.

'None. I have none.'

'Where are they, Doll?' – his skin so black sometimes that it shines, even though he is quite light-skinned. And I hear him upstairs now, coughing, even his cough has an American accent. Where do the lines cross between 'loving' and being 'in love'? That is, for me, a serious question.

'There were some pictures. Mother had some.'

'Can I see them?'

'They're gone, Rich, they're all gone. I got rid of them. I couldn't stand the look of them, they're gone. Up in smoke.'

I had to tell him what I looked like. Such detail. Such questions. I wished I'd kept the photographs.

'Well – I had long hair like all the girls in the parish. Long hair, down to here. It was the thing, then. Mine was blonde. And I had sticky-out teeth a little, sucking my thumb. Well, you know that kind of thing anyway, that's universal.'

'These?' He traced my figure with both thumbs. I remember the afternoon vividly. We were sitting on the grass.

'My downfall.' I laughed, and looked down at my figure. But it was true. 'My bloody downfall, Rich.'

I did not tell him why. It feels so outlandish to believe that Mother envied me my figure. Feels true inside me, though. I've never envied any woman her figure, but I think if I was fat I might often be a little crazy with envy.

My figure caused the first true awkwardness between Mother and me. And, I think, the second, final one. I was fourteen, almost fifteen the first time. One damp morning I awoke with a bronchial difficulty. They pronounce it 'bronicle' around here. Dr Greene, a foolish old man, was one of my father's 'friends'. He asked my mother to stay while he examined me. Even then I found him distasteful. He was better at curing greyhounds.

He said, 'Moya, my nurse isn't here, she's on her

41

half-day. You were a nurse yourself, weren't you, and she's your daughter, so you'll stay, I s'pose.'

No word to me. No did I mind, or anything. He talked to Mother all the time over his shoulder while examining me. One question made me intervene.

'Has she started yet, Moya, h'm?'

I knew what he meant and quickly I said, 'Yes.' That was true and Mother knew it.

In the mirror behind me I saw Mother smile her little smile. She shook her head.

'We'll talk about that another day,' she said.

Their exchange excluded me. Old Greene coughed in acknowledgement.

At the end of his stethoscoping he looked straight at my figure.

'Grand girl, God bless her. Grand. Great form so young, Moya, eh? She's going to be a beauty, isn't she? She'll break hearts.'

The old drunk. He talked about me as if I were a filly.

Outside, Mother looked straight ahead, flinty and vehement. We walked down Hill Street. Black and red she was. Black in her mood, and anger had burnt red spots into her face. I supposed that she was angry at the old doctor's lack of ethics. Too much to hope that she might have been angered by her own lie. She actually shook her head at his question. She actually contradicted what I knew about my own body.

I began to wish for a different shape. I think it is deadly when you wish for something different but don't know what it should be like, especially when what you have is so good.

It got worse. One summer morning a year or so after that, I was dressing in my bedroom. I can still see in my mind the spiders' dew on the apple branches. Birds sang, thrushes and blackbirds. Our orchard that morning was like something out of King Arthur and the Knights of the Round Table, misty and golden.

Mother stopped by the door of my room. I was moving sleepily, wearing only the bottoms of my pyjamas. Vaguely among the drawers and shelves I would find a top to wear. She saw me standing between the mirror and the window. I turned and caught her staring at me. The sunlight trapped me.

I came down into the dining-room later. She looked up from breakfast.

'There you are. My darling girl.' She smiled. Then she said twice more, 'My darling girl.' And she rose and left the room.

When next I saw her about two hours later, she was turned into a pillar of ice. It was a mood I had never seen in her before, apart from that one cold glance at her dressing-table, apart from that flash of hard frost outside old Greene's surgery. I didn't know what had happened, I didn't know what I had done, and I felt disturbed and uneasy without knowing why.

The week after that, for my sixteenth birthday, she gave me money. Not her usual, thoughtfully chosen, feminine gift of beads or underwear or shoes. She gave me impersonal money. And she gave it impersonally. I found it on my dressing-table in an envelope with a note. No birthday card. The note said; 'Buy yourself something. M.'

No, 'dearest Ann', or, 'from your loving Mother'.

What in God's holy name had I done? I still don't know. If only I had a witness. If only someone would come to me and say, 'Listen. We always knew your mother was jealous of you.'

That was when Mother went into what I think of as her 'silences' towards me. Sometimes she cut me dead for two, three, four days. The silences did not occur every day, but even on 'good' days she kept a distance.

I tried to start conversations. No, not a word. At best I got a wall of monosyllables. And her face was a lantern of disapproval.

I was so bewildered I thought of asking my father if Mother was unwell. Over a few weeks I watched carefully to see if she was going to the doctor. Day after day I sat in my room in tears at her latest rebuff. She turned her head away if I asked a question.

That was the passive end of it. At the active end, she frowned at my clothes. Or she asked me to wear different shoes. Or, if I were going out, she'd ask me at the last minute to change my outfit completely. No argument, just a cold face and a dead voice. I felt as if I were being struck with rods of ice. Of course I realize now that silence and disapproval are exercises of power. They were the first of Mother's weapons.

Her next ploy was much more devastating. She put in place a system of disbelieving me. She cast doubt on most of the things I said. She gave an impression that I falsified, that what I said was, at the very least, unreliable. That was the mood she created.

God, the length of time it has taken me to believe myself!

I remember the first time it happened. During supper one night I said, 'I met Aideen Keane today. She's back from America.'

Mother looked at me. She tried to engage my father with her eyes and failed. Then she said, 'Now, Ann. You know perfectly well the Keanes haven't enough money

44

to send Aideen or any of them to Ballyporeen. Much less America.'

'But she was there, she showed me a bag she bought there, it had stars and stripes on it.'

'Ann – ' Mother left the sentence unfinished and reproached me with a cold and disappointed look. Next sentence: 'Why don't you go and write that English composition? It'll keep your imagination busy. Get Janey to bring you a cup of tea.'

All this hammered me. If I said anything with a third party present, Mother looked jauntily at the other person. A little amused lift to her eyebrow. A tiny shake of the head. It was worst of all if a boy called to see me, just to talk or take me to the pictures. Not that I found many boys interesting. But one or two away at good schools had read some of the books I liked.

A pattern developed. Breakfast conversation, both parents present: 'There's a party at the tennis club, is it all right if I go? David Casey is inviting me.'

'Bring him home sure, 'til we have a look at him. Is he Gerard Casey's son? He'll be well-heeled one day.' That was my father.

Mother: silence – or, while looking away, 'Make sure you give Janey your dress in plenty of time to iron it. Not at the last minute.'

David Casey would arrive, or John Cooney, or John Nagle, or Dermot Vaughan, or Ricky Kingston, or whoever: cheery boys. 'Oh, hallo, Mrs Halpin, how are you?'

'Hallo,' Mother would say from a distance, as if the boy had the smallpox.

Then came the unpleasant part, the killer questions.

'Is it true?' she always asked the relevant boy in front of me. 'Is there a party at the tennis club?'

Not only that, she openly got the boy's telephone

number. Then she rang his parents to check. She would murmur in her sociable way, 'Ann, I'm afraid, is at that imaginative stage . . .' I overheard her talking to Don Lacey's mother. 'We can't always quite, you know, rely on what she's saying.' It was the way she said 'rely' – she said it like, 're-*ly*'. It had a finality. I'd have preferred a knife-wound.

She hardened this disbelief of me and the things I said. She made it her version of morality.

'But is that true?' she would enquire. And then raise a doubting eyebrow to my father.

Or she would murmur with a chill, 'Ann, I don't think you should be making up things like that.'

'But it's true!' I would insist. Usually it was something perfectly harmless. A teacher went on holiday to Egypt. That was eccentric in those days, exotic. Mother refused to believe it.

She said, 'I'd have to see the tickets myself.'

A girl we knew got engaged a year after she left school. Mother said, 'Can we have a little less of your imagination, please?'

Her 'please' cut me down like a scythe.

What did I ever do to her? I did not know. I still do not know. My feelings were desperate. If I knew it would bring back her love, I would take my own life. I recall that illogical thought.

Survival became important to me. I became ill often. Periods brought dreadful pain, forced me to bed. Once a month I slept and recouped.

Then one day a woman at the races asked Mother, 'That refined girl, is she your daughter?'

I latched on to that remark. I hunted the word 'refined' in everything from sugar to oil. I tracked down its meaning for me.

46

'Refined'! It was like being shown a map. Of an escape route.

'Refined'! I read more poems than ever, and longer novels. I even read plays.

'Refined'! A road to destiny. No embarrassment. Being respected. Marriage to a man of taste. And ideas. That was my definition of 'refinement'. He would be a man who didn't make his money out of other people's frailties.

'Refined'! I clung to it, because by then I had more or less lost the power to take a decision for myself. I found it harder than ever to know what clothes to put on in the mornings.

It wasn't easy to cling to that little bit of hope – because I could hear Mother's reply to the woman who said it of me: 'We have to take Ann with a grain of salt, I'm afraid. Refinement and all.' And she chuckled.

Whenever I think I should miss her more than I do, I remind myself of the ice in that chuckle.

7

This morning began well, with a letter that opened, 'Dear Mr Hunter, I am pleased to inform you that . . .' Has the mystery bride changed my luck? Over a month has passed: thirty-five days to be precise and I have been feeling less alone; mornings have lost some of their difficulty; I am a trifle steadier and this brings me opportunities. Again, I put in a request last week for a long interview with the Prime Minister – whom they call 'Taoiseach', meaning 'Chieftain', but I can never pronounce it without making it sound like 'teashop'. All my previous requests had been turned down, and it has been almost three years since he spoke exclusively to a British national newspaper (not mine). Now their letter grants me the interview – but immediately.

So – today has been so busy and startling that I have had no time to dwell on emotional matters; tomorrow I drive to the empty fields along the Border in Armagh – but I continue to be fuelled and energized by the memory of her face.

I have found that many men in high office give the impression of being almost too good for the party animals around them. My interviewee, a former athlete, famous before politics, is a courteous man, charming even – but a politician is a politician is a politician.

The Editor briefed me. 'Ask yourself why he is giving the interview now.'

'Why, Charles, what's your view?' Only by asking him questions can one buy time from Charles to think.

'Well, I suppose he thinks that all British journalists double for MI5.' We laughed. 'I also think he wants soundings as to how his position is playing in London.'

'Charles, how could he think I might know such things?' More laughter.

'Be delicate, Christopher, more than usual. We don't need to rough him up and I suspect his position is not that of his party, but he can't say. Therefore he may need a "friend", so to speak. The occasional inspired leak may come your way if this runs well.'

'But what does he really want, Charles?'

The Editor produced one of his famous pauses: they cost the newspaper several hundreds of pounds if the correspondent is in Australia: then he delivered.

'He wants to do two things. He wants to put pressure on Heath to prorogue Stormont. And he wants to appear knowledgeable that Heath is about to do this. And don't forget – tomorrow is St Patrick's Day. He'll be playing to the American gallery.'

The Irish use of language and circumstance always arrests me. As we walked along the corridor the Government Information Officer said to me, 'He has a meeting at four, so if you don't make him late for that you can have a little longer.' Translation: 'Your appointment is scheduled for an hour from two forty-five to three forty-five and you can have until five to four if you promise to see that he is free by four.'

Were these not days of feminism and equality, I would argue that I need a wife. I cannot get my shirt collars to stay sitting down evenly and I am clumsy in matters such as socks and things, which leaves me slightly askew and unconfident before important meetings.

'Taoiseach, your appointment with Mr Christopher Hunter, whom you've met before . . .' and the very civil servant withdrew. The honour of seeing a Head of State always bucks me – and without officials present! I think – I fear – that I may seem a touch pompous when I describe these occasions; I must watch that; it gives offence to my colleagues.

We spent the first half-hour off the record. Taller than me, and younger than on television, he has the gift of bestowing comfort.

'Do you know my constituency at all?' he asked. 'You'd love the scenery. Do you fish?' He poured coffee and asked rhetorical questions, threw in some political anecdotes.

'In the last election I won the biggest majority ever achieved by an Irish parliamentarian, I doubled my previous majority. Fifty-six thousand votes. One of the candidates said to me when he was congratulating me, "You must have voted more than once yourself." That's Ireland for you!'

He offers a heady mixture, this deceptive man; a soft accent, in which he has recently made controversial and provocative statements and, in his office, exquisite china and Albinoni as background.

'Another constituent, a carpenter, he said to me, "Do you know what a parliament hinge is?" Do you know what a parliament hinge is, Mr Hunter, or I suppose you prefer to be called Christopher?'

I made a faraway noise.

'Apparently, a parliament hinge is a hinge of a kind that enables a door to fold back on itself. And this builder said to me, "And do you know why 'tis called a parliament hinge?" So I said to him, "Is it because the opposing sides face each other across the floor of the house of parliament?" Which I thought was a pretty good answer, wasn't it? A pretty good answer. And he said, "Not at all. It's because politicians are two-faced." That's what he said. To me, his parliamentary representative and, if I may say so, his Prime Minister.'

He laughed again, then he sobered and changed tack.

'Dreadful that Abercorn bomb. People having tea on a Saturday afternoon should not have their legs blown off. And that unfortunate woman, same age as my wife, the woman who had her two front teeth blown out: no other damage, just her front teeth. My secretary burst into tears when I read her that paragraph about them shopping for a wedding dress.' Distress floated into his eyes. 'Dreadful if that sort of thing happens. I mean to say, just because it happened in Belfast doesn't mean we don't feel it down here.'

'Here it comes,' I thought, 'here comes the positioning' – but, no.

'I mean to say,' he began.

That is his speech habit – *I mean to say*. He has liquid blue eyes and smokes a pipe.

'I mean to say, still off the record . . .'

She had come swarming into my head, and the eyes of my mind were full with her; her face and her presence like a dust-storm clouding my concentration. The uncanny happened: his next words picked up this great new passion of mine.

He continued. 'This is how the truth works here. I mean to say, a man thinks something and it is true for him. Or, I mean to say, it becomes true. Everything here is possibility. You, the English, you're too rational altogether. You can't understand our sense of possibility.

51

You can't understand us because we speak luxuriously, we make flowers of your language. We do it because it was forced upon us – therefore we took it and subverted it, used it like a weapon turned on its owners. I mean to say, we use it to speak dreams that we can make come true.'

Pulling at his pipe he said, 'I read your piece about the arms find in my constituency.'

I waited for a comment, but he made none, merely said, 'We'd better go on the record now, I suppose, or my handlers will be raising Cain. What do you want to know?' – and we began.

Charles proved right; the position I listened to had more to do with the Americans than Ulster. This man knows he has to walk a tightrope – condemn Republicans yet show emotional support for their aims; but he had long ago spread thick adhesive on his tightrope and he knew perfectly well he would get, barring Acts of God, a front-page lead tomorrow.

He gave me a perfunctory interview, repeating much of his party's known view that Ireland must one day be re-unified.

'This is all Europe's problem, now. We all joined at the same time, together. The first of January,' he said, 'that's going to be a historic date. So therefore we should have a European force, a kind of more local UN force, policing the place.'

By tomorrow, Whitehall and Westminster will ring with thunder – the very idea of an outside, international force policing part of the United Kingdom! A civil servant put his head round the door: 'All right there, Taoiseach? Anything you need?'

'A bigger majority, Dermot,' and they both smiled. 'We have that joke twice a day,' he said to me.

Then he dropped his bombshell (if I may use the term!).

'This is off the record,' he said, and I put down my notebook. 'There's something disturbing that has come up. I want you to meet someone.'

At which the door opened and the same civil servant, called Dermot, ushered in a tall priest, about six feet five with spectacles, one lens of darkened glass.

'This is Father Andy Coll,' said the Taoiseach. 'He has a bad story to tell you. It would be a great help to all of us interested in quelling violence if you keep this story to yourself. When you get concrete information you can have the exclusive. The "scoop",' he said exaggeratedly, with a smile.

Father Andy Coll speaks rapidly in a sharp Ulster accent. He claims he represents three distressed families from the Republican movement whose breadwinners have disappeared, each suspected of being an informer and therefore possibly executed by the Provisional IRA. But it is against the ethic, he says, of the Provisional IRA not to return bodies for Christian burial. What is needed is a respected and disinterested party (he uses strange, almost otherworldly language) to establish whether there have been secret burials and if possible to find the graves so that 'the relicts may observe the etiquette of mourning their deceased.'

I almost gave the irresponsible person's stock response: Why me?

The Taoiseach said, 'You can easily do it. All you have to tell your Editor is that you are on to something, but would rather stay your hand until further developments.'

With cautious interest I have accepted, and tomorrow I meet Father Andy Coll in Dundalk, the border town they are calling 'El Paso' at the moment. Should I be leaving a 'To Whom It May Concern' letter?!

As I leave Government Buildings (today has been very cold, with a low, weighty overcast) I decide to kill two birds by taking a short walk to clear my head and looking out for 'To Rent' or 'For Sale' notices. Ahead of me, walking towards me, smiling vividly comes *she*. I drop my gaze, take on breath, find courage to address her, lift my head – and then see that it is not she at all. Indeed, she looked quite different, but it didn't matter; I saw her there as clear and lovely as before.

Tonight I go to bed elated.

8

My hair blowing in the wind. A beach somewhere, and a handsome and tender man, soft kisses and long walks. With such harmless thoughts I fought sadness at sixteen.

As we get older are our daydreams fewer? I think women daydream less than men do. But I needed them then. I used to practise hugging – on myself. Arms tight around myself in bed. I was also hugging myself because I was generally terrified. A lot of people are afraid.

I was afraid all the time. What was going to become of me? I was terrified, to give one example, of being put on a crass path. In my last year at the Mercy Convent, plans had to be made.

I lost. Mother had put between us a distance that I could not bridge.

She said, 'Your father is right, you should do a Commerce degree.'

My legs shook. Tears seared my eyes.

'But I want to do Arts!'

'Now, we mustn't get above ourselves, Miss, must we? We mustn't imagine we're better than other people.' She turned away, gone again to another land.

I went to university. To Cork, not even to Dublin. To Commerce.

Decline. Decline. Decline. From the first day I declined.

I couldn't bring myself to wash my hair. It stayed under a long scarf. I couldn't do the student life. In the beginning I went out – and found myself unable to cope with the cheeriness. There was good fun around but I couldn't partake, I was too down, too miserable, too afraid.

One night in a pub, a man joined us unbidden, a broad man in a suit, wearing a tie with daisies. One of the girls knew him and we could not send him away. 'Hallo, girls, how's the form?' He spread himself across us. He lugged a fourth chair from the next table. He ignored our withdrawing from him.

'Ned, you've no sense of people's privacy,' said Anna, the fattest of us.

'I haven't, no, girls. An' anyhow what would nice doodley-doos like yourselves be doing being private in the first case? Who's this grand girl here, who're you now? You look like a lovely doodley-doo.' He punched me on the upper arm.

I laughed despite all.

'You and your doodley-doos, Ned,' said fat Anna. 'This is my flatmate, Ann. Ned, we've things to talk about. Girls' talk. D'you get the point, do you, Ned?'

Naturally he did not. He looked at me; a pleasant enough man.

'Listen. Listen here to me. "Ann" is it? I hope now, Ann, that a gang of nice doodley-doos like the lot of yeeze is not going off somewhere playing cards an' not telling the rest of us, Ann.'

My flatmate, fat Anna, had natural sweetness and flair.

'Ned, I heard it about you that you have only to look at a girl and you know whether she's a virgin. Or a married lady. So you know – we're no good to you.' She finished with a chuckle and I laughed too.

'What do you do for a living, Ned?' I said.

'I'm half a businessman, half a cattle dealer and half a shaggin' eejit. An' that half is for not askin' the gang of yeeze have yeeze no mouths on ye, what are yeeze havin' to drink out of a glass? Yeeze must have a bottle of drink?!'

He called the barman. Ned used names a lot.

'Are yeeze asking me, Ann an' Anna an' Carmel, to pronounce on the state of yeeze, is that it?'

'It is,' we said. My outward cheeriness felt it belonged to someone else.

Carmel said, 'What about yourself, Ned? What are you? Are you a virgin?'

'Well, I'll tell you now, so. I think yeeze are virgins now, but 'tis only lately, that wasn't always the case with yeeze, was it? Ah, yes, yeeze're only virgins lately. As for meself, I never was a virgin, never will be. Bad job. Bad for the kidneys.'

'We're giving men up, Ned, they're the bad job,' said Carmel.

'Ach, no, dear woman, that is a case of never meeting the right man; the right man can put a spring in you, isn't that right, Ann? I bet, Ann an' Anna an' Carmel, that yeeze have fellas who leave ye alone an' go off out drinkin'. Is that the case? Bad business, so.'

'You make us sound as if we're mattresses, Ned,' said fat Anna, 'putting springs in us like that.'

'Now, Anna, you're after raising my special subject – the mattress. I'm an expert. That's it. I'm an expert on the mattress. A pure expert!'

The banter continued; Ned bought us much alcohol, to which I was not accustomed. I rose to stagger home.

57

'Ah, Ann,' he tried to restrain me with a huge arm. 'Sure the night is only a pup and we'll make a dog of it, come on to Limerick with me, there's the races there tomorrow.'

I laughed.

'Ah, lord, you're a purebred,' he said, a large hand sloping down towards my hips. 'I'd put you into a five-furlong hurdle if I had you. Will you look at that?' He held me off at admiring arm's length.

From this oasis of good humour I went to the lavatory and burst into tears. I cried for myself. It was time I did. When I came back, Ned had gone.

After that no pubs, no dances, no nothing. Nothing, nothing. I left the flat. Wrote a note to Carmel and fat Anna and left. A taciturn widow out on the Rochestown Road gave me a large room. On weekends when I did not go home, I walked by the river and despair and confusion walked alongside me.

About that time I began to understand something very powerful about myself. What was that business of avoiding men? From all appearances I lived like an old maid. A virgin plenipotentiary. I hid myself away. Liar, Ann! I know now what I was doing.

I wanted people to admire my restraint. Liberation threw fireworks up and down the streets. The virginity count was down. The Isle of Saints and Scholars was awash with what Richard calls 'horny stuff'.

'Lie down here, Doll, and we'll have a bit of the horny stuff.'

Sex was everywhere immediately. It was in advertising, films, magazines, attitudes, jokes. 'If all the girls doing medicine in Cork were laid end to end, ah, they'd be delighted.'

Television had come among us. Clever people and

forbidden things. Divorce, underwear, the Pill. Engaged couples taking holidays together – it was all racy. Night-clubs opened and young fellows up from the country in heavy shoes dancing with married women. Racy-racy.

But I wanted people to have a very good opinion of me so I shunned this randy glow – publicly. As far as anyone could see, I was working flat out. I studied for a first in my degree because I intended a doctorate – to take me further away from home. My work attracted much praise. 'Are you ever ever afraid of taking root in the library?' they asked. I gave the impression that my spare time went on refinement. Reading my novels. Going to the theatre. Learning about what music to listen to, all that. Never stopped working towards what I wanted people to think of me. I still have a ring I bought then, a small garnet. Discreet, maidenly.

But underneath – Jesus! I devoured the new looseness. Especially through my ears. Every suggestive lyric in every song. Every creak and rattle of every parked car in the lane behind my room. Men's voices. I often lurked to hear one of the librarians in particular. He had a voice that gave me ideas.

My mind was a lurid feast. On fire privately. It was exciting and rough. But nobody'd ever know it. No men. I hid my figure. Except when I stayed in at night alone and then I'd sit and walk around in my underwear and my head was alive with hard and lubricious thoughts.

Then came Joey and he blew my cover. It was July, 1971.

I was in Post-graduate Studies. Anything to avoid coming home. Still keeping out of the way of relation-ships. Still the mouse.

Mrs MacCartan, the wife of my professor, said to me one day, 'Ann, you could look very striking.' She said it kindly. 'Maybe you're taking your time,' she suggested.

And I think I was just about ready to start looking for someone. Mrs MacCartan's words lingered. The full-length mirror in my room did not lie. And I was even beginning to meet some nice people, at Professor MacCartan's house and the like, and the slabs of pain were beginning to break up, I could see light coming through.

The bizarre thing is – I was repelled by Joey from the first moment. A man who sucks his front teeth? Who always trawls his hands deep through his trouser pockets? Who spits? Who urinates with Niagarous loudness? As he did that very evening, in the cloakroom off our front hall before we left for dinner.

I look at my little garnet ring now on this pleasant morning and I think, 'How did I hold on to that? And how did I hold on to the idea of that? The innocence of it?' My hands – I'll hold them out for a moment – they don't shake any more at the thought of Joey Martin.

Joey was thirty-two. I was twenty-two. He said he had 'been around a bit'. I hadn't. Joey began as he meant to continue. He seduced my parents, he impressed them. And he was impressive, if you like that sort of thing.

His voice had rivers in it. I admit now that I liked to listen to his voice even when I hated what he was saying. He was big and shining with strong gestures, he was assured. But how could they not see what he was like? Because they did not want to see. 'None so blind as him who will not see': one of my father's saws.

My father actually said – in front of my eyes and ears he said it: 'Ann, girl, c'mere to me 'til you meet my new son-in-law.'

As I did not have a sibling, that pulled me into sharp focus.

'I'll look after her well, Mrs Halpin,' said Joey as he took me out to dinner that night.

When Joey was being Niagarous, Mother poured her ice on my reluctance. 'God knows we pay enough for you to do nothing.'

I was prone to that kind of blackmail. Is that another function of being disbelieved? I should have thought not. I should have thought the disbelieved need never care about blackmail. Being disbelieved erodes you where you are frailest. It makes blackmail look mild.

They knew Joey. I didn't. They had met him after a race meeting in Navan and my father hired him as business manager – on the recommendation of a rival. Why didn't the rival hire him?

I can recall the precise moment Joey and I shook hands. He had bad breath, unpromising. Priests have a lot of bad breath. So do certain sanctimonious politicians. The more sanctimonious, the more sulphurous the old mouth music. Joey's pong would strip the paint off a staircase: 'The Halitosis Kid', Richard calls him, which always makes me laugh. I know all about bad breath.

Mother had met him twice. My father was already long besotted.

But Joey was after half my father's business.

'Family matters,' summoned Mother on the telephone. No questions permitted. 'And try not to put him off when you meet him,' she said.

Mother should have worked for a gang of hitmen. I needed her liking and approval like I needed my next breath. If she would only be kind to me, be nice to me, I would ignore the way she was towards me. I would ignore the fact that she bought superb clothes for herself, dull ones for me. I would ignore the fact that she travelled ten times a year, Spain, Switzerland, Paris, London, and I never got as far as the Isle of Man.

I was a bit excited. Although my parents' taste in people was as safe as razors, this Joey Martin they talked about, he might be a hunk of a man.

I had a lovely, soft yellow lawn petticoat with a touch of broderie anglaise. And a blue-and-yellow shirtwaister I like to this day. I like it for its gentle checks and merry colours. And I like it because it was reduced by sixty per cent in a sale at Switzers. I bought those clothes, not Mother.

Shoes, I have a thing about shoes. I remember those so well – tall, block-heel, straw sandals, French make, black canvas with little yellow daisies on the toes. Joey threw them away into the woods that night.

My father introduced him with pride. 'This is Joey Martin, he's from Dublin, don't hold that against him. This is herself' – he took me by the arm – 'that I'm always talking about.'

'He is indeed always talking about you, and I can see why,' said Joey.

Tall Joey. Heavy Joey. Chunky Joey. Tough Joey, but only when nobody else was there. Weak Joey, if truth were told. He smiled matily at my father. His voice thrummed into me.

'But you never told me the full story.' He turned to Mother. 'D'you know what? She's like you, Mrs Halpin. They always say you should have a look at the mother before you go with the daughter.'

He glittered. All laughed except me. He was repulsive, with fat, wet lips. I was nervous and to this day when I'm nervous I get stomach cramps and I have to swallow hard. Nervousness used also to make me think that I had

62

some mark on my face, a make-up stain or something like that. And I was always certain to get a big spot somewhere before any significant occasion. I didn't that night. Christ! I should have broken out in leprosy.

Small talk followed over drinks. Mother sat regally. She was unusually pleased, smiling. I now believe that she saw immediately the coarse and coarsening quality of Joey. The hairs in his ears were like little nests of wire. She also perceived his hold on my father. And my father's admiration of smooth Joey.

Joey was going to make more money for us all.

Joey was going to increase the Halpin fortunes.

Joey was going to gut their only daughter.

Mother scored a hundred that evening. Of course she did. Look at what she had set up. Her family's wealth would be increased by this big fellow. And her uppity daughter would be brought under control. By a hard-headed young man who would take no nonsense. Eventually Joey and I would run the business. Would fund her and my father in Spain. Or Switzerland. Or the Bahamas. She had it all worked out.

In tones one might use to someone embarking on a cruise, Mother asked of Joey, 'And where are you taking Ann?'

'The Old Rectory,' Joey said. 'Everybody says the food is very good.' Always gave the impression of having done the work, that was Joey. 'Nothing but the best. Right, Mrs Halpin?'

I have never been back to the Old Rectory since. I drive past it often but I never go in there. I never will.

We had some more remarks about business being on the up-and-up. Joey wondered about opening two more shops in the south-west, then Belfast. 'Great punters there.' He asked about improving the on-course presence all across England. Did my father ever think of opening another shop in, say, the Cheltenham area? Or say, Kilburn, or any one of the Irish areas in London, maybe Camden? It could be done in time for next March, for the big spring meetings.

We left. He even opened the car door for me.

I have searched and searched my brain to see whether I did anything to provoke him. No. I had no habit of provocation. My dress was habitually modest. I meant to dress modestly. The shirtwaister, although it buttoned down the front, was quiet. I aimed for 'demure' going on 'classy'. This was the demeanour that was meant to carry me through until I was ready to meet some elegant man. Respectable. That was the demeanour I was wearing that night.

Joey could not spell the word 'demeanour'. But by Jesus he could fracture it. Nobody shatters a concept like someone who has never heard of it. Our civilization is based on each accepting the other's concept. Joey was not civilized. Joey was Pol Pot in a Ford Capri.

9

What is her name?

Heading south from Dublin the car radio tells of the endless mopping-up details; over twenty explosions all across Northern Ireland on Thursday. But I am off-duty; I have put myself out of reach of the office, told them I'm taking the weekend off. What is her name? I did not tell them that I'm driving back into my recent past.

What is her name? I can still see her, standing in the sunshine of her own marriage . . .

For a time this week the memory of her clear eyes became too much for me; that is why I took a decision to come down here again, to the place where I saw her. It was not just the remembrance of her and her wedding day; I want more information; I am a journalist and I need the name to put to her image. On the day I saw her I was too taken aback by my own reactions to dare enquire.

I must try and be more truthful; I also came down here because the journey I made with Father Andy Coll along the Border tore me apart; he has apologized to me for involving me in such hostility. Odd thing was – neither of the two men we met on our visits said much; the first merely looked at me, stared into my eyes and did not once look away, even when he addressed the priest; the second said,

'A soft bullet from a Ruger whirls into the brain like this – '

and he made a corkscrew motion with his finger on my forehead just above my right eye; then he tapped my forehead hard, twice, with the same finger.

'And it comes out the other side. Not that there'd be another side left after a Ruger.'

We have found no secret graves yet, only some murmurs from frightened people of where the informers were killed. Neighbours heard shots late at night out on hillsides.

For now, peace; the rain came in on a westerly wind as I left Dublin last night; I have never felt so welcoming of rain. By the time I got down here to the mountains of the South it had stopped; the night had clear skies. Dinner passed uneventfully, excellent meat, but the waitress was young and had only recently come to work in the hotel from another county, therefore she had no value as a source of information. Yet she demonstrated their values.

I said, 'That was a lovely piece of veal. Was it from somewhere local?'

'I'll ask, sir.'

She came back. 'No, sir, the chef said it isn't local steak at all, 'tis from Fermoy.'

Eighteen miles away, Fermoy; this is scarcely a cosmopolitan society – and every meat is called steak! I sat in the bar reading and drinking and then I fell asleep there, woke up to find that everybody else had gone to bed.

This morning I set out on a long walk after breakfast. Two miles or so from the hotel, the mountains are honeycombed with large, safe caves and I thought I might write a feature; English travellers in Ireland had written of the caves' thrall; Edmund Spenser travelled through this valley. How appropriate; what are those lines . . . 'Her angel's face . . . as the great eye of Heaven shined bright, and made a sunshine in the shady place.' Is she my sacred hunger?

The man selling the admission tickets told me he took the job because he likes to converse with people. No other visitors came and we had time to talk.

'What's your own name?'

When I told him he said, 'Well, I'm living here all my life and you're the first Hunter I ever met. But not the first huntsman.'

He liked his jokes. Next, he asked me where I was staying, and began to tell me the history of my hotel, which had been much used by IRA men on the run in the 1916 to 1921 period.

'They're going to start at building on to it any day now,' he said. 'For bigger functions, you know, more weddings'n that. Places in case people want to dance a polka.'

I can ask questions too; I do it for a living.

I said, 'There was a wedding a few weeks ago, I was passing through.'

He gazed. 'Who would that be now?' he pondered.

'Very expensive,' I said. 'Small wedding, but they seemed very well-to-do. Tall girl, very blonde hair. Very tall mother of the bride, dark-haired, very, ah'm, slim.' I hesitated, both out of delicacy and because I ran the danger of seeming too eager. 'Big, strong bridegroom.'

'Oh,' he dawned. 'That's that Halpin man, what's her name, Ann, that's it.'

I had my name! Ann Halpin! Mrs Ann Halpin!

'They're bookmakers,' said my informant, 'big bookies too, they go over to Cheltenham and everything. Pucks of money, they're rotten with money.' Then he grew thoughtful.

'Oh, yeh, I heard about that wedding, they've that big house, Grennanstown. Ah yes. Ah yes.'

In a knowing tone he drew down the blind of discretion and changed the conversation; he obviously knew that the bride was pregnant, but I did not dare ask. Journalism has a firm rule: you've blown your chance if you do not get all your information from casual, seemingly innocent questioning. Formal interviewing, when the person knows what you're after, is different.

I blew my chance, but I think tonight that I wanted to blow it, that I somehow wished to find out the rest for myself, to uncover (so to speak) my Ann for myself. Nor did I want to cheapen my feelings by slinking around asking questions like a tabloid man; indeed I get into difficulty with my colleagues for trying to insist on some boundaries; such a line of approach has not brought especial success.

Cavernous and welcoming, streaked with red, the caves felt like chambers of my heart; whereas coalmines disturb, caves calm me, and sandstone caves have a benign glow. Emerging, I stood in the sunshine for a moment and traced in my mind's eye this valley curving up and eastwards across Carlow and Wexford and Wales and Wiltshire and on, on, through France to the lands of southern Hungary, this rich seam of dark earth. It passes through my parents' garden.

All around here the rivers are said to pullulate with fish and along their banks stand great limestone houses where, often, trees were planted in colonnades to celebrate Waterloo; colonialism has not long passed. Unhappily the 'ranch-style bungalow' has arrived, some made from prefabricated kits, and they threaten to destroy the natural cadence of the land. Nobody objects, on planning or any other grounds, and it makes me think that greed and violence go hand-in-hand: they pray for peace in the churches every Sunday while outside firm-faced men take up collections for the IRA.

The roads in this county are made of the red mountain sandstone and today I saw the mirage of water that appears in bright light on rising tarmac ahead. I see that I've been doodling her name in my notebook all evening: 'Ann'; 'Ann'; 'Ann'; block letters, italics, little letters, in boxes, in cameos, in circles. She has high cheekbones, I observed, and her lips are almost voluptuous. What will she think of my incapacity to look after myself, my poor eating habits, my neglect of my health? Or my attachment to my cardigan!

Another thought tonight: sometimes, amid the glass and dust of a bomb's aftermath, when the lungs are fighting for oxygen and the mind is fighting for sense, it is impossible not to feel dismay for the victims. Did this or that girl, some secretary in Belfast, some shop assistant in Portadown, did she know as she cycled to work that morning, did anyone at her family breakfast table premonitor that she would lose an arm and an eye because the blast from a car-bomb pitchforked her on to an iron railing? This is the point of my thought: have I therefore with this new passion deliberately filled my mind with something lovelier than that by which I earn my living? Here in this country of paradox I am full of optimism amid attrition, with my spirit singing of love as I count corpses.

Ann! Ann! What do women do in Ireland if they run away from their husbands? Not that I intend to entice you; you will have to initiate any such endeavour your-self. Do Irishwomen keep the husband's name forever?

Mrs Halpin. Ann Halpin. Christopher Hunter and Ann Halpin will marry on the somethingth of something in . . .somewhere . . .

What is her maiden name? Will it be one of those wonderful euphonious names like MacNamara, or Prendergast, or Kennedy, or Cunningham? I hope so. I want to know everything about her, and I will have to be careful when eventually we sit to talk, or else I will ask her so many questions that it will feel unseemly.

The newsdesk has asked me for a think-piece on the statistics of violence for last year: 1,750 shootings; 1,500 explosions; 700 guns found, and two and a half tons of bombs; 170 people dead.

10

'So you're the one,' Joey said to me. The car cleared
the gates.

'The one what?' I chipped. I'm often too chippy – a
defence mechanism, smart-aleckry. 'The one and only?
The one most likely to succeed? The one on the left at
the back in the photograph? The one who won't come
out of the bathroom in the morning? The one in the nice
sandals with daisies on them?'

'The one who's a bit smart on the tongue, I see,'
said Joey.

He had no sense of humour. I should have known
what a bad sign that can be.

'Only joking,' I said.

'That's my department,' said Joey.

Is that why my father sided with him? Because he
demarked so clearly? Everything about Joey was demar-
cation.

He returned to his important conversational gambit.

'The one your father is talking about.'

I find a heavy man with a light touch on life irresistible. Joey, however, was a heavy man with a heavy
touch.

'So what does my father say?'

We drove under the trees approaching the Rectory.
The road signs warn of deer. Flight animals. I should

have been one. I have never known whether I'm 'fight' or 'flight'. Mother did that to me.

'He says he wants me to marry you.'

I often find it difficult to say nothing. Unless forced to, as at that moment.

'That's what he says,' said Joey, who wore aftershave that smelt of chicken.

'Well, it . . . it . . . I . . .'

Just like that. Quick as a flash, as they say, I said nothing.

I had never read anything to equip me for that moment or the next. You won't find such advice in Mrs Beeton.

'By the way, I'd only marry', said Joey – he was trying to wear the air of a man who has always been impressive on the Riviera – 'a woman I can ride easy. And we'll find that out on the way home, Sugar.'

I tried for a small foothold on this shock. But the years of secret prurience called out my name and weakened me.

'Don't call me Sugar,' was all I could manage.

'I'll call you what I like – Sugar.'

It is so easy to see now. Isn't it? So easy. He knew he had the absolute support of my parents. And he sensed that anything I said about him would be disbelieved. What had they said to him? My father had promised him half the business. I knew that from my intuition. In time I was proven right.

What Mother might have said to him about me was more to be feared. Did she say to him, 'She's a bit airy-fairy, but she'll come down to earth. She needs taking down a peg or two'? She must have done. I can hear her say it. They had Joey to dinner twice in the week before I met him. I think they hatched it all then. It meant I met Joey without any parental protection.

He opened the car door for me. That was his way. He had a brilliant surface. (He doesn't have it now.)

'I'm very thick, you know,' he said amiably. We walked from the car to the front door of the Rectory. He is a big, heavy man. 'Will you be able to take that?'

A deaf mute would have known what he meant. When it came to *doubles-entendres* I had heard as much comedy, seen as much television as the next woman. I might not have had direct person-to-person experience of sexual innuendo but I knew what it was. And this wasn't even innuendo. This was public-address system.

I felt the quiver of an unwelcome excitement. The nuns used to call it 'the smear of sin'. But I was so dumbfounded by him and by the images he stirred inside my head that I had no response. Written on the sky of my mind were lurid scenes. Under banners of dark four-letter words.

By the way, Joey never swore. He hates bad language.

'We'll manage anyway,' he said as he opened the Old Rectory door. 'There was never a gap couldn't do with a bit of widening. Right, Sugar?' He said it consolingly.

My mother walked me into that man's arms. One day I may do a doctorate in how mothers betray.

I can't say that first evening with Joey was the worst of my life. Because there was worse to come. But it was the third worst. He began it as he meant it to continue.

We had a waitress neither pleasant nor unpleasant. Common, though, and a heavy woman.

'Backside', said Joey, as the woman departed to the kitchen, 'big as the side of a church.'

He ordered chicken (to match his aftershave, I thought).

'Make sure you give me a bit of the breast,' he told the waitress when she took his order. She was entranced. She

73

couldn't take her eyes off him. Waitresses are like that with Joey.

The English language changed that night. Just a little change. The word 'leer' lost adequacy, lost definition. How could a man so young have grown so filthy an expression? I felt cold over and over, a warm night like that.

And over and over I went to the Ladies with my stomach cramps in full cry. When I came back from one trip, Joey had taken the linen napkin. He made it into a woman's torso and legs. With a tiny opening at the crotch into which he kept pushing his thumb. I blushed, even though I had determined to resist. My father wanted me to marry this?! At the same time I felt that kind of worrying, dirty excitement in me. I pushed it away but it kept coming back.

Joey told the waitress a joke. I hate jokes. I like humour but I hate jokes. Men like jokes.

'There was this woman,' he said. 'Out the road, not far from here, you probably know her, so no names, no pack drill, right?' He said 'right' after every sentence, especially when he'd had a few drinks. 'And she was a maiden lady, like. You know, a hedge growing on it, right?'

The waitress laughed.

'But,' gleamed Joey, 'she needed the cows bulled, right? Anyway, the neighbours told her about the AI guy, the Artificial Insemination man. "All you've to do," they said to her, "cow in the shed, washed down, fresh bucket of water, bar of soap for the man – and a towel to dry his hands," right? So she sends for the guy and the guy comes in his waggon and she takes him into the shed, right? And she says to him, "There's the animal, there in the stall. There's a clean bucket of water and a bar of soap for you and a towel, and there's a nail there on the back of the door to hang your trousers on." Right?'

The waitress laughed so much he tipped her five pounds when we were leaving. The Halitosis Kid.

Shock upon shock. I reeled to the car. That dinner painted the word 'lewd' in new colours. My shock also came from anticipation. It proved accurate and connected with bits of me of which I was ashamed and afraid . . .

Imagine – during the evening he asked me not one question about myself. He only made pronouncements.

'They say you read books.'

'I hear you're handy with the lies.'

'You have notions, I hear, stuck-up, is what they say.'

'Sugar, did anyone ever tell you you've one ear a bit bigger than the other?'

That last one was true and it hurt most. Why does a physical insult cause more pain?

Down the hotel steps, once again he opened the car door. As if it were a carriage, and I a lady, and he more improbably a gentleman. In the car he pawed my thigh. I grasped his hand and pushed it slowly away. He laughed, pawed me again and drove down the avenue.

Minutes later he said in the woods, 'We'll turn in here, right? I scouted it out the other day, dead quiet.'

I suffered paralysis, said nothing. My father wanted me to marry this man. My father never took much notice of me, true, but this man? My father. Wanted me to marry. This – this appalling male creature. I sank and sank, defeated by thoughts and realizations I could hardly assemble. There was going to be no honeyed courtship. At the same time a sewer of excitement tried to force its way overground.

On a forest road Joey Martin stopped the car and turned off the engine. He then sat back to open his trousers.

I said, 'No.'

'What "no" is that, now, Sugar?' asked Joey. 'Is that, "No, I've never seen anything like the thickness of that"? Or is it, "No, I've to lie on the flat of my back"? Or would it be, "No time like the present." Right?'

I answered, 'It's just – no.'

He said, 'I hope it isn't the "no" Joey doesn't want to hear. Right?'

'No. Just – no.'

I had never been kissed. True, I'd had country hands thumbing my breasts as if they were the pages of a phone book. They did it from the side during dancing. But they accepted when thumbs were pushed aside. Never this.

'Get out, Sugar.'

'No.'

'Out of the car. Right?'

'No.'

No seatbelts in those days. Joey got out of the car. He walked harshly around to the other side – and said, 'Out, Sugar.'

'No.'

'One more time, right?'

'No.'

'You're not hearing Joey clearly. Out, Sugar.'

'No, Joey. Please.'

'Is that "please" as in "I'm going to please you, Joey," or, "A grand summer night, you can do as you please, Joey"? Because, Sugar, they're the only kind of "please" Joey is interested in. Get out of the car!' He hammered with his fist on the roof above my head.

In fright I got out. Then occurred the brief and terrible

incident that aged my heart by several years. And confirmed unhealthy things about myself I had not wanted to know.

Those sandals, my French sandals with the yellow daisies – he flung them hard and contemptuously into the trees, into high bracken. I never saw them again.

First he forced me to my hands and knees. He opened my mouth by pressing my jaw . . .

But did I stop anything? Or did I scream? Even one scream? No. But I suppose I couldn't scream, could I?

'That's the introduction, Sugar, right? Now, Sugar. On your back. For Joey and for Ireland and St Patrick.'

The sky caved in. He rolled me this way and that.

On my hands and knees again, Joey behind me, a monster at the mouth of a cave . . .

'A job has to be done right,' said Joey at last, kneeling back and searching for his cigarettes. 'That's Joey for you – marking the territories. Right?'

I looked into the wood. High ferns shone their large fronds at the moon. The phrase 'virgin territory' came into my head. I began to weep, at the outrage and at my own dark part in it.

'Great ride,' said Joey in the car on the way back from the woods. 'Joey liked that. Joey loves a good ride.'

I shivered, too shocked to weep. Or to scream. I now believe I was in the grip of foreign powers. Of my own creation.

'By the way, Sugar. Joey wouldn't like it if the parents, like, got the, you know, wrong impression, right? Anyway, Sugar, I'll deny it and they'll think you made it up.'

The house in darkness welcomed me. I washed and washed and washed. You know that relief when you have a bad dream and find out it was never real? In the morning when I woke, my first impression was the exact opposite.

I had to go to Dr Greene next day (there was no other doctor in town those days).

'Well, I don't know,' he said. 'A bit over-enthusiastic, I s'pose. That's the way 'tis with young men.'

Which hurt more – Joey's nonchalant savagery or Greene's joviality? He gave me ointment. Ointment? There is no ointment for the heart or the spirit.

Fait accompli: I came home from Dr Greene's surgery to hear my father at lunch sing Joey's praises.

'God, girl, you made an impression. God, an impression and a half. Moya, you shoulda heard. Credit to us, she is, "as ladylike an individual as you'd meet in a day's walk." Those were his words. The man is a goner on you, a dead goner.'

Then came another of Halpin's Familiar Phrases for Everyday Use. He said, 'D'yeh know what it is? God must be praying for us.'

I always thought mothers were supposed to have special, instinctive alertness towards their daughters' femininity. Mother smothered hers. If she ever had any. She showed no interest in my physical wellbeing. She picked up no signals on her female radar.

'That's nice,' Mother said when my father went on about Joey's view of me. 'That's nice.'

But she was hijacking his compliments and rubbing them on herself.

Nobody asked me did I like Joey, did I hate him, did I this, that or nothing. My feelings never crossed their thoughts. My likes and dislikes had never been entered in the normal ledgers that enable people to keep ordinary account of each other.

Soon, Dr Greene told my mother of the pregnancy. He rang her. I never got the chance to say.

We had none of the natural consternation I believed customary in families. I would have welcomed it. My father handed me money. He told me to buy some wedding clothes.

Mother said, 'I don't know how you got away in Cork all these years. I suppose you were doing something immoral, like those contraceptives.'

So much for my silent, sad days.

11

Drove back this evening; the hotel is crowded with paediatricians in Dublin for a conference; it has been raining since I left Silverbridge. I found Grennanstown House this afternoon – it is an impressive place, Georgian, with old trees powerful along a curved avenue towards limestone portals and tall windows. The directory in the village telephone kiosk confirms it – 'Halpin, J., Grennanstown House, Silverbridge.' Her husband must be John, common name around here, or Jerry, short for Jeremiah. Mrs John Halpin. Or Mrs Jeremiah Halpin? I could always telephone and ask . . . No, let Life take care of this, let Time do it . . . But – but: I dialled the number tonight, then hammered down the receiver before the connection could be made.

Was their house originally a glebe? Nearby stands an old Anglican church and graveyard (they call it Church of Ireland here), and I walked through it in the sunshine. No Halpins on the tombstones; *Ruth Thompson, George Hunt, George Hyde, Ernestina Stephenson, Richard Edwards; Rhona Ulverton and her beloved son, Munchin*; the names of Connors, Hazeltons, Bertrams, but no Halpins.

I must face my life better; I must shed this fear that I carry with me always; I must terminate this worry, this dread that people will dislike me. Is that why I took on this weird priest, 'the tall Father Coll' as I think of him; he has a most nasal voice – and I think I fear his sentimentality. My call to the newsdesk brought the uncomfortable news that 'someone called Coll' has been looking for me; I fear he may try to 'adopt' me. He has appointed himself the representative – 'the moral spokesman' he calls it – of these three families who have lost menfolk, they believe, to the IRA. Certainly the Provisionals have condemned them publicly as informers, which means they have been killed. Usually, the bodies of informers are dumped where they can be found; this has not happened now in these three cases and one other suspected case, although no condemnation came from the Church.

'Scalp Hill,' Father Coll said on that frightening, lowering day, 'we'll make that our first port of call, so that we . . .' He rarely finished his sentences, a most irritating mannerism.

I had stuffed my notebook into my pocket as we climbed the steep side; I find it hard to believe that it only happened last week.

'We're looking for fresh earth,' he said, this lanky and desolate priest, 'so that we might have some idea of where . . .'

Under the overhanging rock slabs at the top of Scalp Hill we turned – and saw, down on the lane, a car, a white Ford Cortina, park behind our car.

'Who would that be now, that'd be . . .' The priest squinted.

We saw no freshly turned earth and, so, walked down; a small man stood rigidly by the gate waiting for us; he was the man who looked at me all the time he answered the priest.

'Good day to you,' said Father Andy Coll, 'and who might you . . . ?'

'I'm a man. Get out of here,' and he looked into my eyes.

'We're Christians, hoping to secure a Christian burial, in consecrated ground for . . .'

'I'm a Christian, too. Get out of here,' said the man. I decided to say nothing.

The priest said, 'There was a man buried here secretly, he's entitled to a funeral with a priest and a . . .'

'No-one's-entitled-to-nothing-get-out-of-here,' said the man with his eyes of flint.

I could feel my brain whimpering and I saw the priest tremble.

Father Coll said good-bye to me in the main street of Dundalk and walked away; I drove south; that is when I decided to come in search of the woman I now know to be Ann Halpin – Mrs (regrettably) Ann Halpin. Perhaps her husband owns the woods I walked through this afternoon; he is certain to have land; men like that in Ireland make sure they own many acres. The woods cooled me; they restored some of the equilibrium I lost last week in south Armagh. A deer leaped away up on the hill by a beech hanger, in that curious jumping panic of deer; how often I feel like that. I stumbled on a rotting sandal that once had daisies stitched on it, left behind in the grass and ferns by some laughing local girl in her love-error; and in the trees magpies yelled at me.

I had lunch in a hotel on the edge of the woods, the Old Rectory, amid photographs of prize horses. The overweight waitress had a cold, and we spoke little.

12

Do I believe in weddings now? A girl from a house across the fields here got married last week. No, I don't believe in weddings. That's another part of my femininity that I lost. Or had ripped from me.

At Mother's insistence I wore cream: 'Well, Ann, you know who white is for only.' My bump hardly showed. I had a new doctor by then, a Dr John MacMenamin. He said it must be a boy, boys keep hidden the longest.

I said, 'But I'm nearly seven months.'

He looked at me kindly and said, 'Where are you hiding it?'

None the less I wore a looser dress than I ever imagined I would marry in. 'Empire line,' I said to the chatty assistant in Switzers.

The wedding, my father said, 'all went off famously'.

For all of them. Not for me. I swung between fighting my despair and wallowing in it. The only relief I got was from blaming myself. I was snagged on my own fatal flaw, wanting my mother's affection to return.

That flaw turned into a deep hole in which I lay. Richard always says that the holes we fall into are the holes we dig ourselves. I could have fought my way out of that betrothal to Joey Martin. Times were not such, even in Catholic Ireland, that a girl could be forced to marry. I could have aborted. Abortion ferries clogged the Irish Sea.

But I also did nothing towards myself because Joey Martin with his abuse and disrespect (how some words are too mild) slung some sort of hook into me. That snagged me too. Another fatal flaw. Deeper and deeper was the pit at the bottom of which insult and sex were joined to each other. That was what I believed.

Joey had a saying when he watched football: 'The ball bounces for a winning team.' They were the winning team. Everything went the way they wanted. My aged uncle, my father's brother, died. This gave them a reason to keep the whole wedding business quiet.

Joey came to live with us, Mother's idea. 'Makes planning easier,' she said.

Every night Joey came to my room. 'I'm just going up to tuck her in safely,' he winked to Mother.

She smiled to my Aunt Alice Beresford, 'He calls her "Sugar". They're like a pair of lovebirds.'

And so Mother smiled as he went to tuck me in. Because she felt there was decorum. Because Joey was always back within five minutes. Five savage minutes of cold, determined violation.

My only protest was the turning away of my face. I would not look at him. He pinned me down contemptuously and then discarded me.

But, the pit, the pit, I did not walk away from it. I did not climb out of bed one morning and walk unstoppably away from that house. And I did not say to them, 'Here's the truth. If you don't believe me, I'll find someone who'll be glad to.'

Why did I stay? Why does anyone hang on to receive more and more damage? I still wanted Mother desperately, I missed her. If she half-smiled at me my heart went on red alert, hoping for a glimpse of that old, sweet affection. I would have crawled to her for a touch of concern. A million miles for one of her smiles. Dear God!

Every night, I heard the heavy plod to bed of my father. After the distant crack of Joey's door closing, Mother came padding by. Her room was nearest mine. I kept hoping she'd open the door. And come in. Be friendly, as she was when I was small. She never did.

The house settled. I lay awake, with no capacity for thought. Only stricken loss and hurting orifices.

We had the wedding Mass in Rosegreen church. Mother had 'a family connection' there. Her uncle had been parish priest. Therefore, no questions were asked.

Joey's brother, Liam, was best man. My cousin, Angela Beresford, was Matron of Honour. Sitting on my side, in the same pew as my parents, were Aunt Alice, Auntie Jo and Uncle Cormac. And, 'to balance things out,' said Mother, my other cousin, Tina Beresford.

'The Halpins and the Beresfords are the closest alliance in this whole family,' said Mother, as if we were a local branch of the Habsburgs.

Joey's parents and his twin sisters came down from Dublin. He has a sad father, a tough mother and filthy-minded siblings. Kilnoran Lodge seated the dozen of us in their 'Meadow Room: Private Reception'. We were a discreet wedding – good food laced with brandy. In the entire day I probably had one minute to myself. Even when I stood at the door to get a breath of fresh air and look out at the mountains, Joey came after me. He could not believe his luck. All that money now coming his way. He did not want to let me out of his sight.

There was a man, I saw his back, having his lunch alone in the dining-room. I imagined suddenly running away with him. I had a very big fantasy that lasted about a quarter of a minute. He'd come out of the dining-room and we'd run to his car and we'd be gone. What would they all say? Oh, God, it was a lovely thought that day. But – no dice, as Joey used to say.

Liam made a speech, crass as concrete. My father said maudlin things in a bogus voice. As we cut the wedding cake the priest blessed us again. He was a man who held himself as if he had come down from a mountain with an important message. My dress looked lovely and felt lovely, but I could not enjoy it.

At about half-past four I went up to change in the bedroom which the hotel had given us. Joey arrived fast as a jet.

'Joey likes a quick ride,' he said, and he was more than half-drunk. 'Quick is right,' he said. 'I can do what I like with you now, right, Sugar? Martial rights, right?'

He meant 'marital'. Or maybe he didn't.

He left. 'Three and a half minutes, a personal best,' he said. 'Joey sets a record.'

The uncomfortable but exciting dark wish for such humiliations began to pass once I saw through what was taking place. Nowadays nobody tries to control me. All I knew then was – this was Joey's interpretation of 'knocking the nonsense' out of me.

I still believe that Mother would have been shocked if she knew the whole story. But she would not have believed me. That would have been her defence.

The collision of fantasy and reality causes terrible damage. My secret life had often imagined scenes like the ones Joey served up. Soon, I loathed every shred and shard of any such thought or event. The word 'enjoy' came nowhere near. Pleasure was not even a distant shape in that blooded sky. I think I wouldn't have minded if he only pretended to humiliate me. As, say, in a game.

Joey, though, was no game, Joey was for real.

My father had the old sentimental tears in his eyes as he waved the bride and groom good-bye. Sad bride. Bullying groom.

'Ann, girl, look after him. He's like the son I never had,' my father said.

Mother said nothing.

The priest made the sign of the cross over the car. Would you believe that? The sign of the cross. A mile down the road Joey stopped, throwing up.

13

The Editor tries to browbeat me and threatens to fly over and see me. I do not have to share his opinions of my work, nor will I tolerate his comments about me.

Yesterday we had brief relief from all the bombs and bullets at lunch in the Embassy Residence. The Ambassador's wife has a serenity that washes over everybody, and I cannot make up my mind whether she knows this and uses it like a good diplomatic wife, or whether it is a completely natural gift. Three other couples there: the main Guinness man and his Spanish wife, utterly charming; a barrister who kept the table heaving with laughter at accounts of cross-examinations in country courts; and the newest arrival at the Embassy, the Third secretary and his wife: I wonder if they're the standard MI5 contingent. My 'opposite' was a Classics lecturer, a woman in her fifties, who spoke scarcely at all.

These occasions have little use in them. Nobody mentions the Troubles, and if indiscretions begin, such as opinions on the local politicians, the Ambassador or his wife stem the enjoyable tide too early for any useful revelation – but the ex-Finance Minister came in for a lot of comment: he rides to hounds and a newspaper columnist has christened him 'the Heel of the Hunt'.

Pleasantness ended for me during the main course; the newsdesk rang the Residence to tell me of a bomb. His

Excellency accompanied me to the door and dismissed my apologies, said he felt quite wistful, wished he could accompany me. To which I replied that what I found when I got there might not be very pleasant – how small is the talk we make.

Three-quarters of an hour later, I stepped through the rubble of a pub wall where a Belgian tourist died with his map and camera; another man, a retired lorry-driver, also died: blood on the wallpaper, grey matter on the beer-pump handles. A police sergeant told me that the compressed-air blast, i.e., the force from a bomb, goes up and out, and therefore if the bomb is planted at street-level, the carnage begins at about knee-height.

The oddities remained: a full beer glass, intact, with blood on the beer's cream head; a shoe, the laces still tied; the Belgian's map of Dublin fixed perfectly to the wall above his head where he died; the Guinness sign on the beer pump neatly holed so that the word now reads, 'Guess'; the front page of the *Racing Post* stuck on the ceiling as if wallpapered there; patterns of plaster dust embedded in the green wall as if someone had been applying a marbling effect; a chair standing as a chair should – when the police touched it the chair fell apart.

I spoke to the barman, who had been walking towards the pub about to come on duty as the bomb exploded; their descriptions here are so graphic: 'It was like as if the whole front wall breathed out smoke very fast, a huge, fast belch, like a train coming out of a tunnel,' he said, 'and then the noise followed it like someone imitating an explosion. Look, I've rubble in the turn-ups of my trousers.'

A parking meter outside the door had a beermat pasted to its little glass window: I scraped it off with difficulty.

I had a long discussion with the Editor about how much description to include – what a cynic! He made me tone down the gory descriptions, the details of injuries, saying, 'The Belgian, if it had been a Brit, perhaps . . .' I so disagree with his point of view. Charles then twisted the knife a little, saying the copy-takers had been suggesting my phone calls always seemed more lucid before lunch.

If it weren't for Ann Halpin's presence in my mind I might daily regret that I came to this country; my brain is full of blood and despair, because this life increases moment by moment; it feels like a wild undulation with ambushes; I rise to every emotional or professional crest and then shoot down the deep slope to exhaustion, anti-climax and doubt. Images haunt me and taunt me: flesh from a bombed car, the black and cream and red of that bloody pint left standing in that shattered pub, dead faces grey with dust under a splintered table.

Tonight I am in Jury's Hotel, Sligo, having attempted once more to rid myself of south Armagh; we tried again three days ago, Father Andy Coll and I. In the car from Dundalk to Crossmaglen he attempted some exhortation.

'I'll take you to see the families and then you'll . . .' he said. 'You talk to those wives and you will see the pain that they're . . .'

I fought the powerful mix of irritation and fear, hoping to put together more details; if nothing else I will get a major piece out of all this crazy and dangerous meandering.

'The usual method they kill them by is bad enough,' the priest intoned. 'You know, the banknote pinned to the pocket like Judas's silver, the shoes taken off, the eyes and mouth taped, the bullet in the . . .'

'In the what?' I almost snapped.

'Everybody knows about the bullet, I mean that's the most infamous bit of . . .'

'You mean in the back of the head?' I said – again rather tersely, for me, at any rate.

'Turn up this road, Mr Hunter, the unfortunate man's last-known associates live here and we'll . . .'

'Is this dangerous?' I asked, and he misunderstood on purpose.

'The road's a bit bumpy, could do with a bit of tar, but . . .'

That is when I sat in a man's kitchen and he walked across the floor to me, from the other side of his own fireplace, squatted before me and made the corkscrew motion with his finger and then tapped my forehead.

'And it leaves a big hole. The pathologist can take the bullet out with his fingers' – which brought more tears of fright to my mind's eye.

I wish I had children; I wish I had married and had a little boy and a little girl; there is a line of Robert Frost's that upsets me so much: 'Home is the place where, when you have to go there,/They have to take you in.' I feel as if I have no home. That is how I came to Sligo; I telephoned from Dundalk, saying the pub bomb had unsettled me. 'Go and see a bit of the countryside,' said the Editor. 'Do a colour piece if you like – but you don't have to. Are you all right?' He sounded irritated with me again.

Bombs and blood and Crossmaglen's fright; I came to Sligo to find the land of love expressed by Yeats's poems. Instead I found doubt; beneath the table mountain of Ben Bulben so magicked by Yeats, my heart began to drift into gloom and doubt and self-doubt. What preposterous emotional situation have I created? What position have I invented? Why does my life need to be filled with these snapshots of dust-streaked blood and torn limbs, my forehead tapped in threat – I feel the hard tap now? A slew of uncertainty dogged my life in the past more than once and now it does so again. Once before in my life I had this kind of difficulty and found myself unable to speak a normal sentence, normal phrases, words even. Have I now the resources to haul myself onward?

Moment of truth: I must have given myself the fantasy about this quiet bride in order that I would have a place within me to which I can always return, because that is what I have been doing – returning to her grave face amid moments and aftermaths of the greatest carnage and disorder one could encounter. How do I know this? The doubts tell me. Doubt is – for me – the key to truth: I believe that which I doubt.

But if these feelings are not genuine, if I am making them up because this kind of worshipping-from-afar unrequited love is the only kind of relationship I can have – then I am seriously adrift.

It is one o'clock in the morning. I have written too much. Tomorrow I will try and climb Ben Bulben, unless it rains again, or find the lake isle of Inisfree, nine bean rows and a hive for the honey-bee.

'Sugar,' he called his bride. I thought she did not merit the commonness of that touch and I thought she did not quite like him, but can that be? Is that not again my wishfulness? What was plain was that she had developed a way of dealing with him.

'Right, Sugar?' he said, and he wiped his hand across the air like a plasterer skimming a wall.

She nodded, standing a little sideways to him, contained within herself.

Back at my table, my newspaper lay open; the waiter – further intrusion – had plonked the glass of brandy on it; the sun had started to set. I had the foolish hope that this remarkable young bride followed me with her eyes. I wonder where they chose to honeymoon; a resort in Ireland, perhaps, or – they looked well-to-do – some inevitable Spanish Costa; or is she more sophisticated than that?

I paid my bill, went and stood in the car park. The mountain range rises from pasture in the water meadows of two or three valleys. My first thought was: this is the powerful feeling, the grand emotion that I have read about but have never experienced; this is the knowledge of love that I have encountered only in books. That is still my thought.

That road between Forkhill and Crossmaglen in south Armagh is the most terrifying stretch of land I have ever travelled. Tap. Tap. My skull remembers. Tap. Tap.

14

I used to laugh at things I found funny. In school the other girls said that my laugh set them all off laughing. Much deeper than my voice, my laugh. Can't stop when I start. Never laughed like that with Joey. Never. How could I?

But in my new life I do. I was laughing like that this morning and everyone here started laughing too. When I laugh like that it reminds me of lying in the grass with Richard in the old days.

I will not describe the honeymoon in detail. I cannot. Not for reasons of delicacy, but for reasons of awfulness. The first seven nights, Joey got insensible at dinner, then headed glittering and swaying for the Bamboo Bar. I went silently to bed. Hours later he stumbled to the couch, slept on it. Some time during the night he fell to the floor.

I had early breakfast alone every morning, on the balcony, watching the meaningless rise of the sun, my hands on my stomach trying to give the baby a peace I did not feel. Pregnancy was this bewildering feeling – at that stage – of dreadful worry and placid thought. Joey rose bleary and silent at eleven and we said not a word to each other.

The end of the first week, walking to the pool I heard Joey behind me gasping, 'I don't believe it. I

94

just don't buckin' believe it. Well, stone the buckin' crows!'

A woman greeted him, small and hard-faced with her black straight fringe painted on her forehead. She walked like a man, legs apart, determined. Of course, it was all staged. I could not prove anything. But it had the smack of planning. Although I was an infant in terms of shrewdness, I did know myself well enough to register the truth of something.

Simultaneously they said, 'What're you doin' here?'

I never received a satisfactory answer from Joey to my later question, 'Was all that arranged?'

Something dogged me for a long time afterwards. Married to a man I loathed. Married to him by, I believe, a foolish and greedy father. By a mother who wished me coarsened. Yet – why did I feel a lurch of jealousy? Even though her arrival took his attention from me? Even though I did not want his company?

'I know you to see,' she said to me. 'You're Joss Halpin's daughter, aren't you? I know your mother to see, too.'

She knew well. She knew more than that.

'I suppose you're as stuck-up as your mother?' said this vulgar piece.

Joey roared a laugh.

'You didn't ask me if I had a mouth on me,' said Josephine Scannell. She blinked against the sun of Gran Canaria.

'Oh, sorry, girl,' said Joey. He called a waiter. 'Get this woman a vodka and blackcurrant.'

Never asked her. Knew what she drank. Didn't care that I observed what he knew about her.

Our first major row came that very night.

Joey said, 'Sugar, I've invited Jo over for a drink before the grubstakes. Have you any cigarettes?'

'When did I ever smoke?'

'Ah, Sugar, I'm always waiting for you to surprise me with a little stash for Joey. Like a good wife.'

I nearly said, 'I'm not your wife.' But of course I was.

'I'd better go for some, so,' he said. 'I won't be long, Sugar, keep the sun warm for me.'

A cloud crossed my heart. He had gone to see her. I knew. Feeling rotten, I lay down on the bed. When I awoke, Joey was tiptoeing around the room, half-dressed. I pretended to be still asleep. He tried to hide his underpants. I found them the following day. With lipstick marks on the waistband.

He slept with her several times during the honeymoon. And drank with her. Insensible they were, most of the time. He abused me terribly. He abused me verbally, socially, physically, emotionally. Especially physically. This chair I'm sitting on now, I feel myself flinching a little on it when I recall. That is why I cannot describe our honeymoon in detail. And all I ever wanted to do in my life was be nice to people. Be decent, a decent human being. The number of people I've known that I've wanted to hug. I do it now, I couldn't do it then.

On the flight home Joey never drank. Ripley's Believe-It-Or-Not. My father read its extraordinary stories aloud each evening. His favourite bit of the newspaper after the racing pages. A man in Wales died aged seventeen showing all the symptoms of old age. A dog in Nebraska had a head at each end of his body. Boys-ah-boys. Joey Martin endured a two-hour flight without a drink. Ripley's Believe-It-Or-Not.

Waiting for our luggage by the carousel, I could

scarcely stand. Squeezing into the Ford Capri made me wince. Twice we stopped for me to be sick. Joey looked worried, first time ever. He worried that he'd gone too far. His physical approaches to me had always been violent, always contemptuous, always intended to humiliate and control. The honeymoon contact was the worst ever.

'Can't you straighten yourself up?' he asked. He was flittering with anxiety. I flinched with pain and with the desperate anxiety of the baby. He smoked and smoked. I'd guess he did twenty cigarettes in the hundred miles, smoke one, light one. Could the baby smell the smoke?

We got to Grennanstown House in the early evening. You would have thought that Joey had won a war. My father clapped his hands together. Mother embraced Joey: 'Joseph! Welcome home!'

'She got sunburn on the old thighs,' he said to my mother, to explain my hobbled walk.

'Boys-ah-boys,' said this vast-palace-of-the-spirit father of mine. 'Look at the sight of you. Brown as berries the pair of you. And ye loving yeerselves as much as Mammy and myself.'

My mother beamed on Joey. She said sideways to me, 'Auntie Lisa's here, we never expected her.' Then she lit up again. 'You're just in time for dinner. I bet you're starving, Joseph.'

'I could eat the hind leg off the Lamb of God,' said Joey.

My father laughed again. What – what, what, what! – did they see in him? *Halpin's: We're the Best Bet!*

While I lay on my bed after a bath Auntie Lisa knocked and came in. Auntie Lisa, my father said, 'took Paris without firing a shot. Her and her million-dollar smile.' Lisa worked in the fashion world. She had a mystery man, said my father, very rich but an invalid.

97

No such thing, of course. When she died I learned the truth. She did piecework for some of the designers. Auntie Lisa trimmed hats and travelled through life a footstep ahead of poverty. Her fabulous lover also came from my father's gallery of fakes. He was no wealthy merchant. He was the accountant for a firm that made car batteries. No wife, he was just too selfish to marry this good woman. Although she had it well concealed behind sweetness and fun, Lisa was one of life's doormats. My father got one thing right – she had a great smile.

'And how are you, Ann? My God, your husband is a smasher. That curly hair. Isn't he big? I love big men.'

'I need a doctor,' I said.

She sat on the bed beside me. 'Honeymoon troubles?'

I turned my head away.

She stood. 'It's urgent, isn't it?'

Dr John MacMenamin arrived within half an hour and gave me two stitches. Auntie Lisa went downstairs and Joey came up, as sent for. He shifted his feet.

Dr MacMenamin with his red, flaky skin said askance to Joey, 'You the husband?'

'Yeh. Yeh, I'm the man. The man with the van. Joey. That's me.' Joey rubbed his hands.

Dr John looked straight at him and said, 'Don't do that to your wife again.'

'Listen,' said Joey. 'I'm the husband. I pay you. Right?'

Dr Mac closed his case very quietly. He said to Joey, 'You're obviously not up with the law. Times have changed.'

Joey went white in the face. He left the room and left me in peace. I lived the next two months for myself and my baby.

The mornings of pregnancy now became slow and warm. My permanent anxiety began to fur over. We had no house yet. It had not been decided by 'The Committee' as I secretly called them – Mother, Joey and my father – where we would live. Until then, I found peace in Grennanstown, the house where I had been a solitary child.

Joey took evasive action. He buried himself in work, went away often, stayed away. To give him credit, he used the time productively. Every venture became lined with gold. Profits skyrocketed from that year.

Did I have pride in him? Not at all. If he had run the Paris Opera House – perhaps. But Joey probably thought the Paris Opera House was a five-furlong handicap.

My father spoke ceaselessly to Mother and me of 'our gold rush'.

'Girls, 'tis only like the Yukon.'

We had something in us that made people come to us to lose their money. Joey spent a lot of time in Dublin and in the west, and then in England again. We opened a betting shop in Liverpool, one in Chester, one in Wolverhampton. *Halpin's: We're the Best Bet!*

This 'boom' kept Joey away from Grennanstown House for two weekends out of three. If he phoned, he and I had little to say to each other. Knowing the range of Mother's earshot I gave him news of her and my father. I asked him questions about hotels and weather. Then he spoke to Mother. She laughed at length. When he did return at a weekend we met principally at Mother's dinners.

These meals were never taken without several other guests. To show, I suppose, our ever-growing wealth. And Mother was turning herself into a lady of the manor. At one stage she wondered whether my father should dress for dinner every evening. That was, as he said himself, 'never a runner'.

Joey and I did not even have to look at each other during these long-table events. We sat on the same side, with guests' between us. Everybody talked to him about the money he was making, about his travels, the new Halpin's shops. Quite extraordinary, really: nobody queried that a young husband should spend so much time away from his new bride. I hoped that everybody was going along with some unspoken understanding about our marriage. No. They were only interested in the money.

Sometimes when he was near me, a certain sadness seemed to come over Joey. He kept looking at the bump in my stomach. But he said nothing. I think he knew he had blown the chance to share in something essential.

Anyway, he was seeing a lot of Miss Josephine Scannell. Black hairs on his white collars. Lipstick on the front tails of his shirts. Receipts for many meals for two. He wore clothes I knew he could never have bought for himself. But I had become placid with child and this daily serenity helped me work out a future means of living.

When the baby had grown enough, I would find a means of independence. I would tell Mother that I wanted things that way. If she objected I would tell her some of the truth. Then I would threaten to tell her all the truth. Then I would threaten to tell everyone. If Mother made trouble I would hand her a letter permitting Dr MacMenamin to break his confidentiality towards me. Nobody in the world could disbelieve a man so direct.

As for my baby, I didn't do Commerce in Cork without learning about trust funds (Joey worried about this knowledge in me). When the time came, whatever income I had or could earn, at least the baby would be fed and found.

Until those days I would attend Mass every Sunday

morning. I would be a dutiful wife if Joey were home. A dutiful daughter if not. I had to appear thus. People did not leave their husbands in our parish. No divorce anywhere.

I think a lot now about that fleeting glimpse of Joey's sadness, about his looking at my stomach. He knew, I am certain, that he had excluded himself from something precious. But he needed his coarseness and his control more than he needed me. He had his half-share in the business. Joey got what he came for. And he never touched me again.

It was at this time that I developed my fixation with weather. I began to get very interested in sunset times. I watched the direction of the wind. Or whether it would rain. We had a barometer in the hall at Grennanstown House. On the window-sill beside it, above the umbrellas and golf clubs, sat a compass in a black round box. It belonged to my mother's uncle, who had his master's ticket out of Limerick port. During clear days, I sat out in the garden, well wrapped up. I twisted the compass round and round, familiar with all points. It was as if I were mapping my life, searching for a direction. I gave myself the pleasure, too, of thinking about everybody I liked. I wasn't lonely, then, like I was before, but I wasn't lonely because of the baby.

My room had a deep seat in a window alcove. In this alcove, dressing slowly, I sat or knelt on the window-seat. Looking out on the day and the weather. Richard says that when he came to live in our county, the first thing he noticed was the cloud formation. He says the cloud formations around here are unique. He spends a lot of time looking at them. Richard has travelled the world, so he knows about clouds. He had few clouds, he says, in the skies above California when he was a boy.

For hours daily, I sat in that window. A line of poplars near the house changed colour with each gust of wind. The birds came and went like angels. They made such a contrast to the news on the radio. We had endless politics and current affairs. We had Unionism and Nationalism and Republicanism and Loyalism and Civil Rights. Richard to this day is fantastically interested in all that, says America should settle it. I never had any interest, at least not until the IRA proved useful to me.

Most days I walked, perhaps several miles at a time. Always the same journey to begin with, until I reached the woods. Then I hardly ever took the same route on two consecutive days of that mild winter/spring.

My face bloomed and my hair grew even glossier.

'Nature's boon,' the women nearby said, the women I met on my long walks. I became quite friendly with one or two of them. I saw their babies, accepted their good wishes.

There was, is, one walk that took me to the edge of the woods. My Granddad Halpin grew up there. He was a railwayman, who went on to buy shares in the railway. (Like Richard's great-grandfather, James John Huttle.) That is how the Halpin money began. Granddad lived in a tall, small house out by Bishopswood. I often thought of buying it. Too close then, three miles, to home. The house had a red door then and has it now. It's bigger now, a little terrace of tall, small railway cottages knocked together and lovely inside with views on to wooded uplands.

These are the same woods in which Joey violated my body. These are rich spreads of horse chestnut and beech and ash and elm and pine and larch and lime, all mixed up. Once I saw a jumping deer.

By undergrowth full of scurrying noises, there was a

102

log seat. On this bench several times sat a small, elderly man. He was a retired forester who had never fallen out of love with the trees.

'You always know where you are with timber,' he said to me.

I asked him things and he told me. About the ash coming into leaf long after the others. About the hazelnut slipping out of its cluster when it's ripe. He taught me about the two colours of horse chestnut flower, white and pink; 'the chestnuts of India'.

He said, 'The hard thing is, about squirrels and wood-peckers, they're pests too. Ordinary vermin, rats and that, no bother getting rid of them. But how could you kill a woodpecker and it looking so handsome?'

Men who work in the country have a delicacy towards women. My old forester man suspected there was some trouble in my life. He never asked me outright. He made gentle, gliding remarks.

He would say, 'There's nothing like looking at a tree for calming down trouble inside a person.'

He would say, 'When I was ever in bother, I'd always come out here and count the leaves.'

He would say, 'After Hannah died, I always came out up here to think into things.'

Then one day he looked at me. He knew I had about two weeks left and that I really should not have been out walking. But my slimness held the pregnancy so well. So he said, 'A lucky child you'll have, to have such a nice young mother ahead of it. Good luck now with yourself.' I love men with instinct.

I took the hint and went walking no more. There and then I decided to call the baby after Johnnie Ross or his late beloved wife, Hannah.

Mother proved interesting during all this time. She

watched me intently. I eyed her even more keenly in case she was giving any signals of drawing nearer. Wrong. She never did. Being then placid blunted my regret.

One dramatic day, I watched her from my window-nook above as she walked across the gravel from the stables. Suddenly, I saw her both in reality and in my imagination's eye. This walking woman seemed to have grown a square aluminium box where her head was. Another, larger and shinier, encased her hips.

She walked along, completely recognizable. But instead of head and pelvis, she had these two strong and gleaming boxes.

15

All day today we have had high winds and molten sunlight, a combination I think peculiar, like the marvellous cloud formations, to the south of Ireland. I have just driven back from another stay at the Kilnoran Lodge and my heart is high. No work; I refused to speak to the office for the past two days; they are so rude – all those questions about my health. They complain that I have not filed copy for two weeks and will not accept my excuses that one bomb is much the same as another.

Never mind: I saw her; I saw Ann – on two occasions, the second at length! Every doubt I ever had has evaporated; I am more smitten than ever. Fanfares, please – on golden trumpets! A glimpse would have satisfied me; my heart and my soul convince me that I have not been dreaming, that I have been right instinctively all along. She is the woman for me and I don't care how long I have to wait for her. A major fear has evaporated; I have worried that my original sight of her had become a fantasy; I was wrong.

Yesterday afternoon, I had to find once again the road angle which revealed the house through the trees. My right shoe has a hole in it, and the water in the puddles got in (I forgot to pack socks).

Suddenly I saw her in my rear-view mirror; she had evidently been for a walk alone. She walked down a small slope of the narrow road, between bushes already beginning to bud, her head high, hands deep in the pockets of a heavy grey coat. She has purpose in her walk, but I cannot begin to guess what the purpose may be. Her hair flowed.

I raised the newspaper so that she could not see my face and she strode down the hill past the car without looking; she seems placid, lost in thought, rosy of cheek; all I saw was her profile. I am glad she did not see me; I have not had time to wash or shave. My hands trembled, they are shaking now, because my visions of her in the past have all been true, but of course I now have a new picture.

There is an old saying: 'Enough is as good as a feast'; I had a feast. Yet – such good fortune: I was about to banquet! I now have several more images of her to carry around in my head because this morning I became a journalist in the interests of my own heart's desire. As though she were the subject of some news story, I adopted the simple ploy of waiting outside that Georgian house on a Sunday and following the family car. In the church at Mooreville, she, her parents and her husband (and I have to concede that he is a big, handsome man) took pews in the centre aisle. By taking a side aisle and sitting a little back from her, I observed her quite fully.

She did not take Communion (nor did her husband); thus I was denied a full frontal view of her; nor did I dare to let her see me, in case (vain hope) she recognized me from the wedding day. I nevertheless had great sweet sight of her and the more I saw the more I loved. Her beauty has increased and she has the remoteness of the truly beautiful woman. My heart lurched, my thoughts became random and excitable; I am still flushed.

How I wish to protect her! How I wish to see the

106

blue veins of milk on her breasts! How I wish to be the man who raises her child! But such a woman, so firm and distant – will she leave a man she has decided to marry? I think not. Will, perhaps, my aspiration become impossible? Oh, God!

Her father seems amiable, a long man dressed expensively, although, I think, self-made, because he does not wear his clothes as if they were his. He has a lean, weathered face and though his eyes seem unsharp, he may not be without cunning. At second impression the husband seems a lively fellow, much younger than me, looking around him constantly and outside greeting people as cordially as a politician. I raced from the church at the end so that I could get an unobvious vantage point.

Ann made straight for the car with her mother and they stood for a moment or two waiting for the men to catch up. I watched them from beneath a tree while pretending to fumble with newspapers. My lips kept forming the words, 'love' and 'Ann', and then her husband came to the car; all opened their doors and, sitting in the back with her mother, Ann Halpin, the woman that I know I am right, so right, to love, drove away in her husband's black Mercedes.

What is the picture that stays most in my mind? My original view of her survives, and now I have two others, very strong, to place alongside that of the wedding day; the first of that tall, loping gait of hers as she strode down the road, through the gate and up the drive to her home; the second as she stepped carefully down the steps of the church, her elegant coat falling open a little, her fair hair sweeping about her face as she bent her head. She has high cheekbones, and eyes spaced widely apart. What I am left with now is a tremendous hunger to see her again, to watch her with fuller advantage, to observe the weather of her moods as they blow across her face.

I have not yet had a good view of her hands and amazingly it has only just now occurred to me to wonder what age she is. Is she thirty? No – but she might be, there is a maturity in her, it shows in her step, in her carriage, in her slight distance from everyone; twenty-four, I should think, twenty-five perhaps. Her clothes are exquisite, unusual in a town this small, but I suppose her husband gives her a large clothes budget. I hope he does not buy clothes with her; that is something to which I very much look forward. Soon, I may think of making a move, but – but: even as I say that I still hesitate. Perhaps . . . Perhaps . . .

16

All girls think of birth. At school we feared the pain. But thrilled to the thought of it, too. We didn't know it was so wet a business. The pain? I never minded the pain. I hadn't much, any. As easy as sauce from a jar.

I had two midwives. One had just qualified. The other had years of experience. Strong as horses, both were irreverent. They ooh-ed and aah-ed over Joey. 'God, Mrs Martin, he's a hunk.' Then talked about me when they thought the drowsy drugs had kicked in.

'Will she keep that figure?' asked the younger; I liked her priorities.

'Ah, I'd say so,' said the older who always said 'Ah' when she opened her mouth. She must have met too many doctors. 'Look at the bones on her, she'll not spread into fat. That long bony back.'

'But did you see the bones of him?' asked the younger who had had an exchange with Joey, stopped him throwing his weight around. 'Fine thing. Where'd she find that? Has he a brother?'

And then – oh, the baby! He was a darling, my Ross. He was small and wrinkled and bloody and red. He was a darling and he was mine. He was all mine. His legs were as bandy as a jockey's. His eyes were as tight as tuppence. He was lovely.

I had hardly to push at all. He slid out like a boy going

to a dance. The only uncomfortable part of the whole business was being driven to the hospital by Mother. She immediately found a way to telephone Joey. And told him to come home. I never wanted to see him.

But Joey is Joey, and Joey always wanted to be seen doing the right thing. So long as he could be seen doing it by the right people. So Joey came with a bunch of flowers bigger than himself. At least he was open enough to say, 'It impresses the nurses.'

Joey seemed awkward. He never asked to see the baby, who was brought in anyway by the nurse. He was sitting there when my father arrived.

'Will you look at that, the happy parents with their lovely little baby. Boys-boys, I wish I had a photograph of that.'

Then he did something sentimentally awful. He pulled a cigar out of his top pocket and gave it to Joey. I winced and must have looked very uncomfortable. The older midwife, who also worked as a staff nurse, came in and read it right.

'There's no smoking here. Mrs Martin, you're over-doing it, are you? Ah, you promised me you wouldn't, and it'll soon be time for the baby's feed.'

She shooed my father and Joey out. 'The pub's the place for men at a time like this, not here under our feet. Isn't that right, Mrs Martin?'

She winked and they left, my father generating what I am sure he thought was an amiable, biddable pro-test.

And then Mother arrived and in the neutral distance that passed for warmth from her to me, we had a con-versation about names. I lied – and won.

'So it's just plain "Ross", is it?'

'Yes, Mother.'

'I was hoping' – here it comes – 'that you might call him after my father.'

Not a word from me.

'I was. Why are you calling him "Ross", it's such a Protestant name?'

'Not among Scottish Catholics, Mother.'

A big lie always works with people who lie to themselves.

She brightened. 'Scottish Catholics? Do they have a St Ross?'

'He's not canonized yet, Mother, but I have great devotion to him. He was called James Ross, and he was martyred by Calvinists.' The nuns told us that a lie has only one leg. It needs another lie to stand on. I might have given 'James Ross' four legs it worked so well. Mother looked pleased. 'James Ross' was one of my best spur-of-the-moment inventions.

'It'll be the first "Ross" in the family, I'll say that for it,' she conceded. She left the room and came back a few minutes later. 'Joseph is thrilled.' She had caught up with them in the hallway.

'At the name?'

'Oh, yes. He told me he thought it had class, real class. I must say I began to agree with him.'

I can still scarcely bear that my family only believed me when I told them lies. It was a trick I had slowly been perfecting.

And Ross? Oh, the feeling, the almost panicky excitement! The joy of holding him in my arms. That very first moment of being left completely alone with him! His little mouth seemed like something you see inside a shell on the seashore, all pink and puckering in and out. His perfect little fingers and toes were personally counted by me.

I never read any book or saw any picture that told me what it is like to hold my own son in my arms. Only recently have I been able, without gasping or weeping, to come back in my mind to that moment. It was the most particular moment of my life. He was a butterfly out of the chrysalis, my own wonderful butterfly who lay in my arms with his squeezed little eyes and tiny toenails.

17

Father Andy Coll has become so possessive of me, and he at last has betrayed his true interest – he wants publicity; he wants to be seen as a saviour. But he has taken me nowhere in these enquiries; I did not need him, I never needed him; therefore I went it alone – today, yesterday and the day before I conducted my own investigations.

This is the sensational result: I was kidnapped by the IRA; I was kidnapped and tortured by them but shall tell nobody – and I have seen a kingfisher like an angel come to save me.

That unpleasant priest droned on about the three secret burials; told me a dozen times that three IRA members had been taken from Belfast by the IRA and questioned at length in a number of different houses out in the countryside near the Border. After torture sufficient to make them confess to the extent of their collaboration with the security forces, they then spent some time with Republican families until the high command decided their fate. Found guilty of informing, each received the verdict of death and each was taken into the dark fields at night to be shot dead by two IRA members simultaneously. Something the priest said (I now find him extraordinarily irritating) triggered an idea; the family with whom one of the men spent his last days had grown unusually attached to him and pled for him – in vain, but

113

it suggested to me that they might mourn him and thus, perhaps, speak to me. In this I made an error.

They agreed to see me; I telephoned, told them who I was, concealed nothing, and when I drove down the lane to their farmhouse eight miles from Newry, I saw that two cars followed me; where they came from I do not know, nor did I attach any importance to them at the time. A dog greeted me, wagging its tail – but that was the last friendly act of the day or the next thirty-six hours.

I had spoken to a woman on the telephone, but no woman came to greet me; a man waited by the door, did not shake hands – and that did strike me as unusual; the Irish have natural courtesy. I followed him indoors, walked behind him to the fireplace and the door behind me slammed. The kitchen was full of men wearing balaclavas. One came forward and kicked me with a heavy boot on the right knee – I thought the patella had been shattered. I stood there, not knowing what to do – to scream or to be stoic; something hit me on the head and I staggered but did not fall; two of the men pushed me to a heavy wooden kitchen chair and slammed me down. Then they stood before me; the rest stood behind the chair; I could hear their breathing; something trickled down the back of my neck – I put back my fingers to feel: it was blood from the blow and for some reason the sight of it on my fingers comforted me.

'What's your business here?'

I said, 'I telephoned. I told the woman.'

'What's your business?'

'A priest. Father Andy Coll. I'm a reporter.' I had heard that the paramilitaries, needing publicity, did not damage journalists.

'Reporting what?'

'This priest. Father Andy Coll.' I had wet my trousers

114

and my tongue did not work well. Into my mind came a vision of walking peacefully near Maiden Castle with my father on my eighth birthday as he explained to me the long history of the hill-fort; I achieved a closeness to him that day which has not returned. Tonight I telephoned my father and was surprised to hear him ask, 'Everything all right with you?'

'What's a priest got to do with anything? What are you reporting?'

'I heard – the priest told me – that some men had been shot and buried near here. I wanted to find out if it's true.' Might as well come clean.

'Why?'

'To write about it.'

'Why?'

'For my newspaper. For the readers.'

'What's it to do with them?'

I did not know how to answer that. A woman wearing a scarf wrapped around her head so completely that I could not tell her age walked in carrying a pan of boiling water. She laid it on the table with a hypodermic syringe beside it; the men tore the sleeve off my shirt and tied my wrists savagely. I must have passed out.

When I woke up, I had three thoughts that I can recall: my father's presence – he is, like me, tall and thin; Ann's face – again; and thirdly, the damp of the small room in which I lay. I stretched and found I was not bound, was fully dressed. Some light came through from a small, dirty window; this was not a room but a barn and I lay on some old canvas on the floor. Nothing seemed to have been taken from my pockets. Some wires curled beneath the door; I wet myself again; I smelled rank. They had imprisoned me with a booby trap and I did not know where I was; I fear that I began to weep.

The tears eased me and I climbed softly to the window; darkness was falling and this hut or barn or shed stood out in the middle of the countryside with, as far as I could make out, nothing near it. While I still had enough light, I inspected the window: too small to escape; then I examined the floor – rough concrete and no obstruction between me and the door. Did the door have a lock?

A wind blew and the door creaked open a little, enough to give me a view of the wires – they led nowhere: a joke. I opened the door further and saw nothing but an empty field and a lane with my car parked on it.

The kingfisher flew across in front of my face, a small piece of lovely voltage.

In the car someone had courteously replaced everything as I had left it – my contacts book, my spiral-bound notebooks, my small case. Had I met a roadblock tonight on my way back to Dublin I should have been in trouble, because I rarely drove beneath ninety miles an hour.

The cleverness of these terrorists has never been fully charted; no trace of the hypodermic injection, no trace of soreness on my knee, not even a bruise; I searched my head with my fingers to find where the blow had landed – but they had washed and ironed my shirt, they must have, because the collar had no trace of bloodstains. And they had even stitched my shirt-sleeve back together so expertly I could not find where they had ripped it.

I must speak to the hotel manager about the invasiveness of his staff. One of the porters called to the room without telephoning and when I answered the door said to me sociably, 'Oh, there's a man, Mr Hunter, always wanting to meet you, do you know Dr Leamy at all, he does a lot of the work for the hotel, you know the guests and that?'

A man came forward and said, 'Hallo, nice to meet you.'

I closed the door on him: I am much too busy.

18

It never dimmed, that pleasure of holding baby Ross. Feeding him. Touching him. Stroking his little face, his little cheeks of down and his soft skin. That pleasure, whatever my later despair, never faded. It sustained me many a day, that memory. He was someone I could smile at, someone I could be nice to without it being doubted or suspected. I gave him the hugs I dreamed of when I was a girl.

He slept in my arms after his feed. I kept his little feet safe in the hollow of my hand. And I looked down at his dear face which for a time became my crystal ball. There is no loving like the loving of a baby. Nor is there any anguish like the anxiety of a mother.

What's wrong with love? I know what's wrong with love – the fear of losing it, that's what's wrong. The joy of Ross was soon accompanied by some terrible nameless apprehension. My pregnant tranquillity evaporated. I felt scooped up again in a system of danger.

Three nights after Ross was born, Joey turned to me in the hospital while I was nursing. He didn't like to see me breast-feeding. Everybody tried to stop me. Except the nurses. 'Don't listen to anyone, Mrs Martin, you do what you want to do. Isn't it only Nature?'

Joey asked in his lethal mock-innocence, 'Them arms

of his, they look very rubbery, does he have bones yet that can break?' And he smiled at me and winked: 'How'ya doin', Sugar?'

I didn't leave Joey then. I should have, because I jumped with fear every time Joey approached the cradle. Every time he lifted the carrycot into the car. And whispered, 'I'd better not drop this, heh, Sugar?'

Once at Sunday lunch Ross dribbled all over Joey's new dove-grey suit. Mother, even Mother, saw the fast annoyance. Cool Joey wasn't able to hide it.

My father tried to pacify. 'Sign of good luck. That's what my mother always said. Time to have another soon, so.' He was embarrassed.

'Here,' cut Joey at me. 'Take him.' His eyes contained illimitable rage.

That night, first steps to an escape route, I rang Professor MacCartan. Could he clear the way for me to do a doctorate in Dublin? He said, in his pleasant way, that he knew they would be delighted with me in Dublin.

Then Joey said he would come and stay with me in Dublin. 'Ideal to have a Dublin flat, Sugar. Talk of the town for Joey.'

Mother's idea, it transpired.

Joey wanted to take the first flat we looked at. Hatch Place. I twigged why. She, the Scannell creature, had a flat in Earlsfort Terrace. Three minutes' walk away.

So be it. I found a mews house off Adelaide Road. Near Leeson Street Bridge. I could take Ross for walks along the canal. See the swans. Joey could hardly contain himself. Scannell was now not three minutes' walk away, but two. She lived near enough for a quick call. Under the guise of slipping out for twenty Players and a box of matches.

I was a hoarder then. God, please forgive me. I noted

and hoarded every occasion Joey went out. Every twenty Sweet Afton or Senior Service. Every box of matches.

'The fix, Sugar,' he'd call, and rush through the hall while I was upstairs with Ross.

Should I have been grateful that Scannell took his attention away from me? Joey's hook in me was now drawn. But no. I hoarded every one of his 'cigarette' outings. Was I still suffering jealousy? Which would be 'weird', as Richard would say. Was I hoarding grievances to avenge? I cannot now say.

Joey was otherwise physically docile. This surprised me. Then, one weekend home, I found out why.

'That baby's doing well,' Dr MacMenamin said. 'A pound heavier than he should be.' Ross drooled and smiled. 'But I never mind that with boys.'

He patted and prodded gently. Ross still smiled. He smiled at everything, that lovely boy. Even at spiders, and wasps.

'And you?'

'You know me.' Fending off, fending off.

'I do, but how are you?'

'Same old scrapings, Dr Mac.'

'Did he tell you he came to see me?'

'Who? Joey? He didn't, did he?!'

'I think he was trying to get me on his side, afraid of what I knew. He said he had bronchitis; funny place to have bronchitis, I thought, in his stomach.'

I laughed. Dr MacMenamin was like a red mullet. His psoriasis blared where his hair receded.

'What did he say?'

'It was more what did I say.' More than Dr MacMenamin's skin was dry.

'That's why he's so quiet.'

'I hinted you'd have a job having more babies.'

'You're a star, Dr Mac.'

'How are things in that department?'

'Joey hasn't come next nor near me. You must have frightened him off.'

'He's fond of the law.' Dr MacMenamin, a thin man, smiled.

'Judge Joey. He's always quoting it.'

'So I did the old thing,' said Dr MacMenamin, patting Ross's tummy. 'I poisoned him with his own favourite food. I told him I was in a hurry, I was giving evidence in a court case. "What kind of a case?" he asked me. "Domestic violence," I told him. I said I was an expert witness.'

'Dr Mac! You all-time great! If I wasn't a married lady I'd marry you all over again.' When he blushed, his psoriasis disappeared into the blushes. 'What'd Joey say?'

Dr MacMenamin inclined his head like a pigeon. 'He gave me a tip for a horse going that Saturday at Leopardstown.' I waited. 'The animal is still running, for all I know.'

I left, laughing and laughing. And not telling him about Joey's taunts.

'If he fell on his head now, Sugar, at this age, or was dropped, what would that do to him?'

Or – 'Would hot water burn him bad, Sugar?'

And – 'I often heard, Sugar, 'twas good for a child to fast twenty-four hours.'

Or – 'They hate flame, don't they, Sugar? But they're puzzled by it.'

When I was little, Grandfather Halpin took me to the junction. He had worked there as a boy out of school. Cleaning signals, working sidings, greasing points. He showed me the mail grab. A large metal arm hung out over the track. As the night mail flew through the station, a metal ring, draped with a strong net of white mesh and attached to the side of the train, reached out its paw.

At top speed the paw grabbed inwards the mailbags hanging on the arm. Tossed them into the sorting car. I began to feel that Ross and I were like the mailbags. Life or some force was grabbing us at top speed. We were among tearing hands – and I knew it.

One Sunday, Liam arrived. Ross's godfather, for God's sake! I was outmanoeuvred and outnumbered on that one. Nothing I could do.

Liam brought a bottle of vodka and a bottle of Bacardi that Sunday.

'The whore's cocktail, Annie. Bacardi and voddy.'

Why do I mind so much being called 'Annie'? Or was it that lout's presumption of intimacy?

Vodka looses people's senses and Liam dived at the couch where I had let Ross lie to kick.

'And Slattery has the ball. He's streaking down the wing. He dummies past one man. He dummies past two. He's running into heavy defence. But he's got young Martin outside him. And he slips the pass to Martin, who SCO-ORES!' He half-handed, half-threw Ross to Joey.

Joey got up and was about to repeat the performance. My preservation overcame my horror. But when I reached for Ross, Joey handed the distressed infant to Liam above my head. 'Here, Liam.' As adults play with children and a ball.

This frantic scene went on for minutes until I bit Liam savagely on the arm. He would not have the nerve to strike back and I grabbed Ross and left, into the fog of a Dublin Sunday afternoon.

Who could I tell? Nobody – because nobody liked the

way I loved Ross. My father didn't care. Janey was afraid of Mother. Auntie Lisa was in Paris. Dr MacMenamin didn't practise in Dublin.

'The child has too many clothes,' said Mother sourly one day.

I went out immediately and bought more. Ross looked great in dark green, or navy blue, or a kind of deep yellow. The auburn hair shone.

But I'll say this for Mother: she handled Ross with great affection. She may not have said wonderful things to me about him. But that was about me and not about Ross. When he was in her arms or on her knee, she treated him with a tender warmth she had long stopped giving me. Nevertheless, she was not nearly as nice about him as she was about other people's children and grandchildren.

Joey never to my assured memory, never ever, not once, bought Ross a gift of any kind. Not even a rattle or a ball or a little truck. All the gifts Ross had, he had from me.

But Joey pretended to behave as a good father. He said to my parents, 'I've put the lad's name down for both Clongowes and Glenstal.'

This is Joey who was slung out of Synge Street Christian Brothers because he was too unruly. Too unruly for the Christian Brothers – who would beat you numb for watching the wrong brand of football. 'Oh, yes, Clongowes and Glenstal,' he said in his assured way. 'If the Jesuits don't make a man of him, the Benedictines will.'

The only Benedictine Joey ever knew comes in a tall thick bottle.

Yet – people flocked to Joey. Men I respected. Women I admired. Any time we went anywhere they surrounded Joey.

This was the same Joey who said, 'I caught you giving me a funny look there, Sugar. Do that again, Sugar, and you and I will – '

He never finished the sentence but looked at Ross. No wonder I was uneasy. From then on, especially when Ross began to walk, I never left him and Joey alone together.

Oh, God, if there is a God – save my soul, if I have a soul.

19

I shall never forget today. Was I speaking aloud to myself as I walked through St Stephen's Green, past Henry Moore's big-shouldered statue of Yeats? I do not know and it does not matter.

Maybe I felt her presence; it now seems that way and that perhaps explains my agitation. Certainly I knew how she walked, how she held her head, the set of her shoulders, the fall of her hair; these have been my daily mind-furnishings. Should I have used the word 'Draconian' in that piece yesterday? I slipped it past them – Charles was away – and the steam has been rising ever since. Perhaps the term was too strong and subjective – but not inaccurate, especially as Whitehall has criticized Dublin for not bringing in stringent anti-terrorist measures, and today they have done so.

I reject the accusation that I used 'Draconian' simply because I have in some way come to sympathize with these people whose country I live in, and one of whose women I passionately and secretly love. I do not believe the other comments warrant a successful libel action, but now I have to write this completely unnecessary report for the lawyers.

Those were my thoughts. Then I saw her.

A son, she had; I had been wondering; a son. She held him in her arms to see the ducks who waddled along the path. He gazed as children do, with the eternal gravity only they possess; she kissed him and they laughed.

I found a deck chair at hand and fussed with my brief-case: they stayed nearby, not more than twenty yards away. I have not seen her for so long; it seemed proper to stay away during the last stages of her confinement and I think I know that in the early days of motherhood she will scarcely have emerged; I think (and I laugh at this) that I had phantom pregnancy pains too.

This morning in the lambent sunshine I simply feasted my eyes on Ann. She wore a green coat, and a scarf flowed loosely around her neck. When she crosses a street, she walks first, pulling the baby buggy behind her, not letting the child take the risk by pushing it ahead as most parents do; I so approve – I so approve.

She lives, I discovered, in a mews house near Leeson Street Bridge. Now I will drive by when I can and watch for her; no Iron Curtain or MI5 surveillance will ever have been so tactfully deployed. And all the time I fall deeper and deeper into love and sometimes despair. Now I love her child as well, a sweet, sweet boy. Like lovers, they kiss and laugh, and they play and chuckle and hug, and when she lifts him from his buggy he puts his cheek to hers, or laughs and excitedly points to things.

I love them. Can I, I wonder, think myself into a thought system where I can give them protection – even though they do not know that I exist?

Sometimes I halt myself in my reveries and ask myself whether all this is not too outlandish. Then, something happens which brings home to me the power of even the most outrageous possibility on this island, the element of the unexpected in life. Last week three IRA prisoners were air-lifted out of their prison exercise yard by a com-mandeered helicopter. Difficult not to laugh and laugh and laugh. To date they have not been recaptured; the helicopter landed minutes later on a racecourse and the men vanished into the suburban hinterland; they might as well have gone into rain forests.

I cheered when I heard it but all I could do was report the facts: in the middle of the day, while prisoners were exercising, a helicopter came right down into the prison yard and as the other prisoners held the warders at bay, three key IRA men ran to the helicopter and were taken up, up and away.

The air is full of politics. This afternoon, the Home Secretary announced the formation of a new Executive of eleven members to sit at Stormont and I had a row with the newsdesk – they will not let me cover the story. More annoying is the fact I was due to go to Sunningdale in two weeks' time for a Council of Ireland meeting. Nor have they said I can attend regularly the meetings of the Northern Ireland Executive from January next.

Have had my hair cut, not for any reason other than that I have begun to tire of its length. A telephone call this afternoon from the Editor's secretary, Paula; pompous woman, she tells me that Charles is coming over to see me; she was evasive; there must be a race meeting on. My general calm has become, to me, extraordinary; I have forbidden the hotel maids to take the empty bottles from my room.

This afternoon I strolled up and down the canal bank near where Ann lives – and I was rewarded; they emerged and I was able to walk behind them at a respectful distance as she and her little boy went to the Shelbourne; I settled myself in an armchair near them; people looked at me a great deal – any stranger in town excites interest. The little boy has begun to crawl and to stand. The people having tea all smiled at him: impossible not to;

then his mother collared him and brought him back to her chair some feet away from mine where I gazed on them with pleasure, excitement and the massive, almost tearful relief of seeing them. A waitress approached and I heard Ann speak. She has a slow and cultivated voice, a country accent but a refined one; she speaks very clearly with broad vowels and an interesting vocabulary.

Ann said, 'Someone's expecting to come and meet us. We'll have coffee when she reaches us. For now I'll take orange. Himself' – indicating the little boy – 'will enjoy orange also.'

Short sentences, softly spoken; unusually short sentences; I leaned forward to listen and she half-glanced in my direction; had the Editor been punctual, he would have seen me blush. She was wearing a navy linen coat; at her neck a scarf with a red and navy geometric pattern, and superb shoes – high block heels, and a single strap over the instep. Her long hands moved slowly; she did not remove her coat, but opened it; I could see a loose-pleated tartan skirt in red, navy and white plaid.

Her demeanour interested me most – because that, after all, is the gap I have never been able to fill in. All of the speculation and fantasizing had to do with how I might first approach her, where we might travel or live – Lisbon; Bath; Connecticut; Provence. Watching her now I think she will be all the things I want – self-contained, elegant of spirit, passive and fiery, naturally intelligent, not hysterical, can be stimulated to argue, does not drink too much. Her face suggests an under-used intelligence; her movements seem quick but she showed little interest in her surroundings. In those (few!) seconds when the little chap rested, she seemed preoccupied; if he gave her a moment's respite her gaze drifted, as if more drawn to thoughts of the faraway than the here and now. Perhaps that is what I wish her to be; perhaps I wish her to think of days when she could have a different life, and perhaps the force of my wishing thrust those thoughts into her head.

This is fabulously presumptuous of me, but I do not speculate or fantasize as I did before; I feel more sensible, and not a little amused at my egotism. In this I have begun to discipline myself: it would be so easy to have the fantasy that her life is not happy. Last night I dreamed that I was being dismembered; the night before I dreamed that I was flying like a bird; wonderful dust-storms whirl inside me. I am convinced that Ann's life has turned out foully and I prepared to approach her as she sat alone.

The little boy more or less made the acquaintance of everyone in the room. He is a distinctive chap; he crawled everywhere, played little games, especially with old ladies, and then crawled away. Every time he broke away his mother went after him and fetched him back; she stemmed his objections with a heart-warming affection; it lifts the heart to see it, even the heart of someone like me who has virtually no experience of children. She bent down and kissed him, perhaps tickled him.

I have never had occasion to study a child and his mother before, except in paintings; I have always loved Bellini's grave Madonnas in Venice, in Rome, but I feel certain that it would be difficult to find so simple and rich an affection. Others noticed it too; I saw people looking and, judging from their expressions, approving. Once, I touched the little boy's head as he crawled to my chair, he is almost able to walk; then he made urgent noises and crawled off again, and the pianist distracted him by beginning to play.

At that moment I half-rose from my seat about to speak to Ann – but the expected friend arrived, greeted

Ann warmly and extravagantly, an attractive woman quite a few years older than Ann: she seemed to have an American veneer. Ann fetched the little boy (yet again!) and the newcomer kissed him with enthusiasm. How annoying!

20

If you're badly hurt in your heart you become a Recording Angel. Survival does that. You measure your score. Make sure it isn't getting worse. Keep an eye on what was done to you. Make sure it doesn't happen again. Mothers are natural recording angels. They have to be, to clock up experience. Experience creates safety. I can't give up the habit. I still enter everything in my mind's logbook. I suppose that is why I am writing all this down.

I was thinking this morning as I stood at the upstairs window. Richard was still asleep (if you could call it sleep). I was thinking, 'Did anyone like me in those days?' Not a nice thought. Worse than that, I had no idea what people thought of me nor had I any idea of what I looked like. I couldn't fix a picture of myself in my mind.

But I charted every day of Ross's early existence. Many, many times I have thanked God that I did.

At six months he could have gambled in any poker school. A year old, he could have ridden in the Grand National!

I kept photographs that nobody ever saw. The notes on the back of them had every detail of his little life. I took them with a camera Joey never knew I had, and I suppose those pictures vanished with the rest of my things.

When he began to crawl, trust Ross, he did it differently from anyone. He did it backwards, heels first, then legs and tummy, followed by the Grin. Then he learned to crawl forward and he was like a rocket.

And when Ross learned to talk, Ross talked all the time. To me. To his grandparents at weekends. To the people next door in Dublin. To a dog we would meet on a walk. To the birds on the window-sill when I spread crumbs for them in the winter.

'Dog, Mamma, dog.' It was the first word he learned. For a time, everything, a dog, a cat, a tree, a bird became 'Dog, Mamma, dog.'

'That child is going to turn out stupid, Sugar. Bleedin' do something about it,' muttered Joey.

'Dog, Mamma, dog,' said Ross, pointing to an angora goat at the zoo.

Then came the garden party, dreadful, dreadful day. It began as Joey's idea, 'to be held annually, Mrs Halpin.' In Grennanstown House – 'good for contacts'. But I knew why Joey wanted it. First, to legitimize his relationship with Josephine Scannell. She was now his 'secretary' in the Dublin office. Secondly, to get his family's snouts into our general trough. Then it became Mother's idea.

'I'm givin' Joey his head,' said my admiring father. 'I never seen a man make money like him.'

Fine by me. The summer of 1975 shone all day and balmed us all night. Hence the garden party.

We had never seen much of Eamonn Martin, Joey's father. He's a harmless, sandy-haired taxi-driver, retired now. Kay is his worse-than-appalling wife. We had seen too much of Liam. Of the Martin twins, Majella and Jacinta, I had seen nothing for three years – not since the wedding. That was even too close an acquaintance. I have nothing against working-class people. I remember with affection the forestry labourer whose name I gave Ross.

The Martin twins simply jarred with me.

'Oh, howya there, how much d'ya pay for that?' the twins whooped in chorus when they saw me. They stole toothpaste and eau-de-Cologne from my room. Two years younger than Joey, they huddled like lemurs, giggling. God! They were in their thirties! I wonder where they are now?

Joey, Liam and the twins had obscene four-way conversations, all about 'getting your ring', meaning sex. 'Gee' was their word for female parts. They had a joke about a Dublinman called 'Ulick McGee'.

'You're a bit stuck-up, Annie. Like your old lady,' said Liam.

I shut him up by saying, 'Would you like me to tell her you said that?'

Joey's standing with Mother rose skywards. She more or less fawned upon him.

'There, Sugar,' he would say to me, holding out a cupped palm, 'there is where I have your old lady. In the palm of my hand. Sprawled there like a crab.' Joey had a poetic touch at times.

The day of the garden party began hot. July again, bloody July, July and Joey. I woke early and went to the window. Hammers and ropes astrew the lawns. Marquee yet to be rounded off. A hen clucked somewhere in the bushes. Dew. I remember a story I read about footsteps across a dewy morning lawn.

My heart felt heavy. I put it down to Josephine Scannell – coming here, to my family home, and by Jesus I did not want her touching Ross!

Then Ross woke in his little room off my bathroom. Oddly, he started to call me; he never did that. Sometimes he climbed out of his cot, hit the floor with a thud. Then clambered into my bed. He grinned and whispered like a soft, chubby, pink conspirator. Then snuggled into me, lifting my arm so that he could get his little head on my shoulder.

Not this morning.

'Mamma. Mamma.' Not an insistent or a distressed cry. Just a gently troubled, soft call. I had been wearing nothing, such a hot night. I picked him from the cot and held him tight. He fretted and I climbed back into bed.

'Mamma?'

'Yes, lovey boy.'

'Hot, Mamma.'

I checked him, in case of a fever or a heat rash. No, no trace.

'Ross, I'm hot too.'

'Poor Mamma.'

But when I held him tighter to me, in his favourite position, he wriggled and then fretted further.

'Poor Ross, Mamma.'

'Yes, lovey.'

'And poor Mamma, Mamma.'

Then he smiled and wiped my forehead with the corner of the sheet and then wiped his own face. He never bounced or laughed that morning. He just lay quietly. I should have known. No, I should have listened. Some terrible voice was speaking to me and I ignored it.

And we had been having such a lovely time. The day before, I went out in the car to see whether Janey Little would come and help with the drinks. Janey fussed over Ross as if he were a crown prince. He fell in love with the twin kid-goats Janey kept in her quarter-acre. He had long ago fallen in love with Janey and she with him.

'Little?' he asked with his quick way. 'Me little.'

134

'Yes, I'm "Little" as well,' smiled Janey, giving him biscuits.

In the car on the way home Ross and I sang 'This old man, he played one, he played knick-knack on my tum,' and I poked Ross in the tummy.

When I went on to the next verse, 'Knick-knack on my shoe', he called, 'No, play one, Mamma, play one.' Which had guarantees of tummy-poking in it. His eyes looked like mine. When I see myself in the mirror each morning I can see Ross's eyes too. That resemblance has cut slices off the sides of my heart!

The sun hit Grennanstown hard that day. River in the distance looking metallic. Bridge at Silverbridge turned white. All sights, I now think, harsh. By three o'clock, people poured through the gates. My father's purchasing power had hired two of the local police: 'Come in yer uniforms, lads,' he said, although they were off-duty.

Mother throve, a one-woman receiving line. A knot grew in my stomach. I suffered a deepening nausea of apprehension. Why? Was it simply the imminent arrival of Josephine Scannell?

Ross never let go of my skirt.

She came in a new car. Joey saw me look at the car. She, unlike most other guests, was allowed to drive in and park with the family cars.

'Yeah, Sugar. It is, you're right. It is a company car, right?'

I said nothing.

'Hallo again,' she said as she came to meet us. 'Long time no see. Is this the son and heir?'

Ross hid behind my skirt.

I said, 'Hallo,' but I was not going to allow myself to shake her hand.

Ross said, 'Mamma, we go drive.'

135

'I can't, lovey, not now. But we will later, just you and me.'

'Mamma, we go drive.'

I picked him up and cuddled him.

'Can I give him a hug?' asked Josephine Scannell.

Ross flung his head away from her, dug his hands tight into the back of my neck. I could have cheered him for having the sense to reject that anaconda. She was even dressed like one. She wore some kind of tight snakeskin print with a crocodile-skin clutch bag. Appalling.

'He's a mammy's boy, I see,' she said. 'He'll grow up a cissy.'

'All OK, Sugar?' asked Joey. 'Great to see Jo here, right? You two should get pally. Swap things, like, y'know. Clothes. Or lipstick and stuff, right?' And he winked at me.

In a moment or two I heard Joey introduce her to Mother. 'They tell me you're marvellous at your job.'

Ross either sat in my arms or clung to my skirt. I made my way slowly to the marquee, chatting to many people that I knew.

In sunlight as heavy as brass the afternoon moved on. I had to mingle. That scene stays in my mind. The slow waltz of conversation. The contrast between the genuine people and the slippery ones. The genuine ones talked to anyone – and the others to anyone they might one day be able to use.

Dermot Feary was there, a man of obscene bonhomie.

'I was saying to your mother, Ann, that there's a new restaurant in Marbella and Jesus the seafood is as fresh as Kinsale.' Ten years ago he couldn't tell a prawn from a wristwatch. 'D'you know when they park the Jag they washes it just because it's a Jag.' He had a suit whose lapels shone like mirrors. His wife, Hazel (she changed it

136

from Hannah), clanked with gold and said, 'We're going to Florida next week, Dermot done a big deal there, he have two apartment buildings bought.'

They're bankrupt now, the Fearys. He was seen in the car one night out at Castle Lake with a girl who works in Lowrys Hotel – and she boasted about it. Hazel without thinking of the consequences went and sang to the tax inspectors. Mother said, 'She went down with the ship.' My father said, 'But wasn't she the iceberg, wasn't she?'

Lucy O'Connor wore a Sybil Connolly dress. And lied about it. She said Sybil Connolly had asked if she could make for her because she had such a good figure: 'A natural model, Moya, she said I was.'

Mother always believed people when they told her something that made her feel inferior.

A waiter crashed into the side of the marquee and fell, splitting his chin on a champagne glass. My father said, 'That family make their living out of insurance money.'

As I moved from group to group, I felt I floated on a cloud – of poison gas.

In the hot sun, Ross picked up my dread. Or I picked up his. Inside the marquee we sweated. Outside we roasted – a heatwave.

Ross said, 'Bikky, Mamma?'

I said foolishly, foolishly, foolishly, 'Go into the kitchen, Rossie, and ask Janey. Janey'll give you a biscuit.'

'You come, Mamma.'

'No, I'll wait here, lovey.'

'No, Mamma, you too, you too!' He started his little tantrum dance. Sometimes he grew as wild as Africa.

'Lovey, I'll be right here. I'll be just here talking to Gran-Gran.'

He went a little berserk. I crouched and held him tight and in a while he calmed down. Then I sent him away. He trotted off to the kitchen with great reluctance. Looking over his shoulder at me he gave his little wave. I watched his fat little legs and his white socks.

Five minutes after he left I became uneasy. I excused myself. In the kitchen, dear Janey said, 'He was here, and I gave him a biscuit. And then his father collected him and took him off for a walk.'

'His father?'

Janey always knew more than she ever said. 'What could I say?' she asked me helplessly. 'The child's own father?'

'No, Janey, that's all right. Where did they go?'

'I think he said the wood.'

I ran. I knocked a glass on the hall table, but I ran. I ran silently, with my brain screaming. I ran like one of those people you see fleeing the man with the knife in black-and-white films.

At the edge of the wood I saw the flash of white first, her very white thigh, the snakeskin skirt. She was half-standing, astride Joey. They had chosen a place in which they could not be seen. Unless you came in from the old path behind the garages.

I screamed, 'Ross? Where's Ross?'

She, being a woman, got the truth straight away. She pushed Joey away, pulled down her skirt. Joey could not even hide himself as he dragged his clothes together.

'Where's the fire, Sugar?' He looked foolish but tried to downface it.

'The kid, the kid!' Josephine Scannell spoke with a real force. It made me see why he fancied her.

'He's OK, right?'

'Where is he?' I screamed.

'He went back to the house, right? Keep your hair on, Sugar.' But he knew something had gone wrong.

'Which way?' I screamed. I knew which way.

Our land looped around by a neighbour's field and byre-yard. From that fence you can look straight on to our lawn, fifty yards away. But there was an unprotected grass-covered slurry pit in between. Ross must have seen the marquee and made straight for it by slipping under the fence.

I saw his shoe, his little shoe. I saw his shoe with no sock.

Part Two

21

Statistics for 1973: 250 people killed; 5,018 shooting incidents and 978 explosions, 1,595 weapons found as well as over thirty tons of explosives – and the police charged 1,414 people with terrorist offences.

Statistics for 1974: deaths arising directly from 'The Troubles': 216. Of 1,113 bombs planted, 669 exploded and almost twenty-five tons of explosives found; shooting incidents, 3,206 – security forces found over twelve hundred weapons; the courts heard more than thirteen hundred charges of terrorist offences. These are the facts that cannot be evaded; I reported on few of them; I have been away for some time. For some time.

Reading back over this journal I find I lied repeatedly to myself; I will not do so again; from this entry onwards I shall be as blunt about myself as I can. The euphemisms 'overworked' and 'exhausted' and 'battle fatigue' will not be used any more, at least not by me. I shocked Charles last week in his office when he said to his new secretary, 'Have you met our permanent Dublin correspondent, Christopher Hunter?'; he emphasized 'permanent'.

She smiled and said, 'How do you do?' a perfectly civil young woman.

Charles said, 'Christopher is on his way back to Dublin, he's been out of there for a time. He hasn't been well.'

'Oh,' she said, 'I'm sorry.'

'I had a nervous breakdown,' I said. 'A complete collapse. Nearly went loopy.' Then, fingers on my lips, I went, 'Blubba-lubba-lubba.'

'C.!' Charles twitched. 'Steady, old man.'

'No, Charles. I'm more comfortable with the facts. Probably because I'm a journalist.' The young woman laughed; I felt good about it.

Throughout my long absence, my fear has been that my (until then inexplicable) passion for Ann Halpin caused or crucially informed the breakdown. This line of thought led me nowhere with the doctors; I spent much of the time in a Hampshire 'sanatorium', where eventually I found courage to tell Dr Verne the story of how I first saw Ann and what I felt, and of my subsequent emotions and then pattern of sightings and responses within me. He listened, made no comment and later checked my dosage again, increased it slightly. I countered by taking a tablet fewer daily, and slowly led myself to clearer thought and an improved, more optimistic outlook. And that became the pattern of my recovery – such success as I have had came through my own efforts; in time I weaned myself off my medication.

I award myself marks for character – but I was left high and dry not knowing what to think or feel as to the true cause of my collapse. In the English calm of Hampshire I also felt that it was occasioned or, rather, clinched by the awful Father Coll, but I feared deepest of all that it connected to Ann Halpin. I expect I will find out the true source quite naturally.

How strange – and how delightful – to be back. In my absence the paper rented a house for the Correspondent and for any reporters passing through: this is now my home: no more hotel rooms (except on forays). Charles has been good to me; he wrote to tell me of an increased expenses budget, and today he flew in from London to see that I had settled in; I am writing this in the hour I have to spare before seeing him again (for dinner). On the telephone he commended me awkwardly for my 'bravery' – he was referring to the fact that I arranged to meet him this afternoon in the Shelbourne Hotel.

'The Shelbourne? Are you sure, C.?' – scene of my debacle, my ignominious departure, screaming and falling, when he, having been much worried, came to fetch me back to London.

'Yes, Charles.'

'Oh, well, I expect you know what you're doing.'

It made me think back – which I wanted and needed – to the occasion he mentioned, the time I last saw Ann as she and her little boy met her friend for tea. It plays in my mind now like the scenes of some film I had to leave before it ended, and was now viewing again: 'Shall I see her today?' I wondered idly, and I am thankful that the thought contained none of the dangerous, stalking *frisson* of before.

Yet the texture of that deleterious afternoon stays with me not entirely uncomfortably. Tea ordered, chairs arranged, the women interrupted each other with delight, each asking how the other was, how life dealt with them; they talked much of the little fellow, and then the conversation deepened. I recall that her friend liked Ann hugely, a good sign; I tried to angle a little closer (how embarrassing of me!) but the piano began to play again and their words were drowned. Serious business was under discussion; the faces of both women became grave, with her friend showing concern and Ann, quite animatedly, obviously telling a tale or tales. I remember wondering whether I should begin to wave and try to get

Ann's attention. Or perhaps pick the boy up in my arms and play with him, so that she would come after us and we might meet in that fashion. However, the little boy on his hands and knees became enthralled with the piano – and Charles arrived unexpectedly early (as distinct from today when Charles arrived more than an hour late; to be fair he had warned me that he might have difficulty in being punctual).

Those who have never met him, who only deal with him by telephone or in his memos, receive an incomplete impression. In person, Charles is a sensible, mature man, with none of the cynicism expressed in his written communications. Even when in the past he infuriated me, I have to say I remained aware of great sensitivity in him: people of choler often possess it; perhaps that is why they get so heated. I did not go to the airport to meet him; a Sinn Fein press conference (once again infuriatingly smooth) took me out of circulation.

The cartoonists love Charles; he has wild hair and those bulbous, thyroid eyes. This time, I greeted him civilly! We joked about his last meeting with me in the Shelbourne.

'You shouted, you know.'

'I'm so sorry,' I said. 'I'm really sorry.'

'You fell over, C. Or rather you tried to throw yourself on the floor.'

'Oh, God, Charles.'

I recall now that I had scarcely registered his presence that day. Until I heard him say, 'So, therefore, just for the time being. You can, well, I suppose, yes, you have parents, haven't you? Down in the West Country somewhere, somebody said.'

Such a moment! I looked at him and I think I said, 'Go away! Go right away, go away from here! Now!

Go now! Get away from her! Leave her alone!' People turned their heads and a hush fell.

Now Charles tells me that what I said was much ruder than that, more voluble, to say the least, and very vociferous. 'I was so taken aback, C. You talked to yourself all the time. Kept telling me to keep away from some woman or other.'

Oh, dear! I said nothing.

So this afternoon he said, 'You owe me a drink.'

I said, 'Champagne. On me, not on expenses. And you know I will not go glass for glass with you, don't you?'

'No champagne,' he said. 'The black stuff, please. This is the only place to drink it. It tastes foul at home.'

As if I didn't know; as if it and many such brews had not contributed to my recent history.

I like Charles; he has difficult ways, especially when he loses his temper, but he has kept his marriage intact and has raised two completely delightful daughters. His presence today has helped me to replay that dreadful afternoon. He and I left the lounge in a halting fashion, to put it mildly; the women still there, engrossed in conversation, took no notice – at least I hope they took no notice; perhaps by now Ann has forgotten the incident, or might never recognize me from that moment; I feel hopeful that she won't – their noses were almost touching, so great was the confidentiality with which they conversed.

Her little boy, whose name, Ross, I overheard (and have retained), had fallen asleep on the couch with his head on his mother's lap. I made to go back into the lounge but Charles had a firm grip on my arm. Then he had one of his coughing fits in which he whoops alarmingly, searching for breath; it distracted me – as he hoped it would.

147

Tonight, I can see Ann's face as clearly as if we all still sat in the Shelbourne Hotel that sunny afternoon; the little boy must be quite big by now. How I wish (but it is a milder wish than of old, if no less tender) I could drive down now, this instant, immediately, to her countryside beneath the big clouds; I could stay there until the weekend and perhaps I would meet her then and her little boy and speak to them – he would certainly speak to me and that would break no rules. The prospect, even if still only a fantasy, has none of the old feverishness in it.

But I have to play myself back in here first; Charles told me this evening that in due time he intends me to have more responsibility than ever before, more editorial freedom. Tomorrow I have to research a piece on local opinion and have it ready to run when the Birmingham bombings trial ends at the Old Bailey.

Oh, this is better! Ann's face hangs like a moon in my mind. On Dublin's streets today I again saw her walk in the walk of every woman, that lope, and she rests in my mind so much more calmly than before; gone is the fever and it has been replaced with certainty and resignation. It is good to be back; someone in the house next door is playing Haydn – I think it is the Nelson Mass.

Dublin is hot and quiet; I have time to think; tonight I sit in the garden of this house in Monkstown wearing only shorts and short sleeves, not missing a cool beer, not pining for unnameable things I never wanted anyway. Charles has gone on holiday; his deputy does not like me and therefore I shall receive less space for a few weeks or so; fine with me.

I have discovered a curious mechanism in my mind – a device like a time-lock: it will only open up to certain reflections after a period of time, and I have begun to wonder if this may be some deep, in-built safety device with which I protect myself. Certainly I could not until now consider fully my recent past; I feel that had I done so I might have had a recurrence or caused some new damage to myself. But tonight the time-lock has opened that room a little and I can look in more detail at what lies inside.

The harshest truth about a breakdown is that nobody cures you, not the psychiatrists nor the other doctors, not the nurses, not the pharmacists nor pill manufacturers – you have to cure yourself. I began that self-curative process when I reduced the medication they heaped on me every time I reported an emotional concern. No, nobody tells you about self-cure, you have to work it out for yourself. As a consequence of working it out, I now think I know how a breakdown happens and how it is cured: correction – I know how my break-down happened and how I cured myself and how I will go on curing myself. Charles's confidence in me helps too.

The primary thing I have had to understand is that the breakdown did not happen overnight: it was cumulative and came about because my spirit was not respectable, that is, not something I could respect. I know that my obsession with Ann may have precipitated it because she struck me at first glance as the kind of woman I could respect – and that is something I have never done. Nor have I really respected anybody, with the exception of Charles and one or two others and, albeit vaguely, my parents. How can I respect people when I am earning my living from their griefs and their efforts? I have been twenty years or so a journalist and in all that time I have been reporting on, by and large, the worst aspects of life; that is what makes news. But I never stopped to ask myself what it was doing to me and I believe now that it had a number of devastating effects on my inner life.

First there was the quick-fix element. Living on adrenaline from story to story, reporting a dreadful life-changing tragedy for somebody I never saw before and never would again and then passing on to the next crime, betrayal or death took me through a series of blood-filled shallows: much was awful but nothing of it was deep. This gradually made me hollow, a man with no chance of a consideration more profound than the next story, the next fix.

Each story had deep and tremendous meaning for those to whom it had happened and had I been a more considerable man I would have permitted myself to absorb consciously some of the experience of the events I was covering. That I did not, that I immediately strode without reflection through the next pool of blood, made me as unfeeling as a mercenary soldier. I know, I know – that is how professionals are supposed to behave.

The – often violent – transitoriness never permitted me time to think of my interviewees within their experiences as people; I asked the questions, but I never thought the thoughts and I never felt the feelings. Thus, in any one situation, if, say, some politician had been caught flogging – or being flogged by – a prostitute and I achieved an interview with the wife, I might – and did – ask her the question, 'How do you feel about this – from the man who has lain beside you at night for X years?' but I never stopped to ask myself, 'What does her pain really feel like? What is she feeling about the warmth of his body, about the sound of his night-breathing which she once must have loved and perhaps still does? Does she feel any better because he did not treat her in this humiliating way he obviously needed to express – or would she prefer that he had?'

People became commodities with me: I never stopped to think myself into anyone's thoughts and griefs; I stamped on any shoot of sensitivity that poked above ground. And then, when I saw a woman who so star-tlingly seemed to me the antithesis of a commodity, I was dumbstruck. That is a little over-simplistic, perhaps, but there was something in Ann that made me stop and think, made me think, 'I want to know what she feels, what she is like inside her heart.' At the very least, she was not a fix, she was not a means of earning praise.

My life on the newsdesk in London and here in Dublin was always one long round of incidents and events – and rushing from event to incident does not breed thoughtfulness. The fact that I was addressing such momentousnesses and never giving them anything other than superficial and fleeting attention meant that I never let my deeper spirit develop; I never once, for example, put together a sequence of events in my calendar year and asked myself whether they and their presence and arrangement in my life amounted to any kind of meaning. To have done so might have seemed egocentric – but it would have taught me to begin looking at patterns in myself. In fact I never looked at any patterns in myself and thereby missed the trends that would have warned me I was cracking up. I assumed that life is a random thing rather than an intelligent force.

It has also become important to me that I now attack and dismantle the system of self-justification by which I then lived. One night, a television producer – he later became head of his department – told me proudly of an interview he had done with a bereaved woman; her husband died in a London car-bomb.

'It took me an hour', he said, 'to get the bitch to cry, but I got her – I nailed her!'

'Oh, well done!' I warbled gaily – I am horrified now at such crassness.

Drink, and the appalling habits that went with it, passed airily by as an occupational hazard. While in London, when the paper went to bed we hit the pub and then the restaurant and then, often, someone's bed. We had a girl in the office, a copy-taker, and we joked about her 'friendliness'; I, too, used her, and I, too, used many others like her and I, too, distanced myself in embarrassment when such women made claims, or became distraught, or got sacked brutally, or showed signs of incipient alcoholism.

As for the breakdown itself – it is as if each event I followed and each justification I advanced had now begun to pursue me, and attack me and punish me for my failure to take them spiritually, for my insistence in seeing them only as career fodder.

I think tonight of the deepest days of my illness. They said to me that I should shave and dress carefully every day, that I should try and get myself into a routine of rendering small services to myself in a methodical way; they told me that I could rest assured I was not an alcoholic. I had no chance of resting assured; what they did not tell me was that rivers of anger and self-pity and fear and inferiority and worthlessness would flow with such power through me. First, I vacillated; I dismissed with hate all those that I had ever interviewed or trivialized or used, or I swung the other way and felt tearfully sorry for myself. Then I grew afraid of retribution, because I could never in ten lifetimes apologize to everyone I felt I had wronged. Finally I knew – knew truly – that they all had been superior to me and that I had come into their lives only to learn how fundamentally lower I was on the general scale.

There is an awful moment in a man's life when he ejaculates into the body of a woman he neither knows nor feels for; it demeans not only him and her but a whole, deep system of mankind, of breeding, of love and love-based desire. Drunk or in anger I had done that too often; literally and metaphorically I had also done it in my professional life. In eight hundred words of copy, no matter how large the headline, how can anyone possibly make sense of mothers and daughters and sons and breadwinners blown to shreds? I have seen a bloody shard of human flesh curled around a bombed telephone kiosk and immediately thought of the kudos I could earn from a good description of it.

Did Charles, cunning soul, know the cathartic possibilities of a journal when he asked me to write one? More cunning, did he know I would need it? As I write increasingly confessionally, good memories return – of my father singing 'I am the Captain of the Pinafore' at a wedding when I was about five.

The stars are exceptionally bright, and as I look at them I wonder where Ann is. Is she nearby, a few miles away in her mews house by the canal, or is she too sitting out in her garden down there among the mountains and rich rivers? If she is, I hope she is peaceful, her child safely asleep. How old is he now – between three and four, I reckon. I expect that not much will have changed in their lives during the past eighteen months and I like this new, tranquil contemplation of them.

However, I still have to retrace my steps and ascertain the facts (or otherwise) of that extraordinary event (or was it a hallucination?) along the Border. Was I kidnapped – or did my wild mind dream it all up? I dread that journey, and since I am being honest I dread too my next sighting of Ann. Will I still be in love with her?

22

My garnet ring. I have been washing dishes. No need
to. But sometimes I prefer not to use the dishwasher. So
my garnet ring shines this morning. I have a necklace of
small garnets. Mother's. I am interested to observe that
I can wear it to Mass or to a funeral but I cannot wear it
to an event of natural joy. The bread van has just called.
Tommy Halloran, with his cowlick. He knows I need
soda bread for Richard. Tommy Halloran keeps giving
us little presents of bread. He shows me the pictures of
his children.

Of the days that immediately followed the garden
party – nothing.

Days? To this very morning, with frost on the beech
trees outside this window, I know nothing of the following weeks – and weeks. Not just from grief or incapacity.
My senselessness came principally from sedation.

They sedated me immediately. I learned that years
afterwards. They said I had gone dangerous with grief.
That was the excuse they used. They used it for all the
measures they took. Why? Why? Did something snap in
them? Was Mother's jealousy of me so out of control?
It must have been. I can think of no other explanation
for such wickedness. To be a victim hurts; to survive
victimization heals.

Dr Greene, a guest there on the lawns, ran to the fence

with the others to stare at the slurry pit. The police-men stripped off their uniforms and began to search. I screamed and tried to join them. Several hands, doubt-less compassionate, held me quiet. Old Greene gave me an injection. I heard my own screams subside, a voice in space.

A week later, with one signature, Dr Greene wiped out all his betting debts.

'Confinement in a psychiatric hospital is essential.'

I know now that they snapped.

'For her own safety.'

Greed took them over. I was under control at last.

'And the safety of those around her.'

Halpin's: We're the Best Bet!

What became of me in those days and weeks? I know I felt grief. Grief? What a slight word! I felt grief so great that I spent many hours thinking sunshine thoughts of childhood. When I was four Mother bought me a green dress with smocking on it and I would wear nothing else for months.

Ginger-snap biscuits suddenly dominated my mind. They reminded me of the first time I tasted them. I was about three. I was happy then with Mother's smiles and the sunshine through the house. I asked for ginger-snap biscuits and St Heber's gave them to me.

But mostly I looked at the wall of my room. And I kept mouthing the words 'happy' and 'happiness' to myself. The wall was the only place I could not get lost. If I moved from that wall I would get distressed.

I remembered something. The day after Ross's birth, a woman in the next room became frantic with labour. They had given her a spinal injection when inducing the birth. She had a fashionable but incompetent gynaecologist. The epidural had not taken. She moaned and roamed, then she came to me seeking change to telephone her husband but in her hand she already had the coins she needed.

In those early St Heber's days I felt like her, but I was much more astray from myself than she had been.

A doctor and nurse sat in my small room. They asked me numb questions – or was it that I gave numb answers? With each assertion of mine they looked grave. They ticked their forms. Not one word did they believe.

'I am in mourning for my baby son, Ross, who has drowned. My husband went off into the bushes to ride his secretary. They took my son with them and they let him wander off and he fell into a slurry pit. Where are his socks? Did they find his white socks?'

It all seems fairly clear to me now, the facts do anyway. Do you think they could risk letting a story like that off the leash? Mother? My father? And my husband, Joey? The force of the emotion behind it remains a mystery to me. How can you do that to your own flesh and blood? To your only child, to the mother of your child?

Nobody came to visit me in St Heber's Private Psychiatric Hospital. Where the doctors made their money from accepting people declared unsound of mind. But I was of sound mind and therefore they had to make my mind unsound, otherwise I would never fit the hospital's shape. If I did not fit I could not be treated. If I could not be treated, the doctors and nurses could not be said to be doing their jobs, could they? They would take people under false pretences. But not money.

So would they try to make my mind unsound? Fear mingled with grief, fear of what they would do to me. My devastated state protected me. I had had a spinal injection of sorrow and all of me was numb. The frost has started dripping from the trees and the condensation is running down the window-panes.

I didn't even have to pretend they needed to do nothing to me. In the beginning I needed no controlling. For several weeks I lay passive. Richard calls it 'lying doggo'. Trying to cope. Trying to cope. I didn't need to be made mad. I was already mad. I was mad with grief.

They observed me very closely and I think now that it was because they feared me. Washing my hands a lot pleased them. I couldn't help it even though it hurt my skin. My hands became red, like a cleaner's. Every time I washed my hands I felt the slurry come back again and smear me.

A private mental hospital has fewer patients than a public one. A private mental hospital out in the country fewer still, and they are of lower disturbedness. We had very little screaming at night, very few ructions. The quiet helped – and it also hindered. As I watched the cows grazing outside the windows I talked to myself. I walked in frayed circles. I plucked at my person. My brain wailed and I looked mad because I was mad. Mad with sorrow and loss.

As well that I was. They vacuumed the personality out of me. Or they tried to. They meant to. But it didn't matter because most days I felt like a shell.

After the isolation of the first couple of months, they freed me a little. I was allowed to feel but not contact the outside world. We all watched television quiz shows. And advertisements. A few bits of news reached us. Two villages away a house burned down and several of the inmates lit up in animated echo. Somebody in the Royal Family got married. Or divorced.

One local buzz made the truly mad inmates flap. A businessman had been kidnapped, a Frenchman, I think.

The whole country was being turned inside out and they were busy nearby. A local pub, the Thatch, was searched. One evening, a few days later, they caught me watching television news alone. A nurse, John Holmes, switched it off fiercely.

That was how I began to know how nervous they were of me, and the realization triggered some sense of survival. Before, I seemed mad because I was mad. Now I was growing calmer. I began to observe what they wanted from me and I gave it to them.

I gave it to them because the fear of what they could do to me had grown and grown. Electric shocks to the brain. Lobotomy. Permanently stupefying medication. I stayed quiet as a mouse. To get them ever more pleased with me, I pretended to relapse a little. I sat in my room behind the locked door and wept aloud even when I didn't always need to. Wept and wept. Aloud, aloud. This quietened them and reassured them in their diagnosis.

I told them I heard voices. They smiled gently. I did hear voices – well, one voice. I heard Ross's voice, 'Mamma, Mamma, "This old man, he play one," Mamma.' I heard Ross's whispered voice, 'Mamma awake, yet? Ross awake, are you awake, Mamma?'

I talked to Ross. I asked him out loud where had he gone, was he in Heaven?

'Can you see me, Rossie? It's me, Mamma.'

My failure, my failure – my mind was seared with my failure. I failed to keep my only child alive, and that is the biggest failure a woman can have. Ten more children would not replace him. My thoughts were like red-hot knives. My self-recriminations were like bombs. It wasn't difficult to act mad.

I can recommend madness as a means of bereavement. You can hide behind it. Meaning you can shout and scream all you like. I surprised myself with my capacity for madness and gratified those who observed me, made them feel they earned their money. Consequently they left me alone. They gave me no electric therapies and very few pills or doses. I won that battle.

Each day floated past on angry pink sails. Each evening coloured my heart savage violet. In the deeper night I tried to pray. I tried to count the times Ross and I had wonderful days, but I always failed. Sometimes the only relief I could get was by lying face down on my cold floor.

Today I am a lively woman who laughs a lot and I would never have thought that possible. I am giving the impression that I felt only sadness and fear in St Heber's. I did – I felt profound sadness and terrible fear. But soon something else began to dominate. Rage.

Rage. Rage. Roaring rage. Deranging rage.

I cannot describe the rage that hit me. It was so ferocious that I asked myself – maybe they did make me a little mad in those early months? The place affected me, no doubt about that because I still have no memory of certain things, such as the food in St Heber's – it has slipped my mind completely. And the laundry arrangements. Nor can I remember my scarves of which I was once so fond and proud. During my absence they too vanished from Grennanstown, never to be found again. I cannot recall them to describe them, which seems to me very odd, because I have always liked scarves and now have several. In fact they are about the only things I cannot recall.

But I can remember the rage.

For a time though, I forgot, or chose not to retain, other things. The way to Granddad's house. The name of Johnnie Ross's wife. Janey's birthday. The name of

Professor MacCartan's wife. Now I believe that I let all of these things drift from me. I needed my whole mind for survival. But at the time their loss surprised me.

As the rage bit, a bigger surprise crept over me. I began to improve. By which I mean the grief began to level off. It submitted to the power of my understanding. How shall I describe that improvement? I didn't howl as much inside myself. It was not that I missed Ross less. Not at all; in fact, as the days wore on, I missed him more and more. But one day, hard logic wrote a statement in the sky outside my window. 'You must have had some responsibility in Ross's death,' the skywriting said.

I flinched at this thought, as who would not? I wept. I screamed. But this time the scream lacked earlier conviction. I said to myself, 'By all means put on an act for them, the nurses.'

Now, however, I was beginning to act to myself. That was not good. I had terms to come to. So – the question hardened: where was I to blame in the loss of Ross's life? No salvation would arrive until I admitted some responsibility, some blame.

I did admit – to myself only. I admitted that I was wrong. Wrong to stay with such a horrible man as Joey. Wrong to hang on within my family in the hope that Mother would return to me. Wrong to deny myself an identity in the hope that Mother would return to me. Wrong, wrong. Mother was not my identity. She was different from me and always would be. I would not accept that because I knew who she was and I did not know who I was.

Sometimes I think that if I had not been an only child none of this would have happened. I may be right. It may be the case that an only child depends too much upon its parents for its identity. I had none of those thoughts then, refused to think them.

In other words, I did not have the courage to look at the truth. Mother, in her envy of my looks, had moved on from me a long time ago. And then, having married Joey, I should have walked out – whatever the discomfort or disapproval.

Of course I am putting all this very lucidly now. The thought process, the 'improvement' did not happen like that. Day followed day in a kind of sludgy procession. For weeks at a time I never – as far as I know – thought about things. I just lived in dullness, punctuated by emotional pain.

On my calm days they always let me out among the other patients and I was so tempted to stir them all up into a rebellion. But these were mostly extreme cases of Down's Syndrome, or old folk gone senile. One or two young people simply mooched, had no contact with themselves at all. Therefore, the nearest I came to rebellion was that effort to watch the television news.

So we sat and looked at each other in our brown nylon floral coats and trousers. Some drew pictures. Some played with decks of cards.

The Occupational Therapist came to see me. I said the same thing.

'My name is Ann Martin. I am not mad, I am in mourning for the death by drowning of my little son, Ross. He died because his father, who never liked him, wandered off to ride his secretary. And Ross whom he was supposed to be minding fell into the slurry pit beyond the fence.'

This convinced them of my derangement, because, as I later discovered, I did not repeat the same story in exactly the same words each time. Then I discovered that had I repeated the same story word for word, they would have recommended more intensified care. They would have believed I was more deranged than anyone else in there.

As Richard says, 'You lose some, you lose some.'

23

So this be the life that I live! For three months Charles has run – almost uncut – every word I have filed. The texture of my exhaustion has changed, thank God; now it feels like honest fatigue, a worker's tiredness. It no longer has despair in it: no self-accusation, no self-pity – and no temptation to drink again! In these particular circumstances I am surviving excellently, because my life, if professionally jubilant, has been necessarily ragged. I have zigzagged back and forth across the country in tune to a huge manhunt where facts are elusive, where roadblocks and rumours have replaced hard news.

Late last night, a company chairman, an elegant Frenchman from near Bordeaux, was kidnapped violently in the south-west. The Provisional IRA disclaimed responsibility and this morning a breakaway group got a message to a radio station. Their motives include Republican ideology and cash, the standard mix of all guerrilla politics. (Coincidence in this country sometimes has a freakish light. Directly I heard the ransom demand on the radio news, I opened my letters to find that my sickness insurance claim had been paid – an average two hundred pounds for each week I spent 'ill'; fourteen thousand, six hundred pounds: I am rich!)

After a mad hundred and twenty mile dash to the police press conference in Limerick we were given no clues, no idea as to where the searches might get concentrated; and the spokesman, a personable Superintendent, stonewalled all questions. So good to see all the old gang, the agencies, the slightly flamboyant but very funny BBC man, the edgy locals; people waved and smiled to me, and mouthed, 'Welcome back.' Only one, a man I don't like, pressed unpleasantly when I refused a drink at the hotel bar; all the others immediately accepted my request for 'something soft, or mineral water'. I bet they think I've been away drying out.

My local informant – he calls himself a stringer but he has never worked for a newspaper – has a sandy moustache and he smells of licorice.

He said, 'Ask me where I'm going now, Chris.' (He has an awful tendency towards intimacy.)

'All right. Where are you going now?'

He answered, 'Can I come with you, Chris?' It took me a moment to work out what he wanted – that I should drive him to where he wanted to go. 'My car jacked it in,' he said. 'It got a pain in the alternator.'

I asked, not without asperity, 'Where, then, are we going?'

'Have a look near Inchkelly. I heard they was packing the place with cop cars this morning.' The language here swings from archaic to mid Atlantic – with loose idiom thrown in.

Police at Inchkelly stopped me from driving up the track but I found another road (there are roads to everywhere in the Irish countryside) and approached the back of the house on foot where police and soldiers stood around smoking cigarettes.

'The bird has flown,' volunteered a dry police sergeant, who then – probably against all orders – told me everything: that the kidnappers and their victim had been here two days; that someone was injured – they found blood traces; that they had had little to eat; that someone in the group suffered headaches – they found a pill bottle; that at least one of the gang was a woman, although he stayed coy on the proof of that fact.

Their blind eyes allowed me to inspect the interior: squalor, damp and three fetid mattresses; one empty catering-size baked-bean tin, three filthy tea-mugs and police-chalked circles where they found the shells of four bullets. Doors and windows had been barred with old sheets of corrugated iron dragged in from the roof of a lean-to. I filled three pages of notes and tonight, so far as I can tell from radio and television, I have beaten all colleagues to the draw; my eyes are tired after that slow, uneasy drive on narrow roads that have no markings.

Ann has been much on my mind – perhaps because I drove within twenty or thirty miles of Grennanstown House. In the distance I saw the mountain range and for a moment it almost felt as if she had joined me in the car; certainly a mildly unsettling, but benign feeling of her presence materialized. In the past, I might have conversed aloud with her and now unease dominated the return of such a thought; I felt guilty; I did not want any return to the old and destructive conjunction of daydreaming and passion. That is why I have not tried to see her; since my return to Dublin I have avoided the canal area where she lives. Looking back, it almost feels (another uncomfortable thought) as if I stalked her in those days.

It began to rain and to reassure myself, I decided to ring the office. I found a telephone in a roadside pub called the Thatch where, naturally, the barman listened to my phone call, then told me, 'The whole Jaysus-country should be in the asylum out the road there, we were always mad, only 'twas never taken notice of up 'til now, bombin' and kidnappin' and guns, 'tis the same as shaggin' Chicago, and wasn't that all done by Irish fellas anyway, Legs Diamond, wasn't he born down near Athlone, Jesse James, wasn't he from Lixnaw?'

In this country all the power lies with the rhetorical question. The barman smeared mustard on every quarter of my sandwich and continued his monologue.

'I mean, Jaysus, they searched us, here, this pub, the whole Christin' idea of it – where wud we hide a gang of kidnappers, is it up the shaggin' chimney? The local cops has it in for us 'cause we got done for a small bit of after-hours drinkin' a year ago and we wud'a got offa that if we'd 'a given the boys themselves free gargle. Jaysus, Al Capone wasn't in it with them lads. Would they've ever searched us if we'd 'a given them the run'a the place?'

Day by day I confirm to myself that nothing has changed in my emotions towards Ann; what is different is the way I manage those feelings – calmly, undemonstratively, unexcitably. Time will take care of this, I tell myself. Time will do it. Yet all day I had a powerful and lovely feeling that I was somehow in or near her presence. Perhaps the notion came merely because I drove within sight of the mountains where I first saw her. Calm, though, has supervened; I am tranquil in my heart. That combination of my passion for her and the atrocities I report – that fusion has lost its lethality.

I have had to stay overnight in this bed-and-breakfast place, Avondhu, in this silent village. The household watched the news on which I was interviewed; they showed no signs of recognizing me; they will kick themselves if they realize it after I've gone. An entire country has been galvanized by this kidnapping; on the head-lines and in the think-pieces it feels like a wild time of adrenaline and snap judgement, but that is not how it is forming in my mind; I am astride this story and I have both strong objectivity and compassion; I truly feel I have them in good balance.

'My God, C., you're back on form,' exulted Charles when I rang him. 'Lovely copy. Loved the barman. How are you feeling? Are you all right?'

Charles is the one who told me about the Duke of Wellington's deathbed remark. Asked as to regrets on his life the Iron Duke said, 'I should have praised more.' Charles has made a conscious effort to avoid such a regret and all his reporting staff love him for the encouragement he gives. When a greedy and bad-tempered gold-digger from another paper tried to hook him, said she meant to marry him, a surprising number of people warned her off; that measures how loved he is.

'Charles, I'm enjoying this.'

I said it exultantly. I have had hours of long slog up lonely lanes, avenues and tracks, to deserted or remote farmhouses, barns, long-forsaken cottages, and I feel wonderful, that is to say, responsible and at ease and more secure than I have done for years.

Four and a half months since my return; I miss Ann and I do not miss her; the words echo again in my head: 'Time will do this. Let Time do it. Time is also an intelligent force.'

24

Ross! Ross!

With my finger I traced his name on the damp wall, on the floor, in the dust. With two crayons in one hand as we did at school I wrote his name twice in doubled writing on the white drawing-paper they gave us. Each time I wrote it I prayed. Not so much for him as to him. Prayer calmed me. That makes it sound as if I got myself under control fast. I did not. It took time – and devices.

One device – I picked good moments from my memory. At school they taught us dancing. I waltzed by myself in my room at St Heber's. That became a very good thing. It helped reinforce their view of my state. But it helped me even more. 'Back-Side-Close. And. Left-Side-Close. And. Forward-Side-Close. And. Right-Side-Close.'

I also picked out moments from my life that might teach me something. My time at university wasn't all morbid. I had a few wild occasions. One weekend we all went to Gougane Barra and my sides were sore from laughing. Two of the boys were musicians and they found two more and we had a dance in a pub. I wore out a pair of shoes. On the few occasions that I danced, it made me popular. I was admired at tennis club socials and one or two university hops.

Why did I not do more of that? Especially as I love

dancing. No confidence. I had not even the beginnings of self-esteem. I had this true, deep belief that once people got to know me they would dislike me.

I brought faces back to my mind in St Heber's. I had to look somewhere for a normal face and my memory was the best place. We had an Arts student who made everybody laugh. He asked me for a date. And he asked me so nicely.

'Look,' he said, 'I'm a bit afraid of you. They say you wear iron knickers. But my father owns a factory that makes tin-openers.' He called me 'a famous virgin'.

We made a date – and then I broke it. I went down the road to the telephone box, rang him up and said I wasn't feeling very well.

He said, 'Aw. Jaysus. That's a real pity. And here am I with half a dozen different makes of tin-opener and no use for them.'

I rang him back later but they said he had gone out, and I sat in my room feeling stupid and lonely. The next time I saw him he was with a girl who looked not unlike me. But in St Heber's the remembered jokes about the tin-openers at least made me laugh.

That led me to another device. I tried to recall the people who had good opinions of me and what they said. Even if Mother never admired my looks, women of her generation often complimented me. There was the woman who called me 'refined'. And the professor's wife who talked about my 'raw material'. Or Mrs Hegarty, in whose house I lived at university. She had no sense of humour. That was fine – neither had I in those days.

One afternoon, though, she said to me, 'I should say this to you. You're as nice as ever stayed here. You've'n't an ounce of the pig in you.'

170

Whether she meant my tidiness or my hoped-for good manners, I don't know.

But when I remembered that, I cried, because I also remembered that it was something I had stored for Ross's later years. I hoped it would become a cant between us; 'You've'n't an ounce of the pig in you.' I had been saving many sayings such as that for when he was older.

Slowly I brought the fits of true, i.e., the not-acted, weeping under control. I still sat for long periods in my room sharing my thoughts with the wall and began to think of escape. Now I realize that it had never been my intention to stay in St Heber's, but I was so exhausted by grief and so sedated in the first few weeks.

When I began to improve, I sat and let things flow over me. I decided never ever to stop myself from bursting out into a high fit of wild crying and bereftness.

I also decided to get out of the place. After several months, I could see that the doctors were beginning to have some discomfort with me and this filled me with the fear that if I became too much for them they would do something awful to subdue me. Ryan, the smooth thug who owned the place, had sharp eyes. I saw the worry in them when I asked him, the first time, 'How soon am I going to be discharged?' It turned out to be a stupid question. And the beginning of a bad mistake.

'Now, we're very pleased with your progress, dear.' He smiled and turned his back on me.

Dr Barnabas Ryan is wealthy and politically connected, a pillar of the community, with very expensive spectacles and a moustache. He tilts a little to one side, like a wind-pressed tree. My bad error was provoked by him speaking to me like that; 'Very pleased with your progress, dear.'

I had seen him in the corridor with the Occupational

Therapist. More than once they stood at a knowing angle to each other. Mrs Ryan with her eight children would not have liked their friendliness. I hated Ryan. Wrong approach. I should have kept him at a distance in my mind. Every time I said something, he made it seem abnormal: 'So that's what you think, dear, is it?'

I decided to use my alleged madness to have a game with him.

'I think it would prove instructive,' I said to him one day, using my very best vocabulary, 'were you to make some of your routine observations of me while I am in occupational therapy.'

He took the bait – and I was right. First of all I watched them more closely: I spied and my hunch was right. Sheila, a nice enough woman, was having a fling with him. Most days of his visits their cars followed each other from the car park under my window. Fair enough. People are people – but Ryan had expanded his practice by getting a reputation as a big Catholic husband and father.

A nurse took me to the therapy room. Ryan sat there, in his countryman's worsted suit. He positioned himself so that he could see Sheila's behind as she bent over my table. In the glimmer of his pricey horn-rims I could see his greed for her.

'Hallo, Ann,' said Sheila, on her best professional ticket.

I whispered to her, 'He's staring at your arse.'

Me! Speaking like that! Then I created and held a silence, answered none of her questions. Next I looked up at him while saying to her loudly, 'How long has Dr Ryan been riding you, Sheila?'

I said it so calmly it got in under the armour. She blushed. He flinched – and recovered.

'Miss Dalton, how do you think – the patient – is today?'

I spoke on, so fast he couldn't stop me. 'How often does he come round to your bungalow, Sheila? Does he park round the back in case anyone'll see his car from the road and tell his wife? Does he take you away for a few days to a hotel while his wife is on the Lough Derg pilgrimage?'

Then I planted the knife. 'Did he tell you about the other one he's riding, down in County Waterford? I bet he didn't.'

I took a gamble. A man like Dr Barnabas Ryan always had a woman down in County Waterford. That's what men with moustaches are like.

They concluded the session there and then. Ryan had livid eyes.

That was a bad night. I feared electro-convulsive therapy. Wrong; I under-guessed; I under-feared. Ryan was a true savage.

This is what he did. He waited. My medical records noted that my periods had now returned to normal. I had timed it badly. This little game had been played the day before a period. Twenty-eight days later he taunted me, alone.

'It was really your fault, wasn't it?' he said. 'The little lad wouldn't have drowned if you hadn't been negligent. You only concocted that story to shift the blame on to your husband.'

I screamed at him again and again. I tried to scratch him. But he had provoked me with perfect timing. Through the glass panel in the door he had seen the nurse approach. Nor did I know until later that he had recorded my screamed responses – but not his own words.

They straitjacketed me. The sleeves never end. White heavy canvas. Then they wrap the sleeves all around your body so that your arms are trapped in a permanent self-hug. I never saw a bigger irony than that self-hug, I who used to practise hugging in her daydreams. They put the 'legs' on me too, another canvas tube – it slips over both legs and is padlocked above the knees so that the thighs and buttocks can be free for injections.

Two more months in a row he did the same thing. When I was in the blues he timed savage taunts. Each time, I went for his throat. The fact is that if he had said those things to me at any time I'd have tried to kill him. And rightly so. But I never saw what he was up to.

After the third time, I saw Ryan in the corridor. I was only out of the straitjacket that morning. He was saying good-bye to Joey. I tried to get to them, but the nurses held the door locked. I went berserk and they came with the jacket again – they call it 'Jacko'. And the 'legs' again.

They got written permission from Joey, my husband, to remove my womb. On the grounds of pre-menstrual violence they held me down and injected me with anaesthetics. When I recovered I knew what had gone on.

I don't think I will ever have the ability to describe my desolation. That is how I finally began to learn who I am – by learning what I could not be.

25

Nine days ago, the kidnappers fired shots from a house on a council estate in a small flatlands town and found themselves cornered. I have been here every night since then; I arrived almost with the police, and an hour ahead of the army; two other reporters, neither of whom I knew, stood against a wall in the rain; two hundred reporters later converged and many of them live in rented caravans sprawled across the town commonage. The three American networks came with crews and dollars and we have become a gold rush for the fifteen pubs, the two boarding-houses and the only hotel.

This is what I am reporting: two people, a young man and a young woman, hold a third, a much older man – who was a significant *Maquisard* during the war – in a boxroom of a house already too small when it was built. My compassion flows towards them, up there in that cramped room where, we have been told, they lie on the floor. It forces me to consider the assumptions people make about each other in this country; the assumptions we make about our fellow man define our level of civilization.

The French protect as many people as they can from as much as seems important. In England we believe that our public figures do not deserve privacy. The Irish operate through an intimacy that is in some part genuine humane

175

concern and in some part hunger for any knowledge that will give them a degree of power. I had a conversation along these lines with the *New York Times* man tonight as we stood in the strange moonlight and gazed at the siege house. Inside, these three people lie inches from each other: the rebels' cause, notionally at least, is the adding of another layer to a political shale that has piled up over many centuries. Or, to be more accurate, the licence to try and write history.

Every time I think of them, I feel sorrow on their behalf: sorrow for the vehement yet taciturn young man who has taught himself to be a crack shot because he found that words have not the effect he needs; sorrow for the young woman who has grown up in a system of the vilest preferences, watching her family in Ulster, generation after generation, being denied work on the grounds of religion; sorrow for the dignified and successful businessman who so brilliantly led his cell of the French Resistance against the Nazis and who now has to endure these new indignities, these violations of privacy, in a country he has come to love. My mood tonight is therefore melancholy – but not self-endangering; my emotional recovery holds.

It needs to. Today, I took time out and drove to Mooreville, specifically to Silverbridge. Fact is – I have been missing Ann as certainly as if she has been someone whose company I have relished. And, this is so strange, I have also been missing her little boy; I have been so desirous of seeing him again. Tonight, but for reasons utterly other than I expected of my visit, I am drawing on all my resources. I am almost a bereaved person, a mourner – my disappointment and sadness are so great that I can scarcely describe this sequence of events. Therefore I must write this calmly, so that when I return to this journal in years hence, I can remind myself how I was.

Grennanstown House now has a closed and locked gate, with a large 'For Sale' notice. I climbed out of the car surprised and slightly upset: no sign of life, no trace of recent traffic on the short, curved avenue. Where was everybody? It felt like a house from an old poem; the trees and chimneys still, the atmosphere unquiet. I was inspecting the 'For Sale' notice when I heard a footfall on the road behind me and looked back; I must have hoped it might be Ann.

'Thinking of buying it?' a middle-aged woman asked pleasantly.

I smiled back. 'Probably not. Too big for me.' Her dog snuffled the hedgerows and then the wheels of my car.

'You could always fill it with a wife and six children.' She smiled.

'Only six?' This is Ireland.

She smiled again. 'You must have money if you're thinking of buying this place. It's sold anyway. Or that's the rumour.'

'Merely looking,' I said. 'Why are they selling such a lovely property?'

'I live about four miles away,' she said. Any half-good journalist senses when people are clamming up.

'Aha! So you're thinking of buying it,' I said flippantly, 'and you were sizing me up in case I might be a bidder?'

She shook her head and something in her attitude kick-started worry inside me; I had, I realize, been uneasy all day.

'People never stay in a house where there's bad luck.' She called the dog, who ignored her.

Heart now pounding with that awful sickness of something beyond control, I said, 'Bad luck? Oh, dear.'

'Their child drowned. Small little kid.' She pointed to somewhere beyond the trees. 'Over there, he fell into the slurry pit. Terrible story.' Her eyes glittered with the relish of other people's difficulty and I wanted to punch her.

'So have they left?'

'The mother's gone. Disappeared. After the drowning she was up and gone. One night or early morning she left the house and took only her coat. They're saying she went mad and ran off somewhere. She might have drownded herself for all anyone knows.'

I looked at the woman: what could I say? In the days when I went to France a great deal I became fond of the countryside around Coligny where in the winter the Marne overflows, leaving silver birches marooned in fields of water; I felt like one of those trees. But somehow I do not believe that the Ann I have been worshipping would take her own life.

Do I have hope tonight? I drove back to this little town like the driver of a hearse. There is something in my heart that will not let me buckle under this sadness. Time to go and check the siege site; the stars are high with frost and tomorrow is Hallowe'en.

26

A woman on the radio this morning said, 'All cooking is chemical change.' I like that. I had often wondered about it myself. Watching a sauce change its consistency. Exciting. If only we could do the same for ourselves. I think that must be my goal. Watch every change in myself. Then eventually I'll know what I taste like!

Night was great in St Heber's. Great and dark and still. It brought silence. There were some snufflings, a few sleeping wails along the corridor. But mostly silence. I loved that. All I ever wanted in life was to love someone, to be tender and silent with him. I wanted an endearing man who would forget things, who needed care and love. Who needed reminding of things. Who needed warmth at night in bed, and teasing, and a welcoming smile every time I saw him.

The silence of those nights had something of that imagined love in them. Peace and safety and gentleness in the dark. At that time, before Richard, the silence was the next best thing to love.

One silent night I looked through the window of my room. There was a moon. As a child I used to hope the moon would suddenly have my father's face. No face on this moon. A dark shape came and vapourized in through the glass. It was Revenge. It stood beside me dark and strong and shocked me and invigorated me.

Through that surge of vengefulness I gave myself a purpose. I said I would avenge myself and Ross. It may have been an immoral purpose, perhaps an evil one. But it was a purpose such as I had never known before. It lifted my heart if not my soul. The pain began to ease that night. It has been easing ever since.

After the hysterectomy, my body had fallen into Limbo. No monthly record left to me. No monthly reminder of the possibility of another Ross. No possible daughter one day. No possible ten children to replace Rossie. No more babies for me, who loves babies. No more periods for me who had never had a difficult period in my life.

No nothing.

They butchered me too. I caught infection after infection. To this day I do not know where the operation actually took place. St Heber's did not have surgical facilities. I have a vague recall of being transported lying down. I suppose I was in an ambulance.

I almost had to learn to walk all over again and because I could not move swiftly they relaxed. Someone must have said it was safe to let me into the garden. Slowly I walked to it along the stone flags of the passageway.

I walked there like a snail, I even felt I was leaving a snail's trail. But not silver – red. Of blood oozing, leaking, from my damaged body, and slowly I walked around the garden.

Like those prison camps with watch-towers, there was one angle of the garden that had no window looking on it. It was like the corner of the garden where it was always summer in the story about the giant.

When I first got my bearings that's what I headed for – that corner. I walked slowly to the wall. Another wall to look at. A high wall, of grey stone. To this day I love walls – we have a wall here at the far end of the house and it catches a lot of sun.

One day, there at that stone wall, I met Richard. It seems extraordinary now. I knew at the time that it was extraordinary. I went along with it.

Weeping, I leaned against a high pile of timber. It was one of those days when I was asking myself what would happen to me. Was I in this place – like most of the others there – for life? I was particularly sore that morning and they would give me no more painkillers. Still distressed, I was half-yelping in pain.

A voice above me called, 'Hey, Doll. Hey, hey!'

I thought it was God. But is God an American? I remember asking myself that queer question. Maybe I read it years ago in the *Reader's Digest*. I looked up and there he sat. Much later I of course realized who he was – the man my father and the local people referred to as 'the nigger in the fields'.

Richard says he's what they call an 'octoroon', an eighth black in him. Nancia, his Negro great-grandmother, was a slave embroidress. Richard's white ancestor, James John Huttle, met this beautiful black girl. When he found he had made her pregnant, the decent man married her. Richard says that the powerful wealth of the family kept James John Huttle free of all stigma.

'Although', he says, 'God alone knows what stings those wasps buried in Nancia across the drawing-rooms of San Francisco.'

Nancia and her man must have had handsomeness in abundance. Richard has a high forehead and a golden, chocolate-brown skin and a mouth like an ice-cream. Everybody knew about him, even those who had never seen him; he was probably the first black man ever in our area, probably in the whole county.

Richard still calls me 'Doll', which I like, and sometimes 'Babe'. I can still see him on the wall that day. Tall and lanky and fit and strange, he looked like a young-ish wizard. Even then he felt a whole generation older than me – I wonder if that's because of Vietnam.

Some days now, though, the condition he's in makes Richard feel like my baby. I think the octoroon thing is most noticeable in the edges of his frizzed hair. He still wears a bandanna with the stars and stripes on it. I tease him about his bandanna.

'Would you ever take it off, Rich, I mean in any circumstances?'

'Doll, it'd call for legislation.'

His looks often took my breath away in those days. In morning light I have never seen such a lovely skin on a man. He's less full of anger now, although he still hums all the time. Tunes I know, tunes I don't know. Sometimes his humming is dangerously tuneless.

Richard said again from his high wall, 'Hey? Hey?'

I wailed, 'They butchered me. They operated on me.'

He asked, 'They take your brain?'

'No. My womb.'

'That's evil.' His vehemence made me smile. 'Gimme up your hand.' I reached up. 'Hi. I'm Richard. Who're you? You're some person, I'll say that, those cheekbones. Don't think much of the drapes, though.'

I laughed in my tears and he slid down the wall.

'Brown floral print?' He pinched the fabric at my hip. 'Whooooo-h! Out! Not good this season, Paris has said "No!" to it.' He shouted this and I laughed again. 'I just want to look at you,' said Richard.

He looked mostly into my eyes and I had difficulty holding his gaze, but I did.

At length he said, 'You're not crazy. No way.'

I blushed. 'Who said I was?'

After that we met every two or three days. Never an appointment made; I walked there; there he sat.

We talked. 'Didja ever see me before?'

'I don't know.'

'You shoulda done. I've helped in the kitchen. And I've brought deliveries. I come here a lot.'

'Why do you come here?'

He said, 'So's I can know I'm not crazy.' I now know he was being evasive, I now know he came looking for me. No wonder I love him. He came looking for me! That makes my heart weep!

'They say I am crazy.'

'Not everyone.'

'Not everyone what?'

'Not everyone says you're crazy.' A bright light slammed on.

'What do they say?' If others knew I had a chance of defeating all this.

'They say things. Your name Martin? Ann Martin? Husband big guy, thinks he's bigger?'

I nodded. 'Let me sit down.' We sat behind the trees.

'Is it true you're a fugitive? From a chain-gang?'

'I'm not a fugitive.'

'Figure of speech. Old song. The word on the street is you have a story to tell.' He was testing me, looking at me closely.

'What kind of a story?' I could feel my lip trembling.

He leaned over and patted my sad, unfecund tummy. 'A bad, sad story. A story of past times with lonely things. The story of a little boy gone missing.'

I looked away and I knew that tears were going to come.

'In the watches of the night,' said Richard, 'you will learn to talk about these things.'

'No,' I said.

'Listen. Do you know what a gook is?'

I shook my head.

He sat up, adjusted his bandanna, stretched his body.

'I can tell you. I alone, in this vicinity, can tell you what a gook is. A gook is someone comes after you to kill you. And then if you kill the gook he comes after you some more.'

'You're talking in riddles.'

'Do you know when people can't talk in riddles? When they're holding someone in their arms. Come here.'

He put out his long brown arms and I folded into them. His breath on my hair smelt like an uncle, tobacco and peppermints.

'Nobody can see you here. Talk now,' he commanded.

I didn't. I couldn't. Not that day, not for ages.

Richard repeated the same performance several times. He would mention 'a small person gone missing'. Would talk of 'sad days' and his favourite phrase, 'the watches of the night'. He said, 'And I am a nightwatchman.'

I began to divine his technique. He talked a lot merely to establish the principle of talking. Then he fell silent and that was when, he hoped, I would talk a lot too. To this day he seems to have unlimited kindness and yet everybody has always said he was a wild man.

Richard focused me, though, and he helped me through bad time after bad time. The control of myself I sought after Ross's death had brought a new problem. I felt I would have difficulty staying alive – inside St Heber's or outside. Inside, what was the choice but to die? If I ever got out – well, who knows? The actual act, the moment of what I might do to myself, never offered

184

itself to me in a vision, although I thought fondly of high buildings.

An accident seemed more likely. An event would take place, on the road, or wherever. I would cause it and my life would be taken from me without fear or favour. And most important without fuss.

I think that was how St Heber's essentially incarcerated me. It imprisoned my possibilities as well as my physical presence. I grew afraid of the outside world, afraid of what it – or I – might do to me. Certifying me as mad rendered me unable to think of a life outside their walls.

Richard stopped that kind of thinking. That is also why I love him.

27

My thoughts are with her all the time. How does she feel after losing her beloved little boy? Where has she gone – has she fled abroad? Has she become deranged? Is it not now more important than ever to find her, so that she may have more children? What an absurd thought! Such thinking led me into my previous difficulty; I must stop it; I am not a saviour – but my work is my saviour.

For seventeen days now I have not left this town, apart from Grennanstown House (I went there again today). This small hotel, the Hawthorn, has given me a block booking – a fortnight at a time on the understanding that if the siege be called off, even at the beginning of a new fortnight, I must still pay the balance. It has rained so much that the field of caravans has turned to mud; little news filters through from the police, but my stringer has given me a valuable piece of advice.

'The clergy, Chris, they always knows the SP.'

I must have looked as if I needed a translation.

'SP. The starting price. You know, the races, the horses. What's the SP, like, what's the score on that?'

I befriended a local priest who translates Homer for relaxation – 'And I have two greyhounds the which I race twice a year.'

All the clichés in Ireland have the weight of truisms. From Father H. I have been able to get to a mystery figure the local papers call 'the Sandwich Woman'; she is a policeman's wife who is catering both police and besieged. In great secrecy – I am the only one who interviews her – she tells me what they eat day by day and how the kidnappers make their hostage taste each sandwich before they themselves eat. Her cousin works in the town pharmacy and I have learned of the analgesics, plasters, tampons and pills hoisted to a rear window of the siege house in a basket. Charles, professing himself delighted with me, talks wryly of Ernest Hemingway liberating the Ritz in Paris.

A major scare broke in the siege and again I did well. (All my copy still appears every day – which means it has taken me just four and a half months to get back into my stride; Charles has stopped worrying, and said as much: 'Normal business has been resumed.') Last night, a moonlit night with an east wind coming straight off the boglands, an army marksman climbed a ladder and drew a bead on the window of the room. He had not, we were assured later, intended to fire and had no such orders. Nor did he receive the opportunity: two shots rang out and I saw the marksman half-race, half-stumble down the ladder shouting, 'Jesus! Jesus!' Those of us looking on took cover; we had not expected such an incident and I had been there as part of my routine. I learned later what had happened. As the soldier raised his rifle to sight the window, the girl in the siege bedroom fired one shot and blew a hole in the glass for her co-kidnapper to fire through. His shot then blew the top off the soldier's finger. Ambulances raced, police cars swerved: 'What larks, Pip, old chap,' quoth Charles.

Today the stark and, to me, painful word, 'SOLD' had replaced 'For Sale' on Grennanstown House; a new padlock has secured the gate. I drove all around, on lanes behind the house and to the distant hill where I could look down; I parked far off and walked; beneath the trees lining the approach to the avenue, a gap opens in the fencing. Not all the shutters have been closed and I managed to look into quite a few of the rooms.

Few people vacate houses in such good condition. Apart from some marks where large furniture has been standing, everything seems excellent; undamaged paintwork, and lovely curtains – brocades, velvets, silks; the carpets also remain and one of deep Chinese yellow seems almost new. Ann must have bought it not long before the drowning.

The rooms feel impersonal, though, as if their decor has been chosen for expediency rather than with love. This, I fear, worries me – but of course I know so little of Ann's taste nor do I know how much her husband overrules her. The house has been well secured; I could not gain entry; I wanted to find Ann's room, see where she lived and slept and bathed. Where is she? God, where is she?!

I climbed on the broad window-sills seeking an open or loose window catch; I tried doors harder than I should have done – and had no success. After a while I walked the gardens, found the slurry pit and stood at the fence looking across to it. My shoulders shuddered and a cold wind passed through me as I remembered the little boy I saw being caressed and cared for by his mother in a Dublin park on a sunny day, whose head I patted as he crawled by my chair in the Shelbourne Hotel.

For a moment I had the sensation of being there at the time of the tragedy. Some feelings of tenderness prove as difficult to cope with as sorrow or loneliness (my old familiar friend), and the contemplation of that afternoon's events became too much for me. I turned away from the fence, re-crossed the wide lawn and walked into the stableyard and the outbuildings. The first large door I came to opened easily. Some ancient broken harnesses hung on the walls; straw spilled out of a disused iron feed-brazier; bales of hay formed a fallen stack and I sat on a bale.

What does one use for faith at a time like this? In Paris, there is a statue in the Centre Pompidou gallery by Gaudier-Brzeska of a ballerina: the dancer has, my mother says, the most perfect hip movement. Tintoretto, on one of his panels for the San Rocco in Venice, painted a powerful Christ exhorting the halt and the lame, Christ sweeps his arm upward as if urging them to take up their beds – my father loves that painting.

Above my head to the right I heard a noise. A white barn owl rose almost vertically, flew around for a time as if asking me to leave, then settled back on its beam, watching me. The ancients would have said it was the soul of the dead little boy.

28

I'm looking at my fingernails – due for an overhaul!
Mother had so many bottles of nail varnish. Gorgeous
names. Pearl Pink. Oystershell. Egyptian Nights. Jewelled Carmine. Old Topaz. But Mother never let me
wear any. Oh, well.

Nobody ever followed me to that corner of St Heber's
garden so I pretended infirmity longer than it lasted
and everybody left me alone. They thought they had
destroyed me.

Over there by the piled logs my tears developed a
long-lived habit. They liked to be dried on Richard's
sleeve. They have dried there often.

'Oh, Rich, if Rossie only knew you! The things you
could have told him, the stories.'

How strange we must have seemed. Even to God
looking down on us. I can see why people think Richard
is crazy. When I knew some time later that I had heard of
him, I recalled neighbours telling my father about him.
But nobody ever knew his name. Sometimes children
from the school in Deanstown, the next village, tried
to sneak a thrilling glimpse of him, that strange black
man who lives out there in the fields, eating wild birds
and talking to himself. 'Know better company to talk
to, Doll? I don't.'

Came a day when Richard kidnapped me. He hauled

me over the wall of St Heber's and we fled. In the car he protected me so obviously and spoke to me so sweetly and gently it made me cry. And to this day I cannot remember a moment when he did not speak to me with tenderness.

The previous day he told me his plan. 'I thought of surprising you. But you might wanna take something. A souvenir.'

I stole the certificate old Dr Greene had signed. And I stole Joey's letter of consent to the hysterectomy. They don't lock the office at night. The night staff can sleep in their chairs because they sedate everyone. I was always 'asleep' when they came for me, so no sedation. Long ago I stole one of the spare keys to my room. That is how I managed to creep out that night.

'Where are we going, Rich?'

He chose the west coast, Galway.

'Two reasons.' Distance was the first. 'Far away for long enough. That is the secret of remaking yourself. And that is what you will be doing.'

I didn't know Galway at all. It is an old city and it looked strange to me. People said it had dark-eyed, Spanish-looking people, and good wit. I was able to impress Richard with the origin of 'lynch law'.

'The mayor here, Rich, centuries ago, Mayor Lynch. He hanged his own son who was found guilty of a crime.'

Richard said, 'I'm pleased he never knew my old man.'

Richard's second reason moved me.

'The sea, the ocean. Doll, you need to feel cleansed. So – first, a hotel. Then we hire some holiday house for the winter, walk the sands in the rain. There'll be plenty of rain.'

191

We stayed in the city centre, the Great Southern Hotel. The reception staff freaked a little when they saw Richard, and I freaked a little when I saw the hotel. My parents always stayed here for the Galway Races. But that was always in August, so they wouldn't be here now.

I became very weepy in our room. Richard went for a walk. When he came back he ordered a sherry for me and it made me drunk.

We dined in our room and I was awkward and embarrassed. A single foray to the main restaurant proved bad. I had to leave within minutes, couldn't face the other diners, burst into tears. We never did it again and anyway, I could scarcely eat.

That night Richard picked the lock on the swimming-pool door. We swam silently, naked, in the dark, with utter modesty towards each other. In bed we hugged. My whole being felt as if it were both freezing and thawing. Richard never tried to touch me. It never felt strange having him in my bed. I had only slept with Joey. By comparison Richard was lovely – but Dracula would have been lovely after Joey.

Next day came the first of my tantrums.

'What do you want me to do next, Rich?'

'If we get someone excellent to cut your hair it might get you a fresh start.'

'No, Rich, no!'

He grabbed me as I started wrecking the room.

I got my hair cut short, first time ever. Not even Barnabas Ryan had tried that. Richard sat near and held my hand and wiped my tears. They must have thought we were mad. I spoke not at all and they believed we were both Americans. I went back to the hotel and fell asleep until morning. Richard began to look for a house to rent.

The house he found brought good omens.

'Vibes,' said Richard, 'they talk to me, they talk to me.' He snapped his fingers and did a little shimmy.

We moved in at the weekend and I found an old newspaper lining a drawer. It was dated three years earlier. From it smiled the face of a man I had completely forgotten. In this photograph this man was presenting prizes to a local Chamber of Commerce.

He was, is, a bank manager. In Dublin I had been able to do many things without Joey's knowledge because he never asked how I spent my days. Joey had no interest in us. Ross tried in baby talk to tell Joey about feeding the ducks in St Stephen's Green. Joey never listened.

The photograph brought it all back to me. This was the bank manager of the Baggot Street branch where I had opened a deposit account. I used to walk Ross along the canal to see more ducks.

Joey was immensely careless with certain aspects of cash. Drunk after the races he often brought cash home in his pockets. Siphoned away from the taxman. I did a little siphoning-off too. The account was in a false name: Ann Beresford. All correspondence was to be kept at the bank.

'My husband's a heavy gambler,' I remember telling this smiling, prize-presenting face now looking up at me. 'I want to create a little protection.'

'Ah, sure. Understood. Understood. Will we keep the deposit book here, Mrs Beresford?'

Nothing pleases a man more than to feel righteous on behalf of a woman. At the expense of another man.

'Richard, we have to go to Dublin,' I now said.

Nobody knew of this account. Therefore they could not have had it frozen when they locked me away. As I was sure they had done with my known bank account.

193

'No Dublin,' he said.

I told him.

'Transfer it,' he said.

'But don't I need to be there in person?'

'They'll do it on your signature,' he said. 'If you do it to a local branch of the same bank.'

With interest it came to just over eleven thousand pounds.

'Big siphon, Doll,' laughed Richard.

September's gales brought the next omen. Smoke poured into the kitchen. Richard and I sat by this lovely fireplace each night and whenever I looked at him he smiled at me. (I am going to go upstairs in a minute and give him a hug, just for that memory.)

'We need a sweep,' I said. He had never heard of such a thing. There was no fireplace where he grew up in California.

The chimney-sweep was a man called Patsy Naughton. He said, 'A sweep is a lucky thing. Did you meet a sweep the morning of your wedding, did you?'

Richard laughed.

Patsy came out. We sat on a stone wall near the house wrapped in warm coats.

'Told ya I was lucky. Here.' He handed me a small black package. 'Open that. No, she hasta open it,' he said to Richard.

I plucked gingerly. A dead kitten, mummified, wrapped in soot-saturated cloth. It was as preserved as a smoked fish.

'Aach!'

'No need for an aach! about it, Missus. That's a sign of luck, they put them up their chimneys long ago to bring the house luck. That's dead lucky. All yer ventures will prosper.'

'His, too,' remarked Richard. 'He charged us forty pounds for twenty minutes' work.'

Luck came. We had wonderful sea weather on that shore which nobody else visited. Fish beached at our feet. We found a small crate, watertight, of leather luggage fallen overboard from some cargo ship. It had leather-bound notebooks, completely untouched by the sea water. A local farm adopted us. They gave and sold us food. Richard told them he was an American writer finishing a book.

I never spoke if we bumped into people. We let them assume I was American too.

The winter bore us along on soft winds with no dangerous extremes. Those famous westerly gales stayed mostly offshore. When they came close we walked in them. They exhilarated, and they cleansed us. Our roof, our chimneys, were never threatened. No frost, no hail.

We had heavy rain, a great deal of it. Our greatest misfortune came from that. Rain flooded the shed that acted as a garage. The car refused to start. Richard replaced the plug leads and we never had that difficulty again.

I had some very bad emotional dips – my 'deep-sea dives', Richard called them. Then I began to strengthen. The day we left St Heber's, I recalled an item of furniture in Mother's bedroom. She smoked ceaselessly, ashtrays everywhere. One stood on the floor, chrome, about two feet high. It had a weighted base. If knocked it always sprang back upright immediately.

Ross played with it. He pushed it and watched it jump back. Once it hit him on the forehead. He enjoyed knocking it down thereafter.

I bought him soon afterwards a little coloured man on the same principle. He too sprang back when knocked, in his red coat and yellow trousers and black boots. But

I never liked either the ashtray or the red-and-yellow black man. I found them a little sinister. On that drive to Galway I discovered why. If things bounce back too quickly they can hurt you. Recovery must take some time, otherwise it has no value. No depth. I wanted my recovery to be profound. It needed to be.

By that Atlantic coast I sprang back very, very slowly. Two days forward, three days back, two days forward, two and a half days back. Days I could not get out of bed. Nights I would not come to bed.

After three months a little progress could be reported. Two days forward. Two days back. I moved between anger and weeping and silence, even while we walked arm-in-arm along the beach.

We had become lovers as naturally as we washed in each other's presence. I was not afraid or disturbed by it. It comforted me and I loved Richard's bed manners with me.

But there were days when I removed myself from him. Days I spoke so abusively to him. Days I screamed at him. Days I undermined him. He took it all and I bless him for that every time I remember it.

All the thinking I had done in St Heber's had been superficial. Or so it seemed now. Nowhere could I see, or feel, or think towards any lasting coming-to-terms. The words 'tranquillity' and 'serenity' had been struck from my language.

'Coming to terms with what?'

That question surfaced around Christmas. We spent it bleakly. I was deep in bed and Richard sat in the room reading. (Of course I now realize that he never let me out of his sight.)

'What terms do I have to come to?'

No answer. I had asked the question of myself, but had

spoken it aloud. Richard, untypically, never answered me, just came to the bed and stroked my hair. I wish now that I had been nicer to him in those days – but I didn't know what I was doing.

One day early in January we went for our long daily walk, three hours and a half of solid beach. The tidemark looked like a foamy, dirty handwriting and was punctuated with flotsam. We turned over charred wood, cans, plastic bottles, strips of plastic.

Richard said, 'I'm going to speak.'

I said, 'Go ahead.'

'I've spoken nothing.'

'True.'

'Nothing at all.'

'Yes, Rich.'

'I gotta.'

'Why?'

'Something's wrong, Doll.'

'What?'

I let go of his arm. He grabbed me and said, 'No, no, no, no, no, Babe. Don't scream at me, there's no need.' His face seemed extra black in the ocean light. 'Now come on.'

He held me and stopped me screaming. Then he said, 'Describe the insect.'

'What?'

'We had a saying, if you got bit in the canes – '

'The canes?' Huge clouds rolled in from the west, darkening over the shore. Far, far away a man loaded a tractor's trailer with seaweed at the water's edge.

'The bamboo canes. The Mekong. The Delta. All that. We had a saying, the medico asked, "Describe the insect", so's he could fish out a cure. So – "describe the insect", Doll.'

I turned away, then I turned back. 'Coming to terms,' I said.

'Yeah?'

'I don't know what terms I can come to.'

'Go on.'

'I can't. I don't know what words should now follow.'

'Like – there's something missing, is that what it's like?'

'Yes. I think I'm going to die, Rich.'

'No. I'm here to keep you alive.'

He spoke so softly in the wind I could barely hear him.

'But I might – I might kill someone.'

Richard never answered. I remember that so well.

29

The time at last seemed right to do the thing I feared, and yesterday I began to do so.

'Is this wise, C.?' asked Charles a little aggressively on the telephone.

His secretary reported what I was up to, that I had been asking for some of my old reports from the files.

'It is simply that I want to measure how ill I was, Charles. Some days now I think I was very unwell. Other days I am not so sure.'

'Yes,' he said trying to be patient and understanding; but his choler flared. 'That bloody country you're in. No bloody pathway to sanity.' He grew anxious again. 'You are all right, though?'

'Yes, yes. I simply want to read some things I wrote. You know – go back there and judge how off the beam I was. Scene of the crime, so to speak. Come on, Charles. You know what I mean.'

'One day and one night, C., no more. OK?'

I agreed. This morning the various bits of unpublished copy arrived, a record of my instability. As to Charles's idea of 'sanity' – an hour later I stood behind a police cordon awaiting the explosion of a bomb inside a bank. It never went off, much to the regret of several bystanders: 'I'm waitin' for it to blow up my overdraft' – and much similar banter. After which I reached my car safely and drove north and spent the afternoon looking for my own footsteps along the Border. They did not exist, I had never been to such locations – and tonight I am both worried and relieved: worried that I could have been so ill and not known it, relieved that I have a fuller picture of myself as I was when ill: knowledge cures me.

It remains difficult (and so embarrassing) for me to believe that I imagined or invented being kidnapped. To have written about it makes me cringe: thank God Charles had the good – or sixth – sense not to run my story. I have more than a little difficulty in the shame that I feel. I can analyse it all (and doubtless will, over and over) but factually there was no farmhouse, and factually there were no thumping men in balaclavas, and factually there was no barn, and factually there were no wires leading from under the door. I have the descriptions, here in my own copy; I was specific as to directions and route details. There was, I describe, a pub, the Four Horsemen, my final landmark, and the crucial farmhouse had a half-thatch, half-slate roof; the former exists, the other not.

By seven o'clock this evening I found the Borderland Inn with its inexplicably vast car park; by seven thirty faced the inevitable steak and onions of an Irish country hotel. As part of the deal they serve a pint with dinner; mine sat there like a threat and the waiter disapproved as he took it away untouched and flat. Over dinner I checked again my notes; I highlighted every geographical mention in the copy I had filed and I meant to retrace every step.

'Do you know a pub called the Four Horsemen?'

My feeling was that I knew it had existed but I questioned it; now I know that nothing I described thereafter made sense – although one might not immediately know that reading my copy.

The factotum at the door replied so quickly I could hardly catch a word; I think he said, 'Oh, surely, over behind Forkhill.' He became irritated when I indicated incomprehension and then spat, 'Go by the Jonesborough signpost. You've to watch yourself over there' – a remark which irked me; 'watch yourself' is what I had come to do.

In England, especially in villages like the one where my parents live, a pub called the Four Horsemen might have a painted sign, perhaps some wood panelling, and a sense of tradition, old atmosphere; not here – a great deal of plastic is in evidence, and a slot machine with coloured flashing lights and noise that does not turn itself off for several minutes after play has stopped. I recognized the place; yes, I had been there before, but even tonight the memory of that first visit remains hazy and sinister. On that occasion I drank a lot very quickly and left; this time I did the opposite.

As before, I asked for Michael McConnell and – not as before – I met him. He remembers my name, this old and rather fierce man whose demeanour I liked immediately. He was the original contact I was given by the unpleasant Father Coll. Mr McConnell, a stalwart of the old IRA, fell out with the local Provisionals. They left him alone because of his age and because of his 'involved' son, and Father Coll said that he was the one who most challenged the Provisionals' denial of Christian burial to the informers they shot.

'You never showed up the last time, did you. I used to read your paper, listen, years ago. Never agreed with it then and 'tis worse now, I do often see it on the bus or at the doctor's over in Newry, he's a Protestant. Good doctor, our own fella's an ikey ould hoor. You've nearly to pay him before he knows what's wrong with you. I will, I will, I'll have a small Jameson. And I know you're not here about the smuggling?'

I said, 'No, but tell me.' He might have a key in his back: wind him up and out come consistently long bursts of speech.

'Listen, they've a great Eee-Eee-Cee thing going, the same lorry of pigs over and hither, over and hither, three different border posts and Brussels giving them nine pounds a pig, forty pigs to the lorry, eight lorries working, work that out. They get a chit for every pig and some of them pigs do cross that Border six times a day. Different from my day. What was it like in my day?' he continued, seeing the question form in my face. 'Listen, we had to go at it through the night, a pig at a time in a wheelbarrow and we'd have a sponge, listen, soaked in whiskey or poteen and the sponge stuffed in the pig's mouth so that the pig'd suck it the whole time and not squeal. And by the time we got him over the Border every pig was as drunk as a skunk.'

He laughed; I like him, even though he feels as foreign as an ancient Egyptian.

'The, ah'm, burials?' I nudged. 'The informers?'

This time his speech shortened to curtness. 'It never happened. Leave it alone.' Immediately he diverted me – in dramatic fashion – by nodding towards a drinker at the bar: 'Our spy's in tonight, I see.'

'Wha-at?!'

At the end of the bar a big handsome man in an old green greatcoat speaks with his hands to two young women. He is younger than me by several years, his eyebrows meet like a pair of dark, hairy caterpillars, the ones we used to call 'woolly bears'. He looked out of place; what I might call his 'physical culture' did not fit. Mr McConnell continued.

'Ah, 'twould be better for everyone if you were here about him. He's our local spy.'

Gently, gently: my nose was working. 'Why do you call him that?'

The eyebrows man saw us looking and walked towards us.

'Because sure that's what he is. Tommy the spy. He's one of your crowd – English. He's an army officer stationed in Bessbrook, pretending to be a mechanic from Larne. But will you look at that pair of paws on him. A girl's hands aren't as clean. A mechanic never had hands like that.'

'How are you this evening, Michael?' greeted the big man. This, I thought, is not an Ulster accent, this is a man thinking he can put on an Ulster accent.

'Hallo, Tommy,' said Mr McConnell.

'Tommy' is six feet four and no matter how he tries to conceal it, middle-class English, with a Home Counties marrowbone.

'Ah, listen, this is my friend, Mr Hunter, over from London, a reporter.'

Tommy asked which newspaper and I told him; then he asked, 'Mr McConnell, you promised me the words of a few songs.'

'But can you sing at all, Tommy?'

They laughed, an artificial camaraderie and Tommy moved on; seen from the rear he has shoulders as broad as Ann's husband and that same heft of bulk.

Mr McConnell had another whiskey. He has in his eyes that mixture I see so often in Ireland – sadness and violence. He returned to my line of enquiry.

'No, now, there isn't any place round here that's half-thatch, half-slate, ah, the thatch on houses is nearly all gone. You do find it in the folk museums, but that's

203

mostly all. You can't get thatchers and even if you could, don't they have to go to Hungary for the reeds? The combine harvesters killed off all the long straw.'

'Are you sure, Mr McConnell?'

'Am I sure? Amn't I eighty-one years of age? If I'm not sure now when will I ever be? And don't I have a son on the run? But we'll not talk about that. Them army helicopters. You should write about them. My wife has the arthritis and she can't sleep the best of times, and when she can, don't the fuckin' army helicopters come over, down over the house? Put that in your paper, will you?'

From the end of the bar Tommy raised his eyebrows at me and moved towards the door marked 'Gentlemen'.

'Our spy is beckoning at you,' said Michael McConnell, drawing a fingernail across his stubble. 'Go along after him and see what he wants, why don't you?'

'How do you know he's a spy? I mean – isn't it dangerous for him if it gets known?'

'Dangerous for a lot of people if it doesn't get known. And 'tis his own neck, anyway.'

In the lavatories, Tommy changed his accent. 'Look here, you're one of us.'

I recoiled.

'No, what I mean is, well you know what I mean.'

I said, 'In the name of God, what are you doing? Are you dotty?'

Tommy smiled. 'No, no. They think I'm kosher. I'm a mechanic from Portadown as far as they're concerned.'

'Bessbrook.'

'Yes, Bessbrook, same thing really. I have quite a deep cover. Do you know any songs?'

'Who are you really?'

204

'Artilleryman, but that's not the point.' He has curiously small eyes. 'Do you know any of their songs?'

'I know a verse of one.'

He asked for a page of my notebook and I dictated a song that played on the radio every day in the south; I had failed to keep the words out of my head.

'"Oh, I am a jolly ploughboy. And I plough the fields all day. 'Till a sudden thought came to my mind. That I should run away."' Tommy has bad breath – yech!

He asked, 'Is the tune difficult?'

'No. You'll pick it up quickly. "So I'll take my short revolver. And my bandolier of lead."'

'Good show,' said Tommy.

'Don't say that here,' I said. 'Don't you know where you are?' He laughed; this man, when a boy, read too many adventure comics. '"And live or die I can't but try. To avenge my country's dead."'

'Oh, wow!' he actually said.

'"So we're off to Dublin in the green. Where the helmets glisten in the sun. Where the bayonets flash and the rifles crash. To the echo of a Thomson gun."' I gave him the words of the chorus and beetled out of there.

Mr McConnell smiled at me.

'I think he's mad,' I said.

'I think he's dead,' said he with a little smile. 'Ah, listen,' he intervened when he saw my face, 'manner of speaking,' and when I made to go back towards Tommy, he said, 'Leave him alone, they'll warn him off soon.'

I sat down again. 'So. Definitely no half-thatch, half-slate?'

'Definitely no.'

'And no barn corresponding to the one I described?'

'Definitely no, too. I know every stick and stone. I worked for every farmer from here to Armagh city.'

205

The army stopped me on the way back just inside the Border; once again my press card proved a magic wand. Should I have told them about Tommy? No; the man is probably some sort of cranky fantasist; the Troubles attract them.

'Do you know of any house near here that has a half-thatched roof?' I asked the night porter at the Borderland.

'And the other half?' he inquired.

'Normal. Slates.'

'Ey, Kath?! D'you know any house around here has a half-slate roof and the other half thatch? She's living here all her life,' he asided to me.

Kath thought and called, 'No. Never.'

Tonight a new thought approaches – that Ann is the reality of my life in Ireland and that everything else, the violence, the blood, the bombs and shreds of flesh are the hallucinations. In south Armagh, I traced every place I described in those spiked reports: fields traversed, hills climbed, streams forded – I described them all, the landscape contours, the high gates, the high panorama, and yet I found none of it. If I allow myself to take my embarrassment to be a barometer of my recovery, then I have recovered hugely.

Tomorrow I shall ring Charles and apologize fully and finally. Shall I also put an idea to him that has been germinating and that this embarrassing trip has brought to flower? How will he feel if I propose living outside Dublin, if I buy a house in the vicinity of those mountains and clouds in the south where I first saw Ann on her wedding day? I can still do my job – perhaps take a commentating rather than reporting role: that is what Charles has been leading towards anyway.

Tonight I do not know where Ann is, but she is a moveable feast; in her grief she resides so much more peacefully within me. And now that I know, and acknowledge so much about what happened to me, I must respect this instinct that is telling me to go and live in her old territory.

30

Distant sounds. A magpie in the woods. A car passing by. The short blare I can hear faintly upstairs as a commercial break happens on the radio. Richard's up there now, propped up. He listens to the current affairs programmes all day. I love Richard's wildness, his capacity to accept any possibility. That is still his greatest gift, no circumstance is too strange for him.

Except revenge. He always tried to stop my revenge. He was right. I wish I had listened to him. Mother would still be alive.

I drew up such a cold and elaborate plan. It entailed acting in order to deceive. I would return to the bosom of my family and pretend quiet dignity – no rage, no recrimination. I would subdue my personality and give the impression that I had been reduced to a shell. I knew how to do it – appear as a completely changed woman and have them accept me. Acting, acting – modest and silent, I would work my way further and further in.

And then, from the inside, strike.

How beautiful Richard looked the night I outlined it to him. How lovely the sky.

'Look, Doll, the stars, they're winking at us.' He sometimes drank heavily back then.

All that spring and summer I forced talk on him about

my return to the family and I swore him to secrecy, I overrode his objections.

'Doll, are you sure, I mean are you sure – '

'I'm sure, Rich. I am sure. It's the right thing to do.'

'But – using the IRA? I mean – '

'Rich, I am *certain*!'

That was a typical exchange.

He tried hard to change me but I would not allow him to. He even tried, as I then thought, to send me back to my old grief – but that only determined me harder. This is how he did it.

I had been feeling my heart a little lighter, or so I thought. Then July came. I always dreaded the anniversary of that garden party: it still bothers me badly, especially if it falls harsh and hot. That first anniversary Richard took my arm in bed and helped me sit upright.

He said, 'We're going driving.'

I had not the strength to resist him.

The rain hit us as we left Galway city, going south-east. I knew, I knew where Richard was taking us. Dread arrived again.

Deep in Clare, the rain got too much and Richard said, 'We stay somewhere.'

'Rich, I didn't bring any clothes.'

'Neither did I, so we stay in a good joint.'

We did, one of those big Irish-American hotels, vastly expensive. 'They don't ask questions and they have bathrobes.'

Out of grief I slept like a drunk. Next morning, dry and a little recovered, I said, 'Rich, can we go back now please?'

'We are going back.'

I smiled.

'But', he said, 'not the way you think.'

My heart sank further as the journey confirmed itself. Two hours later we drove past Grennanstown House. On the railings hung a builders' sign: 'New Hospital Development'.

'They've sold up, Rich. Where are they?'

He shook his head. 'We'll get those answers another time. If you go through with this plan of yours it means that I will come back to live around here. Wait until you see my pavilion.' He laughed.

I often asked him about this crazy hermit people talked about. To think that Richard had lived six miles away from me for several years.

We drove by my old woods. They are Johnnie Ross's woods too, where Joey defiled me and threw away my sandals. Richard told me he gathered hazelnuts there. He turned down a long, straight, narrow road. They had not had the same rain here. The sun ran high and strong in the late morning sky.

Richard stopped the car. He got out and opened my door: unusual. He almost plucked me out of the seat. And held me as I stood. 'Doll. Easy, easy.'

We climbed a stone stile into a cemetery I had never known of. Ballintemple. The town of the church. No church nearby. This graveyard sat expressionless and alone, thoughtful under the white clouds. I found it difficult to walk. The graves were benign with lime-stone and artisan marble. Richard propped me. I must have looked like those grieving people at funerals on the television news every night.

No pathway in the cemetery was long. Every hillock seemed like the green, sleeping back of someone. Soon we stopped. I stood. I stared.

My first thought: 'Where did I put that second white blouse I bought in Lydon's?'

My second thought: 'The headaches have stopped, they stopped three days ago. I wonder why?'

My third thought: 'The bastards, the bastards, the bastards, they haven't even put a gravestone.'

My fourth thought: 'Why out here?' Then, 'Ah! The family plot is here.' Yes, there was the headstone. Grandfather and Grandmother Halpin.

My fifth thought: 'Poor little Rossie. How much of him is left? Maybe only his little bones, perhaps some of his auburn hair? Could I look? Was he cold?'

Then my heart started to fall apart all over again.

It was an old new grave. Like Ross himself. He was new, with an old soul. All these thoughts ran at the same time. They sounded inside me like different instruments in a music recording. Ah, Jesus, little Ross, my little love. Then Richard caught me and did not let go. But why did I not kneel? I puzzled that for a long, long time.

The clay here has the red of sandstone. Everything started to spin. The sun danced like it's supposed to do on Easter morning. I found it hard to breathe. I also found that I felt no reality there. I could not mourn, could not find the mourning-place inside me. I felt that silent agents were beating me up, things I could not see or hear.

Richard walked me from the cemetery. I must have seemed airy to him. That kind of desperation has long since left me.

I do not know how long we were there. Richard told me much later that we stayed by the grave for no more than a few minutes. Nothing connected. Inside me all my wires seemed to hang loose.

As we walked away there were high ballooning clouds. 'God's cushions,' I told Ross once. Isn't it strange – how I remember that morning so clearly? I remember the grey limestone of the wall, with little green badges of lichen. I remember seeing a small bird dip in flight across us as we walked unsteadily. And I remember thinking, 'That bird could easily be Ross's soul.'

Was I going mad – really mad this time? No. I was going sane.

31

I saw Ann today. And today I have had to remind myself fiercely that I like myself, and need control of myself, and now, of course, I need it more than ever. That is why I am struggling a little tonight. After all the months of hoping and, almost despite myself, watching out for her, looking at every woman everywhere – I saw Ann today.

But I saw the man she was with before I saw her: it was odd – in some knowing or intuitive way I registered his bizarreness and then I saw Ann; he was walking her rather slowly through the lobby of a large hotel and I felt shock.

I disliked him intensely; he is of mixed race, possesses no appearance of responsibility and his face bears the ravages of dissipation. That bandanna he wore on his head could not have been more out of place – on a man older than me for Heaven's sake! He was smiling down at her with a wide, indulgent smile. Had they not so openly been together I should have suspected him of perhaps kidnapping her; although I must put that down to the fact that kidnapping has been on my mind ever since the siege ended.

Yet, perhaps he did kidnap her; apparently kidnappings have that effect; they call it 'Stockholming' – where the hostage one day marries her kidnapper; one of the news agency chaps based in Dublin covered the kidnapping in Stockholm where it happened. No, I must be sensible; this was not kidnapping – but it might have been Stockholming; she looked up at him adoringly and responded to his lead. I feel convinced that had I seen him without her I would have felt a not dissimilar recoil from him. My response cannot simply have derived from bias and self-interest – or, since I have promised myself to be honest, jealousy.

No, no; I must hold on to myself; of course he did not kidnap her, no occasion to, and of course I was shocked, because I had kept alive the fantasy of meeting her in circumstances that I would have prescribed – a walk across green fields, or a moment in an art gallery: in other words, a romantic encounter, and I never, therefore, allowed myself to think of her being with another man.

The shock of that adoring look she gave him has hit me with the force of an accident to the heart; and she seemed so dependent on him. How had he interposed, how had he won her? Where had I failed? An instinct seized me – it said, 'Disregard this: this will pass: she will be there when you move towards her.' I am prepared to allow that this is the voice of self-preservation, but I will accept its comfort.

Ann's hair has been cut severely and that upsets me – but I have to remind myself of my vow: I have no proprietary rights here – I have no rights at all. She seems not to have changed much otherwise, amazing in one who has been through what must be the ultimate pain – of losing a child. So little has she changed that I almost walked up to her as to an old friend. I have not seen her for so long. Has she returned to her old territory – which is about forty miles east of here?

She did not see me, she did not see anyone, so rapt and

dependent was she, and regrettably I could not follow them. Nor did they say where they were going. When the receptionist asked, 'May we help you with your next hotel booking?' he said, 'No, thank you.' I think he is American.

He took Ann's arm as if he owned her and said, 'C'mon, Doll.'

Different hairstyle, different clothing. Gone is that simple, elegant taste; the clothes she wore today, though completely acceptable, had none of her previous style; they look ordinary, and they look as though she had slept in them.

High summer or no, the day rained (as they say here), that driving rain off the Atlantic that gives the west of Ireland its vivid colours and limpid air. They drove off at great speed and I turned back from the doorway. My mind scrambled to some kind of foothold; but I spilt milk, I spilt coffee, splashed myself heavily. I sat by my window for almost an hour recovering my grip on myself and only moved when the receptionist rang to ask what time I hoped to check out. Despite my upset at seeing her attached to another man – and such, I think, a churl – my heart was able to say repeatedly, 'She's alive and she's safe and she's in this country.'

Has she left her husband? Marriages often break up after tragedy hits them; perhaps that is what happened here. Perhaps she blames him for the drowning or blames herself so much she cannot face him every day; or perhaps she can no longer look on the face of the man who bred the child she has lost. Who can say?

I came down to County Clare covering a massive bank robbery. In the raid a policeman has been shot in the head; he lies in a coma at the Regional Hospital. His wife

agreed to let me see her and I interviewed her this afternoon in the kitchen of her home, with two small children
watching like chipmunks. The woman's account had a
lurid quality, as if she needs to talk about the shooting in
detail – which she did, entry wound included. She found
the situation complicated by the fact that her grandfather
had fought with the IRA in 1921. When she spoke, her
face remained unusually immobile, even though she has
expressive speech. None of her gestures suggested shock,
and she fulfilled my angle on her – a young wife and
mother far away from the Irish border, yet caught up
directly and appallingly in something over which she
has no control, and for which she has no greater than
a distant wish, i.e., the unification of Ireland. And that
vague wish, like the wishes of so many in the South, is
encouraged only lightly – by, at most, the occasional
ballad with her husband when off-duty in a pub late
at night.

The interview pleased me; this has been my first opportunity to reverse my habitual unfeelingness in these situations. In line with my new resolutions, I asked questions
which considered her and did not put my own career first;
I listened closely to her, took in what she said, divined
her true worry – should her husband be permanently
incapacitated, their lives would have no chance of the
improvement she could normally expect.

'When do you worry most?' I asked.

'The evening. And the children going to bed. They
have no play much these days with their Daddy sick.' She
paused. 'And he not knowing them, like, not knowing
their names, he not being, I mean, he being unconscious.
They ask if he asks after them.'

Time and circumstances are wonderful allies; this story
came along at the precise moment when I needed to write

something that would support my case for a more reflective role. For such a role I could not live among richer material: the contrasts of Ireland invade one inimitably. Driving to the next village I stopped for petrol and ended up with a story that will make the front page.

The garage proprietor took me to the back of his workshop where he proudly displayed a large yellow contraption – a submarine he himself had built. He spoke without punctuation, as they seem to do down here.

'I built an airplane but them in the Department of Transport and Power wouldn't let me fly it, they wouldn't give me a licence, so I thought well if I can't go up I must go down and I go out now and I sail her along the bottom of Lake Dysart 'tis a limestone lake and you can see the length of it when you're on the bottom of it.'

'Yellow?'

'Yeh, the song, "Don't we all live in a yellow submarine".'

I found him wonderful. He had powered the engines with huge car batteries that pumped empty the tar drums he used as side tanks, and the batteries also drove the propellor that took him to the surface.

'How often do you submerge?'

'When I do have a row with the wife.'

At the newsdesk they almost disbelieved the story; I shall have corroboration for them when my photographer flies to Shannon in the morning.

All day my heart has ached at the sight of Ann and the freight of sorrow she must carry: the truth is she looks unquiet; her bloom has gone. She has ruined my capacity for placid sleep – but I have the compensation of hearing the Atlantic outside my window, and although she looked reasonably well, I associate Ann's face with the rain driving tonight across the stony fields. Where are they lying tonight? Are they making love? This is so awful.

32

When I was little I thought I would always remember everything that happened to me. What I can't remember now is when I began to formulate The Plan. I dug out some old letters and notes last night. Had to put them away. The pain of all that.

The Plan. It began with a letter. We posted it in Dublin, drove there to do it – at my insistence. We found a letterbox by the canal. Was it the same canal whose ducks Ross loved? I don't know. We turned and drove directly back to Galway.

> Dear Mother,
> May I come home, please? I have been away and somewhat down, but I think I am getting better. How is Daddy? I came to Dublin last week to see a doctor and now I would like to see you. If you would like to see me, please be at the Junction to meet the Kingsbridge train on Monday at a quarter to eight. If you're not there I can catch a train back.
> With much love,
> Ann

I took three hours to draft that letter. I still have the copy I took. The last sentence about catching 'a train back' was the best passage. Mother has always desired things that might slip away from her.

'I'm going to be the prodigal. Play the prodigal daughter. Look at the timing, Rich! Monday's perfect – therefore I'm going, she'll think, for a quiet week. Definitely not just a weekend trip. They'll know I'm serious. Early evening that first evening – time for supper, which I won't eat, and bed, not much else. Eat little. Plead tiredness. They'll expect that. Let her seem to care for me. She'll enjoy that – for a day or so!'

'What're you going to wear, Doll?'

'Downbeat. Brown. With a bit of black. Dowdy. I want her to buy me clothes. I want her to be my saviouress. I want her to take charge of me, give me a new wardrobe. If she does – I'm home free.' I felt exultant and Richard looked gloomy.

Mother stood far away down the platform, far from where the train stops. As ever, she let me come to her. I walked slowly. My bladder had weakened since the hysterectomy. I coached myself intensely. 'Stay a little vague.' 'Walk slowly.' 'Don't laugh for weeks and weeks and weeks.' 'Submit. Submit.' But I was whimpering inside my head.

She had not changed at all. Not fundamentally. Her hair was a bit brighter black, perhaps. Same shade of lipstick, same high shoe, same expensive knitwear, Italian, I'd say.

What had she been thinking about me while I was away? *Had* she been thinking about me while I was away? She shook hands. Then she hugged me. Briefly, briefly.

'Ann. Ann.' That was all. Then she walked beside me. Erect of head. That hard profile. Not a tear in the eye, not a trace of sadness that I could find. A tightness of mouth, perhaps.

219

'What kind of woman are you, Mother?' I wondered to myself. With all my bravado and all my cold, vengeful anger she could still get to me.

Richard and I guessed she would be there at the station out of fear that some scandal might emerge. After all I had escaped from St Heber's. Who knows what I might do? Did I fear they might return me to St Heber's?

'If they do, Doll, I'll come and get you again.'

Mother wasn't there because she loved me. When she dumped somebody they stayed dumped. I saw her do it with friends. She never spoke to them again. If they rang, as Eleanor Power did, Mother merely put the telephone to one side and went on with what she was doing. After a quarter of an hour or so she listened to see if they were still there. They never were, so she replaced the receiver. No emotion crossed her face or eyes.

She fell out with Helen Quinn who, a month later, came to the door. Mother opened it, looked at her and closed it again. Just like that.

We walked together, she and I, down this long cattle platform. God above! I told Richard I would act. He didn't like it. I told him I would act my heart out. But I didn't know it was going to be this difficult.

'How are you, Ann?'

And still she looked straight ahead. I knew why. She had to be alert in case we met someone she knew.

I gulped. Never mind. Over the years I had learned to cope with those sudden rushes of nausea.

'I'm all right, I suppose. Up and down.'

'You look well.'

'Yes, Mother.' My lips fought desperately to obey my exhortations. Do not purse. Do not grimace. 'Yes, Mother.'

Then I said, in a rehearsed blurt, 'I will not embarrass anyone. I will behave.' It was easy to burst into tears. She saw me fight them back.

'Where is your suitcase?'

'I don't . . . I haven't . . . I have no – ' I indicated the clothes I wore. All rehearsed. But fear of her disapproval nevertheless hit me.

Fear dominated my memory of my family. In Cork, if they telephoned my lodgings my stomach lurched as I read the landlady's message. Or my hand trembled as I answered the telephone. Joey intensified this response. I can still hear the note in Mother's voice. Knock on my bedroom door at Grennanstown House; that tone of Puritan satisfaction: 'Oh, Ann, your husband's on the telephone for you. It's Joseph.' She spoke his name as though it had meaning in Nazareth.

Now the fear had not only come to the surface – it lay there like an oil-slick.

Mother said, 'Oh, my dear Ann. Not still losing things, are you?' That was one of her big complaints about me, that I lost things. 'Never mind, we won't talk about lost suitcases now, we'll get you home.'

I felt like a prisoner being frogmarched.

Mother introduced me to a man. 'This is Kevin. Kevin this is my daughter, Ann. She's been abroad, and now she'll be at home.'

'Have she any luggage, Ma'am?' He spoke as if I weren't there: this man knew who the boss was.

'It's coming by a different route, Kevin.' My smooth, unhesitating mother.

A driver. Kevin. Whose arched eyebrows made him seem permanently surprised. A chauffeur. Oh-ho! Mother had arrived. He wore a grey suit, but no cap. Mother was learning discretion.

'I thought we'd just have dinner, you, me and Daddy this evening. Daddy was so excited when your letter came. Although it was slow in coming, but that was because it was re-addressed.'

I had deliberately sent it to the old address at Grennanstown. And Mother could still do it. She could still make me feel that the delay in the letter, that the entire postal system, was my fault.

'Re-addressed?'

'Yes. You'll see.'

I did. Two miles from the Junction, Kevin turned right. We went under the railway bridge, past Clanbreen Stud Farm. In a plush avenue stood a board marked 'The Fields: Private Property'.

'Mother?' I began to ask. I was at last beginning to be an actress.

She bestowed again. 'Not long now. Look out of your side window.'

Kevin pressed a button. Glass moved downwards and I got a clear view. I saw the long and powerful red roof. White chimneys and picket fences and peacocks. Peacocks! Jesus! Another gate, long, wide and narrow, sighed open alone. We rolled on to beige gravel. The house came straight out of a Doris Day film. White clapboard and red brick and windows everywhere. It had a little clock lantern tower.

'Kevin, are you collecting Mr Halpin?'

'I am, Ma'am.' He stood by her door.

'Tell him we've arrived safely, will you, please, Kevin?'

No mention of Joey.

Mother said to me, 'We've only just finished. At last. Indeed my interior designer only went back to London last week.'

Interior designer. Mother needed an interior designer

222

– but for her own interior. She had changed her mode of speech. Now she spoke through tighter lips, with a hint of a sibilance. Had I ever spoken like that she would have called me 'affected'. And wouldn't another mother have said something like, 'Lovely timing, it's as if we were getting it ready for you'?

Kevin crept away, not even revving. We stood and looked at the house.

'Wait until you see inside.'

I could have been misled by the fact that she seemed excited. It was not at my arrival. Her house was finished. Brand-new. Up to date. For a while she was ahead of the posse.

'We sold Grennanstown, did awfully well. You know Daddy's nose for property.'

But as she walked inside, I experienced a shock of great sadness. Her bearing reminded me of Ross. I had not prepared for that. I had not expected it.

Mother turned and saw the tears in my eyes.

'Ann, it's really quite nice. I'll tell you tomorrow how much it cost. I never told Daddy the final figure.' She giggled at her naughty secret.

I fell in with everything, accepted all she showed, responded as she demanded: 'Lovely. Lovely.' I developed an impressed murmur. Room after room, curtains, towels, paintings, silver, glass. This was not a wife or mother. This was a curator.

Eventually we sat down. A young woman walked into the drawing-room and surveyed us; she wore a firm grey skirt.

'And this is Agnes. Agnes is Kevin's wife. Agnes, this is my daughter Ann, that you've heard so much about.'

Agnes looked at me without smiling, a cool, unhostile look. 'Hallo.' I knew I was going to like her.

'Hallo, Agnes.'

We drank. Mother drank champagne. I drank orange juice, part of The Plan. No alcohol when in their company. They had to have the impression that I did not drink. Agnes appeared every time Mother's glass needed refilling.

Mother talked. I wondered whether she feared our conversation. But soon it became plain that she did not. She merely wished to talk.

Of the difficulty the interior designer had finding the right blue silk for the hall curtains and walls.

Of her own trouble when her couturier in Dublin died. Of the maple on the floor of the dining-room.

Of her idea to commission a dining-table that could be one large table. Or five smaller ones.

I had rehearsed my position. I would indicate a desire to stay for a few days. If in a few days she asked when I was leaving, I would 'break down' and put myself in Mother's hands.

No need. She never asked. She assumed I had come to stay forever. In fact she assumed it so totally I had a paranoid flash. Did she know of The Plan? No. She blithed on.

'So for tonight and perhaps tomorrow, stay in the guest room and then by the weekend Kevin and Agnes will have The Enclosure ready.'

I smiled a nervous joke-smile in her direction. 'The Enclosure?'

Mother smiled back. 'There are three houses.' She spoke as if from a brochure. 'The Stables is the biggest, the name is your Daddy's idea, we're The Stables. Then there's The Paddock. And The Enclosure, that's for you.'

I did not ask who lived in The Paddock. I suppose I

already knew. Not that it mattered. Mother showed no concern or embarrassment. Or perhaps she did. Perhaps her practical air, which I knew so well, had always been her rescue device. Her embarrassment valve. No. The fact is, she expected to have utter command of me.

Again! There it shone! That flash of Ross! Oh, God and Jesus, the pain of that!

'And then, we must talk clothes. Oh!' She harked at a sound. 'I think that's Daddy.' Just as she did in my childhood.

The drill of that household fascinated me. It still does when I think of it. Agnes opened the front door. Kevin handed to Agnes my father's coat and hat. My father climbed from the car. I could see that my acting's greatest difficulty was going to lie in the suppression of anger. So these were the values they had always aimed at. These ordinary people in a small country town should have known something about modesty.

'And she's here. Well, well, well.' He had a joke when I was little. 'Did yeh ever hear the story of the three wells?'

'No, Daddy.'

'Well. Well. Well.' A hundred times he told that joke. I never minded.

Here he came now. He looked like a pink and kindly version of Boris Karloff.

'Well. Well. Well.'

He stood, head to one side. Genetically, I should have no difficulty acting. My father acted every moment of his life. Toss a coin to judge who was falser. He or Mother. He put his head to one side and held out his hands.

'Let me look at her. Isn't she grand? Mammy, isn't she grand?' He wore a light grey suit that cost a thousand

225

pounds, trouser-creases of steel. 'Ah, there's a God in Heaven, my little girl is home to me.'

I rose and let him hug me. His embrace did not feel as sinister as Mother's.

He sat on the couch. I wondered did they have those other accessories of the new rich – extramarital lovers. Talk began. What was said I cannot remember. Nor do I need to recall. He spoke at length, mainly memories of me when young. At which I knew to smile.

'D'you remember the time you fell off of your bicycle that Santy Claus brung you? And you kicked the road and then you kicked me and I laughing at you. Boys-a-boys. Well. Well. Well.'

Mother smiled. She had learned the power of unison.

I scrutinized them both. Time in a mental hospital teaches you how to look at people without them knowing you are looking. I inspected their faces. No trace could I find anywhere of bereavement at the loss of their grandson. I thought any grief they might have felt could return when they saw me. If I mentioned Ross what would happen? I did not have a clue. It wasn't grief I should have been looking for. I should have been looking for fear in their faces.

Mother amazed me, even by her detached standards. She never asked about my clothes. Nor my plans nor my means. Did she never wonder where I had been? Did my father? Did Joey? Did they ever ask each other – or themselves – where I had gone? I do not think so. I never found out.

Mother merely sailed on. Each evening she directed Agnes where to place the bowls of food. Each evening she gestured Kevin towards my empty water glass. Each evening she knew her champagne glass would be filled routinely.

226

'I'm still hoping my little girl will come into her Daddy's business,' said my father before long. It was night, some weeks later, and brandy had slackened his tongue.

'We'll talk about that,' said Mother in tight mode. She never dropped her guard – even after a bottle and a half of champagne.

Some new ghost came riding through the trees at that moment. It was not hatred. It was not love (certainly not love). It was not affection, nor disaffection. The ghost rider was the spirit of family blood. Of ties that transcend all bitterness and damage. Had I ridden with this ghost rider The Plan would have collapsed. When the ghost rider returned, pale amid the leaves and branches of my heart, I faced him down. Because there and then I needed those plans of revenge. Even now, long after the outcome, I still argue this and I still mean it and Richard still disagrees with me. But primal family affection could have destroyed the rest of my life.

Mother said good-night. I did not sleep – in my bed so piled with pillows I could hardly climb into it, so deep with down mattress I could hardly climb out. At one o'clock I fetched a towel so that tears would never reach the pillow. At two o'clock I slipped from the room. Mother always snored, always slept soundly, especially after champagne. This fact enabled her to twitter a justification about her 'sleeping-draught'. I stood still as I heard my father go uncouth to the lavatory.

He returned to his own room. They still slept apart. I sat in a chair in the long corridor until he too began to snore.

Richard says that people who need night-lights suffer from bad conscience. My parents' house never darkened. Every room, every corridor, every corner had night-lights. In the kitchen, dimmed lights stayed on all night. I found milk in the fridge and drank a little.

I searched the house that night. It had always been my intention to search it as soon as I could. I searched every corner. I even tiptoed into Mother's bedroom and stood watching her asleep. Then I searched quietly. But I knew I would come back one day when she had gone out. And I knew the result would be the same.

Nowhere in my parents' home did I find a trace of me or of my gone little boy. No trace, no hint that either of us had ever existed. Me and my son. Their daughter and their grandson.

33

Charles asked me today on the phone whether 'events, C.' had had an effect upon me. 'You know, the endless round, the bloody bombs and things?'

I felt able to reply, 'No more than they should have – I mean in ordinary, human terms.' He meant yesterday's atrocity, which I alone witnessed. My good control of its potential effect upon me reassures me: my emotional health has improved consistently.

By arrangement, I went to a Dublin suburb called Cherry Orchard, lower-middle to middle class (even though such definitions here are, I think, either blurred or do not exist). My appointment, made more or less in secret, would give me an 'exclusive' interview with Aidan Kilmartin, the man who last month created a breakaway party from the Provisionals, the Irish Republican Democrats. I had seen him once or twice, when he was a background Sinn Fein figure at their press conferences, and he now has suddenly emerged with a maverick reputation; two gruesome killings in Monaghan have been attributed to him directly. London proves enormously interested in him: perhaps some word had reached them from Whitehall: certainly Kilmartin was expected to destabilize the mainstream republican process considerably. Were our crowd running him? Has he been feeding them information about his erstwhile comrades in the Provisionals?

I saw his car and followed instructions: drive past him and hold up my splayed hand twice – to indicate the ten minutes he said I could have with him as he sat parked outside the house of a friend. Coming towards me in another car, I saw the BBC correspondent. Some 'exclusive': Kilmartin had evidently agreed to see us in turn. As instructed, I parked far away from Kilmartin's car but where he could see me. I was to wear no coat or jacket and have my notebook and pen visibly ready: no groping in my pockets. He conducted his telephone conversation with me in a low, matter-of-fact, rather placid tone, saying, 'No tape recorders, d'you hear? I want to be able to deny anything I say to you. I might decide to frisk you and if I find a tape recorder, or anything I think you shouldn't be wearing, I'll have a soft word with you. OK?' I have never felt such menace.

Kilmartin rolled down his window as I crossed the street: in another precaution he had parked with the passenger side to the pavement and told me to approach the driver's side from across the road 'where I can keep you in my sights'. His greeting might have been that of a neighbour seeing me walk by, or a casual acquaintance; he leaned back a little, both hands behind his head.

'Are you going to make me famous?' he asked with some joviality.

I asked him where and how he wanted to talk.

'Like this. You stay out there and I'll stay in here. Then we'll all know where we are.'

This man was highly intelligent – and completely frightening; he had a pleasant and easy manner and a complete lack of care for anything in the world. We all of us covering Ireland, press and security forces, got the Republicans wrong; just because many of them had not had much education did not mean they were thick.

I leaned back against the car, addressing him from a half-sideways position, and in this unorthodox way the interview began; he insisted that I leave his wing-mirror unobstructed.

Kilmartin spoke freely and alertly, responding with interest, but with an implied intimidation that froze my blood; for instance when I asked him his age, he said, 'Thirty-seven. A few years younger than you.' I looked up and down the road – so did he; he checked his rear-view and wing mirrors unceasingly; in the distance I could see the BBC man waiting in his car.

Then it happened, and nobody could have known what to expect. The door of the house across the road opened and a woman emerged, tall, heavy and perhaps in her late forties, with unpleasant hair. She carried two plastic sacks, one of which she dumped in the dustbin at the gate. With hindsight, I registered her more than I should have done: 'something odd there,' I remember thinking. She looked across at us, and turned to go back to her front door, then she changed her mind, and wandered vaguely towards us. Had she walked straight she would have reached the rear of Kilmartin's car, therefore by eschewing a straight line she moved just out of his peripheral vision; she still held the second plastic sack by the neck.

As she reached the car she turned fast and stepped towards Kilmartin's open window. Before my eyes, one foot away from me, she raised the sack and blew his head off. When a head is blown off that is exactly what happens. Kilmartin's head crashed sideways, hit the window on the passenger door, cracked the glass and dropped to the passenger seat like the head of John the Baptist. A fountain of blood spouted upwards and sprayed the ceiling of his car – and me. It all took time to become real – in fact I finished my note of his last answer. The woman – who turned out to be a man, hence my registration of something odd – simply dropped the gunsack to the pavement, nodded to me, walked slowly back across the road, produced some keys, reversed the car from the drive of the house 'she' had been in and drove away unhurriedly.

For what seemed like several seconds I did not move, could not move; my ears felt muffled from the violent crump of the noise. Next, perhaps because the tenor of the occasion had been set, I walked away too – and kept my nerve. I knocked at a door, asked for the telephone; the elderly owner looked at me in consternation and that is how I discovered I was dripping with sprayed blood; I rang first the police and then the newsdesk and then went back to the car. The BBC man has not spoken to me since; he complains that I ought to have beckoned him forward; by the time he realized something had happened – he was too far away to see detail – the police had prevented anyone from nearing the car.

My position with London grows more and more secure; the report on Kilmartin's death has clinched it. Charles urged me, 'If you're up to it, milk it, C.!' – and thus I did interviews all over the place; both the BBC and ITN led with it, as did all the other newspapers. My return to full orders, said Charles – but he was not being sarcastic – is now complete. I should say so.

This afternoon Charles rang and I was about to put to him my thoughts of moving out of Dublin when the urgency in his voice stopped me.

'C.,' he said, 'can you tackle something for me?' He briefed me with a breaking story. 'I was wondering whether it might chime with you. Given your previous experiences with, so to speak, matters under the ground.'

A significant officer, serving out of Thiepval Barracks in Lisburn, has disappeared.

'But see this as a template story. You know, "Our Fate in Ireland", that kind of drift, hard but poignant. I want the lot,' said Charles, 'the family, the education, the hero's role. And the fact that Ireland breaks through into another level of Englishness, our bastions, the middle classes.'

'What's happened to him?'

'Nobody knows.' Charles has ameliorated further and further his way of dealing with me and I am grateful to him for that. 'That is one of the main questions. The word is he's supposed to have been buried secretly. They took him and slaughtered him. That he's in a wood near the Border. Another source, though, has it that they put him through an abattoir.'

I winced. 'Why?'

'This is the worst part almost,' said Charles. 'Worst part for you, I mean.' He paused. 'Given your past experience. You know. He was taken – if he was taken – in your old turf, south Armagh. Secret burials again. It's a bit of a high ball. Field it?'

'Yes, I think I can.' Even if I felt that someone had just walked over my own grave.

Captain Philip Graham Graves: 'Battle-of-Britain type,' said Charles, with decorations already: a classical English boy-soldier – rowing blue, a Balliol man after Harrow, son of a Harley Street rheumatologist whose mother had 'come out' in 1947, that first memorable debs' season after the war.

The tabloids had the lot; Charles's secretary read some of the headlines: *Boys' Own* shock-horror – 'WHAT HAVE THEY DONE TO OUR HERO?' I flew out of Dublin this morning to Heathrow.

Graves's parental home in Marlow touches one of those rare pockets of deep countryside that still remain – almost as oddities – in the Home Counties. I drove past old hangers of beech and ash to a pair of unassuming gates, by a tennis court under old trees, across gravel in front of white bow windows, to meet a sad, pretty mother answering my doorbell; she had spoken to no one else – Charles pulled strings.

We had tea, Philip Graves's mother and I, and chatted a little until her husband arrived; to my surprise he seems (and Charles says it's true) a good deal younger than his wife. They responded differently to my questions: he proved angry and she proved unendurably sad; for some bizarre reason I expected the opposite as they took me through the details of their only child's life.

When Philip was five his father took the decision to become a consultant rather than remain a professor and their quick resultant wealth bought them the house at Marlow. Philip learned boat craft on the little reaches of the Thames and became one of the first weekly boarders at Harrow, where he got into difficulty over bullying. But his father smoothed that out and Philip's aggressiveness found release on the rugby and cricket fields where 'quite naturally' he made the first teams. His academic results took him to Oxford where he failed on the sports fields (temperament again, I gather) but rowed for two consecutive years.

He had 'a little difficulty in adjusting': he was suspended once for (no matter how they disguised it) grievous bodily harm. Oxford raised a corner of the university carpet and wielded the brush; Paul Graves guaranteed his son's good behaviour after that, meaning that he probably posted a large financial bond: 'Surely you don't need such minute detail,' he flashed at me.

Otherwise, they told me with some pride, Philip had been 'colourful' at Oxford. While reading Law, he kept bats and snakes in his rooms, rode to hounds in the holidays, and took up the martial arts. His mother smiled at the recollection of 'girlfriend after girlfriend' and mentioned 'Naomi' as having endured. I asked for a photograph of their son and they jibbed; for the moment I did not press the point.

When have I had forty-eight hours as diverse as these have been? Watching a self-declared 'terror-monger' having his head blown off and then saturating the airwaves and the printed page with my impressions of same; 'Terror,' Kilmartin said to me, 'I'll show them what terror is. They call me a terrorist – I'll live up to it'; and next, taking tea and cucumber sandwiches in deep and discreet middle England. I said all this to Charles tonight and (this is what gets him the loyalty he enjoys) he never asked what might have been a justifiable question, 'Bearing up?'

As the Graveses sat talking to me I knew I had to find Naomi next: Charles said the story has no urgency because in this case he prefers comprehensiveness. Then came the shock and answered the eeriness I felt when Charles briefed me. Paul Graves and his wife changed their minds about the photograph, and when they showed me their son, Philip, in full uniform, I recognized him as 'Tommy' the ballad-singing spy from the Four Horsemen.

34

Must keep a balance. Must remind myself how they, Mother, Joey, saw me in the old days. Snooty. Arty. Looked down on them. Scorned their friends. Made sarcastic remarks. That is what they thought. Maybe I did. In my defence all I can say is that I seemed to live in a state of permanent hurt. In fact I have more difficulty than ever trying to understand the depth of Mother's jealousy. It must have been awful for her – if it was awful enough to drive her to such lengths.

Others liked me. People were, are, very warm to me. All sorts of people, in shops and banks and so forth. Did Mother like me? No, no, no – but I know my father did, does.

The early weeks with Mother passed in a haze of attempted self-control. And Mother-control. In both directions. Her control of me. Me of her. And control of my reactions to her.

Her insensitivity takes my breath away. On my pillow the second night sat a long, brown legal-type envelope. Inside I found the annulment documents of my marriage to Joey. On the grounds of my 'mental instability'. Being Mother, she left in the envelope a letter from the Archbishop. He praised her – which means they paid handsomely for the annulment. 'A donation.' How much? I'd say ten thousand.

Largely I coped. I could spend time in my room alone. There I regrouped. As long as I remembered to act, I won. Richard and I were not due to speak for a further two weeks. A month's immersion, he suggested. 'The deep end's the safest,' he said. 'Ask any swimmer.'

I went along with Mother's clear intent. She was going to take me back into the fold – but under iron control. For her (as I saw it at the time) the deal seemed excellent. She could 'redeem' me at no cost whatsoever. And she could show me off to her friends. In my muted state it was clear I would not be a nuisance. She had no intention of raising the past, I could tell that. So there would be no trouble and no embarrassment. Her life would not change. And it didn't.

Two mornings after my arrival she said brightly, 'Lucy O'Connor's asked us to lunch. Isn't that lovely?'

I nodded. We were sitting at the usual ridiculous daily breakfast. Linen and china and interminable cutlery. I saw afresh why Mother adored Joey. She cannot resist vulgarity. It releases something in her. She gets lighter in its presence. It is her escape.

Lucy O'Connor talks quickly and competitively and her house is equally ghastly. She desecrated a Georgian manor (terrazzo over the wonderful old flagstones). Her entire conversation is peppered with names. She claims to know only celebrities, or prestige destinations. Here is a sample.

'Jack and I are going to Marbella with the Cronins [former Finance Minister] but we're thinking of driving because the Iberia Airline first-class seats are hardly first-class at all, Jack says we're as well off in the Bentley, and anyway the last time we flew, we were going to the Bahamas for New Year, I lost two of my best Louis Vuitton cases. The Nolans [major supermarket owners] are going to be there, the men have arranged their golf already.'

Mother and Lucy O'Connor spoke all afternoon in two separate soundtracks. Neither addressed the other. Neither answered the other. This was a contest lunch.

Lucy O'Connor said to me, 'Have some figs, ah'm, ah'm . . .' Had she forgotten my name? 'I got them specially sent down from Dublin this morning. You know, Moya, they barely survive the hundred miles.'

On the way back from Lucy O'Connor's I had to postpone other emotions. Kevin took a different route from the outgoing one.

Mother, quite sharply: 'Why are we going this way, Kevin?'

Kevin: 'The road is up, Ma'am. 'Tis closing today for two days, there's notices about it.'

Mother tensed and sat back, lit another cigarette. Soon I saw why. Kevin's new route took us past the corner of the lane to the little cemetery where Richard had taken me to mourn Ross.

I know that I am today a woman of considerable resources. Moments like that made me so. I did not look straight ahead. I looked all round me, out of this window and then that. As if nothing mattered to me. As if nothing life-rending mattered to me. Back in my room I lay face down on the floor.

At the weekend Mother took me to The Enclosure.

'At last,' she said.

For some reason I had not yet fathomed, the decor offended less. A smaller house, it spoke in a gentler tone, greens and soft blues and terracottas. Within minutes I received the explanation.

'You know,' said Mother confiding, 'I've hardly seen this. Jan did it more or less by herself. Lucy O'Connor says she always lets her designers have their head on at least one section of the house. And I was so tired after doing The Stables I just gave Jan a budget for this. I told her to finish it before she went back finally to London.'

Mother had not chosen the beds nor the bathrooms, nor the pictures nor the wallpapers. In a way this freed me and I felt the first good relief since my return. I knew that ghastlinesses lay ahead. But now I had a haven inside me. I could think. I could go forth.

Then Mother said, 'Kevin and Agnes live here too. But they're very quiet.'

So – I live with the servants.

The first week became the first month became the first six months. Mother never left me alone. Every day I had to go somewhere, meet someone, attend some function. Sometimes I called in my old capacity to invent malaise and when I did she began to show relief and left me alone with my 'migraine'. Soon, the novelty of redemption wore off. I was too mousey for her and she stopped dictating my day. As long as I remained meek, in my new 'modest' style, no questions arose.

I saw to it that she had a benefit. I was her prize. I was her proof of good works and forgiveness and she touted me around the place like some refugee she had saved. And she had no need to waste time on me when nobody was looking.

So when people came for lunch or dinner I was brought out as some kind of freak show. I was the badge of the family's naturalness. I was the reason they had been rewarded with so much money and 'good fortune', as Mother put it. Here before their eyes sat the black sheep. The mad daughter. For her enduring of me, Mother deserved all her good fortune. I was the down of their up.

I played my meek part among these guests. I had become so ghostly that I was able to flit around the place almost unseen and unnoticed. Thus I heard – and overheard – all their conversations. I actually heard her ply the lie, 'When we went to bring Ann home from, you know . . .'

With me alone her conversation never varied. She repeated the gossip of her neighbours. We studied the upcoming social events, such as weddings or anniversaries. She took the magazines and ordered their latest offerings. The antiques trade telephoned her nearly every day. Its beauties or its discoveries never beckoned her. She asked who was buying what, and how much did they pay for it.

There were mornings when my shame at her crassness showed on my face. I allowed her to misconstrue it as my sadness at my own life. What mattered to her was the next possession. Or some acquaintance's newest acquisition. A table, a brooch, a piece of silver or an apartment in southern Spain – these were endlessly debated on the telephone.

I hated it all. Everything about it offended me. No bookshelves had been built. They had bought one bookcase and it contained a local history book (for which Halpin's had been the sponsors) plus some volumes published by Tattersalls and other racing bodies.

The pictures on the walls had been bought on the gossip of other people. Some of them were good. Artists who become fashionable – either dead or alive – often do so on merit. But the hanging was atrocious. And the lighting of them, and in some cases the framing, was barbaric. They had a gently erotic, rose-pink Roderic O'Connor nude in a spitefully thin, chrome 1950s frame. And no music. My old record player was gone, like everything else of mine. I had no way of playing a record. I never heard Beethoven or Mozart or my lovely Schubert in that house.

How did I endure this? The game I played was a long one. So all of these observations I kept to myself. I controlled my outward expression completely. And if I needed time to myself, I had only to walk in a particularly depressed gait. At which moment Mother would become slightly agitated. She would say, 'I have a few things to do. I'll be occupied for a while, Ann.'

She addressed me as 'Ann' in two ways. Either in front of others when all her solicitousness was hanging out like flags from a window. Or when she couldn't bear the sight of what she thought was my depressed self. Thus was my freedom earned.

What truly enraged me was the fact that Mother and her friends came from a simple society. They had all been born of humble people who lived in the deep and old countryside. Land was powerful then, not money. Land also forged a bond of responsibility. Neighbourhood was the most valuable commodity. If a man's barn burned down his neighbours donated the shortfall. If need arose he would do the same in return. Not now. Not with these Get-the-Money grunters.

Where did these vulgarians spring from? Some of these women no longer went to funerals. They had heard that in London and in some parts of suburban Dublin women didn't attend funerals. Yet their mothers and grandmothers had prized the closeness implicit in such ritual gestures. Societies deteriorate with wealth.

Hardest of all for me was the memory of Ross. Or lack of it. He might never have existed. Not once did Mother mention Ross to me. To this day I find that as callous as cannibalism. My best hope is to suppose her guilt so great she was unable to speak.

But – the human spirit is unfathomable. I was about to take a fierce revenge. I hated everything about their life. Yet I still loved Mother. Deep inside, I loved her as I had loved her when a little girl. Nor would I let go the idea that somewhere deep within her she still loved me passionately.

On good days I tried to rationalize, tried to form the charitable view that her difficulty with me came from a love for me that she was unable to speak. And I loved my father, too. For all his foolishness he could touch my heart with his little finger.

And I had a new love. Richard's place in my heart was deepening. Every time we met we made love. He never made disapproving noises at my tears.

Richard, my love.

I managed to see him quite often. Mother assumed I was out in the country walking, 'finding' myself as she wrote in a letter to a friend. I read it before she sent it off. In it she sainted herself.

'Drop it, Doll. Please!' Richard pleaded. 'Drop The Plan.'

I shushed him and we lay in the grass and made love in the sunshine. Seeing him kept my nerve together. I needed him every time my father talked about the business. *Halpin's: We're the Best Bet!*

'When is my girl going to come into her daddy's business?' he said repeatedly. I, of course, resisted the move. Because it meant I would see the footprints of the one person who had been carefully manoeuvred away from me all that time. Whom I dreaded seeing.

I knew he was about. I knew Joey was near. In the next house, behind the trees, The Paddock . . .

Joey was driving a Mercedes. I saw it and I often heard him revving it. Once, I thought I heard his voice, but his

242

car wasn't there. Other than that he had never been mentioned. Not once. At the thought of him I shivered. Partly through loss. Partly through shame. Partly through fear. Mostly through rage. And revenge.

Then one day, I was sitting on my small terrace in the sun. At a footfall behind me I looked up.

'Howya doin', Sugar?' said Joey.

35

Another blow today – something dreadful happened to me. It heaved me brutally into an arena of feeling where I have little prior knowledge and no previous experience. But it is a measure of how I have grown that it has not destabilized me. I saw Ann lying half-clad and drinking in the open air with the man who accompanied her at that hotel; he was virtually naked.

I have been trying to concentrate on work, trying to keep Ann out of my mind – because I now have within me the confirmation that I was always genuinely in love with her. It was not an obsession; it had nothing to do with my breakdown – that was coincidence; I have been in love with her since the day I saw her and I may have to live with that as an unrequited fact for the rest of my life. Thus, I have been working harder than ever.

Charles came over on a flying visit last week; he said he came because he had been invited to an Embassy lunch, but I know that he wanted to check on me. He liked what he saw – he said so; we discussed the Philip Graves story; he gave me what he called 'A *carte* that is much blancher. I want to move you off day-to-day reporting – we're going to use Dublin as a training ground. I think, if I may say so, C., your new-found thoughtfulness needs a more appropriate outlet.'

I have come to believe that Life's timing tells one of

the rightness or otherwise of one's decisions. A good moment had therefore arrived and when I proposed to Charles that I move out of Dublin he merely said, 'Not north, I hope?'

'No, Charles, south. A good deal further south.' I could scarcely hide my relief: I had been expecting a veto.

'Fine by me. That will help give you the broader picture I want you to think about. It gets you in among the people.'

He telephoned when he was back at his desk and had returned to his old caustic self, a sure sign that he has given up worrying over me; the 'broader picture' changes my role; he wants me to take 'a taller view', in other words, more editorializing; reporters on three-month tours of duty will do what Charles calls 'the turf work' and I will write significant think-pieces, investigations such as this Graves story and occasional leaders on Ireland.

'And you are sure you can do those from anywhere in the entire island?' he said, and went on, 'Is there a woman in the case?' – but I simply chuckled.

Events seem to have swung my way too; at the moment commentary is required in abundance because reportage can find nothing new in the main story – IRA prisoners at the Maze have decided to stage what they call a 'dirty protest': they have smeared the walls of their cells with excrement and wrapped themselves in blankets. We are confined to Northern Ireland Office or Sinn Fein press releases, truly an undesirable Scylla and Charybdis. Thus, I have to editorialize, get tangential opinion, write reflectively; thus I have had time to search for a house where I wish to live – and that is how I came to take one step back.

Am I forever to be bound up in conflicting positions?

Here I am with this excellent career development – yet my heart is hurting so much tonight. I am trying to overcome my shock at seeing her again with her bizarre companion and at the same time I think I may have found a delightful house; or houses – a little terrace of three old railway cottages stands out in the woods about three miles from Ann's old home, and two hours or so from Dublin and by a mainline railway station. The buying and furnishing excites me already: they have excellent fabrics and pottery in Kilkenny, about forty miles away; I shall have a stone floor, some fine old chairs and an elm table. Mustn't get carried away, must be successful at the auction; the solicitor tells me that if the sellers know it is for someone like me they will puff up the price, so I shall keep out of the bidding. But – it is so difficult to keep one's emotional faith alive in such circumstances. Had I not been viewing the house I would not have seen Ann lying in the grass.

After lunch I set out on the first of my explorations, not merely for pleasure. An old castle nearby was, they say, modelled on Versailles and has interesting associations with Swift and Hazlitt. Reaching it entails parking the car on the main road and walking a mile or so by fields of pasture.

The castle has a fascinating atmosphere; not, I think, a real castle originally, it feels more like a fortified house but with tremendous and intricate embellishment – spires, turrets, false ramparts, galleries; I found traces of a library, with the page of an old book buried deep beneath rubble, a diocesan record of some kind. Ivy dominates the walls, but much of the stone remains visible – cut, especially on the quoins, as if it had been silk. In the near distance to the north sits the hamlet once attached to the castle, and some Edwardian village architecture survives: ochre walls and dormer windows.

I found that long, old avenue they call the Bell Walk; the hot weather had made the gravel reappear through the dried grasses; it leads to the bank of a stream which I followed to the old kitchen-garden. Suddenly I heard laughter, voices, then more laughter.

My boyhood adventure books gave tips used by the Red Indian trackers: when you hear voices you must stand still to establish whether the speakers are on the move or stationary. These voices came from one position and I drew closer. With careful manoeuvring I got myself to a position where from a low, great branch I could see through a gap in the old wall of what must have been the kitchen garden. Beneath me on the grass lay Ann, lying on her stomach. She was covered only by a shirt, under which she clearly wore few clothes. The man with whom I had seen her in that hotel sat nearby, also without much shame; he drank from a bottle and they talked and laughed.

In all my contemplations of Ann, it had never crossed my mind that I would have to deal with sexual jealousy. Loss – yes; I have faced loss every day, both on the days where I knew where she was, even – perhaps especially – on those days I had seen her. Pain, too: the pain of unrequited (and in this case, unspoken) love produces anxiety, confusion.

This experience today has made me even less comfortable with myself and I do not know what to do. I tiptoed away, then almost ran from that place; I never looked back in their direction, and when I reached the car I think I was in tears. It is difficult to describe what I feel: fear does not sum it up, although livid fear burns me; I have lost her. She seems to have left her husband, but she seems to have a new man in her life. Have I missed a tide in my own affairs?

It is now midnight and still warm. I have kept my resolution firmly. I know that if I had liquor near me I would tonight be back among old difficulties. Perhaps they are preferable to new troubles.

Naomi has not replied to my letter but I did not expect her to; Mrs Graves tells me that they were having difficulty contacting her; her family say she has locked herself away in grief – apparently she had expected to marry her soldier. I had better try and find her. Today I took an unpleasant plunge and telephoned Father Coll in his parish along the Border; he says he will give me no information other than telling me that yes, the officer is dead.

And so the Philip Graves story rolls on with tension and pace, and with it I roll between the dilemma of pain in the matter of Ann Halpin and the satisfaction of work – and on good days vice versa. This switchback experience keeps my optimism in good shape. That is the best I can say to myself tonight; I think I shall concentrate on work now for a time.

36

Yes, the blood does thin at times. At crucial moments in our lives it thins. Fear thins it, and sudden loss. I know. I can feel it thin now, just from memory. You move a limb – to stand, or extend an arm. And it won't work right. The arm or the leg feels empty. It is without its usual thickness of liquid pumping through.

As when Joey walked in saying, 'Howya doin', Sugar?'

My right arm would not work to shake hands with Joey. It flapped a little, then it flopped back to my lap.

'Howya doin', Sugar?' Jesus! As if he saw me yesterday. As if – as if. Thoughts failed me.

Some flesh had come to him, on the face and in the waist. His face seemed darker as if pigments had congealed. The eyebrows were the same bushy black smears. He took out a cigarette, tapped it on the packet as he always did. Then he half-shoved the packet in my direction. I waived and he lit his Zippo like a soldier in a war film. With his thumb up came the flame and with it rose my hatred.

'Hallo, Joey,' I said. 'How are you?'

I could barely see him through my mist of fury. All the skin in my throat tightened with rage. I felt myself blushing. He – or anyone – would misinterpret that as shyness or embarrassment.

'Good call here, Sugar,' he said, exhaling. He looked around appreciatively at the house and garden. 'That's the form, right? Good call.' He tapped his toe on the flagstones of the little terrace. 'Bricks and mortar. Best call of all. Twelve per cent per annum appreciation. Eight years' return on investment. Yeh, good call. How's the form anyway?'

He drew up a chair.

'That's your Merc?' I asked. That was the tone I had cultivated for Mother and Father, an I-will-please-you-without-thought-to-myself voice. I sounded mildly interested but docile. My fingers twitched slightly. They wanted to reach forward and gouge out his eyes.

'Yeh, the Merc. I hadda think, automatic or manual. Joey stuck with the manual. She shifts, Sugar. Put the hammer down, nought to seventy in six seconds. Drinks a bit. But don't we all. Right?'

He was, I realized, treading water, trying desperately to have things normal.

I thought: Well, what can you say if you do finally confront your estranged wife? Whose orifices you have assaulted within hours of first meeting her. Whom you have abused vilely. To whom you have been openly unfaithful in front of her eyes. Even while on honeymoon. If you contributed at least massive negligence to the death of your – and her – only child. Then committed your wife to a mental hospital. And signed the papers for having her entire womanhood eradicated. What do you say? What can you say?

Joey pressed on. 'I thought of a BMW. Your old man wanted me to go for the Jag, same as himself. I said to him, all due respects, Boss, Joey still has all his hair and teeth, right? Joey'll get a Jag when he's losin' his hair and teeth, right? Your old man just laughed. Fair do's. They're lookin' good, doncha think, the parents, Sugar?'

I said, 'I like your suit.' It was vile; large check, larger lapels.

He looked down. 'Joey always fancied a good whistle.'

He dragged on the cigarette. In one pull he consumed half an inch of the paper tube.

'The old lady, she says you're comin' on. Old man's like a pig in the proverbial since you ... since you, well, you know, sort of ... you know, got back in the photo, right?'

I asked Richard: do pictures go through men's heads when they feel violent?

'Carved flesh, Doll. Bullet holes. A pair of blackened eyes the mildest. Disembowelling.'

Are women different? I wanted to boil Joey. And I wanted to slice slivers off his ears and off his thighs. I wanted to stand him naked on tiptoe, string him wide apart by the wrists between two pillars and then blow-lamp him. I wanted him to eat a poison. It would act very slowly. Violent, slow-motion agony. I would stand before him. I would watch him. I would tell him. As my savagery within grew, my outward docility deepened.

'You're looking very well,' I said softly. 'Daddy says you're now being acknowledged as a business genius. Apparently one of the newspapers is going to do a big profile of you.'

Joey made a gesture I recognized. He held his hand open and turned it behind him.

'All grease. Newspapers, too. Backhanders. We adver-tise. Same as politics. First cousins, Sugar, you musta heard me say it before, first cousins the greasy pole and the greasy palm. First buckin' cousins. The boys locally

251

want me to run. Next election. That's the idea behind the newspaper piece. Dublin, they say, think it's the biz.'

Joey the politician!

Richard mused when I told him, 'The higher a guy wants to climb the more he exposes his balls to the knife.'

I had Joey, I had him! He was the one I feared. His manner and his being rankled – but he was sharp and tough-minded. In politics he would be vulnerable to scandal. And already he needed my approval. Or so it sounded. My mind lit with flashes of lightning. They needed me. They needed to have me under control, not racing around telling my story. That was why they were thrilled with my meekness. This was going to be brilliant.

Joey lit another cigarette and forked the old one into the hedge.

I said, 'I, ah'm, maybe you heard – I still have to rest up a bit.'

He jumped to his feet. 'Yeh, sure, Sugar. Hey, listen. Against myself, against the firm. Quick double. Vincent O'Brien's two at the Curragh Saturday, right? You might trouser a few shekels. God, Joey must be gettin' soft in the head, tryin' to do the bookies outa money. Joey the Charity. OK, Sugar? Keep in by the wall, right?' And he walked away.

I made it to the lavatory off the utility room. I threw up more violently than I had done since St Heber's. This time it wasn't from thumbing my throat to cough up the Largactyl. It was Joey. And it was Ross. Ross's father.

The erotic books I read when a virgin said things about women knowing men. That once a woman made love to a man she knew him best – better than his own mother or sisters. I began to worry that the converse was true. Did men who had entered women understand them uniquely well? Joey might catch on to The Plan. I still think he did. Or thought vaguely that something about my return did not fit. But he allowed himself to be overwhelmed by his need for my approval. That is more accurate than saying he feared my disapproval.

Father came home early that evening. Agnes came to me.

'Your mother says will you go over for a drink. And are you to be eating with them? She hopes you are.'

They had been talking about me when I arrived. I know because they stopped.

'Is there any chance at all you'll break out offa the orange juice?' said my father. 'Boys-then, I need a bottle to myself this evening and favourites after winning all over the show. Everywhere. Redcar. Leopardstown. Wincanton. 'Tis on handouts we'll be next. And Goodwood next week, always favourites winning at Goodwood. We'll have to dip into Mammy's purse, won't we, Mammy?'

Kevin handed me a glass of orange juice. Mother's champagne had been opened. It stood beside her in a cooler. Father had his tumbler of whiskey and his glass of water on his marble side-table.

'Well, here's how, anyways,' he said, raising his glass. 'Good luck who stood.' Kevin withdrew.

Father looked to Mother who nodded.

'Girl,' he said to me awkwardly, 'that was a powerful day's work you done today. Sure he came back with tears in his eyes.'

I dropped my gaze.

'Joseph is more sensitive than he sometimes shows,' said Mother.

'Ah, Jesus, Jesus!' screamed my brain. My next thoughts were, 'Maybe they were right. Maybe I was insane.

253

Maybe I am insane. Is it insane to think that I am the one with the greater right to be sensitive here?'

Mother always had an air when she talked about Joey. In his company she became a little girlish. She giggled and fluttered. I found that disgusting. In his absence she was a touch proud. His name made her sit a little straighter. As she did now. And she touched her hair, tossed it a little on one side.

I have never mastered the art of invective. Not even inwardly. And I needed it at that moment. Instead, according to The Plan, I nodded. A difficult nod to judge. Not contrite, no longer too docile. The screaming in my brain made it more difficult.

'Ann,' said Mother, 'we are very, very appreciative.' She smiled her Joey smile.

'Chip offa the old block,' said my father. 'You have your Mammy's way with people.'

They both nodded. That was the beginning of the end of them.

I said tentatively, 'He has changed a lot. He really knows what he's doing, doesn't he? He'll make a great Minister. Or Parliamentary Secretary.'

'Ah, he told you,' said my father. 'That's better again.'

Mother cut in, 'It is a secret, Ann, dear.'

'A state secret, you might say,' laughed my father.

'We don't want to say anything. Because obviously, dear, nothing may come of it.' Mother's speech had grown so affected. It irritated me more and more.

'My God, they could do with him,' I said, just fervent enough.

'I'll tell him what you said,' chuckled my father.

'He has all the qualities needed,' said Mother. Her piety had begun to flow.

'Yes,' I said.

And yes, you said it, Mother – all the qualities needed. Arrogance. Brutality. Corruptness. Dishonour. Egotism. Foulness. Grease. Hollowness. Insincerity. Jocularity. Killer instinct. Lewdness. 'M' for money. 'N' for neck. 'O' for obtuseness. Powerful. Quixotic. Rapist. Swine. Thug. Untrustworthy. Venal. Mother's voice cut in with something even 'W' for worse.

'We think he needs a clean sheet. That's what we think.'

'W' for whitewash. 'X' for extraordinary, this devastating crassness. 'Y' spells 'why' – why I came back.

'Z' – to zero Joey. That is what will be left of him. Zero. 'He will be called,' said Richard, 'Joey Zero.'

'Yes, Mother,' I said, 'ye-es.' I pretended to return to them from far off. These little reveries came into my repertoire quite naturally the evening I first arrived. Over the months I used them repeatedly. This helped persuade Mother I was on a slow recovery.

'He'll be perfect,' I replied. 'Perfect.'

But now I took serious time off in my mind. To think. To regroup. They talked to each other all through dinner and my attention was free to escape.

Greengages line the walls outside Richard's 'pavilion' as he calls it. I have lain there in his arms so often, looking at the night sky. Richard had clear water every day. Where the stream goes underground, he laid stone flags. They made a kind of platform and gave him a little cascade. He carried the slabs one at a time down from the castle grounds. And he turned this arena – they call it locally 'the Sluice' – into a kind of water-garden.

We still tend it, this wide and clear pool. One side of it must be kept clear of all growth. Here Richard dipped his filling-mug. All around the other edges he cultivated pretty weeds. Things flick in and out of the mud, small fish and boatman insects.

One morning in the clear pool he found a dead badger. The creature must have been banishing some small animal. Or he fancied something that looked exotic to him. The badger stuck his head inside, under the flagstones where they form a square arch for the stream to go underground. He dislodged one of the large flagstones and it fell on his throat and cut it. A badger's most vulnerable spot, Richard says, is his jugular. The pool where Richard gets his water filled with blood. He told me he was afraid it meant he was going to die. At noon he walked to where the stream comes out. The blood had all gone.

One afternoon, after he made love to me in his pavilion, he started to weep. I asked him what the matter was and he said, 'Did you hear that noise?'

'What noise, Rich?'

He said, 'I heard something.' He was snuffling hard tears.

'What did you hear?' I cradled his head.

He withdrew a little and said, 'I guess it was only the clouds slipping across the sky.'

I said, 'Anything else?' trying to keep him close to me. 'Did you hear anything else, Rich?'

He said again, 'I heard the clouds slipping across the sky.' And he covered his head panickily with his hands as if he were being kicked. The insides of his dark fingers are pink.

I never saw him like that before and I burst into tears.

He lived for fifteen years there – 'the nigger in the fields'. The roof is aslant, with some galvanized iron he 'borrowed' from a farmer not far away. Some poles prop it up. The walls are also made of galvanized iron. In the lush seasons some branches act as doors and beds. He erected planks across barrels as tables and desks. The floor can be grassy green or earthen. He had carpets of newspapers when I went there first. They got deeper and more absorbent as the seasons rolled on. I bought him new lightweight blankets and a big sleeping bag.

In those early months back with Mother, Richard filled my mind. Night and day, every waking moment he was there. I am certain he was also in the dreams I did not remember. I thought of him all the time. He seemed to feel deeply for me too. But I did not ask. We just hugged forever when we met. So there seemed no need to ask if he loved me. To borrow a saying of Richard's, 'Never push the river, especially if it's flowing your way.'

'Ann, dear,' said Mother. I hauled myself back. 'Your father wants to know.'

My father grinned. 'I want to know if my little girl would give us the benefit of her education. Take a look at the books, like. Tell us how we're doing.'

I said to Richard, 'See, Rich. I never had to ask. They did it for me. That means The Plan is right.'

Richard smiled. He still disagrees with me on this issue.

37

Philip Graves is proving both a problem and a fascination; he was not what he seemed and the details of his life emerge as unedifying, but he fought like a hero before they killed him. Charles has emphasized again that he does not wish the story rushed, he wants all the facts only when I feel certain I have them truly. I return to the story piece by jigsawed piece and can report more than partial success; whether we ever run it in its fullest detail depends upon Charles's consideration for the Graveses.

So far I have discovered that Captain Philip Graham Graves did indeed pose as a mechanic called Tommy and pretended to work in Bessbrook. He neither knew nor accepted that the Provisional IRA blew that cover of his a day or so after he embarked upon it – and for several months they allowed him to operate in south Armagh in order to feed him misleading information. But what they did not know was that under another cover he had been a member of an elite hit-squad targeting Republican leaders in other parts of the province for the previous two years. Had they known that they would have given up any notion of 'turning' him – the main reason they allowed him to live so long.

I went back to Michael McConnell and found him tight-lipped.

'Listen, what are you going to do with the information? If I give it to you?'

I said, 'Either I'm going to print it, if it stands up, or I'm going to use it to lead me to more information, or both.'

'My son wasn't ever involved in it,' he said.

'I have not come across your son's name,' I told him.

'How big is your hurry?'

'Not big – provided at the end of it I have a full and accurate story.'

'He was a hard soldier,' he said and changed the subject. 'Did you come up here only on this?' – and when he heard I was also going to Belfast he asked me to meet him on my way south again.

I spent Sunday in Belfast, intending to write a piece on Lent among the Catholics of the city; some had talked of holding vigils for peace; some had talked of fasting; some had talked of civilian hunger strikes in sympathy with IRA prisoners, and one couple, with two sons serving life sentences in the Maze, said they would take liquids only for Lent. In their house I met student friends of their sons, who invited me to report on the rag-day procession, a kind of Lenten carnival parade with drums and mummers.

Yesterday at noon I stood at the corner of Ormeau Avenue and watched this large procession jolly towards me. Two harlequins led the way, one in red-white-and-blue diamonds, one in green-white-and-orange diamonds; they linked arms and capered, their white faces in permanent grimacing grins. Behind them pranced pixies and columbines and pierrots; a character in a gorilla suit lumbered along; girls played fiddles and young men played banjos; a pipe band skirled at the head, another behind.

The harlequin theme recurred throughout the procession; there must have been two dozen of them in red-white-and-blue diamonds and two dozen in green-white-and-orange diamonds. They all pulled the same stunt – they grabbed spectators and danced with them for ten, maybe twenty yards; they grabbed me – a girl, judging from the perfume (but who knows nowadays) – and I spun around in her dance, then fell in beside the long procession, as many did, to hear the rally in Donegall Square.

I was now halfway down the parade and I saw ahead of me two of the harlequins dance with a policeman and then with a policewoman. In the way that lightning strikes the earth I knew that something was wrong – and both officers died at the same time. As their harlequins swung them deep into the throng two other harlequins came by and shot them in the throat: the handguns had silencers. Their bodies were lain with speed and surprising gentleness on the roadway in the very middle of the procession. Floats, marchers and bands passed over them and only then did their deaths become evident. It was the perfect terrorist killing; what could the security forces do? Arrest the entire parade?

I have better faculties nowadays for dealing with shock; I know I am going to suffer from delayed shock and I know I am going to suffer grief at each and every death. In this case I saw the eyes of the young policewoman before she died – she had brown eyes, fair hair under her green cap, and she had a face that was both hard and open. Last night I shivered a little but, where in the old days I would have headed for the bar, I went to my car and left the city.

Michael McConnell asked me, 'Any news outa Belfast today?' and he knew – I know he knew. He made me

260

describe the incident in detail, and the impression came across that he was putting me to some sort of test. When I had finished he asked me whether I might do him a favour – deliver a coat to a friend of his in Dundalk.

Another borderland farmhouse, another barking dog: another hard man to greet me, the youngest so far. He strode across the uneven muddy ground.

'You can give it out to me through the window,' he said.

'You've been expecting me?' I said in a friendly way.

'Did he say anything?'

'Only that you were a friend of his.'

'So – what d'you want to know?'

Aha! This was the promised source. I handed him the jacket and decided to go for broke. 'What exactly happened to Graves? On the night?'

They have this look about them, these men that I have met, cool, direct and unresponsive; I am understating.

He answered. 'They're saying around here that he put up a hard fight. They're saying it took six of them and that he got one and hurt another.'

'Was he armed?'

'They're saying not, that he had a gun in the car and never got to it. They're saying that they got him in the car park.'

'Of the Four Horsemen?'

'They're saying that he went off with them in a van to the woods at Crow Rock. They're saying that there's marks on a little bridge there.'

'Was it because they knew he was a spy?' Sweat trickled down beneath my armpits. 'Look, can I get out of the car? I need to make some notes.'

'No. Stay where you are. You can remember it. They're saying that what happened is, two lots of fellows were coming for him, and they never knew about each other. The second lot was coming to lift him sure enough, but to "turn" him. The others got there first, and they were harder men.'

'The man he killed before he died – how was his death explained?'

'They're saying he died in a road accident. 'Twas reported that Friday in the *Courier*; 'tis easy to find, there wasn't that many twenty-five-year-old men killed by a hit-and-run juggernaut around here that night.'

'So what happened – on the spot – at the time?' His dog growled now and then, and I found that almost equally unnerving.

'They're saying there was a great scrap. They wanted to hang on to him for a while and ask him things, but he was that hard to hold down they had to do for him.'

'A considerable fighter, then?'

'They're saying around here that he was what they'd call a good soldier. All right, now?' He tapped the car in a valediction. 'Watch yourself turning, there's a sheugh full of water there, 'tis hard to see.'

'The grave?' I asked a little desperately. 'Can I find it? You know, for the family, take a photograph of where he's buried, that sort of thing?'

'Hold on a minute.'

He walked to the house, went inside and emerged a moment later carrying a shotgun. I thought of starting the engine but, somewhat paralysed, did nothing. He rested the shotgun on the open window-ledge of the car, pointing upwards, a foot from my head, and cocked both hammers.

'There's a slurry pit over there, my grandfather dug it, 'tis forty foot down, nobody'd ever find anything, 'twould take the car an' all. Don't get me wrong now.

'Twas never used as a grave. So far. So – don't go looking for that grave. At all.'

At no stage in our three minutes of conversation did he betray any emotion of any kind: he is, at most, twenty-six or twenty-seven years old. He removed the gun from the car and stood back. A year or two ago I would have cack-handedly reversed without fail into the water-filled drain he warned me about. Now I did a perfect three-point turn in his yard and drove out slowly, my left thigh and leg soaking in my own urine.

38

Joey began to call round more and more.

'We've all new staff now,' he told me a little furtively. He was so uneasy then in my company. 'I have this new secretary, she's a scream. She must be fifty, Sugar, if she's a day and she goes dancing every Sunday night. And the Isle of Man for her holidays. Grab hold of that, Sugar. The Isle of Man, right? Every buckin' year. Nothing in the Isle of Man bar two cliffs and an ice-cream stall, is there? But she says she has a great time, right?'

What was he saying? That Josephine Scannell was no longer on the scene? I could not bring myself to ask.

Two days later Agnes came up to me. I was cycling out on one of my 'mystery tours' as she called them. Mother had gone to Dublin. Those were my best days. Mother went away often. To shop, or to lunch. To avoid seeing me, her hangdog daughter. I had many times since searched the house in her absence. No trace of Ross did I ever find.

'I have something for you,' said Agnes, in a flap. She handed me a small brown paper parcel. 'Don't tell your mother, will you? I found them when we were clearing out some old suitcases.'

I opened the parcel. A pair of Ross's shoes. They were blue with little buckles. I bought them at Saxone in Grafton Street. Ross fed the ducks in St Stephen's Green that day. I never made it to Richard's that night. I was too unsafe, too unsteady. I was often unsteady when I met him, but he always calmed me, then tried to talk me out of The Plan by calm, reasoned summary.

I fought him. 'No, Rich, this is for Ross. And they banged me up in a nuthouse. I never got to mourn. I never got to the funeral. They took away my procreative source. I was going to be left there to rot. And they don't even acknowledge that their grandson ever lived.'

'But, Doll – forgiveness is part of life too.'

His accent thickened as he fired up. 'Look at me. Do you want me? I know you do. I know it from the way you handle me, I know it from the way you are inside of you. Then you must believe me. If you believe me when you're lying in my arms, you must believe that what I tell you is for life. Forgiveness is for your life, Doll. You're on this planet for a life sentence! We all are.'

It is probably how I will remember Richard – at his most powerful within himself. When I look at him now, the Richard I see is that pacing, uttering, air-stabbing Richard. He still has powerful views on everything.

I argued, 'Rich, I have to do it. It was what was done to me.'

The power with which I drove The Plan through forced from Richard one day the story that I always knew must be in there – it burst from him.

'Forgive, Doll, forgive! I've had to. You know I'm not religious. But I forgive. I forgave the gooks. Found my friend Andy Shankleman crucified. I was thirty-three. Andy was thirty-three. The Great Reconciler was thirty-three too, when they tacked Him up. And six feet tall. Anyway I'm more than six feet tall. I think about crucifixion every day. I think what it must feel like and I think about it because near the town of Pen Long, the administrative district for Da Lah, they used the bottoms of bean cans as giant washers for his hands. And never bothered with washers for Andy's feet. They even shoved a machete in his side.'

Richard's force is part of his being.

'I was the man found him – Lieutenant Huttle, second tour of duty. He was taken in Da Lah, inland, green and wet, big leaves and fatigued soldiers. Three days earlier, we took a village and wasted it. Had to, the gooks were dug in under us. Bad times. We knew the local commander around Da Lah spoke good English. We assumed Andy had been tortured, which is how they found out, presumably, about his devout faith.'

He lapsed into an official voice, a dull drone.

'Eleven hundred hours: with air cover advanced on local reference g 1412 r stroke l 13: all areas clear: entered evacuated compound: found Signalman Shankleman wounded, in vertical imprisonment E.N.E. of compound. "Vertical imprisonment"? Oh, Christ!' His voice reverted. 'How do you take a man down from a cross, Doll? How? How? I know how to do it. I got the guys to lift the cross up from the earth and lay it gently horizontal. I had the arms of the cross and the single timber plank to which his feet were nailed sawn off short so that we could at least put Andy in the helicopter with only small pieces of wood attached to him. We had to do this at top speed. The gooks were in the bamboo. He died shortly after the Chinook took off. That was Easter Sunday. Would you believe that for a sick joke, Doll?'

Richard, my passionate love, did a great imitation of Mr Ed, the talking horse. He could do Donna Reed and *I Love Lucy* and *Green Acres* and the sadder dialogue from *Peyton Place*. Now he screamed at me. 'First they drilled the hands and the timber behind it, then they shoved the bolts straight through. Andy had a week's beard. I bet they liked that, he looked the part. That's why I say – *forgive*.'

39

I know all my neighbours here, and I get on with them, and they show an interest in my work; I receive nothing but helpfulness from them, nor do I feel censored or censured by them in any way over my views on the Irish. I know they buy the paper and read my pieces, because the newsagent, Donegan, told me that my presence has been good for his sales!

'I hope you're going to stay,' he laughed.

Some of the people I meet are now beginning to discuss my reports with me, and ask interested questions, sometimes in wonderment at the horrors I describe, sometimes in genuine interest at an Englishman's view of the situation. At a party on Saturday, several said to me that the only question they want answered, is: 'What is the solution?'

I was about to say that I could never offer an answer, because I do not have one, but before I could open my mouth, they offered their solution and I think it will become a kind of notional, national solution south of the Border:

'Declare a day,' they said, 'call it twenty-five years from now, when the two parts of the island have to come together and work as a unit within Europe. Take the troops and the civil servants out and we'll all sort it out together.'

It is very difficult not to comment on this, especially late at night in someone's kitchen (do they ever go to bed around here?) and so far I have managed to sound non-committal – but it makes the most useful background against which to survey the Irish and judge them. The more I meet these people the more I realize how out of touch our politicians are with Ireland.

I am moved by their respect for me; since they discovered that I have given up drinking they have never forced a drink on me. I feel certain they wonder whether I have some 'story' of my own, whether I am a man with a past; what I cannot tell them is that I am convinced I am a man with a future. That I still think so persuades me (now that I have begun to think of such things) that faith is love, and vice versa.

Most of my neighbours have family names that have been in this area for more than a thousand years – but I have not yet found a local person who has been north of the Border, nor do they exhibit any wish to go there and they feel slightly abashed at this. They ask me questions about the new Peace Movement, about the folk singer Joan Baez with the Peace People on the bridge at Drogheda. It is said that a busload of women from a nearby town went to that rally, and certainly some of the wives here identify with the two women who founded it. Mainly, though, they keep it all at the distance of newspaper reading, and television news and current affairs which they devour.

Life here will be more placid for me: I can see peace in the distance; it is approaching in the way one can see weather coming across the plains beyond the woods. When the Graves story is complete I intend to move into less turbulent waters.

Charles has confirmed his agreement to this.

'All there for you, C. – politics, religion, history and imagination. You've had enough violence for a while.' And lest I thought he feared for my emotional health again, he told me that in his view I am now 'one hundred per cent all right'.

Paradoxically, now that I am in her territory, as it were, much of my time has been spent in an effort not to think about Ann; not, in any way, to 'cure' myself – but I feel that if I can learn to manage this obsession (and I am now calling it that openly to myself) I will be making a significant contribution to the good resolution of the matter. I have not mentioned her name to anyone and I have not, for example, steered the conversation round to bookmaking, or the village of Silverbridge or any such topics! However, I do admit to listening extra keenly when names are bandied about. What I must not do is fall into the trap of living in the future.

But mercifully my good instinct to buy this house and make it delightful has proven helpful. Essentially it has taught me that my life can now be divided neatly, for the first time, into the professional (still a large portion) and the personal. In the professional I finally met Naomi, Philip Graves's 'fiancée' (his mother's term, not Naomi's); that story is now almost ready. And in my personal life, it is time to mend my fences with my only close living kin, my parents – because there seems to me no point in getting a house ready for the woman I love if I have not, so to speak, put my own house in order.

Naomi Suter resembled nothing that I expected of Philip Graves's woman. I suppose I had half-anticipated a willowy rose, a Home Counties 'gel', who danced at the Sandhurst Ball; perhaps I based that on his mother's looks. When I eventually saw her (five requests turned down – then a curt acceptance based on getting rid of me) I found a small, overweight woman, of German origin, tough-minded, critical of her lover's media canonization and almost disrespectfully clear-eyed regarding her own grief.

Older than Graves by about eight years, with sheenless dyed hair and a hard-looking bosom, she asked me at the door, 'Are you phobic?' When I said 'no', she said, 'Pity. I am – and it would give us something to talk about.'

In the hallway, as we walked to the sitting-room at the back of the house, she said, 'I was not his fiancée. I won't have that. That's his mother's idea. It's because I have money, or at least my family has. She wanted him married to me and never hid the fact. Oh, by the way, he was always impotent when he came back from Ireland.'

We sat in a room that had one of the most exquisite pieces of furniture I have ever seen – a walnut Georgian tallboy. She saw me looking at it but did not comment. This is a woman with a noticeably odd characteristic; she never grooms herself. Most women I have observed touch their faces, finger their hair a great deal, they smooth their fingers and cheeks, they smooth their sleeves, they tug, caress, ease, stroke, fiddle, push, pull, correct, make little physical adjustments. Naomi Suter sits with her hands either folded in her lap or dealing with the cigarette she is smoking. Even then she makes little of the cigarette, moves it to her mouth in a minimalistic gesture, then rests her hand on a chair-arm so that the ash will always hang over the ashtray.

She speaks minimally too, but curiously so. Although she gives the impression, in tone and inflection, that she says little, it transpires after some time in her company that she is actually speaking all the time. Not insistently, not domineeringly; she has a personal style that enables

271

her to grasp a one-to-one social situation and keep command of it. I found this style of hers pleasant.

That meeting with her seems strange to me now and not a little devastating. I had prepared myself for any revelation, for declarations of love and I knew in advance (or so I thought) that it might all seem odd, perhaps perverse. Here she would find herself sitting before a stranger and declaring her passionate love for a dead man who might in other parts of his life have been less than perfect.

She is one of those people who – inexplicably – bring images to one's mind. She reminded me of an afternoon when I drove around a corner on a long Italian road and caught my first glimpse of the walls that guard Mantua; they sat above still water reddened by a setting sun. The evening ahead promised dinner with a woman with whom I thought I was about to fall headlong in love. She, though greedy in her wish to be entertained, talked throughout dinner of her love for the man who had just ditched her. Now, here was this image, this pattern again – even though I had no intention, and never would, towards Mrs (as it turned out) Suter.

She proved quite willing to talk about Graves.

'He was a man who changed,' she said. 'When I met him first, yes, I did think we might marry. That is where his mother got the idea. But he changed.'

'In what way?'

'I'm still not quite sure. He lost something.'

'Lost?'

She has a sarcastic streak. 'I don't mean his keys. Something went from him, from inside him.'

I waited.

'I don't want to use the word "innocence". But it is not unlike that. He acquired a . . . I don't know. A glitter, is how I think of it. Not in the show-biz sense.' The sarcasm

272

again. 'I don't want a headline – "Dead Hero's Show-biz Dreams".'

'When did he change?'

'Two, two and a half, three years ago. After his second tour of duty. I felt he was being made to do things he didn't want to do. Very male things. That he had always thought about. And then when he did them he was, I don't know, "upset" is too slender a word.'

Two, two and a half, three years ago – the period when he ran hit-squads in and near Londonderry; I could say not a word.

I spent an hour with her, but she gave nothing detailed; he had told her very little. She returned twice to the change in Graves as if talking to a stranger might help her to puzzle it out.

'No laughs,' she said. 'Not that he was ever a laugher. But the boyishness, I liked it in him, and then it dimmed.'

And: 'He said once that he thought it was the job of a hero to kill people, that he knew it when he was a boy. But the army changed all that.'

'Do you miss him?'

'Mr Hunter, I am not going to weep so that you get your human-interest story.' Her eyes flashed. 'And please do me the favour of not disclosing my address. I do not want these murdering bogmen shinning up to my balcony, if you don't mind.'

'Of course. Of course.'

'No "of course". You do not belong to a delicate profession. One of your colleagues described me as a swarthy blonde. Thank you for that, you lot.'

'Is there anything I can do for you, Mrs Suter?'

She started a little. 'No. No.' But in the hallway she said, 'If you do find, if you find – I mean, if there is a grave . . . I don't suppose there is one?'

Met my father at Heathrow and we flew to Shannon together this afternoon (hares sat on the runway as we touched down). This will be the first occasion in my adult life when my father will have spent time in what I can call my home; I am almost irrationally excited about it, even though I scarcely know what he is like adult to adult.

As if such leaps forward are not enough, I saw Ann today – and as I have never seen her before; I saw her in Main Street, Mooreville and she was dressed like an executive. At first I could not be sure, thought it a trick of the light, or an optical illusion. Then I turned the car at the next corner and drove back slowly; she stood in front of us, waiting to cross the street, and as I stopped my father indicated that she should cross; she smiled at us. I find tonight that I can remember every detail of what she wore: a red suit and red shoes: that bald description makes them sound cheap and unattractive, but this was expensive red; and an ivory blouse with quite large lapels. She carried a clutch briefcase and was emerging from the bank when I saw her; perhaps I should transfer my account to that bank; perhaps they have social gatherings for customers at which I could meet her.

How many versions of her have I now seen? I can scarcely put together the woman I saw today with the bedraggled, rather shattered woman I saw in that hotel on the arm of the man with the bandanna; with the woman I saw lying naked in the grass drinking from a bottle in a summer grove of greengages and hazel trees; with the young mother helping her little son to admire his new shoes; with the pregnant and yet *soignée* wife emerging from church on a Sunday morning in a country town; with the grave and distant bride I first saw five years ago in February '72.

Father has aged a good deal and I have the fervent hope that he will not die before – well, before my life becomes at last what I wish it to be. If I see more of him he will make me old-fashioned, which might do me good. He suspects that there is some secret in my life but he does not pry. Contrariwise, he himself has opened up in a way nobody would ever have thought possible.

40

Names are problems, aren't they? I never liked the name
'Ann Halpin'. It annoys me that I liked the name 'Ann
Martin'. A stronger name. It's what I still sign myself –
'Ann Martin'. But 'Ross' – oh! I was so proud at the
christening of 'Ross Martin'. Lovely, distinctive name
for a lovely distinctive little baby.

The Plan rolled on. I put Richard's reservations behind
me. I sort of postponed forgiveness, too busy looking for
the one final piece of the jigsaw, the killer punch. Then
– 'Opportunity follows Inspiration.' That is one of my
father's sayings.

'Take me dancing, Rich.'

He looked at me and laughed. 'No.'

'Please, Rich.'

'Dancing?'

'I don't know why.'

He smiled with his big, perfect teeth. 'I don't want to
dance, Doll.'

'But you move so beautifully.'

'No. Guys'll come and hit me.'

'Well, stand and watch.'

'OK.'

I never did it when younger. Others went to Dreamland
or the Sound of Music Ballroom, and in Galway we
often saw the crowds going to the Hangar in Salthill,

two or three thousand people. But I never went – too snobbish.

'Where will we go?'

'The Oyster, Rich.' We laughed.

'Ann, you're not thinking of going to the Oyster, are you?' said Agnes. She suspected things about me but she never said, would have been glad if I had an admirer. And she would never, not on pain of fire, have told Mother. 'God, Ann, last Sunday there was four and a half thousand people in the Oyster. You'll get crushed.'

Whence Richard procured the car I did not enquire. Safer not to. We had never been out together anywhere local and now I feared that I might meet one of the clerks from the Halpin's office. They were slowly getting to know me. Responding to my father's pressures I went into the office now and then, did the banking for them and things like that. I also knew that was where the action was. And the business was probably the best place to attack.

The extraordinary thing to me then was how they trusted me. (I know now they did it out of fear.) After all they had done to me they trusted me completely. Mother told me of profits and business plans. My father showed me balance sheets and asked me about the management of overnight cash. Joey did not participate in these exchanges but looked on approvingly.

The office girls were very friendly to me. I cultivated them, sources of information. But I knew they were inquisitive about me, wondered about my private life, and I very much did not want them to see me at a dance. So I did my hair differently and wore bright make-up and teetering heels. They would have to peer to recognize me. I would avoid the 'Ladies'.

Pat Fox & the All-Stars had hit the bandstand before

we got there. They were well down Memory Lane –
'Hands up here anyone who ever danced the Hucklebuck.'

A wild cheer arose and we danced it again. I could
see Richard on the balcony, smiling from beneath his
bandanna.

The smell of hair lacquer is recognizable universally.
And talc and perspiration and ropey aftershave. Everybody seemed to want to sweat at this dance hall. That
was the object of the exercise – to sweat.

The painted walls also had only one function – to
look wonderful on the night of a dance. At all other
times they must look as gaudy as cheap prayers. But
now the swivelling lights made them as thrilling as the
walls of a jewelled cave.

Whoever painted these interiors had gone geometri-
cally mad. Diamonds and circles and rhomboids and
chevrons slashed their way across to the balcony and up
to the ceiling. The bar was lined with green crêpe paper.
You needed a drink when you got there just to cure the
eyes, but the people were so pleasant and friendly it made
me want to cry. My Hucklebuck partner, a nice-looking
man in a check jacket, asked me if I'd like a drink and
I said no. He seemed disappointed.

I went back to the wall where the women gathered,
waiting for the next dance. Men went to the far wall
and laughed raucously and punched each other gently. People who had come as couples never left the
floor. They swayed a little and clung to each other defi-
antly or uncertainly, depending on their relative sophistication.

'Eurovision time!' blared Pat Fox amiably. 'Which
one of youse remembers Butch Moore and "Walking
the Streets in the Rain"?'

We all did and a slow waltz took place.

'You're not from around here?' asked my next partner. He had a check jacket too.

'No. Galway,' I said.

'Were you ever at the Galway races?'

'I go every year,' I lied.

'My uncle had a horse won the Galway Plate,' he said. 'You interested in horses?'

'Ah, yes.'

Then *Caramba!* as Richard would say. I saw Joey, standing in the doorway talking to some men. He was not looking towards me.

'Who's that man there?' I asked my partner.

'You'll be voting for him soon,' he replied.

A girl in a yellow dress bumped hard into us, hit my instep with her heel. I winced and it gave me the opportunity to stop and watch Joey.

I asked, 'Why? Is he a politician?'

'You should know him if you go racing,' said my partner. 'Big bookie. Joe Martin. His wife ran away and left him.'

I felt like collapsing. Instead, I asked the inspired question, 'Who are the fellows with him?'

My dancing partner laughed. 'Ah, sure he's a generous man.'

'Maybe he'd be good for a few bob, so?' I smelled it, I smelled that I was on a hot trail.

'Not unless you're a Provo,' laughed my dancer.

'Is that who . . . ?'

'Them boys are, ah, well, sure you know yourself . . .' My partner laughed again. He had good irony. 'The band should be playing "A Nation Once Again" – or "The Patriot Game". We should all be speaking Irish.'

'Jesus,' I said, holding the vernacular mood.

'Put up a request to the band,' said my partner. 'Ask

'em to play "The Broad Black Brimmer of the Brave IRA". Then you'll see the capers of them boys.'

I said, 'Jesus, I hope they're not going to bomb the place.' That ended the exchange.

Everything began to fit. One day, while preparing the banking, I took a small sack from the safe. One of the girls stopped me.

'That don't go,' she said.

'Oh?'

'Mr Martin handles all them himself.'

'Are they ledgered?'

'No.' She hesitated. 'They're the laughing bags.'

'Laughing bags?'

'Because as long as the tax fellas don't find out, we're laughing.'

Then she thought she shouldn't have said it.

I reassured her. 'I wanted to be certain I was banking everything.'

'That's not what they're actually used for,' she said in the glow of my reassurance. 'But nobody's supposed to know.'

Before Joey could see me I left the dance floor, and with Richard after me almost ran to the car. Incoming dancers got the wrong impression.

'How's she cuttin'?' called one man.

'Make sure you get it back!' yelled another.

In the car I exulted. The Plan was to bring Joey into a disrepute that would make the entire company suffer. I had not expected that Joey would hand my revenge to me on a plate.

Part Three

41

Silence pours from the newsdesk – how welcome. Father has a more pleasant, less anxious presence than I recall from my childhood, and he is unusually domesticated; it is almost like having a wife about the place – in the old-fashioned sense of being cooked for, and of living within an aura of general care (something neither Father nor I know much of from our family history!).

He has also begun to divulge himself; an occasional remark of mine may prise open a rounded aspect of his existence. I commented two mornings ago on his neatness of dress: always 'collared and tied' (as he calls it) even when wandering into the garden.

I said, 'You put me to shame. I ought to dress more thoughtfully.'

'Learned it in the army,' he said, 'and never lost it.'

Thereupon he unveiled a chapter of his military history; he spent most of his life as a surgeon in Bristol Royal Infirmary; before that he fought in World War Two, but has never spoken about it. To my astonishment he said that my reporting of atrocities from Ireland has slowly caused him an unloading of his experiences, as if (although I failed to ask him the question) the link between us gives him a kind of vicarious catharsis. I discovered that he parachuted into Arnhem as a doctor.

'What one never reads about', he said, 'is the number

of men who died merely in the parachute drop itself. I cut bodies down out of trees. Parachutes don't always open. They certainly didn't in those days. Lesson for life, I suppose,' he mused.

Then he became an observer and a medical officer in Berlin with, he said, a visit to Dachau in late 1945; he says he finds it difficult to discuss what he has seen and has never told my mother anything of his experiences. I expect he used the passing of time as a cloak, like so many of his generation, yet this week he has been reminiscing like a man drinking quickly.

As I listen to him, I consider the dignity of my father's behaviour. For years he knew that my mother was having an affair with his friend from school and university, another doctor. That affair began in my early childhood and was pursued all through my teenage years. It drew me in too, not just in the tension I now realize it caused in the home, but in two sightings of them which have long troubled me.

One took place during an afternoon when I came home unexpectedly from a visit I had been making to a school chum and from which I was not due to return until much later. Afterwards I waited for days to see whether she would raise the subject with me, but she never did. Some time later we had a blazing row, Mother and I, about something trivial; now I realize that the quarrel – in which I bitterly accused her of never looking after me as well as the mothers of other boys did – had to do with the things I was unable to say about finding her naked in bed with her naked lover.

The second time I saw them together she was wearing the dress I knew my father most liked on her – a blue and ivory dress that buttoned down the front and seemed to have an underdress of flowing muslin. To this day her wearing that with her lover seems almost like a worse betrayal.

I never peached on her, and she must have known I would not. Instead I tried to draw closer and closer to my father – it has just occurred to me that my feeling for him must have inculcated in me the idea of how wrong it is to entice a woman away from her lawful wedded husband. Even though adultery goes on in my world all the time and all around me, I want no part of it. Not even in my worst days did I ever have a relationship or go to bed with a married woman.

As for Father, although he knew my mother had been having a long-standing affair, I believe he took the view that he had given his word; she was his wife and he would keep his word, no matter what. To do otherwise would have exposed her to allegations of sleazy behaviour, something he would not have countenanced: it was all straight and old-fashioned. But he withdrew to quite a far distance – from me as well as from her. My mother terminated her liaison not many years ago, and I think – and I hope – that the relief has begun to show in their improved attitudes to each other.

Thinking about all this, I had a jealousy attack this morning, probably as a result of seeing Ann so desirable once again, and probably because I asked myself whether history, so to speak, has repeated itself. When I saw her, almost unclothed, in the woods it was like being back in my parents' bedroom on that afternoon I found Mother; I had once again innocently stumbled across another woman who was part of my emotional life, part of my inner security, and I had found her doing something hostile to my sense of intimacy with her.

Undoubtedly in the case of Ann and the man she was with (I cannot think of him as 'lover') I have abrogated to myself rights I do not have in this matter. Yes, it is a high-handed position to take – this complete possessiveness of a woman I have seen no more than a dozen times, never spoken to, have observed at times rather creepily. Thus I place myself in the curious stance of expressing a morality to which I have no right of any kind.

These times pass by in a kind of anticipatory haze – waiting for something to happen. A novelist speaking on the radio last week mused on Samuel Beckett's source for the much-discussed and mysterious title, *Waiting for Godot*; Beckett, this woman said, will have heard the Irish term, *Go Deo*, meaning strictly 'Unto God', meaning colloquially, 'Forever'. Is that me? Waiting forever?

As for reporting news, the words of the politicians, 'acceptable level of violence', had a haunting ring when first we heard them; now they prove true day by day. Last year's figures have just been released, probably the lowest since 1971; we have become so inured that we forget the meaning of each bomb, each bullet, we forget the torn flesh, the families destroyed by grief.

Down in the undergrowth beneath the statistics, surreal impressions arise. I have been telling Father about my interviews with victims of 'punishments', teenage boys in Belfast hospitals who may never walk normally again. For a myriad misdemeanours, such as stealing cars, petty theft or street-corner drug dealing, youngsters are 'lifted' by the paramilitaries, taken to some deserted or commandeered house and tied to a chair. Once they have been made to 'confess', they have holes drilled in their kneecaps by their captors – who use power-drills; for speed they use handguns with silencers.

One boy, Pius McKeown, did not know why he had been kneecapped; his speech had the vividness I have come to expect.

'I was standin' mindin' me own business, not lookin' anywhere, and this wee man gets up at me and says to me, "You're for the bit," meaning the masonry bit, like.'

I needed a translation – and the surgeon showed me the X-ray plates; difficult to imagine that a group of bones could be so fragmented; the masonry bit hit the boy's patella twenty times.

'The only good thing about it,' said the surgeon, 'the pain is so excruciating the victim passes out. But if this happened to anyone much over forty, I would not be surprised if they took a heart attack and died outright.'

I am now able, more or less, to distinguish between Protestant and Catholic accents; the surgeon was a Protestant; his patient a Catholic. I asked the dreaded question, expecting a withering reply.

'Oh, I'm often asked that. I don't ever know whether they're Catholics or Protestants. And to tell you the truth, I think they often don't either.'

The victims gave me their X-rays, hoping that I could publish them as if they were photographs. Father devoured them, and made a good point: this kind of injury has never happened recurrently during what he called 'a real war'. In deference, acknowledgement and, I think, affection for Father, I called my piece, 'Incidents Not from a Real War'.

Father and I have been able to spend a great deal of time walking in the woods; when we come home my fire burns brightly; the local logs make high, colourful flames and fill the house with a woody smell that lingers. My books have finally settled on the shelves, collated from childhood and from storage and from Dublin; I have sold the flat in London to its tenants, which means, I suppose, I have made the statement of where I wish to be.

42

I wear very little make-up now. And wear it very rarely. Last night, taking it off, I had an odd feeling at the mirror. 'No longer lonely.' That was the thought. 'No longer lonely.' And then the odder thought. 'I almost miss loneliness.' It was always the worst thing. Growing up in that house when Mother turned against me was an experience of crippling loneliness. She had been so nice to me – then, nothing.

I have such sympathy for anyone who feels lonely. Should I have said it to her? Should I have said, 'Mother, are you jealous of me?' I'd say it now. If I had the chance.

The Plan. If you lift people up before you drop them, they feel the fall harder. As I did from Mother. That's how I knew, and that was my thinking. Take Joey up to a great height and then push him. By stating political ambitions he was nearly as high as I wanted. I wanted Mother up there too. I had a vague idea of planting guns on Joey, but that raised problems. But if I could link him to the IRA ... That's why our dancing trip thrilled me so much. I didn't need to invent anything. Or do anything illegal.

As for the heights, I found the Mountgoldens. Not face to face. Not in some pub. In the newspapers. They were all over the business pages and often in the gossip columns. They were looking for acquisitions. And it was I who recognized their potential appeal. If I could get them to make an offer for Halpin's I could then shanghai it devastatingly.

The Mountgoldens had casinos and hotels and helicopters and yachts. That was Joey fixed – Joey, who would only go for a big name and flash. They owned racehorses. Like most bookmakers my father's real passion was for horses. Finally they were Anglo-Irish with a castle – but Catholics. Irresistible to Mother. To take her hostage utterly they had property in France and a brother a bishop in California. The idea locked itself shut.

I decided how I would plant the thought. Why not sell them Halpin's and all its shops and licences for shares. Get Joey and my father seats on the big, bold Mountgolden board. Accept a tied deal, no independent trading for anyone on the Halpin's side within, say, three years. And then my father and Joey could start all over again. Brilliant! I'm still proud of it – clinically speaking. The shame – that's a different matter.

I started with Mother and planted the idea – shouldn't Joey maybe get in touch with them.

'Everybody's doing this kind of thing,' I said. 'Making their fortunes twice over. We did studies on it in college.' That pleased her – 'That they should all profit from my education,' I thought savagely. 'This would make him a Cabinet Minister the moment he gets elected,' I said.

She flashed at me like a lighthouse. And must have told Joey that night.

Joey asked me next day what I meant. 'I mean, buck me, Sugar, they're like the Royal Family, right?'

'Look at what they've been buying,' I said. 'And they're Irish.'

My father and Joey together, guided by soft suggestions from me, opened an approach through our Dublin lawyers. Joey came by to tell me. Agnes let him in and he stood in the hall.

I said, 'Good,' in a way I knew he would like.

Methodically I advanced – like a small army filled with rage and hate. I got Emer, the lanky, talkative clerk, to show me the laughing bags one Saturday morning. My father and Joey had gone to Mallow Races.

'Do we have, Emer, you know – any record of who gets money out of these?'

A pushover. 'Only Mr Martin has any record. We just give it out when we're told to. But he mostly takes it himself.'

People should not lock things in safes. A safe is not safe. Joey is a clever man. He was too clever to leave names, but so controlling he kept dates. No matter what name he gave to his 'donations' he was caught. Traceably caught.

In an inspired moment I said to Emer, 'Does he, Mr Martin, does he ever actually, do they ever actually meet here in the office, you know, our friend . . . ?' I smiled and indicated the laughing bags.

Wild grimness had taken me over. It was helped by my physiology. Every time I saw or met Joey, my body where my womb had been stabbed me like a knife. Emer is one of those girls who must talk. One sentence can never be enough. She talked on and on. How some of the money was taken to racecourses. That was mostly how he did it.

'That's where they meets him. They pretends to win bets. But that's getting risky 'cause people are getting to know who they are. Sometimes she, Mrs Parker, comes in, you know, if her husband's off somewhere. Nobody

290

ever asks where he is, like, and 'tis all right to give it to her.' She giggled.

'Is this for some kind of protection,' I asked.

'Ah, no. I mean they're great friends, them and Mr Martin. And Mr Martin's wife.'

I'm a gambler's daughter. I was on a winning streak.

'You mean Jo?' I gambled.

'Yeh. Although she hasn't been here for a while now.'

Not since I came on the scene. Is that why Joey was so furtive? He had married her. He had married Josephine Scannell! The bastard! That was why he wanted the annulment. The grimness inside me kept me even, kept me level.

Emer said, 'I s'pose, well, you know, with the kid and that. She don't have the time.'

Christ! Joey and Josephine Scannell had a child. I went cold instead of hot. Is that a measure of how I had grown?

Emer rambled on. 'But Mr Martin and him, you know, Mr Parker, they often meets for a chat.'

I went home with a headache. And, despite my best intentions, a heartache. The old jealousies had never died. I felt defeated.

Until the name made Richard jump.

'Big buck, Parker,' he said. 'Been done twice for membership. Never pinned anything violent on him. A big, big guy. Son of an Englishman. Like so many of them. Weird.'

So – I did not need to lie after all. I was prepared to. I was prepared to swear it blind, but not in court. I would never have to go to court. A police superintendent's oath was all it needed. I knew that. Richard confirmed it for me.

'If a superintendent swears that he believes a man

291

is a member of the Provisional IRA – twelve months minimum, Doll.'

There were such cases in the newspapers every day – an automatic prison sentence. And if you're setting yourself up as a pillar of the community – a ruined life. Joey's friendship with Redmond Parker gave us our break. Otherwise he could have claimed it was protection money. That he was being coerced.

I did my work behind the scenes. I watched the laughing bags. I found paid cheques endorsed by Redmond Parker. Careless Joey. And I encouraged the Mountgolden deal.

With a glitter Mother watched the merger from the sidelines. She had the controlled excitement of a football coach. I fed her the quoted Mountgolden figures. And for my father I informally valued Halpin's. The asset base included the freeholds of all our premises. My father had always insisted that we own everything. I calculated the cash flow from all shops and racecourses. Our income stunned me daily.

I figured how much the merger would bring each of the three of them. The Mountgolden shares had stayed on a plateau of just under seven pounds. New results were expected to lift that. A business profile hailed the brothers as stars. Their politics were described as arch-conservative, even Anglophile. Perfect.

Joey stood to pocket around seven million and he would still have shares. Plus a Mountgolden main board seat. The Mountgoldens were as respectable as God and as safe as Fort Knox. The deal would catapult Joey to the top of the business community. Joey who blew his nose into linen hotel napkins when he went out to dinner.

My parents would share massive money. Mother automatically inherited my father's. And vice versa.

A galling point jabbed me. My marriage arrangement had meant the company shareholding was divided into twenty-five per cent each for all four, Mother, Father, Joey and me. As Mother's share was my father's, mine was Joey's. Wives were chattels.

Where now was my quarter? I never asked. I knew, and in the office one night alone I confirmed from the old documents and certificates that Joey got my shares when he sanctioned my hysterectomy. I wanted, I longed, I was desperate to hear the trap snap shut. It was closing. Soon, I heard the overture begin to play.

It made a big brassy clang when several weeks on, Mother said, 'We have some very interesting people coming to dinner tonight.' Then she whispered, 'The merger.'

She told me all about their personal lives. And she took credit for the whole idea. Barefacedly she told me she had thought it was time to climb on to a new plateau. And that my father 'and Joseph' (still the reverence in her voice) had agreed.

That afternoon at four o'clock, a quiet time in the town, I went and spoke to Superintendent Hinds. New to the area, untouched by human hand, that is to say not bought off by Joey or my father. He read carefully the pieces of paper I gave him. His behaviour was correctness itself. I asked that my name be kept out of it. He said there was no need to mention anyone. I told him Joey was going abroad tomorrow for some time. A lie.

At half-past seven one, two, three Mercedes came in convoy up the drive. Joey's was the first.

'Boys-what,' said my father, 'isn't it like the Government was arriving to meet us?'

Alastair Mountgolden remains in my mind. He was the smoothest dealer I ever saw. Red wavy hair, pinstripe suit, silver rings. He walked on the balls of his feet like a little dancer, short and powerful. He smiled all the time and the smiles had nothing behind them but his teeth.

His brother, Barry, slightly taller, much heavier, played the straight man. He too watched everything. I could see why they were taken so seriously. They had natural power. But both had small eyes. I hate small eyes. Joey has small eyes.

Such a double act. Tonight! For one night only! The Mountgolden brothers! See them catch each other in mid-air! Alastair homed in on Mother and Joey. Barry took my father. They had evidently strategized – but did not know what to make of me. Good.

'Ann's part of the financial control,' said Mother. 'We're a family firm, too.'

I was the daughter. I was a cipher. That's how they must have played it.

They had all had several meetings. Nobody told me, but I knew. Mother was away for days at a time. Excitement had hit them like a prairie fire, as Richard would say.

Share prices. Share options. Share performance. That was their new talk. Joey placed an order at Donegan's for the *Financial Times*. When he swaggered into Kiely's for his lunch-time pint the pink paper jutted under his arm.

Now at dinner their slavering eagerness turned my stomach. Anger roasted my insides. Did these people – my family! – have no sophistication of any kind? Anywhere within them? At any level, no matter how meagre? My rage was not fanned by guilt. I never felt any guilt then. They led themselves like lambs to my knife.

I watched the Mountgoldens. Wealthy, powerful and sleek. Each played to the other perfectly. They described their properties. Hotels in France. Casinos in Britain. Assets disposed of in Italy – 'Too many problems, a problem for every Italian,' said Alastair. 'They're a bit too Don Corleone for us.' They smiled broadly.

Joey loved it. Joey has seen *The Godfather* five times.

The business talk became fluent. Such dazzle. They dropped names the way Marco Polo dropped gems. Never overtly, much more cleverly. To Mother, for instance, 'You probably know . . .' and they would name some luminary from the gossip columns. Taking the smooth with the smooth.

Mother rose to it.

'Of course,' she replied. I could see her thinking about her social future. World domination was on its way. Lucy O'Connor would be reduced to what Richard called 'zilch'.

The Mountgoldens had brilliant technique. Alastair asked Mother a question. It assumed she lived at the highest levels of society and accomplishment. Then he did not wait for an answer. This technique both complimented her and spared her the embarrassment of getting it wrong.

They missed out on me. I had been branded. 'A story there somewhere,' someone will have told them; 'that closet has its own little skeleton.' Literally, I thought, literally. I was the daughter for whom something in the company had been found. They were told that I worked quietly – not importantly upfront.

Over coffee and brandy Alastair turned to my father. His little barrel frame blocked my view.

'Mr Halpin – '

'Ah, call me Joss, for God's sake. The dogs of the road call me Joss.'

The brothers laughed.

295

'Joss. This', he pronounced 'is good business. I have rarely met such civilized and hospitable people. Or such a well-run company.'

'I'd like to get alongside those sentiments,' said the more awful Barry.

'Private jet,' gleamed Joey to me when we met in the hall on his way back from the lavatory. 'Grand job, Sugar, grand job. We have the use of it. In the deal, right? Hey,' he whispered, 'Barry was the man who persuaded the film guys to give James Bond an Aston Martin.'

'*Molto schiffoso*,' I said, the only piece of Italian I knew. I think it means, 'Much shit.'

But I felt the uterine knife again.

In all this time I had paced my own behaviour. By no means had I ever come back to my family fully. No trace of the feisty and opinionated self who first married Joey. The word 'docile' continued to fit me. I did not push myself forward in any situation. 'Defer' remained my most active verb.

When faced with meekness people mostly behave as they really are. They do not have to answer to you. Or so they think. This is perfect – if study of them has become your motivation. I had continued to play the brown mouse to perfection. And would until the day came. The day had come. Tonight.

Nicola, Barry's wife, seemed extraordinarily bored.

'How well do you know Italy?' she turned and asked me suddenly.

'Not at all,' I said.

'You're the Financial Controller?'

I said nothing. I wanted to say, 'Not a lot of finance and very little control.'

That was Nicola's last effort at conversation.

I tried. 'Where did you go to school?' I asked her.

She didn't answer.

I knew from the society columns and the profiles. Her father had a small stationery wholesaling firm on the Long Mile Road in Dublin. When she landed Barry Mountgolden her mother thought they had spawned a natural princess.

She wore a slight touch of red eyeshadow. I have never liked that in another woman. Her sister-in-law, Alastair's wife, Dinah, who used to spin the wheel in a television quiz, had a diamond brooch I would have killed for.

We were having a glowing evening. The wives when they arrived had ooh-ed and aah-ed over Mother's taste. But I saw their glances.

Just once Barry zeroed in on me (I have begun to think like Richard, I use all his words).

'Tonight's the night we sign it, tomorrow's the day we announce it,' he said. 'I suppose you've already checked the horoscopes.'

Mother had enough knowledge of me to interrupt. 'Did anyone take notice of the date? I'm superstitious about dates?'

Barry played an ace. 'Did you read your FT this morning?'

Tycoon Joey had not understood the shorthand for *Financial Times*. I saved him.

'The newspapers never arrived. It was that kind of a day,' I apologized.

'A lift in the share price yesterday – and again today,' said Barry Mountgolden. 'Eight pence up yesterday, eleven pence today.'

I realized the Mountgoldens were as anxious that we might not sign as my family were that they might not.

Mother and Joey looked at each other. Each calculated how much this increased their wealth.

More toasts, then the inevitable solemn moment. Alastair clinked his ring on his glass.

'I just want to say something, if I may, Moya. And it's this. And I know I speak for Barry too. And for Dinah and for Nicola.' All nodded. 'We do a lot of business. Obviously you know that, I mean, that's why we're all here. Don't get me wrong, I mean, we like you and all that.'

Laughs all round, my father booming.

'But there's something different about this deal, there always was. For the first time we're getting into business with people whose values seem to fit so exactly with ours. It's uncanny. I mean, uncanny.'

How right you are, I thought. How right you are. Interesting to see a man tell the truth even though he's lying.

'I mean, we try to be, well, we try to have good standards as well as doing good business.'

I have long noticed something about people who really do have good standards. They never feel the need to say they have them.

'But until now we have never found people who both think and feel – and that's the important part – *feel* the way we do. So I believe in my heart, that, well, this is going to be our most successful venture yet. And yours, I hope. I feel that in my heart.'

Joey's face had begun to shine. It does when he's drunk. Mother reigned as she never had done before. My father had tears in his eyes.

I knew the Mountgolden deal embraced everything. Halpin's would become a subsidiary of this giant, smooth public machine. My father and Joey would ascend to the main board. I was, and would remain, nothing.

But – I had taken out the deeds of The Enclosure. The property I lived in was free of all company encumbrance. I had made over the house to myself under my father's signature – and hidden the deeds. When the company was being restructured it would simply not arise. 'Perhaps because I had no shareholding' – that's what I would have told the due diligence people when they arrived.

Tonight the forward papers were being signed, the intent. The signing gave the Mountgoldens all the power they wanted. It enabled them, a public company, to make an announcement. Signing of the final contract was a formality. Both sides accepted that. That is what greed does. We were perfect for them too. They liked cash-flow.

No doubt assailed me. I never thought beyond the moment of triumph.

Alastair Mountgolden finished his speech, wiped his mouth a last time. He wiped it a lot, as do all men who slaver. Joey wipes his mouth a lot. Then Alastair reached down for his briefcase.

'This is the moment the lawyers earn their money.'

He handed the papers to my father. And a pen. We all sat back in silence. I could hear Mother breathing.

My father signed. Joey signed. Mother signed. In that order. Everybody around that table knew I would not be signing.

'Congratulations,' murmured Barry. I did not know whom he was congratulating. Himself, perhaps, for getting the grabs on so much cash.

I looked at the three faces. My father had reached a pinnacle he never knew existed. Mother believed she had become a Cunard liner. Joey had gone into the stratosphere he read about in *Business & Finance*, or *Fortune*. Joey smiled at me. He smiled. I remember not caring what the smile meant.

The blow fell. It fell from the skies like a black jagged bolt. It did not hurtle through the roof. It came in at the door.

Agnes, discreet even when dismayed, slipped into the dining-room. I had heard the cars outside.

It was simple. It was banal. In they came. Like a play. Like a film. Like a story. Two policemen and a man. Like in the old song. My father's line again, 'With the help of God and two policemen.'

I heard every word that was said to Joey. He was seated between the Mountgolden wives. The plainclothes man did the talking. Arresting you on suspicion of being a member of an illegal organization. You do not have to say anything. But if you do. It may be taken down and used in evidence against you.

I also heard my own words.

'On your back, Joey,' I murmured to him. 'For Ireland and St Patrick.'

I watched the Mountgoldens next. The wives didn't know what was happening. Rage followed fury. 'What kind of people are you?' Barry, first, then Alastair. 'Christ!' Fury followed rage.

Then I knew what I had been trying to put in place all evening. They were twins. You get one, you get both.

Perfect.

Two uniforms escorted Joey through the door. Two policemen had come running when I screamed by the slurry pit. The Mountgoldens rose in rage and embarrassment. But they took the contracts with them. The signed papers.

My father sat stunned. I looked at Mother. She knew – I think – the whole truth at that moment.

And I said to her softly, 'In loving memory.'

43

This is a confusing time for me, and I have to resort to my journal to see whether I can tease out the sense of it all. I seem to be involved in events and investigations that take me further and further from my goal (my goal being Ann) and yet I have a sense, almost of foreboding (can foreboding be promising, as distinct from threatening?), that the very events I investigate are drawing me closer and closer to her; it is all very bizarre.

Not that life does not go on as usual: it does; for example, I spent this past week in Northern Ireland, including a day in Armagh interviewing the Cardinal who has called for a British withdrawal.

I have also been reading the histories and the mythologies and am struck by how much the ancient informs the new. I tasked myself with not reading newspapers, not hearing news bulletins to see whether by digesting the mythologies I could objectify the situation in general and, thereby, the Philip Graves story in particular.

This man, this prelate, in whose leather-chaired study I sat, might have been a druid. He laughed when I said that but his sense of history dominated our conversation and if once or twice he came right up to date by discussing the events of the last few years, it simply heightened the impression that in this country the line of descent from the ancient past is only a footstep backwards.

The Cardinal spoke of events that took place from the seventh century onwards; he lamented the forced extinction – 'by the neighbouring island' – of the golden monastic age, and described the Elizabethan plantations as 'attempted genocide'. He might have been talking about something as recent as the Holocaust instead of the span from Henry Fitzempress to Oliver Cromwell, in other words from 1169 to the 1650s!

I find it so difficult to steer a firm editorial course through this time-warp and I took the sensible decision of saying so to Charles. He cheered me greatly with a cold flash of objectivity.

'The balance', he said, 'is in the old saying; "What's politic in England is passion in Ireland." Stick to that, old man.'

Again (and I found this cheering) Ann's face came to me as I lunched with the Cardinal, and it came to me as the face of a wife must come to a husband – in simple comfort and reassurance. I do not panic about her now; the conviction that she will be mine entered my soul a long time ago and it resides there unimpatiently.

Yet again, I am pleased to have such a private set of thoughts; I find them and the very fact of them sustaining and nourishing. Also, I need firm privacy because it is difficult not to get the impression that everyone here knows everything about one. Early in our conversation the Cardinal said to me, 'You weren't well for a while back there. Are you all right now?'

How do they know these things? How do they know?! But his concern enabled me to relax and we had a long and pleasant conversation about life as a churchman.

Then he said, 'I have a brother a doctor, he practises in a village not far from here and I'm often struck by the similarity between our trades. Of course in the old days the priest also cured the people. The druids, if you like,' and he laughed; he laughs a lot.

I told him my father had been in medicine (I felt a slight malicious pleasure at telling him something about myself he didn't know), and he said, 'I bet he has never had to see the injuries and wounds my brother has to see – especially if the SAS have been in south Armagh.'

I did not let him get away with it. 'What exactly happened to Captain Graves?' I asked. He took the point and for the moment made no more statements of Republican propaganda.

Yet he almost had me baring my soul to him; I think these men take their confessional skills out into the world with them. Now there's an idea: a senior churchman handling his media interviews by using sacred expertise! He was so adroit that I almost found myself ready to talk about Ann when he said to me, 'What is your life like now? You're not married, I believe?' Was this an enquiry as to whether I had homosexual tendencies? No: he understood people, and therefore power, better than almost any politician I had met; so I mumbled something about being wedded to the job and fought back by getting him on to a terrain across which I knew he would feel uncomfortable.

I said, 'Is it true that the Provisional IRA have killed a number of people, informers and the like, and never returned their bodies to the families? Have just buried them in unmarked, secret graves?'

I know that I still smart at not having cracked that story and at first I felt awkward and selfish asking him, but the Cardinal's uncharacteristic discomfort suggested to me that the story, even if I never cracked it, had some merit.

The reason I suggested this interview in the first

303

place had to do with his known Republican sympathies. From his stated views most commentators had generally deduced a closeness, if not to the actual men of violence, to their mentors. Meeting him, I discounted the wilder stories, that the IRA Army Council had met in his house; that he had hidden men on the run; that he knew where caches of arms lay; that he used his contacts in the American church to raise Republican funds. No, he was evidently not such a fool – but my question made him nervous, so I pursued him.

'I've been told they may have buried as many as three men secretly. And – if they've done that, if they have buried people and never given the families a chance to mourn, doesn't such activity run counter to their stated ethic – of coming from the people? Of the people, for the people?'

He said, 'This is a very difficult country to understand. If that has happened – and I'm not saying it has – then it would be very difficult to prove. Or investigate. Even, I'd say, well, awkward to investigate.'

'You mean dangerous?' I asked.

He said, 'Well, it didn't work out for you, did it?'

He had slipped my grasp again.

'Let me go off the record,' he said, which gave me no choice; he has two forces of authority – his own natural force and the power of the Church; together they make him very formidable. He twitched; I thought I had him; then he said, 'I think you should leave that alone, those alleged burials. But you might appreciate some help with Captain Graves.' In essence he offered me a deal – and thus I was introduced to the anonymous but less hostile men who completed the Graves jigsaw for me.

To save face and to give thanks I have written a piece about the Cardinal's background as a Church historian and mediaevalist, and how it informs his pronouncements, such as the one that caused all the rumpus, in which he said, 'We should all pray that England must one day leave Ireland.'

This evening when I came 'home' as I am now pleased – no, delighted – to call it, I heard the sensational news from my neighbours that the Halpin firm is under investigation for giving money to the IRA. I presume, I hope, Ann is not involved. If she is, this news will disturb me more than I want to think about. Father has gone to bed. I can hear a fox barking up in the woods.

44

To be liked. By anyone. That was my goal for so long.
Now that I no longer need it – I feel much liked. And
much loved. Oh, the mistakes I have made. I blush when
I think of them. I go deep red with embarrassment. As
for The Plan! Embarrassment would have been welcome
– to soothe the desperation of remorse.

'Leading Businessman Arrested on IRA Suspicion.'

The newspapers slammed it on to every front page. It
was on the radio and television news.

Bye-bye, Joey.

After he left with the police the Mountgoldens sat
stunned. I heard Barry say savagely, 'Well, we have
interesting times ahead,' and Alastair said, 'Thank you
for your business.'

He knew their entitlements. They had their hands on
as much as they wanted. The contracts had been drawn
up by their lawyers. No room was ever as chilled and
silent as that dining-room at that moment.

Next morning nothing happened at home. Absolutely
nothing. My father disappeared early. I don't think he
had been to bed. Mother went with him. To see lawyers, I
figured. I reasoned that the Mountgoldens would tighten
their grip. They would see themselves as public-spirited
and rescuers of this company that had gone wrong.

Agnes looked both ashen and pleased.

With freedom to escape I went out to see Richard. I drove to meet him. First time he had seen me in a car. I had been taking driving lessons at my father's insistence. It was Mother's car. She rarely used it, but Agnes did. I was afraid someone might recognize it, so we hid it off the road, under trees.

Richard did not ask about the event. I said, 'Did you hear it? Did you hear the great news?'

He stopped me completely, he was in a state. 'Listen, Doll.'

'Richard, you listen! They arrested Joey. It worked. My plan worked. They got him. He's in jail!'

'I have to talk to you.'

'Rich – let me tell you about Joey. Please! The police came. Just after the signing of the contract.'

Richard ignored me, spoke through me. 'Sometimes here' – he went on so fast and powerful that I could not interrupt – 'in these fields late at night, I hear noises. In the hedgerows. Snuffling noises. The kind someone makes in their bed at night. In their sleep. I think, that's the noise I want to hear someone making beside me when I'm near the final heist, Doll. Safety. Safety's love. I'd like some safety.'

I looked at him. Richard seemed luminous. The bandanna had been washed. He wore a faded red T-shirt and had those big boots. A touch of grey lit his black temples.

I tried again, exchanging drama for jokes.

'What do you think, Rich? Will Joey be smoking a cigar in jail?'

Richard sprawled in front of me. 'If I marry here I am safe. I will be naturalized as an Irish citizen and nobody can touch me, even – I think – if I return to the States.'

'Rich, d'you want a drink? I brought you some vodka.'

'I'm giving up drinking.'

'Richard?!' He shrugged off my amazement.

'Zen. The here and now. I'll call it my liver or my pancreas or diabetes. It ain't gonna be easy. Around here they will not let you give up something that weakens them. You, Doll, are my best friend.' He stretched out on the grass. 'In the beginning. Now. And ever shall be. World without end. Amen.' He hauled me over to him and I lay with my head on his shoulder.

'But if you loved me, Rich, you'd let me tell you what happened.'

He never answered; he fell asleep.

I lay there, not moving. Eventually I began to weep aloud. I don't know why. He woke and stroked my hair. The sun had gone in and it was getting cold on the grass. I rose and walked away, still in tears.

In his slow half-shout, he said, 'Forgive! Forgive! Now you have to be forgiven! Bad move, Doll! Look – I went berserk that night. I was put on a charge for threatening a brother officer. If they crucify you, you suffocate. That's how crucifixion works. To care much for anything or anyone since that day only suffocates me. Suffocates me.'

This man had healed me. I had done nothing for him. I thought loving him would be enough.

I said, 'Rich, I love you.'

'Sure you do, Doll. Sure you do.' He was subsiding.

'Am I losing you? Am I going to lose you, Rich?'

'I am the ghost who walks.'

And still we had not discussed what had happened. I tried to tell him. He would not let me. I tried to tell him about my pleasures. Which would satisfy me most? The look on Joey's face? The realization by Mother of my actual power? Or the inner power from a feat of that magnitude?

Richard grabbed me. I refused to make love. He proved exceptionally cruel about it.

'What is it, Doll? I mean, it isn't as if you have a time of the month to worry about, do you?'

I walked away from him. He knew I was hurt. He made no effort to come after me. Since the day he spoke about Vietnam something in him had changed. He had become a child. He threw tantrums. I tried to create a routine of seeing him. He would not have it.

No word still from my parents. No word from them, no sign of them. Nothing. Kevin had not returned. Agnes told me they were all in Dublin. From the television news I learned that Joey was remanded in custody but the lawyers were working. Our front gates were locked. Some reporters tried to get in. They did not know a back entrance existed.

Silence fell everywhere. I slept a lot.

Days later I drove to see Richard. I knew he would be there. Not because it was his birthday. He might have forgotten that. But because he had spent the week on one of his 'hikes'. These were long, manic walks. Once he walked the whole ridge of the mountains.

'You'll be able to see me, Doll. From the main street. Look up, you'll see a guy walking up near the sky. He'll look like a giant. It'll be me.'

Soldiers have failed on that walk. Mountaineers train for it. Richard does it alone. On this particular hike he had intended to walk over the mountains to the sea, forty miles away. Then, following the shore, he wanted to come back across the foothills of the same mountains.

These walks subdued him. But this one did not. When I got there he was cutting wood. He had hauled three trunks of beech from some field somewhere. Stolen, of course; 'I liberated them.'

I lived in fear of his arrest for theft. But his cutting of the trees was dangerous. He used the axe as if he might strike himself with it. Stripped to the waist, in the cold rainy weather, he circled the log as if it were a prey. Blow. After blow. After blow.

'Gimme time. I'm busy.'

'I brought you a birthday present, Rich.'

'Gifts corrupt.'

Oh, God. It was going to be one of those. I sat and watched him. He gave me his umbrella, big and golf-striped. Also stolen. Three hours he made me wait under it. In that time I studied him. Something was wrong, no doubt of that. He walked in circles around those logs but normally he would never have cut them like that because he had fine competence.

Suddenly he sat down. His energy had gone.

'How was the hike?' I asked him.

'Not good.'

'Why not, Rich?'

He tapped his chest. 'Pipes, Doll. I had difficulty breathing.'

My alarms work well. But he did not listen. I tried and tried.

'No doctors, Doll. No. No medics. No quacks. No medicine man.' He always feared they would turn him in, that he would be deported.

'I brought you a shirt, Rich. A warm, wool shirt. For your birthday.'

He looked at it. Then he threw it at me in anger.

'I don't want a shirt. I came for you.'

'Richard? What do you mean? What do you mean, "I came for you"? What does that mean?!'

Something in the way he said it caught me. I knew it was important. His riddles always were. 'Rich! Tell me.'

'Doll.' He spoke slowly. His eyes had become pained and lonesome. Like I never saw them before.

'Doll,' he said again. 'Doll.'

I took his outstretched hand. 'Rich, you never told me fully. Of how you heard about me. In St Heber's, I mean.'

I saw his face deciding to tell me.

'Truth is, Ann. I heard a story. Or half a story. About a woman treated badly. You were that woman. I only heard a bit of it. The guy who told me, he knew no more.'

'Who? What guy, Rich?' He had never called me 'Ann' before. Not even once.

'A guy I play cards with.'

'Who is he?' Something I can only understand today tore at me that morning.

'He's a bell-ringer, Doll. And he plays cards. He told me about this, this "fine woman", he called her. That's you. Her name was Ann.'

Richard stared ahead. The rain was hitting his bare back. I picked the shirt off the grass. He said, 'I hate injustice. They tried to certify me, too. Way back. So I came looking for you.'

'How did you know it was me?'

'I knew you. I had seen you.'

The expression in his eyes tugged at the place my womb used to be.

'Oh, Rich, Rich, why didn't you say?'

'I didn't say in case you didn't like my interfering.'

'Oh, Rich! But you saved my life!'

'So?' His voice sounded like a flat square of lead.

'You did! You saved my life.' I fought through his barriers and hugged him. I kissed and kissed him. He walked away from me and would not come back. I put the wool shirt back in its wrapping and left it in his pavilion. Then I drove home in tears. Nobody there but Agnes.

That night, Richard came to see me. I always leave my bedroom window open. Unafraid, I woke up when I felt a shape lie near me. I knew it was him.

'Is that you, Rich?'

'It had better be.'

'Rich?'

He did not answer and he did not touch me. I know now that he had begun to suffer impotence. It disturbed him terribly.

After about five minutes lying there in the dark he said, 'Will you marry me?'

'I will, I will,' I whispered. 'I will of course marry the man who gave me back my life.'

'No more talking now,' he said. 'Be quiet.'

Eventually I dozed. He was lying perfectly still.

I woke up hours later. To an empty space beside me in the bed. With a sprig of green on the pillow, broken from the oak tree outside the window – Richard's proof, because he knew I would be afraid that I had dreamed it.

45

One hundred and twelve people died last year in 'matters arising', as the Chief Constable of the RUC put it. The security forces recorded almost eleven hundred shootings; they recovered nearly six hundred weapons; twelve hundred bombs and incendiary devices were planted; they found nearly three tons of explosives and they charged thirteen hundred people with terrorist offences.

These annual statistics are losing their fascination for me; maybe I have become frozen to such records, but I prefer to think of my life as still undergoing profound inner change and I have moved on – or am moving on – from being a chronicler of unrest and violence. My house feels finalized, decorated and fully furnished, with a bright garden and a fireplace and an air of welcome.

I took Father to the airport this evening; he has stayed longer than he had intended and my mother did not seem to mind. Next, she must come, and that will be a great challenge – to try and build a relationship with her. She suspects that I have not forgiven her and I feel she must be right. I heard Father describing the house to her on the telephone and then when I spoke to her she said, 'All you need now, darling, is a wife.'

'A wife?' I echoed, and Father, sensing something in me, intervened, took the telephone back.

'I'm sure', he declared, 'Christopher knows everything he needs to know on that score.'

His remark unlocked something in me, and it has led to good inner fortune. He and I went to fetch the newspapers in Mooreville; he has been such good company. Then, we saw Ann; or, rather, I saw Ann, and I pointed her out.

All I said was, 'See that woman, there, in the grey coat. Please take a look at her. Say nothing, just take a look at her.'

'But we saw her a few days ago, did we not?'

We had a particularly good view of her; she saw us looking and Father, from inside the car, doffed his hat to her; she smiled. He said nothing to me, but after lunch he and I went for a walk in the woods.

We paused in the garden: 'Christopher, I hope you're not going to change the colour of that door. I like that red; that's an old railway colour, you know.' Then he reflected on the height of the roof pitch, the tallness of the houses. 'I've always liked railway architecture,' he said.

We walked what I call the top circuit, up the little road to the edge of the forest, then down a forest road to where a roughshod wooden bench gives a view over a small valley.

'This is like Herefordshire,' he said. 'Slightly less cultivated, but perhaps a little the better for that. You know, we went back there last year, your mother and I, and I remembered every stick of it. I was very pleased with myself.'

He is fitter than her, and their relationship has changed; she pays him the kind of slavish attention I recall him lavishing on her. It is as if she is atoning.

'How is she, in general?' I asked.

He waited. 'I – I find it hard to say. Your mother is a dark horse. As I expect you know. I think she has some severe arthritis at times, but she won't say.' Then he looked at me. 'You get that from her, don't you?'

I laughed. 'I don't have arthritis.'

He rapped the bench with his knuckle and laughed.

'That won't do. I meant the dark horse in you. Now – come on. Out with it. That woman we saw.'

I took a deep breath and told him everything, from beginning to now. I did not care that I might sound like something along the scale from idiot to maniac. When I finished, he said nothing, just held his fingers over his lips for a long time.

'What a moving story,' he said. 'What a moving story. And you have carried this burden all these years? How strong of you.'

I did not know what to expect when I began to tell him about Ann, but I know I did not quite expect the response he gave.

'And that was she this morning? That was she? My Lord. What a tale. What a tale. You realize, don't you, that I will tell nobody?' He speaks quite slowly.

'The question is, I don't know what to do now.'

'Time to think,' he said. 'Time to think.'

On the way to Shannon he and I spoke again; he began carefully, then became very excited.

'Look, I've been thinking. All the old things, the old sayings. We used to dismiss them as romantic rubbish but of course we would never have known them so well had there not been some truth in them. I mean, "Only the brave deserve the fair" and, "Faint heart never won fair lady" – sort of thing. I'm not saying you have not been thinking along those lines, but perhaps you've brought the time to its hour? Perhaps the time has come for you

315

to make your move. God knows, you can never predict the response from a woman.'

I spoke my greatest worry. 'What if she refuses me? What if she makes it plain she will not have me? Under any circumstances?'

He startled me with the force of his response. 'Why should she do that? She looked a reasonably intelligent woman. Very good-looking. Your mother will feel the pressure of competition.' He smiled.

'But it is my greatest fear. If she says, if she . . . I mean – I only get one chance.'

He shook his head. 'It does not in my experience work like that. You are not the Hunchback of Notre Dame, you are not even ugly. I am allowed to say so – I bred you.' He laughed. 'No, no. You cannot predict she will refuse you, because we cannot predict what anyone, male or female, will ever do.'

'You're just trying to reassure me.'

'And why not?' He smiled. 'But let me give you some real reassurance. Whenever I have wanted something very badly, I did everything to allow Life to give it to me.' I made a gesture of total incomprehension. 'By which I mean,' he continued, 'I tested my own honesty in the matter and if I found I wanted whatever it was for reasons of good, rather than for reasons of selfishness, if I could answer a whole series of difficult questions honourably to myself – I went ahead and prepared for the thing to come about. Which seems to me what you have done. Now here comes the reassurance. Once I had done all my preparation, I found the thing, whatever it was – once it was the survival of a patient where I knew the surgical procedures, though innovative, were important – I found the thing itself arrived. In that particular case, the patient lived and the procedures were adopted. Had they not succeeded, I would have been in difficulty. I had gone out on a limb. But I had gone out on it honourably. And you have done the same, have you not? And, it seems to me, you may have now done your preparation.'

He made a sweeping gesture with his hand.

'You will know inside you,' he said. 'Soon something will happen. It might be a trip. You might go away somewhere on an assignment and meet her, or somebody who knows her. Or you might encounter her in an unlikely way. Keep your mind open. It may be an extraordinary circumstance or it might be an ordinary circumstance – but I feel certain it will come. Keep the antennae sharp.'

How I wish I had recorded him; this is but a poor paraphrasing of what he said.

I asked, 'What about this man I saw her with?'

'Hah!' He barked rather than laughed – and said no more.

I miss him tonight; he arrived safely, but my mother answered the telephone and said he was in the bath. Never mind; I shall follow Father's advice, even though I shall not quite know what exactly I am doing; I shall follow it because it feels right.

46

One, two, three, four rings on my fingers. Not Joey's,
I never wear those now. One of my mother's. My little
garnet ring. My grandmother's sapphire. And the ring
Richard bought me. I touch them all often. These jewels
are my little private touchstones.

We were married in Galway, the place where I fell in
love with Richard. I organized all the papers secretly.
No problems. I had an annulment, and a donation to
the church helped. Richard, unexpectedly, was able to
produce his birth certificate. He said 'I do' in a voice
like God's. His eyes had gone away into outer space.

Nobody knew. Richard wanted to tell nobody and
I wanted to tell nobody. It did not matter. And so
he became my husband and I became his wife. As we
still are. We had no honeymoon. We did it all in a day,
which was the way he wanted it. He resisted all other
possibilities. Then he went home to his pavilion and I
to my house.

When I got there they had come back, and with them
the ghost rider returned. Mother was my flesh and blood.
That night, after my strange but profound marriage to
Richard, I looked in Mother's face. My blood thickened
towards her again.

Then – then! Then came the split feelings: love for her
and of being aghast. I had ruined her life. Feelings of

being appalled at myself began to rise in me. Remorse has the worst taste in the world.

She knew I did it. Never spoke to me. Turned her face away.

My father, still with a shine on him, said, 'Isn't this all terrible trouble, Ann. Isn't it very sad, isn't it? But God fits the back for the burden. We'll be all right. With the help of God.'

I noted that he did not add, 'And two policemen.'

Mother looked at him as if at a fool. She knew the implications of everything more fully than him. They were preparing for bed. No matter how they handled themselves they were shattered. They could not find things where they had just put them down – Mother's cigarettes on the table beside her, my father and his brandy glass. They were astray. I decided to leave them alone, but to look in on them every day. As I left she never looked at me. The space behind my eyes was red.

Mother took three days to reach me. My panic wildened. Her glances were always bullets. Then Agnes came.

'She wants to see you, Ann – 'bout half-past three.'

Nothing to do all day. Nowhere to go. Richard wanted to wait for a week before meeting again. Such a marriage!

Had Mother been piecing it all together? Strange worrying feelings that I could not describe were taking me over. Dark feelings of fear whose strength frightened me. I defended against them. There was nothing to connect me. I could plead that I made those two remarks to her and to Joey ironically. She had no proof.

God! I was still so afraid of her. Over and over I told myself that my movements had been impeccable. Did anybody see me enter the police station? No. Had a member of the force chatted, in a pub or to his wife? Possibly.

This was not fear on its own, though. There was something else with it, something unbearable, something that twists the heart in frightful discomfort. Something from which there is no ease. This was remorse, fear's close friend. I tried to subdue it. No, there was nothing they could attach to me. Agnes said there had been shouting. That was something I had never heard. In my whole life as their child, not one shout.

Someone had drawn the curtains closed. For a moment I did not see her in the darkness.

Fear hit me like a truck and everything in me clenched. She sat in the corner of the large leather sofa (I always thought it hideous – and it cost the earth). Hunched in the corner, in her dressing-gown, last night's make-up smudged. Mother always had a cold fire in her but that had gone out. She had shrunk. My panic both escalated and subsided. Is this what she would come to?

I consoled myself. I knew why she took three days to see me. She could not face me. Shame. Embarrassment.

What did it feel like? What did I feel when I slowed down and observed her? I must be honest. I felt three things. First was a complete and savage triumph. Second, a compassion that devastated me. The third was an intensifying of the remorse. All – I felt them all at the same time. Add in the fear and it was difficult to walk. I sat down across from her.

'Ann, is that you?'

'Yes, Mother.'

At that moment, for a moment, we were every mother and daughter who ever lived. I never hated her more. I never despised her more. I never pitied her more. And I never loved her more.

'Is it true, Ann? Is it true? The whole way through?'

When I was little she often used that phrase. 'Is it true the whole way through?' Before the 'silences' she used it warmly. After the silences she used it lethally. Now she used it pitiably. I did not answer the question. Instead I asked, 'How are you, Mother?'

'Will I have to sell all my jewellery? Where will I keep my clothes?'

'Mother, maybe you should have some coffee.'

I called Agnes and I opened the curtains. Mother looked like a dying bird. Her smeared rouge looked like blood on her feathers.

'Would you like a bath, Mother?'

'This will kill your daddy.'

About that she was very wrong.

'Nobody will speak to us,' she said. 'Nobody will come to see us.'

About that she was not wrong.

'I'll get Agnes to run a bath for you, Mother. Do you feel like some, maybe, toast? When did you eat last, Mother? Have you enough cigarettes?'

I asked practical questions deliberately. To keep at bay what would now hit her. The missiles of disgrace were already in the sky.

'Are we destroyed? Are we completely ruined? We never knew. But it isn't true, is it? Joseph and those people?'

We sat without moving. We were in silence once more, Mother and I.

'Mother, it is nearly four o'clock. I think you should have this.'

She had some force left. With a hand she swept the tray aside and sent everything crashing. The coffee spurted across the creamy pink Persian rug.

She seemed to have lost the power of her legs. Agnes and I helped her to climb from the sofa. We persuaded her to bed. Dr Butler arrived, placid and decent. In the next two hours Mother's personality changed. She vanished into herself. Never again became the ice empress. Her withdrawal set like concrete. Whatever rope she was holding frayed or broke or she just let go of it. A new kind of silence was born in her, distant and purposeless.

47

I had tea on Thursday at the Shelbourne Hotel where I last saw Ann's little boy: I went there deliberately to chart my feelings, to judge whether they had changed. Yes, they have changed but not so as to threaten the moorings I now have inside me. I can describe it best to myself if I say I can see the gulf between thought and feeling. This position has kept my spirits buoyant tonight and my mind distracted; in other words a conflict rages within me between my thoughts and my feelings. The ridiculous notion came to me that when I did break down here, in this lounge, I was mirroring the fractures I have been reporting in Ireland.

My feelings for Ann remain the same – deep, fond and desirous, but what am I to do about the revelations regarding Ann's family? I have not dared to read the details but nobody can avoid the headlines: 'Halpin's Bet on the Provos' and 'Halpin's: the IRA Connection'. Her husband (her *former* husband I expect, but of course I know nothing) is on all the front pages.

I do not need to read the captions; I recognize him, and ironically the most prevalent photograph was clearly taken on his wedding day. I keep asking myself this question – after the things I have seen, how can I morally have anything whatsoever to do – love, passion, desire, aspiration notwithstanding – with anyone who espouses

323

republicanism and its violence? This is not political on my part; although an Englishman to my bootstraps I can perceive very clearly 'The Cause' as they keep calling it – but I have reported on the methods too often to feel that I could in any way support such people.

Professionally, I have been having an enjoyable time. New academic scuffles are breaking out concerning the authorship of the Lindisfarne Gospels. A professor at Durham University claims that most of the great illuminated texts were created at Lindisfarne. This has left the Irish in somewhat of a miff, especially over the Book of Kells, which lies in the library at Trinity College where a page is turned every day for the benefit of visitors. They told me, not without a little malicious glee, of Queen Victoria: when viewing it she asked for a pen, thinking she was expected to sign it.

Some of the language I heard from those who showed me the manuscript on Thursday felt as beautifully ornate as the Book itself; 'majuscule'; 'cursive'; said one professor. 'We always have to be aware of imperfections; the Book is a bit like life itself; there are imperfections at both ends.'

I have often reflected how poetry lives in the mouths of these people. Why do the Irish use our language so less prosaically than we do? And use bombs more prolifically?

'See there,' said his colleague. 'The scribe caused a flaw and then had to subdue his error. Don't we all have to do the same?'

On the delicate issue of Lindisfarne, they were waiting for me, with another great contemporary text as their authority, the Book of Ulster, which recorded the theft and recovery of the Book of Kells. One of the professors translated for me: 'The great gospel was stolen at night from the western sacristy at Kells . . . it was found after two months and twenty nights, the gold having been stolen off it, and a sod placed over it.' He then smiled. 'Not, of course, "sod" as your readers might understand the word, but a clod of earth.'

'So there you are,' said the second, as if the case had been proven. 'And like all these texts buried in the earth.'

'But', I asked, 'was the Book of Kells begun and finished in Kells?'

'We don't know it wasn't, do we?' said the first.

'Unfortunately,' smiled the second, 'they did not have newspapers of record in those days.'

They gave me lunch in their common-room and I listened to them debating whether the thief had deliberately arranged the Book under the clod of earth in some observance of ritual.

'Well – there is a life here under the ground,' one explained to me. 'The first partition was a division of all the island over the ground going to one faction, the victorious Milesians. And all under the ground going to their rivals, the faery people of the goddess Dana. It all happened at a place called Moytura long before the time of Christ.'

I made them smile when I said, 'You must agree with me when I say I find it difficult to convey such a concept of, well, factual history to my readers at their breakfasts in Surrey and Hampshire.'

'Ah,' dismissed one, with the other agreeing. 'The trouble with the English is they never believe what they could believe. They'd have a cheerier time if they gave themselves more latitude.'

I wryly agreed – and said so to Charles when we spoke.

He mock-exploded. 'Now do you see why I worried about you going native?'

But he and I laughed about it, and tonight I feel that any lingering drifts of our old division have been finally healed and perhaps my breakdown may even have contributed to an increase in my standing.

My head feels peaceful carrying around those Book of Kells images; these illuminations – what they call 'carpet pages', rich in texture and expression – should have formed the education of Ann's little son and sadly never will. Were I married to her I could have gone home tonight and told them what I had seen; that descent of the Genealogy of St Luke (my favourite among the evangelists: how prosaic I am!); the malachite and lapis lazuli colours; the famous doodles and cartoons, the cats watching the mice eat a wafer; the lizards, the hens, the fish.

'You live in Mooreville, don't you?' said one of the professors to me. 'There's a nice proverb from down there.' He said it first in Gaelic and then translated: 'Listen to the sound of the river and you will catch a trout.' I thought, well, I have been listening but have not yet landed my catch.

The layout subs gave the Graves piece a most satisfying display – they scarcely cut it. Charles told me that everyone has been, as he put it, 'mouthing commendations'. I am so proud of it – not for its writing but for all it represents to me, the bridges I have crossed, the rebuilding of myself, the triumphing over old fears; I am going to keep the cutting in this journal.

A Very British Hero – A Very Irish End
by our Dublin Correspondent, Christopher Hunter

Irish history accepts as fact that the first Partition, centuries BC, divided the country in two – one faction took all above the ground and the other, the defeated ones, all beneath it. Later, the island's rich turf hid precious vessels and books from Viking marauders. Today the earth holds new secrets of violence – and may never yield them.

Several months have passed since the disappearance of Captain Philip Graves, an artilleryman on his third tour of duty in Ulster. His whereabouts have excited opinion, speculation and downright rumour. No body has been found, and no burial place been traced; his family cannot mourn and the file may never be closed. Sources on both sides of the Border suggest that one or more arrests may shortly take place, but privately officials admit to little possibility either of Captain Graves's recovery alive or the retrieval of his corpse.

His disappearance has become so shrouded in true and false lore, occasioned in part by his *Boys' Own* hero image, and the army's tacit admission of his undercover duties, that a clear picture has never materialized. However, several weeks of investigations have produced a summary of the last events in the officer's life. The emerging account is acknowledged as being unlikely to change.

Philip Graves was not intended for death. On the night he was taken, a group of senior IRA personnel from south Armagh had already set out for Graves's known location. He had been an habitué of the Four Horsemen, a remote Border pub some two miles inside Ulster. Although he affected a local accent and passed himself off as a garage hand called Tommy, the residents referred to him as 'the spy'.

I met Captain Graves in the Four Horsemen two nights before his disappearance. Ironically, in view of Graves's disappearance, I had gone to south Armagh to investigate reports that the IRA had executed three informers, taken there from Belfast, and had buried their bodies without Christian burial or referral to the dead men's families. For the familiar reasons of fear and/or loyalties, nobody – across a wide spectrum – wished to discuss the issue. While attempting to ascertain some facts, any fact, Graves was pointed out to me as 'the local spy' and then he beckoned to me.

In our subsequent conversation, it became clear he fully believed his cover unbroken. He dismissed my observations that the locals referred to him as their 'spy' and asked me if I knew the words of any rebel songs. Two nights later he returned to the pub, then crowded, and took the stage with a local band to sing two songs beloved of IRA sympathizers.

What happened next has never been hitherto clear, but a collage built from sources who have in the past proved unimpeachable amounts to an image which neither police nor regimental headquarters in Lisburn deny.

The so-called Commandant of the IRA in south Armagh had been observing Graves for several weeks. Local girls had been detailed to befriend him, local men bought him drinks. Their anecdotal evidence suggested Graves had strong Irish, and perhaps Republican, sympathies.

His love of Ireland began early. At Harrow he

formed friendships with the sons of Anglo-Irish families and spent many of his school holidays at their homes in the west and the south-west of Ireland. At Balliol he founded an Irish society. But he was voted off his own committee after incidents of violence which brought him to the attentions of the college authorities.

Captain Graves's parents, who live in the Home Counties, confirm their son's Hibernian sympathies. Paul Graves, a Harley Street rheumatologist, declared himself baffled by what must have been an evident conflict.

'He said to me that he was working it out, that he expected to have a clearer idea of what Ireland meant to him after this tour of duty.'

Mrs Naomi Suter, with whom Captain Graves had been having a relationship for the last two years, confirmed that 'Ireland disturbed him. Every time he went there he admitted to becoming confused.'

In July of last year, Graves was again seconded, as he had been before, to an 'unofficial' operation known only as 'Eleven-D'. The army will neither confirm nor deny the existence of such a unit, believed to have taken its name from the killing in one day of eleven known IRA activists in counties Fermanagh and Tyrone. Republicans in Northern Ireland believe Graves personally accounted for two of those deaths, but, notwithstanding, they also believed that if they could 'turn' him, he could become 'the perfect double agent'. On that ballad-singing Saturday night three senior Provisionals set out to 'lift' their target.

Before they arrived, seven younger Provisionals,

ignorant of their superiors' plan, bundled Graves out of the lavatories of the Four Horsemen and across the car park to a grey van. The noise of the scuffle was drowned by the turning-up of the pub's amplifiers as the band played on. Graves broke away from his abductors and reached his own car, which had a red-alert button with a homing device beneath the seat. He is known to have pressed the button, which remains depressed after use; it should have alerted an SAS squadron in Crossmaglen two miles away, but army sources say the message was never received. (Subsequently, there was speculation that a regimental officer hostile to Graves had disconnected the receiving end of the red alert.)

Graves jumped from his car and ran again, but was recaptured and this time thrown into the van which then headed south across the Border along 'unapproved' i.e., unpatrolled roads. West of the town of Dundalk he was taken to a remote and seemingly uninhabited farmhouse. Here he was concussed and temporarily disabled by a blow to the head.

When he recovered he found himself guarded in a small room by only one man, whom he disarmed and knocked out. Others burst through the door and Graves shot at them, but the captured gun misfired. In the succeeding scuffle he killed one man with a blow to the Adam's apple from the useless gun, and gouged the eye of another.

Graves was then overpowered, tied and gagged. At that moment an army helicopter was heard overhead and Graves's life was almost saved as his captors believed they had been followed. The helicopter, however, moved away and Graves was again bundled into the van.

At about four o'clock in the morning the van stopped in woods a mile or so inside the Republic, and about two miles west of the main Belfast–Dublin road. By a culvert with a small limestone span known locally as Crow Bridge, Graves was tied to a tree and an interrogation began. He was beaten savagely but managed to shatter the kneecap of one of his captors with a kick. Graves was wearing blue jeans and a grey and blue anorak.

When it became clear that he was not going to 'crack', his torturers decided to kill him. Graves asked for a priest and, bleeding terribly from head wounds, he was led to another part of the wood.

Part of the folklore claims that one of his captors pretended, in the dark, to be a priest and purported to hear Graves's last confession. (He had converted to Roman Catholicism while at Balliol.) This did not happen.

They finally dragged the officer by the hair to another part of the wood 'to find a closer acoustic'. There he was killed in the fashion known to be favoured by the SAS: first a body shot in order to disable (although Graves was still bound hand and foot), and then a head shot.

The corpse was stripped and the clothing taken to an abattoir in Dublin, giving rise to the grisly rumour that Graves's body had been disposed of similarly. He was buried in a temporary grave, which was discovered three days later – empty by then – when Southern police with tracker dogs found Graves's bloodstains on a tree by Crow Bridge.

His body was moved twice more, and its final destination remains unknown. Republican sources say he was moved 'west of the Shannon', ferried there inside a lorry packed with sheep. They also describe him as a 'good soldier who fought hard'.

Captain Philip Graham Graves, BA, of the Royal Artillery may yet be awarded the George Cross. Yet many of his personal and military details run counter to the honourable behaviour typically associated with valour. That is one of the ugly paradoxes required of and generated by the 'Troubles' in Ireland, this war that is not a war.

Paradoxical, too, is the likelihood that the whereabouts of his grave will never be disclosed. Thus, he joins untold sacred and beautiful objects that have never been discovered in the earth of this poetic and dangerous country.

Most paradoxical of all, he lies in that underground territory which, if the history of this island is to be accepted as Irish children are taught it daily, formed one half of the country's first Partition.

Charles rang again this evening and said he had been re-reading the Graves piece.

'I know I have a reputation for praising people, C., and you know how bad such a reputation is in London. But, well, full marks.'

This is when my life gets lonely – not when I have sad times to discuss, but when I have good times to share. Rang my parents, no reply; don't yet know if Father saw the piece.

48

May God forgive me. I try now, every day, not to hurt anyone. I am no longer sarcastic. I no longer hate people. My self-pity is all gone. Dear Lord, how I wallowed in it! May God forgive me. He must have done, because I have been given a life that my vengeful actions should have denied me.

Joey got out. On huge bail. They reported on the radio that the case would take nearly a year to get to court. The rumours said that Joey could definitely be connected to 'Republican causes'. Bigger rumours said the firm was a front for the Provos. One newspaper screamed it as a question: 'WAS BOOKIES' FIRM A PROVO BANK?'

They had his wedding photograph everywhere. It made me smile a bit.

Special Branch changed all the office locks. All staff were suspended without pay. Mountgolden accountants were given passes. Joey's house was sealed. So was my parents', but I was left alone. Mother stayed in the Nursing Home. My father moved in with me. They allowed him to bring only his clothes. I had plenty of room – six bedrooms to spare and two drawing-rooms. That's how lavish Mother was in her building enterprises.

Nicola Mountgolden rang me. Agnes took the call. I shook my head.

'She's not here.' Agnes has a very flat accent.

In that week I underwent another profound change. Would the life inside me ever stop changing? This change went deep. This change shocked me.

I had been intent on revenge. Then I felt remorse. Now I felt corrupted. Corrupted by my own brutality. I knew how someone must feel after a crime. In my case the bodies were there in front of my eyes and I had a new straitjacket – guilt. It wrapped me so tight I could not breathe.

I said to myself, 'I feel so ashamed.'

I said, 'This is awful.'

I said, 'I feel like a criminal.'

I said to myself, 'Oh, Jesus, poor Daddy. Oh, Jesus-Jesus-Jesus.'

I had destroyed my parents' lives.

Revenge, I now know, is all shell, all armour. It has nothing of substance inside it. Revenge makes mimics of its users. When you take revenge, you too become hollow and my heart in that week became an echo chamber.

I did not sleep and I did not eat. Naturally everyone thought I, too, grieved. I did – but I grieved for what I had done. What do you do with Revenge once you have it? I still do not know.

When I crossed the threshold of the Nursing Home every day, my mind went white. Guilt has huge pain in it. Nobody would have guessed at any of my feelings because I was competent and concerned but unflappable. I had answers to all questions and I created solutions for intractable problems and I was admired. I was the rock in this swirling sea. Nobody could see how guilt was disabling me.

As I expected, the media continued to make a meal of Joey. That, to my shock, upset me too. He was photographed or televised every time he went to his lawyers. No sign of a wife or child. And no mention of either.

I remain surprised at how ambushed and distressed I felt.

'Rich, this is not going the way I thought. I mean, inside me.'

'Hey-hey-hey! Let me hold you.'

'Rich, it isn't right. What I did isn't right.'

'Shhh, Doll.'

We lay down on his bed and I stayed for hours but we did not make love.

I drove to the Nursing Home.

'How are you, Mother?' Silence.

'Has Daddy been in?' Silence.

'Or Joey?' Silence.

'Agnes and Kevin send you their best.' Silence.

I sat, not knowing what to do. The room had a heavy smell of fabrics. Mother sat in a chair by the radiator.

'Are you cold, Mother?' Silence.

I saw one change, a significant one. No ashtray; no packets.

'Are you out of cigarettes?' I asked.

Without turning her head she said, 'We haven't heard from Lucy O'Connor.'

'No.'

'I haven't heard. Your father hasn't heard.'

'No, Mother.'

'Have you heard from her?'

'No, Mother.'

Mother said, 'That jumped-up bitch.'

She never heard from anyone of her circle. Not once, not ever again.

Further conversation did not take place that evening.

Nor the next. Nor the next. Nor the next. Nor the next. And still I went in every day.

One evening she said to me, 'I need some more of my nightdresses.'

I must have sensed something. 'But I brought you some, I mean you have – what, three, four?'

'I'll be needing more.'

'But you'll soon be out of here.' This was a healthy woman.

'No. I won't.'

This was not good. I went to see Dr Butler.

'I have a problem,' he said. 'Your mother has always been Dr Greene's patient. She has been seeing Dr Greene lately. But he has retired and he won't see her. And I can get no information from either of them.'

I asked him what the position was, ethically.

'Doctors usually forward files easily enough,' he said. 'We're supposed to.'

Greene lived ten minutes away. That night I rang his doorbell. He opened the door and I walked straight in. For some reason he jumped back in alarm. He looked terrified. Did I breathe such visible power, such rage? I had not seen him since the day of the garden party. I found it hard to keep my stillness.

'I want my mother's file,' I said. 'For Dr Butler.'

'No. You can't have it.' He spoke very rudely.

I held up the envelope I had brought.

'In this is the insanity certificate you wrote about me. And a copy of a note from my husband discharging all your racing debts.' I was bluffing. 'You were bribed. You could go to jail. Like Joey. And he paid you well, didn't he?'

He nearly had a heart attack running to get the file. I decided to scare him more.

'Thank you,' I said. 'There's something else I know about you,' I said. 'I have other documents. But I'll keep them in case I need to.'

I left. He had not said a word. Little did I know the truth of what I was saying.

49

Another Irish day comes to a soft close as the woods darken. The contrast almost challenges the sanity; two nights ago I listened once more to the stereo of gunfire from the Shankill and the Falls roads; the children of Belfast can identify the guns they hear each night: SLR, Armalite, Sten. Tonight I can hear an owl – I don't know which kind.

Part of my difficulty in doing this job comes in the maintenance of concentration. For the past forty-eight hours I have reported the visit and its aftermath of 'Our Leader', as they are calling her, to Northern Ireland. At her press conference she reminded us immediately that she leads 'the Conservative and Unionist Party of Great Britain and Northern Ireland' – my friends among the Unionists were much cheered when I spoke to them later.

Again the language can be so striking, north or south of the Irish Border. They have a new official term in the prison administration in Ulster: 'ODCs'; these are 'ordinary decent criminals' – to distinguish them from the political prisoners in the excrement protests and occasional hunger strikes. 'ODCs', we were told in answer to one reporter, include those in prison for rape, child abuse, grievous bodily harm and so forth; I've forgotten who it was said 'Truth is the first casualty of war.' He should have said 'language.'

Such a relief to drive up my quiet wooded little road last night at the end of it all.

This afternoon, I actually walked past Ann; our shoulders almost touched; she did not see me; she was standing on the doorstep of a house talking earnestly to a man I know to be the popular doctor of the town, Dr Butler. I hope she is not unwell and indeed she looked exceptionally well; her image has changed considerably from the bedraggled person I saw in the hotel by the Atlantic. As I passed by, I could smell her perfume and I will now know it anywhere. It seems as though I draw nearer and nearer to her – but I have no evidence for this.

My mother arrives at the weekend; I will take a few days' leave to cope with her. I know already I shall not tell her about Ann, but I do need to speak to Father again soon because I need his input on this problem. The Irish newspapers have been screaming about the likely Halpin involvement with PIRA and one of our chaps in Dublin has written a cut-and-paste piece (not very good, but I kept my counsel). I have been avoiding the story; it is affecting me more than I want to allow. I expect I have been trying to scale down my passion for her ever since the scandal broke – but then when I see her, as I did today, my heart both sings and falls apart.

50

They came to question Mother as she sat in her room at the Nursing Home. That should never have happened. I asked strong questions of the nurses. They told me the men showed their police cards.

I met them both and told them what I told Dr Butler. Mother had had a mild stroke a year before. In Marbella one night after dinner she could not rise. She recovered. It was in Dr Greene's file and I was fantastically worried by it. The detectives left the room, with one saying, 'She wouldn't open her mouth to us, hardly.' I suppose I was nervous too in case someone let it slip that I was the one who went to the Superintendent.

Dr Butler persuaded Mother to stop smoking. From sixty a day to zero. That plus the Special Branch made her dwindle. Plus the loss of her jewels and clothes. Plus the loss of her furniture. Plus the loss of her house. Plus the loss of her status. Plus the loss of her friends.

'Friends.' Not one called. Not one wrote. All those people who lunched and dined. All those people at racecourse marquees. The garden party. The countless dinners at home. The countless restaurant lunches. Not a call nor a note nor a visit.

Mother shrank day by day, hour by hour. She never came back to me. I tried affection. I tried care, both stern and fussy. I tried memory. I tried 'Tramore'. If anything she went further away.

Special Branch came to see my father, too. He spoke to them easily and warmly.

'Boys, ye have ye'er job to do.'

That is how my father is. He touched them, I saw that. He reached their hearts with a kind of innocence. I stood with him on the step as they walked away.

I complimented him on his manners to them.

He said to me, 'Sure why wouldn't I?'

One of the detectives opened the back of their car and rummaged. He walked back to my father with something in his hand.

'We don't need this,' he said. 'We found it in the offices.'

He handed my father a small statue of Tulyar, in Connemara marble. My father made a lot of his early money on Tulyar. Tulyar was his favourite horse ever. How did the man know?

Then we had supper, my father and I. Agnes served. I had cooked.

'This is lovely,' he said.

Dinner began well. Memories traversed the table. My father, at his best, went back to the ESB and Devon Loch Grand National. He went back further to Golden Miller ridden by Evan Williams, and to Tim Hyde, to horses like Lord Nelson and Bell Walk. My father spoke normally, laughed now and then, frowned now and then.

Then we talked of employees, old bookies who had worked courses for years for us. All gone. I had not foreseen any of this.

Women who counted cash on Saturday nights for the last twenty years, local women. All suspended. I had not foreseen any of this.

Clerks and runners, tick-tack men with a line of chat that left us wheezing with laughter. All gone. I had brought mayhem to two hundred and thirty people in a country town and its surroundings. Joss Halpin's people.

I looked across at him. His tear ducts seemed to have no 'Off' valve.

How could I have been so blind? So vain? I had done something unthinkable. I had used my own hurt to hurt others. Unthinkable. An utter immorality. Some of those people would never work again. No redundancy money. No compensation. I had not foreseen any of this.

Look, too, I told myself, at the bind I placed myself in. The story was true. If I had known it – should I have told it? Looking for it in order to use it was as bad as inventing it.

When Ross went, I wanted to die. Now I had that feeling again. Almost as much. Almost. Not quite.

As these thoughts ran through me like scalding, molten metal, survival cooled me. But I well knew when thoughts were settling in to attack me for a long time. I had had experience of that. Fighting back is the only option.

I said to my father, 'I have a question for you.' The moment I opened my mouth he always listened and he listened now as never before. During my 'return' I had become so accustomed to saying nothing that my voice had dropped half a register. Not now. I asked him, 'Do you still have your licence?'

He said, 'No, girl. We have to re-apply for them. We'll get them if we're in the clear.'

I said, 'You're going to re-apply.'

'Ah, I can't.'

I said, 'You'll make the comeback of all time.'

'Ah, I'm not Arkle.'

I said, 'You're nearly as popular. You'll see. They'll flock to you. And I'll do it with you. You always wanted that.'

'No, girl.'

I said, 'I believe we can earn back, so to speak, a huge amount of what we've lost. Prestige I'm talking about. People love a fighter, a survivor. You'll be cheered, not blamed.'

My father straightened in his chair. 'Well, this might make Mammy sit up.'

Then he looked desperately embarrassed. He wanted to say something to me. He couldn't. I felt it was about Ross.

I poured him more brandy. 'This', I said, 'is going to be perfectly straightforward. When they let you, you take a stand at the first local race meeting.'

My father gave a kind of gurgle and stood up. 'I – I have to go to bed.'

I sensed that his embarrassment was too great for him to handle and I said no more. He walked away and I watched him. At that moment I began the forgiveness of him. Even if he was the one who gave me away. To a man who only once in his life called me 'Ann'. In the wedding vows. 'I, Joseph Patrick Martin, take thee, Ann Elizabeth Halpin.'

That night I was mistress of my own house and in command of all under my own roof. I had recovered – or begun to recover – my father. Natural life began to flow again.

As yet, I had not retrieved Mother. My hope had been that in such extremes she would turn to me. No, she had turned further and further away from me.

Richard came through the window again and lay beside me in the dark. He never spoke, just held me

343

and held me. I did not care if Agnes – or my father
– discovered him in the morning. He left on the pillow a sprig from the big sycamore. I have pressed all
those mementoes and Richard smiles when I show them
to him.

51

My passion was bound to come to a poor end. I am devastated. I have not yet absorbed the news fully and I have not yet had time to check it. But it has the knell of truth. The old, threatening sadness has begun and I know that I must occupy myself very soon with something intensive; otherwise I shall not be able to bear what has happened.

Ann has remarried. She has married the man with whom she is apparently besotted, an unconventional American; the marriage has been held in secrecy; her family do not know.

I tried this afternoon to make an appointment with Dr Verne's friend in Dublin, Dr Bourke, but the secretary told me he was in the States and would not return for two weeks, and I fear I said to myself, 'Anything can happen in two weeks.' I think I shall ring Father for moral support.

This is how I found out. I was standing in the doorway of Mr Cantwell's hardware shop having stopped on my way to meet my mother's flight at Shannon. Ann drove by – again noticeably fast – and Mr Cantwell, gazing after the car, said, 'Off to see the husband, I suppose.'

I stood absolutely still and forced myself to ask, 'Who is she?'

'She's that Halpin one. She's after coming down in

the world. You know that IRA bookie they arrested? She ran away from him. She's after marrying a hobo, an American fella, a darkie, he lives out in the fields near Deanstown Castle. They did the job up in Galway. The family don't know, her mother'd go mad.'

As if I didn't quite catch what he said I asked, 'I beg your pardon?'

'There's a very bad story there, y'know. A missing kid. Very bad story it was, and a story that's still bad, they're a bad crew' – and he was about to say more when a customer approached the door.

I walked away and could hardly find my car because my eyes were full of tears; I wept for most of the journey to the airport. Had the incoming flight not been late I should have had difficulty composing myself. My mother, my egocentric mother, tells me that I look marvellous; had I had an amputation since we last met, I do not believe she would have perceived it.

Tonight, alone, with my mother asleep upstairs, I do not know where to look; I do not know how to speak; I write frantically in my journal; I pace this floor. All I have worked for, all I believe in, all I have built towards – gone, gone completely. The old feelings of confusion appear over the horizon. What has all that preparation been for – the move to this house; my emotional muscle-building; my spiritual efforts; my rejection of drinking and of my old way of life – are they all irrelevant? I have lost the chance of winning the woman I love. Worst of all, I have the dreadful feeling of failure – I should have approached her, I should not have been so dilatory. Only the brave deserve the fair.

I know as surely as I have ever known anything how right she was for me; every inclination of her head, every sense I have ever had of her: this was not an infatuation, this was a truth at work, a deep, full truth, and I have now lost my way again. The principal voice inside me whimpers. No original idea sustains, nor can a line of thought continue unbroken without the pain scorching me. I feel like glass that is constantly breaking.

My mother's presence makes it all worse. She is more difficult than I ever expected. But then, since university I have never spent more than a day or two under one roof with her. Perhaps the difficulty of coping with her will distract me from this pain. Tonight I had to try and prevent my mother from destroying my place in the neighbourhood here. She walks among them like a jewelled stork and treats them as though they were serfs.

I also have to prevent her from making throwaway remarks about me, little denigrations which might well dent their opinion of me. The blueness of Mother's blood is the problem, a difficulty I share with Father. When she stepped from the car, she looked at my house and said, 'Oh, a peasant's cottage.'

This was not a joke; she meant it and I know she cannot help this. What does one do if one grew up with fifty servants and a ballroom where they had invented a game they called 'soft cricket' for winter days? Still, I escape lightly; I should not forget how Mother introduced my cousin to someone with the words, 'This is William, he appeals to a certain kind of woman.'

I do not know how wealthy we are, how much riches my mother and the family trust represent – and I do not want to know. Apparently I receive nothing until both parents have died, and I refuse to feel dangled on such a morbid string. She is so irritating! She said tonight how she resents that I no longer drink. I cannot understand it; I thought she would be pleased about the implications for my physical and emotional health. But

– 'No,' she cries, 'I cannot trust a man who doesn't drink!'

I managed to overcome her somewhat tonight – although it took a houseful of people and a charming stranger to do so. We – I – accepted an invitation to Martin Ryan's house; his father is eighty this week and he raised a family of musicians. The music here has a ring to it, and they dance to it on the stone floor of the farmhouse; they tell me the experts can tell by the dancers' steps which parish they come from. Seen objectively, this reaches me most oddly; most of my Irish society up until now has been in Ulster with the army, or among old friends who belong in the Unionist camp where they seem to have little or no such traditions and seem embarrassed when I raise it, although some have said to me privately how they love the music. Seen subjectively, had Charles been here to witness me attempt the dance steps, then we should have had much talk of 'going native'. I can always quell him (as I failed to do my mother) with the presence at the party of Martin's youngest son, a very anglified stockbroker with Lazards.

An idle thought came to me as I watched their dancing and relished again their hospitality: how shall I present Ann to my Ulster friends when the moment comes? She may know the locals here already – but the Sandhurst men? And Charles? The thought made me smile, and then it made my mind quail; it will not happen. It will not happen! She is *married*.

But I am unable to think of her as in the past or the never-to-be – and a different thought followed. I thought that before I could be ready to meet Ann fully, to offer her a life with me, I would have to change part of the attitude my mother threatens to engender in me.

She makes me feel, I think, colonial – as if my being

348

here echoes those in my family who helped govern India. What a good thing that none of my ancestors – so far as I know – ever misbehaved in Ireland. It strikes me now the same colonial attitude hangs about Charles somewhat. He is always too prepared to grasp at the Irish stereotypes of drinking, racing and general roguery, nor does he listen too closely when I point out to him that the reality is much deeper, darker, and, as he knows, often lethal.

I have come, I realize, to dislike this shorthand view of Ireland with which I grew up (even though the stereotypes here so frequently prove so true!), but I have coped with it well in Charles. Father has so little partaken of it that I never thought of it while he was here: it took my mother to crystallize for me a notion whose presence has been in the back of my consciousness for some time.

This is the thought. The man who sits by this fireside tonight writing in this notebook (i.e., me) is not some gentleman landowner with leather patches on the elbows of his jacket, who walks the fields and the woods in the expectation of deferential nods from his tenants as they pass respectfully by. Nor is he an anthropologist, loftily studying the natives and reporting back to the Royal Geographical Society. He is a foreigner in a foreign land.

The party: my mother enjoyed it and she almost behaved. I did overhear her saying how marvellous her Irish cleaning lady had been, and how her husband always said Irish nurses were the best, and how her father had a 'wonderful puckish Irish groom, completely untrustworthy, of course. Pa always said he couldn't take his eye off him. And of course he never washed!'

Oh, God, my mother! Were she making these remarks at home she could be indicted for racism. But they laughed at her in an amiable way and then she met the friendly stranger. He is the Coroner, he took a shine to her and she to him; he proved her equal. In order to keep an eye on her – because still the bad memories attack me, and I do not want her personal history repeating itself under my roof or aegis – I have invited him to lunch tomorrow: better than him inviting her to lunch.

I can feel a physical pain in my chest tonight but I know it cannot be organic.

52

Joey, Ross, St Heber's, the Mountgoldens – all that has
happened to me has done one odd thing to me. I see
myself taking stock all the time. Every day I am conscious
of looking at my clothes on their hangers. I know how
many pairs of shoes I have, twenty-three. If I had to go
upstairs now and put my hands on my best high heels I
could find them blindfold.

What is that stocktaking in me? Control? The control
I never had over my life? I have it now. But I try not to
hurt anyone with it. I wish – well, I wish about Mother
mostly.

Within a short time she gave me no sign ever again
that she heard me speaking to her.

She gave my father no sign.

She gave no sign to anyone.

Her physical health had not deteriorated and Dr Butler
said he found no diagnosable difficulty. She just did not
respond.

'Mother,' I said, 'has Daddy told you? We are going
to put him back on the racecourse. When all this is over.
We are going to get it all back.'

One afternoon she rose and paced by the window.
Never spoke. Never looked in my direction. She said
nothing to no one. I asked the nurses and they told me
she never spoke to them.

My father found it unbearable. He wheezed and fluttered.

'Girl, she won't say nothing. 'Tisn't that she hasn't a word to throw to a dog. 'Tis that she won't say anything.'

She bewildered him.

Joey, believe it or not, rang. But to speak to Mother, not to anyone else. I told him about her. Asked him would he come down and see Mother. He said he'd think about it. He never came. It was the briefest conversation he and I ever had. Which is saying something.

I asked the nurses. They told me a man rang and they put his call through to her bedside telephone. She never picked it up.

I suppose I guessed she wouldn't speak to him. Her pattern had already been established too deeply. For weeks we tried things. Gifts. Newspaper cuttings. Items of gossip. No. No response of any kind. We reached the conclusion that she had chosen this path.

I decided to bring her home. Agnes and I discussed it.

'Tell her you can't afford the Nursing Home,' said Agnes. This was one of Agnes's efforts to extract information obliquely. Agnes is very good at that.

'I will,' I said, not biting, not giving anything away. Because I had money, lots of it. After all, it was Joey from whom I learned about siphons.

Without a difficulty Mother rose, dressed, walked from the room, down the stairs and climbed into the car. She looked neither to right nor left as we drove home. To her surroundings as we arrived she gave not a glance. I led her through the front door of my house to the room she would sleep in. All those rooms had their own bathrooms.

She never left that room again. Nor did she ever speak. We began to feel that we had a ghost in the house. I have never known anything so eerie.

I consulted a psychiatrist in Cork. Could the shock of losing everything have done so much to her?

'She's catatonic,' he said. 'That level of response is unusually intense. Is there anything else that might trouble her?'

I suggested that she might never have mourned her grandson. That she had never condoled with me.

'Possible. Possible. Do you want me to see her?'

I said no. He was too pompous – and the only help I needed was for me, how to cope with my own guilt. I believed I created the ghost that Mother became.

Therefore I flung myself into my father's enterprise. It took a lot of persuasion in the beginning. He was shy of contacting old friends and cronies. Three months had passed since the night Joey was arrested.

'But what'll happen when the case comes up?' he kept asking me plaintively. Eventually he got hold of the spirit of the thing and began to believe that he would be back on the racecourse again. He amazed me, my father, and I learned something huge from him. Life did not touch him deep or hard. He did not let it. His mechanisms were foolproof. For instance, he dealt with Mother superbly.

Every day he took her a lunch tray and every evening a single glass of brandy. He talked to her all the time. She never answered. It didn't stop him. He chatted about this and that. Never about our project. I had asked him to be careful and he was. Then, every day, he felt free in his conscience.

He could say to me each night, 'Well, girl, I've done my best for Mammy today.'

I said to him once, 'Shouldn't we be getting specialists to see her?'

His reply came out of his life-mechanism. 'I'd say, girl, that Mammy has taken her own decisions. Who are we to question them?'

Richard became a different kettle of fish. When I was with him I spent the whole time lying in his arms. He gave me no choice. Richard had become a child. He threw tantrums. Something in him had changed, too. Some kind of fear had hit him. When he was calm he was at his tenderest to me, and when he was troubled I was at my tenderest to him.

53

I was standing at the door looking at the woods when my mother came down to breakfast this morning – looking radiant.

'Such a lovely man, your friend,' she said.

I watched them carefully; my 'friend' – she means the man we met last night at Martin Ryan's, the widowed (as he stressed) Coroner for Mooreville 'and District', as he added. They flirted outrageously, he and my mother, and I feel distinctly conscious of guarding Father's interests; I actually find myself using the word 'Dad' to her, a term I have not used since school.

I want to exorcize the past, which is part of the reason for inviting my mother to stay, but every time I try to have a serious conversation with her she darts away, sometimes physically, always mentally. She can slip from a conversation like a fish in a stream; I cannot pin her down, much less impale her upon the words I wish to unload. I begin to wonder whether I should say them at all, whether this might not be a regressive step.

Mid morning, I came up with what I think was a good solution and inasmuch as it seemed to relax her enormously it must have worked. She was sitting at the table and talking about her mother, my grandmother, whom I never met – friend of the Astors and all that set.

'She had this ivory necklace, darling, so heavy she

could hardly lift it and one of her admirers said he would never take her out unless she wore it and she referred to him as "Rheumatic Jeremy", because every time she went dancing with him she claimed the necklace gave her rheumatism.'

'There is something I want to say.'

I spoke the words very quickly and clearly; I hoped my voice sounded like metal.

'I must just get my – ' and with fear in her face she made to rise.

I clasped her arm and she sat down, looking frightened.

'This is all I want to say. It is all – all right. All right. Do you know what I mean?' She looked so blankly at me that I had to say it again. 'It is all right. I mean – everything, all that, it was, well, it doesn't matter what it was, it is over. It is gone into the past.'

To my astonishment, but oddly enough not to my horror, I had tears in my eyes. She took my hand and held it and we looked at each other for a moment and we looked away. I am faced with a horrifying thought – she did not know what I was talking about. I must accept it as quite possible she has forgotten the moment I walked into her bedroom, still wearing my school blazer.

And so the Coroner came to lunch: I was right to invite him for safety reasons; he had offered her lunch but this way I am able to keep an eye on them both. She was funny and girlish and playful; that they found each other very appealing was proved beyond doubt within minutes. He mocked her Englishness, which took her completely aback – 'I suppose you're not that far from being a Duchess' – and, further discommoding her, asked her whether she had read my pieces in the paper. This was his tactic, to fluster her, which he did – especially when he asked whether she had read the Graves piece, but she recovered quickly and told him, 'Christopher's father does all that reading and he paraphrases everything for me.'

Public officials in Ireland are different; they perceive the philosophy of their positions; they view themselves not merely as the servants of the populace but as commentators on what they do. The Coroner for Mooreville and District is voluble and philosophical; Desmond Hickey is his name, a solicitor, a man of seventy years and more; he has been a coroner since he was twenty-eight; he inherited the job from his father.

'We're interesting people, coroners,' he said. 'We do our jobs there in the edges of people's lives. For one bit of a day, and sometimes for several weeks, what we say – or what we're likely to say – is going to matter extraordinarily to people. You'd think to look at us we have no power, but we do, we have nearly the biggest power of all, we have the power of verdict. Think of that word, Mr Hunter – ah, what, I'll call you Christopher, we're not strangers in this country – "verdict". Are you a Classics man yourself? Because if you are you'll enjoy the root of that word, "ver – dict", to speak the truth. "A good speech is good but the verdict's the thing." That's what Daniel O'Connell the Liberator said.'

I asked him if he finds giving verdicts difficult.

'No, not at all. "Speak as you find and a base man will avoid you." That's all.' Then he picked up my thought. 'My wife used to say I missed my vocation, she used to say I should have been a dictionary of quotations.'

My mother said, 'Christopher's great-uncle was a judge in India.'

'Bad cess,' said Desmond Hickey. 'I bet he hung a lot of people.'

357

'Oh, he was always hanging people for one thing and another.' And missing the point she radiated at him. 'Have you ever hung anybody? Tell us.'

'Pheasants. They have to be hung for a few weeks.' He turned to me and he said, 'That was a very unusual piece, that missing officer, I mean, if you'll excuse me, very unusual from an English journalist. I often thought of that, you know, the sacred things, the Book of Kells and the Ardagh Chalice and that being buried, but I never made the link with Partition. The First and Second Battles of Moytura, that's when it happened, and aren't we still fighting?'

She: 'Why are the Irish always fighting?'

He: 'Now what are you saying? The English have made war on every country in Europe. You're a nation of belligerents.'

I said, 'I like that it, the Partition thing – I like that it is taught as fact.'

He said, 'Burial is a big thing with us. We bury everything. Listen to how often we use the word: "I buried my fist in him." Or you'll hear a man saying in a fight, "I'll be dug outa you", or the commentators talk about a footballer who "buried the ball in the back of the net". Burial is always a big symbol in a country where the land is what matters.'

Upon which I reflect tonight: I am living by symbols; I have fallen in love with a woman whom I begin to see in the same mythic light as I see the country itself, and I have worked on two secret-burial stories as if trying to unearth some fundamental spiritual truth about this bizarre country where paradox is as everyday as drink.

To see it in a deeper symbolic light, I have long desired and pursued Ann Martin as the people whose activities I report have long desired and pursued Irish unity, or so

358

they claim. My cynicism, however, does not permit me to credit them with a longing for wholeness in the way I have longed for it. Was it Plato who talked about 'the desire and pursuit of the whole'? I cannot remember; I must look it up.

The Coroner talks non-stop, deceptively and swervingly; only by listening closely did I grasp that he is a man of enormous erudition and cunning; he might have come straight out of Trollope; and he kept me on my toes because suddenly (again reading my mind) came the question: 'Are you spiritually interested in burial? Because if you are, you should also be interested in archaeology. Or exhumation – and I wonder how much time must have elapsed before exhumation becomes archaeology?'

As I have found so often, the broad, rather flat accents of these parts mislead one into thinking the people are rather slow.

He then proceeded to tell me a story whose lack of credibility at first glance led me to believe it completely; this has happened to me many times; you hear something; you think, 'That's a touch far-fetched'; and whenever I have followed such a story it has led to a good professional experience.

Divided channels of feeling run fast inside me tonight. Upstairs my mother lies asleep in her eye-shades. I sit here, notebook on knee, and I have all the peace and comfort I want, with the foxes and the owls in the depth of the night outside the window; in darkness the wood takes on a watching presence. And my heart is breaking because nearby somewhere, within a few miles of my home and hearth, is the woman I had hoped to see sitting here across from me, the flames throwing shadows on her face – but she is married to another and must be lying in his arms. I try and try to put it out of my mind, I try and try to hold on to my aspiration, but the dreadful question returns: 'What is the point? Why don't you face the fact that she is gone. Gone.'

Back to lunch today; Desmond Hickey said, 'Talking of exhumation, since you seem to have made something of a speciality of secret burials [he pronounced it in the old way, "speci*al*-i-ty"], would you be interested in a local story?' It seemed to give him some discomfort.

I asked rather flippantly, 'Is it dangerous?'

'I'd say the teeth were drawn by now.'

'What's it about?'

He said, 'Did you ever hear of the Russell case?'

'No.'

'Famous case. Famous case. Imprisonment took place in that instance.'

'Is this, I mean – Russell? Is there someone in prison?' I was getting confused.

'There is but there's not. And it isn't Russell this time. One name is O'Connell and the other is Martin.'

For no reason that I know, my skin now prickles as I write down our conversation. I have apple wood burning, lovely aroma.

Desmond Hickey went on, 'The Russell case was in nineteen and twelve, and there was a case since then up in Monaghan, I think. But you'd have to get an exhumation order.'

I asked, 'Can one do that?'

'I'd sign it maybe. It is a bit tricky. There's only two ways in which you get exhumation orders, the first is if you have family rights, and even then that's very difficult. And the second is if you can prove that 'tis in the public good, and I have to say this crime, if it is a crime, comes into that category. It certainly is an offence to conceal a burial or its details in any way.'

I said, 'You've lost me. I am completely lost. Can you begin at the beginning?' But live wires touched inside me. And they are crackling now.

He grew more uncomfortable.

'I heard about it a few years ago, when it is supposed to have happened. If I'd heard anything official, I mean, I'd have had to do something. I mean, I did hear something, but 'twas only talk and there's always talk around here, you know that yourself. I shouldn't be talking, 'tis the congenial company that's doing it to me. Loosening my tongue.'

And he smiled at my mother, then changed the subject. I made coffee and left them talking. Eventually, though, he wove a path back to the story.

'I mean – I heard the same talk as everybody. There was talk that there was trouble in a family and that a child was taken away and for reasons of a complicated inheritance they said the child was dead, and the family paid for another dead child to be put in the coffin in its place.'

I said, 'Can that be possible?' and then I said, 'But that's probably too local for me.'

'Darling, don't be silly,' said my mother. 'Don't you remember what Beaverbrook used to say: "People want to read about people." Don't be silly.'

Just like my mother to explain to me the principal tenets of my profession. She puts on this little-girl voice as if about to flounce her skirt like a three-year-old can-can dancer – but I could tell she was genuinely interested and it was rare for my mother to be interested in much beyond herself.

He said, 'It is only a story. There's no proof' – he knew instinctively how to get me interested.

'OK. What exactly happened? And if so, how can I

361

go about getting an exhumation order? I can make a story out of that. But my editor will ask me why am I so concerned with burials, do I have a death wish or something? And where can I find the people who did it?'

Direct questions often relax people; Mr Hickey grew a little more comfortable and said, 'If you can find the full story and come to me and say there's a gross injustice that's been carried out, then I will listen to you.'

'Do you know', I asked, 'where the grave is?'

'I do. I do. But I'm not telling you yet, because if I get involved at all I have to get involved the whole way. But I'll give you one piece of comfort. You've come to the right man, because there's thirty-one firms of solicitors in this town servicing a population of about fifteen thousand people all told in the whole hinterland across the half of two counties, and I'm about the only one that family never gave any business to. So I'm free to speak.'

Aha! Greed, one way and another, is the best motivation for any source. 'How can I advance it?'

'I have a son a solicitor in Dublin. He'll eventually come down and take over my practice, I suppose. And he has a client, big client too, in big trouble. A man who wants to get things off his chest. That often happens when people get into trouble.'

'Do you want to tell me the full story?' I smiled. 'Should I reach for my notebook?'

He said, 'I'll have to ask my son.'

'Ring him,' I urged.

'I know he's at home anyway,' he said. 'Sunday lunch-time is a great time for getting hold of people.'

I watched him limping down my living-room; what is brewing here? Why am I tingling? I don't know, but I know I am going to pursue it.

My mother leaned across the table. 'Such an intelligent man,' she cooed. 'And he likes you.'

If I am to get on with her I have to allow her dishonesties; what she really meant was that she hoped he liked her.

Desmond Hickey returned. 'Nice room your office. Very nice.'

'Well?' we both asked.

'Yes. But you have to be quick about it. For reasons I can't say. My son will tell you, but 'tis off the record until he gives you the go-ahead. But you'll be on to something bigger than I'm telling you.'

'How much bigger?' I asked.

'Political. Here's the phone number.'

We sat for two hours after that and he regaled us with stories of local society; of the mad Ulvertons, as he called them, of old land feuds, tales of the Civil War. I returned to the exhumation story; it has truly snagged my imagination.

'Why didn't, say, one of the mothers involved – especially of the replaced child – why did she not act?'

'She didn't know. She doesn't know to this day. They never told her. You'd be amazed what everyone knows and nobody says. I had a client here in this little town, in this little town! Three thousand people. He was a bigamist. Everyone knew it except the two wives. Nobody ever told them. People enjoy knowing that kind of thing. It gives them a secret and a secret is power.'

He took his hat and left. My mother was clearly enchanted with him. I have to say I feel relieved that they probably will not meet again for some time.

54

A memory of Janey. I was ten and she knew I was always bumping into things, but she never called me awkward. One morning I spilled a whole large jug of milk, every drop. I was wearing a tartan skirt with a big safety-pin, like a kilt.

Without a scold, Janey mopped up and said, 'Ann, I forgot to tell you. I was at a wake last night, the Connors woman.' Then she regaled me with the drink, the talk, the songs – and the coin in the mouth.

'When I'm dead, Ann lovey, put a coin in my mouth won't you?'

I looked amazed and she said, 'To pay my way when I get to the next world.'

Mother died of a stroke. We had expected it. And we had not expected it. She ended her catatonic state with a gasp.

She never communicated with me again. Even though I brought her breakfast most mornings of her life she gave me not a word, not a look. She lay there white as a spectre. Or sat in a chair fully silent.

I find it all difficult to believe. She died six months to the day – an exact anniversary of the Mountgolden dinner party.

Halpin's: We're the Best Bet!

She died at eleven in the morning, standing by the

364

window, beautifully groomed and made-up by me and Agnes. Despite her resistance we had decided weeks earlier to make sure she bathed every day. Had her hair done. Was made-up. Then dressed as well as she could be. A clean nightdress every day, and a fresh silk robe. She had dozens of such things to wear. The Nursing Home gave her an extra wardrobe.

There she was. In her best silk night set. Clear and white. Agnes had almost finished with the bed. She was chatting to Mother. As we all did. Speaking meaningless words into that void. Unprecedentedly Mother climbed out of bed. Then Agnes heard a choke, a cry. Mother leaned forward, then fell back. Landed on the bed. She was dead by the time she fell.

I knew it was happening. I was in the kitchen and I ran. Not that I had heard Mother make a sound. Agnes had not yet called. I heard Mother's gasp and I saw Mother falling. Stood in the door and saw her falling.

Falling. Falling. Falling.

My first thought was, 'She's dead. She's definitely dead. What have I to wear to the funeral?'

My second thought was, 'I'll never get her back now.'

My third thought was, 'Momma, Momma, Momma.' That was what I called her when I was very little. It is what I called out to her when I was in St Heber's and she never came to see me.

The 'Jesus-what-have-I-done?' did not come until later. Agnes and I rushed to her. But we knew she was dead. So did my father who stood in the door at that moment, filling the light.

He simply said, 'Is Mammy gone, girl?'

Oh, my poor father. My poor, poor father. He knelt, took Mother's hand, pressed it to his cheek, said nothing.

I watched, frozen to the wall I leaned against. He wiped his tears with her dead hand.

That was the moment I learned that women of any age have a last issue of blood from the womb. It will not happen to me. At that moment, too, I became myself for the first time. I no longer stood outside myself watching. I became me.

I did go to Mother's funeral. But the argument with myself was fierce. I argued that I could not face it. That I would collapse at the grave. That my very life was endangered by her death. That this was my closest tie with life.

If Ross had been alive, I told myself, he would have been my reason for living. I had kept myself alive waiting for Mother to return to me. So that we could be as before. Loving conversations. Quiet, fond talks.

How I tried in that ghostly bedroom. Every day I told her something new. Every day I mentioned a designer she liked. I sought gossip for her about fashion and took clippings from the papers and from magazines. I brought her nail varnishes and scents. Ordered manicures and pedicures for her, her own coinage. But I could not keep her alive.

I had killed her. Therefore I must have killed her love. That is why she died. That is what I told myself. Another busload of logic arrived behind that one. I must therefore have killed her love all those years ago. It was all my fault. Joey, everything. I attracted all that.

Down and down went the spiral of despair. I remember a medical dictionary I saw in school. We looked up syphilis. It described an infection that worked like a corkscrew. Something similar got into my emotions the day Mother died.

A saviour arrived – my father. In the car on the way

to the cemetery he said, 'You're the boss now, you have to run things. Your Mammy always ran everything. It didn't look like it, but she did.'

Nobody of Mother's circle came to the funeral. None of the people to whom Mother had spoken once a week, once a day – none came. Her 'friends'. No more than fifty people sat in the church and fewer than that stood at the graveside. A cottier's funeral would have more mourners. Nicky Crosbie and one or two of the old bookies were there. Agnes and Kevin. Some of my father's cronies and their wives. Oddly, I thought of Janey. I missed her funeral. She died while I was in St Heber's. Did anybody put a coin in her mouth? I don't know – secretly I put an old, gold sovereign, her own, in Mother's mouth. I wonder if the undertakers stole it.

Joey never showed. That shocked me.

My father and I stood there arm-in-arm. He kept looking across at Ross's grave. There are some occasions which pass us in a haze. As if we are protected from them. I almost fainted when I realized where Mother's grave was to be. The Beresford family burial plot.

My father asked me, 'What'll we do now, girl?' – just the two of us at supper; I gave Agnes and Kevin the evening off.

I said, 'We sit quietly. You wear a black tie for six months. I'll wear black clothes. I'll maybe go away for a few days for a rest. You read your paper. You go to Kiely's for your evening whiskey. We have all the preparation done. When our mourning has passed its worst points we'll get our plans finished and you'll get going again.'

'I'll miss her,' he said. 'We didn't always get on the best.'

'I didn't know that.' Which I didn't.

367

'I never said a thing about it, girl. That's my trouble. "Least said soonest mended." I shoulda spoke more. Maybe I'll start soon.'

I wondered should I tell him about Richard. Who was turning into an adoring man. Not placid – no, never placid – but very loving. But I could not, I found, tell my father. Instead I told him something else, an early memory of mine. I was wearing very shiny shoes with a strap held by a side-button and green stockings to the knee. My dress was green and yellow. I was playing with Noeleen McCarthy on the gravel at Grennanstown. She pushed me hard and I fell on the path. I wasn't hurt. But I burst into tears because the blood from my knees stained my stockings. Mother soothed me. She smiled and smiled.

I told her, 'Noeleen pushed me.'

She said, 'No, she didn't. You fell, Ann.'

I said, 'No, she pushed me.' She simply smiled more. Then shook her head and said, 'You're a bit of a cry-baby, Ann Elizabeth Halpin.'

That was in the days when she loved me. Or was supposed to.

My father listened. Then he said, 'She was always worried you were going to dye your hair.'

We both laughed. Then he hesitated and when he spoke it seemed difficult for him. 'Any day now, girl, fairly soon, you and me, we'll have a long, long talk. We'll talk 'til the cows come home.'

I know it feels indecent to say so, but Mother's death improved our lives. Within days the house took on a new atmosphere. I am reluctant to say that we did not miss Mother. We did miss her. But not as fiercely as I feared. In fact the relief of her absence is still with me. That was how it was then. After a few weeks I found myself lighter of heart. Richard noticed it in me.

'Easier life, Doll?'

'I expect I'll be hit by sadness soon, Rich.'

'You won't. You've had all your feelings. They were bad, too. And she isn't here to hurt you.'

I did not want to believe him. But it was true. I had experienced all my grief through the remorse I felt over engineering their collapse. That fear and grief was the capsule that contained all my mourning. Richard was right. Poor Richard. So loving. So impotent. He would not talk about it.

Twice a week I went to him and lay in his arms. He did not want to see me more than that. Did not want to be reminded of his impotence.

The new peacefulness most affected my father.

Agnes said to me, 'Your father's a new man. Don't think I'm being critical or anything, Ann. I mean of your mother. But isn't he different?'

I agreed. 'We'll find a nice widow for him one day, Agnes.'

To which Agnes replied, 'I hope whoever it is has never heard the saying, "Ah, sure every cloud has a silver lining."'

I laughed. 'Or, "Isn't it a long road has no turning?"'

Agnes said, 'Nice to see him so easy, though.'

I grew afraid it would evaporate, this new peace. So I took Richard to Galway. We walked the same beach. We called to the house we had lived in. It stood empty. We looked in the windows and remembered fond things.

55

It is Thursday night, and since Tuesday a number of lives have been changed totally and forever. This afternoon the mountains in their clarity and freshness and natural power seemed as near to the touch as the day I first stood there, the day of Ann's wedding. And then, too, the air was fresh as wine.

As a disciplined reporter, with no hyperbole, I shall simply set down the account of these past days as they unfolded.

I took Mother to the airport on Monday, the morning after Desmond Hickey and lunch. She seemed a touch subdued, and en route she said to me in an unusual timbre, 'Darling, I've never told you how much Daddy and I . . . How much we . . .' She stopped, unable to say something; she regrouped and tossed at me the remark, 'We talk about you all the time, darling.' Then she moved back into what I think of as her 'normal' mode – slightly *distraite* and fey and too brittle to get hold of without breaking something.

The following morning, this Tuesday past, I drove to Dublin to see the solicitor who is Desmond Hickey's son. He looks not at all like his father; he is a man who stands at an angle to the world, less distinguished-looking than his father.

Desmond Hickey Junior asked, 'How much has Daddy told you?' The intimate nomenclature surprised me.

'Not a lot. Is there a great injustice in situ somewhere?'

'Did he convey its nature to you?'

'The false burial?' I was being careful.

He looked at me thoughtfully, measuring how much he could say. 'Mr Hunter, this is how it is. I have a client out on bail at the moment. He's on a very serious charge. At times like that people often want to talk. In Ireland a solicitor is a bit like a country priest. Or a doctor.'

'Your father told me so.' I tried to curb my desire to ask a thousand questions. 'What is your client's name? What does he do? Is he a politician, your father said it would be political.' I still had no explanation for my eagerness.

He paused, then decided. 'It's a bit political. As it is known that I represent him I can, I suppose, tell you his name. I'd be grateful for your confidentiality for the moment. His name is Martin, Joseph or Joe Martin. And the other party is called O'Connell.'

I toughened a little. 'So far you have not told me much more than your father.'

He shifted. 'My client told me that, well, he had done something bad to someone. Very bad. To two people, actually. But you see – I have confidentiality to observe.'

He paused for a long time, looking at me as if inviting me to come to my own conclusions. However, I said nothing; I wanted him to go a little further, and he did.

'He lives here in Dublin. At the moment.' Then he paused again. 'I mean, he has a Dublin address, too.'

Time for me to press again.

'Does your confidentiality permit you to divulge his address?'

'Not a problem. It is already public knowledge. He's in the phone book.'

I asked Desmond Hickey Junior for dates and details but he would tell me nothing other than the address. 'I'm only confirming this address for you.'

He gave me the address; he spoke it, no piece of paper pushed across the desk, nothing to connect him with me.

'How soon should I act?'

'I'd say . . .' he paused trying to phrase it so that he gave nothing away – 'I'd say, soon. Soon.'

'Your father is the Coroner. He mentioned exhumation.'

'Not necessary.'

Essentially this is how I read the matter then, and how I read it tonight. Desmond Hickey and his son knew the client intended to skip bail. Their sense of justice in this matter was, as I now know, outraged, but they felt powerless: any information the son passed on would breach his fiduciary trust. The Coroner, who speaks to his son every day of his life, learned of the possible bail-jumping and, upon meeting me, reasoned that an experienced journalist might get a very good result. In essence they used me; in fact they used me well.

I left the younger Hickey's office and walked along the quays in a quandary but thinking clearly; this had to be handled on both the professional and personal levels; therefore I decided to go to the Irish National Library and do some brief research – and on the personal level I went to the office and telephoned my father. He was able to catch a flight that would have him in Dublin Airport by four o'clock. And he never asked why.

I found nothing in the local newspapers for the summer of 1975, no reports of children's deaths in the names of O'Connell or Martin; perhaps local papers do not carry the notices of children's deaths, but that seemed strange.

In the foyer of the Library I lingered a moment before a poster advertising next month's display of some early monastic illuminations on loan from the Stiftsbibliothek in St Gallen, Switzerland. As I made a mental note of the exhibition date I suddenly knew everything in a flash; my mind connected disparate pieces of information and a welter of excitement hit me like a wave that had been building and finally crests. Some confusion remained – I knew no families called O'Connell or Martin, but I felt certain this all connected with me and with Ann.

When I picked Father up at Dublin Airport I said to him, 'Thank you for coming over. What did you give as your reason?'

He said, 'My goodness, I don't think I've ever seen you so excited.'

I said, 'This is so complicated,' and I told him the essentials. 'Don't ask me why but I feel it has to do with – you know. With Ann.' He was the first person since Dr Verne with whom I had spoken her name.

He said, 'I told your mother you were working on a particularly delicate story, it's got a medical aspect and you need my help,' and he laughed.

'I am about to beard him. Do you mind waiting in the car?' I asked. 'I may need you.'

Thoughtfully he murmured, 'Appalling long-term implications.'

I parked the car more carefully than I have ever done. Father sat back, opened his newspaper and settled to a long wait.

The house is in a rich and quiet cul-de-sac. As I walked to the door the man I knew I had come to meet stood

373

inside his bow window looking at me. It was one of those moments whose shiver will stay with me forever. As a boy I once caught a small trout with my bare hands and then I felt it wriggle away. The sense of its flesh stays with me.

He answered the doorbell. 'Hallo?'

From my earlier impressions I expected something brasher. I put out my hand and he did not take it immediately; he looked at me hard but was already grasping the hand as I said my next words.

'I'm Christopher Hunter. I'm a reporter.'

He said, and I realized that I had never forgotten his voice, 'I can't talk to you. I'm not allowed to. I'm out on bail.'

'This is not about the charges you're facing.'

And he knew too. I know he did; his shoulders sagged in the relief and disappointment of truth. Then he recovered and with my awareness heightened by love and his awareness heightened by danger, we faced each other, each knowing what the other wanted. I was on autopilot, postponing all thought and feeling.

He led me to the room from which he had viewed me and closed the door firmly.

'Sit down.'

We did not speak for a moment; he paced, big, bulky, looming – even in what was not a small room. I waited.

'Do you want to report this?' He didn't look at me when he spoke.

I shrugged. 'I don't know.'

A woman called in a coarse Dublin accent; 'Joey, d'you want me to pack any more for you?'

Unfazed, he went to the door and said, 'I've somebody with me.'

I heard a sound like an imprecation.

Then he sat down facing me. 'How much do you want to know?'

He looked towards me without confidence and I fear I may have looked as if I might devour him. I regret to say that I loathed him; I did not mean to and I accuse myself of shallowness.

I began, 'The Halpin connection?' Crazy question if it proved wrong.

He blushed a deep red, for reasons I did not fully understand and he used a gesture I had seen him use to Ann on their wedding day, that plasterer-skimming-a-wall motion. 'In-laws,' he said. 'I married the daughter. I ran the family firm.'

My pen races as I write this down and I know that every time I return to these entries I will feel the same tremors. Then he stopped.

Newspaper of record: I asked, 'You married Ann Halpin and you had a son called Ross?' I had her name wrong all these years.

'Yep. That's the form.'

I said, 'Do you want to tell me the whole story? How you did it and why? And I certainly want to know where the boy is.'

He grew aggressive. 'Listen. I could throw you out of here.'

'And I could be with the police before you could be at the airport.'

He fidgeted strenuously, then he took a quick decision within himself, squared up to something.

'Look, if you keep names out of it I'll tell you the full story. This is what happened. Right?' He hit his stride as immediately as a well-rehearsed actor; this was a man, for all his loathsomeness, in some dreadful anxiety.

'I was hired by Joss Halpin to run his company and

I got on famously with him and his missus. The wife fancied me, right? She never said anything but you always know, right, women give a quick look at your mouth and that. They got me to marry the daughter, Ann. We never got on. I worked my bollocks off for them and she threatened to spend it all on herself and the kid. The kid was in line to get everything. She was tricky with the law, she knew things.'

He began to sweat heavily.

'The kid went wandering one day and his mother came looking for him. Her and I had terrible warfare going on, right? She got the impression the kid drowned and she passed out. Her mother and me got the idea, well, to keep her passed out for a few days, get us a bit of peace like, right? She was always sneering at us, made us feel like shite. The few days she was out of it, like, it was grand, right?'

Not only could I hear his words, I could see them in the air between us.

'We got the kid away that day, my old lady took him, right? When the wife woke up she went nearly buckin' mad, off the head altogether. The old doc who was lookin' after her, he said to us to put her in a home for a while, right? And then the whole shooting gallery got kinda stuck from there.'

My questions flew at him like ravens tearing with their beaks. What happened to the boy? Why had Ann never been told? How did they arrange the false funeral? Who was the other child? How was it covered up? Why was he telling it all now?

To this he answered, 'Because it don't matter now, we're finished, and the old lady's dead, so she can't come to any harm. She never done me down. Look, it went wrong on us, right? We played it up too much.

We said it was a private funeral and that. There was no funeral. We bought a dead kid offa its parents, paid them a buckin' fortune to have their kid as our funeral. That was to cover it over. I mean, we got the whole shaggin' thing wrong. Wrong! We figured that the mother, well, if she thought the kid was dead, she'd stay mad. If she didn't and say the hospital released her like, she'd come, find out he was dead and then she'd go off to America or something. She was like a cat on wires always.'

He finished, wan and lame. 'I mean, it was all shite, right? The others – they took their funeral way off up the country, at least that's what they told people, I mean, they got their kid buried properly, right, 'cause we had a priest an' everything. They said theirs was private, that the doctors told them to. Like as it 'twas polio or something. Right?'

I felt my shoulders as tight as steel but did not interrupt him.

'The whole thing got out of order and once we pretended the kid died, we whisked him away that very minute. So we had to keep up the pretence, and 'twas easy enough, people'll do anything for money. We paid the doctor for a death certificate. But the other crowd, they that had the kid who really died, they're gonna talk soon 'cause their money has stopped, right? They were being paid well every month. Paid cash.'

What about the boy's mother? Why had nobody told her? This made him most uncomfortable of all.

'A few times I nearly said it to her. Then I didn't. I s'pose I was always hopin' someone else would. I hope somebody will. I mean, she came back. We nearly went wild. We all thought she'd find out and we'd get jail. A letter came one day and it said she was comin' home, right? The mother handled the whole thing, maybe she told her.'

I reflected whether this was why Ann had remarried and my heart shook again – but he continued, 'She don't know, though, I mean, she don't know yet, right?'

I asked how he knew that.

'Well, you asked me where the kid is. He's here, he's upstairs, just after coming in from school. And she'd have come for him if she knew. I tried to ring her old lady in the hospital to find out whether we should breast the breeze and get the whole thing sorted. But she wouldn't talk to me nor to anyone.'

Where has the boy been?

'This is where he was always since then. A friend of mine, well, I'm married to her now, right? And my mother, like, they brung him up, right? He thinks his mother is dead.'

Is he well? Is he safe?

'Ah, yeh, he's grand, like, not a bother on him. Right?'

We both fell silent.

Next question. Surely some financial provision has been made for the boy?

'Yeh, there's a fund, a trust. She – I mean, her, like, she can take it over. Right?'

I asked, 'Look, I need all the details. Of everything. Not for publication, even though I will write them down.'

'What's the deal?' He had turned quite white.

'Deal? There isn't any deal you can do, is there? Or do you mean what happens now?'

He thought carefully, and reinterpreted my question.

'What do I want to happen now? I s'pose – I s'pose I want it all to come out for the best. I want her' – he never once mentioned Ann's name: the wrong he did her must have been too great for him to contemplate – 'I want her

to have her kid back. And I want to be out of it. I'm goin'
away anyhows.'

'Get the boy,' I said. 'My car is outside.'

'Hey, hold on – ' he stood up to protest.

I cut across him. 'Get him now. You don't have a
choice. If the boy does not come with me, now, this
evening, you don't get away. But I want the name and
address of the family of the real child, the one who was
buried.'

'Yeah, I'll give you the SP on them. Well, could it look
like, could you make it that it – that it looks like, if the
grandmother could take the blame? Right? If the story
ever gets out. 'Cause she's dead and it can't harm her. I
don't want my old lady rapped, right?'

'Where are you going and when?'

'The wife, job lined up in Libya. Good money.'

'And no extradition?' I said cynically; the IRA went to
Libya for weapons training. He had the grace to blush.

Would I be the one to tell Ann all this? Oh, how I
wished she had not remarried; these would have been
the perfect circumstances and I would have taken it
from God as a sign of faith, as a confirmation. My
rules would have been justified. Now it seemed as if I
would be involved but not gain the benefit I dreamed
of day and night; I am not yet so mature as to see pain
in terms of reward; on my own selfish level this was
heartbreaking.

I said, 'There may be no publication. It would not be
in your son's interest.' He must have thought me very
pompous. 'I will take the boy with me to his mother.'

'Do you know her?'

'Not personally.'

He looked at me and shook his head. 'Jeeze, that's a
handful, that woman is. Her father used to say they never

broke her. I've seen wilder horses broken in. I always felt I was dirty like, right? Any time I was with her, I thought I had shite on my face.'

He left the room and long, long minutes later, just as I was beginning to fear they had all escaped by the back door, his wife clattered in – hard-faced, dyed black hair, a demeanour like a rather tough, small man. She did not shake hands; she stepped aside to indicate a suitcase standing in the hall; she called his name: 'Ross!'

He came downstairs; he had been crying; my heart raced; he looks so like his mother and scarcely like his father – except for his build. I do not quite know what a boy of eight or nine should be like, but he is a meek boy; he shook my outstretched hand but did not look at me. The woman opened the door and the boy and I walked to the car; I feel now as I felt then – that this is not really happening, this is not reality. I glanced at my watch – it was twenty-five minutes past six. He was as vulnerable as a bird.

Father proved so warm. 'How do you do?' Ross scarcely responded to him and Father continued, 'I expect you would like to sit in front?' Ross changed direction without a word and went to the front passenger seat. This boy has had obedience pounded into him.

In the car, I asked him, 'Ross, has anyone told you anything?'

He did not answer, his face white and clenched; Father said comfortingly, 'We will talk about everything later.'

Father was wonderful with him, asked him his interests, told him stories of the war, they discussed television, with Father doing most of the talking; I needed all my concentration for driving. We stopped, Father's suggestion, to have a meal in Naas and as we walked through the hotel together Father murmured to me, 'Normality at all costs.' He told me tonight that he felt rather as if we were a gang of kidnappers!

Ross sat decorously at supper, though still pale, and when we drove away he began to fall asleep. I drove straight here to give us all time to readjust and discuss, and we got Ross to bed. Father slipped a teaspoon of Irish whiskey into a glass of hot milk to make him sleep. I should have taken some.

Next morning at eight o'clock Father brought me a cup of tea and said, 'We had better get things sorted out.'

I rang the Coroner, who came within an hour. When Ross appeared, Desmond Hickey's kindness to him brought tears to my eyes and when he turned to me I saw the old man was in tears too. I felt astonishingly mature, standing in my own living-room, directing matters, suggesting this, that and the other possibility. We made an arrangement; he would fetch Ross's mother. Only my years of journalistic training took me unscathed all through this, and tonight I mean to sleep the sleep of a drunken man.

After the Coroner telephoned, Ross, Father, and I drove to his house; when we got there Desmond told us that Ann had declined to come with him, but would arrive shortly. His housekeeper had prepared soup and sandwiches – none of us took any, apart from Ross. So far Ross had not spoken unless spoken to. We sat in Desmond Hickey's study at the back of the house, therefore could not hear a car arriving. All of us jumped when the doorbell rang and by arrangement – we had talked it through carefully – Desmond introduced me to Ann so that I could break it to her. (I have just remembered this was Father's idea.)

Am I able to summarize what I felt – at shaking Ann's hand for the first time, at looking in her eyes? I think not; besides, perhaps it is too private even for an intimate journal. I had not appreciated how tall she is; close up her face is far more beautiful than I had realized; her eyes show trauma. I am proud of the fact that I put my own responses and interests far behind those of her and her son.

The Coroner said, 'Ann, this is a friend of mine called Christopher Hunter, he's a journalist.'

Did she stiffen a little? Did she expect a trap – to discuss her husband's IRA connections?

'Mr Hunter has an extraordinary story to tell you, he has miraculous news for you . . .' and Desmond Hickey's voice faltered.

Ann looked confused and worried, perhaps fearful, and I began to speak. In my voice rang years and years of love, and if I have ever had a moment's doubt about my feelings for her it evaporated forever in that few minutes. Tonight I feel exactly the same as I did in the very beginning.

I said, 'I believe you were married to a man called Joe or Joseph Martin.'

'Joey,' she interrupted a hint grimly; in emotion Desmond Hickey had his teeth clamped on his lower lip.

'A big man,' I said, 'with black curly hair; he used to run your father's business.'

She nodded.

I said, 'I met him in Dublin last night and he told me that he conspired against you.' She sat back, alarmed. 'He and others gave you, or allowed you to take, the impression that your son Ross drowned in a pit at your home. They sedated you and had you certified as insane.'

'What are you saying? What are you saying?' She pressed her hands together in anguish.

I said very gently, 'Your son Ross never drowned. He is alive and well. He is in the next room.'

She stood up and sat down again, buried her head in her hands, saying, 'It can't be so, but I knew it. I knew it, I knew it! But if I said it who'd believe me?'

Ann stood again, unsteadily and neither of us men knew what to do. She turned away and dropped to her knees; I thought she meant to pray but she lay face down on the floor; we let her lie there for a moment and then helped her to her feet.

Desmond whispered to me, 'Time to bring the boy in.'

I remember the texture of the carpet under my feet; I remember the wood of the door; I remember the stone of the hall flooring, that old house; I still hear my voice speaking gently into the cluttered, long study, 'Ross, would you come here for a moment?'

We had not prepared him well, I think. None of us had known what to say to him. He had been sitting by my father and he rose obediently. I held out my hand, he took it and I led him to his mother.

I feared he might have forgotten her. Not at all. I said a silent prayer for them as Desmond and I stepped out to take the air. The last I saw of them at that moment was the boy's cropped auburn hair buried in his mother's white neck as she knelt to receive him.

We have spoken of nothing since, Father and I.

At breakfast next morning he said, 'It occurs to me that this may be the reason you conceived this passion, to solve this dreadful problem.' As I was digesting this remark, he added, 'I am inclined to believe it a rule of life that tragedy most harms those who cause it.'

We spent Wednesday recovering and today walking it off.

Desmond Hickey came to see us this morning. He said to me, 'This past two days I find tears in my eyes very often.'

Father and I both said, 'Same here.'

'But I thought the English weren't supposed to have any feelings, except for cats and dogs?' – and we laughed more than the remark merited.

A calm has settled over me; a wonderful calm; it feels like a renewal of faith. Father – I am so grateful to him – knew in almost every way what to do; to me this was an extraordinary matter and I suppose I had not expected him to feel likewise. And he has been quicker off the mark than me to raise the appalling questions regarding the emotional care of that little boy.

To think that this is my father – who has never once discussed the pain he must have felt at his beloved wife's affair with his best friend, pain on a daily, hourly basis for several years.

56

I have lost track of the time of all those days. Look at me
now, in a room with three clocks – one on the wall, one
on the mantel and one on this table. I used to think it was
only men who like clocks, but I have always liked them.
But I do not know the times of those days and I wish I did.
I can remember, though, that Mr Hickey's voice on the
telephone so early in the morning filled me with fear.

My first thought was the word, 'coroner'. Was the
post-mortem wrong? Sudden deaths around here have
to have a post-mortem. Had Mother taken poison?

Why this hour of the morning?

Why was the Coroner ringing me?

Why was the Coroner coming to see me?

Had I caused Mother's suicide?

Whatever Mr Hickey wanted I was going to pretend
to be busy. Agnes kept him waiting. Then she came in
and said he was very agitated. And excited.

'Good excited or bad excited?'

'Good excited, I think.'

'What in the name of God does he want, Agnes?'

Why was I so agitated?

He came in. I always thought him a bit of an old soak.
Very suave, very good opinion of himself. 'Likes the
ladies,' I thought. He was often in our house when I was
young. But I had never seen him here since I came back.

And then he came into the room. I was sorting out Mother's endless big brown envelopes. In them she had stored letters going back to girlhood.

And then he said, 'D'you remember your grandfather Halpin's house?'

I said I did. He said that there was an Englishman living in it now and did I know that?

I said I did, a journalist. 'He's supposed to be very wealthy.'

'I don't know about that at all,' said Mr Hickey, which surprised me, since the one thing he does know is how much money everyone has. Mother said he didn't like us because we never gave him any business. But Joey knew his son in Dublin. Maybe that was what all this was about.

'I want you to come out there with me now, out to your grandfather's house.'

I said, 'I can't,' and I knew I wanted to burst into tears but I didn't know why.

'Come on with me,' he said. Then he used the lawyer's phrase that I have always liked: 'And you will learn something to your advantage.'

'I can't today,' I said. But I knew I would.

'Oh, you have to. You have to.' He was pleading with me.

I thought, 'Isn't that what lawyers do, plead?'

'I won't.' I was getting into a state.

'Well, will you come to my house?'

'Maybe.'

'When? When?'

He made me promise to be there before two o'clock. He said, 'This is going to be the most important day of your life.'

But the remark didn't please me, it scared me. I went

and changed my tights. Then I cleaned my teeth. Again? And in the middle of the day? And I found that I washed my hands twice. Then I lay on the floor. Face down.

But I noticed I had started to take a different view of Mr Hickey. I had never liked him, and now I was feeling different towards him. But very frightened, not of him, just frightened.

Agnes said to me, 'There's something up, isn't there, Ann?' and her eyes were shining.

Agnes, as I am aware now, never knew the full story, but she suspected something. Mother made mysterious visits to no race meetings in Dublin. My father was in unusually bad temper when they came back. She saw Mother once filling in a child's birthday card and Mother got very furtive about it.

My father had a saying he hasn't used for years. 'We all know everything eventually.' How it must have haunted him.

I drove as slowly as anything. On the wide grav-elled entrance I parked the car and pressed the big, round, brass doorbell button. Every detail is stamped on my mind.

Mr Hickey came out and I was trembling. I could hardly stand up straight. He spoke to me very kindly and we went into his drawing-room. There is a painting, I think of his late wife, hanging in the hall. She is wearing a cameo brooch.

He went out of the room and brought another man in with him, a tall good-looking man, with a nervous face and very black hair, a thin man with long white hands. 'Face a bit like a greyhound,' I thought. He was wearing a suit made of corduroy.

Mr Hickey introduced us. Often I don't pick up

people's names first time. This time I did – Christopher Hunter. And I will never forget it.

I also know every word he spoke to me. Every word. I have remembered it all exactly.

He said to me, 'I believe you used to be married to a man called Joe or Joseph Martin.'

'Joey,' I said. Was this some trick? Had Joey discovered that I told the police and was this man trying to get at the truth? Would I go to jail? 'Oh, Richard,' I thought. 'Why are you never where I want you to be?' But Mr Hickey had said this would be to my advantage.

'He's a big man with dark curly hair, isn't he?' the Englishman, Christopher Hunter, said. I knew his face from somewhere.

Then he said, 'I met him in Dublin last night and he told me that he conspired against you.'

When I am really frightened the skin on my face behind my outer skin feels as if it is turning white. It stretches. I first felt that in St Heber's. No, I first felt it the day of the garden party.

What can one do? Where can one look? I needed Mother. I needed Agnes. I needed anyone. His accent is so, what, so cool . . .

'He, your husband, and others,' he sounded like a man being tactful, 'built up an impression that your son Ross drowned in a pit at your home. They sedated you and had you certified as insane. Is that right?'

My mind was falling apart. This is what it felt like when I woke up and found they had removed my womb. I think I screamed at him. It felt like screaming. 'What are you saying? What are you saying?' I thought my hands were going to fall off.

Then came the words I want on my gravestone. 'Your

little boy Ross never drowned. He is alive and well. In fact, he's here, he's in the next room.'

Ah, God! Ah, God! There is no way a mother, any mother, can cope with that. That was nearly worse than losing him first day. I stood up. I sat down again. My lips, my speech, they wouldn't work. And yet I was shouting, 'I knew it, I knew it, I knew it!'

And I did know it. I had always known it. But who'd have believed me if I said it? At that moment I knew too why Janey Little had died. Out of grief for me. Her heart was attacked with grief.

There was only one thing I could do. I lay face down on the floor. That was how I survived St Heber's. It was something Richard encouraged me to do if he saw me going off-beam.

But those two men, those poor, good men, they didn't know what to do with this woman lying on the floor. I let them help me up. Mr Hickey said something. The Englishman with his cool voice, I tease him about it now, went out and came back with Ross.

No angel ever came through a door so welcome.

I remember thinking, 'God, is that what he looks like?'

I remember thinking, 'Jesus, he hasn't changed at all. He's still my little Rossie.'

I remember thinking, 'That's a good, warm jumper he's wearing. Someone must have looked after him.'

I remember thinking, 'He's going to be as tall as my father.'

I remember thinking, 'His eyes, his darling eyes. He remembers me.'

And he was the most frightened of all of us.

I couldn't run to meet him, my legs wouldn't work, so I knelt to hug him. The men left the room. I hugged and hugged. Then Ross drew back and screamed at me. I didn't know what he said. He tried to hit me across the face.

I caught his hands. I wasn't hurt. Not physically or emotionally.

He tried to hit me again. He went a little bit berserk. He tried to kick me. He screamed and screamed.

Nobody came and then he calmed down a little. And again he buried his head in my neck so hard it hurt me. He said 'Mamma' a thousand times. I don't know how long we were there. I think we both fell into a kind of little sleep. How else could we cope?

57

Time passes; time has passed; I have not written in this journal for several months and I need to do so now in order to check whether I have changed, whether the earth is still turning. It may be, it may not be; I care not and yet I care more than I have ever done. I want no hurricanes, no earthquakes, no epidemics; my presence on this planet has suddenly become of massive importance to me.

Nothing is quite the way I expected it to be; it is more ordinary and more wonderful than anything I could have anticipated. During all those years of unrequitedness, during all those years of undeclared love, whenever I visualized meeting Ann, I expected the spheres to sing. What I did not know was that they would sing and they would not sing.

Love in practice cannot be anticipated; it is as much a matter of what you must not do as what you must. I must not tell Ann of the love in me for her. She is married and therefore I will behave towards her with the greatest decorum. She will not know how I feel about her and I will not try to interfere in her life.

I have met her 'new' husband and even though I have not changed my first impressions – he is weird, bizarre and brash – I find I can like him; I find I can deal with him and this is largely because of his tender kindness towards Ann and especially towards Ross.

My sense of decorum has not stopped me from becoming a friend as well as a neighbour and Ann is encouraging the friendship. She has said over and over, 'How can I ever repay you?' If she only knew how often the phrase 'I know of a way' has been on my lips.

But no – and therefore I have to perform heroic acts of concealment; I cannot tell her of seeing her in the Shelbourne, or of watching her walk along the canal bank, or on the road near Grennanstown House. Nor can I yet hear her story, although snatches emerge in conversation. I am trying not to see too much of her but she encourages me to visit and I feel I cannot refuse because, she says, the boy is forming an attachment to me.

I do take satisfaction from it all in many ways; I am a fortunate man; endlessly and freely I can study the woman I love; I can be near her, and something tells me that I must have good instincts – if instincts are the pulses to which the emotions beat. This is an exceptional woman, even allowing for my bias. She is far more cultivated than I expected, widely read, informed, cultured, refined in the old sense of the word, without any of the lower middle-class connotations 'refined' has nowadays. She is refined in a deep way and by that I mean in her inner demeanour, although I sense a toughness I did not expect. That must have come from her first husband and I ask myself over and over and over – 'What in Heaven's name did she see in him?' She never mentions him – just now and then I half-hear some remark about 'Ross's father'.

I watch her face; it changes as she speaks; she is uncommonly beautiful; that was Father's verdict, too, and he commiserated with me on not having got there first.

'But,' he said, 'look at the privilege you have been given – of improving someone's life. You will come to know the value of that. I still recall those patients whose lives I improved.'

I watch her movements; she is quite a deceptive woman – taller close-up than I had appreciated, as tall as me when she wears high heels. Her clothes are tasteful, too. I have seen only one drawback: one afternoon I called unexpectedly (people around here do that all the time; at first it drove me wild and now I do it myself). She answered the door but I found her so withdrawn I said I would call back. She did not invite me in and when I called next day it felt as if she never remembered that I had been there twenty-four hours earlier.

As for the boy – he has had his problems and very sensibly Ann has taken Father's advice and not let him go to school yet. He suffers, she tells me, terrible nightmares, wakes up screaming; on at least one day a week he still clings, literally, to her all day and will not let her go. Most of the time she has to be within his sight: for instance she cannot yet take a bath until she is sure he is asleep. In fact for the first week she had to go to bed at the same time as he did and leave her bedroom door wide open, as he also did. Then a swift race down the corridor, a quick shower and back to her room in case the boy woke up and found her not in her bed – which he had to be able to see from his pillow.

I observed one of his tantrums and found myself reacting with unexpected spontaneity. He came hurtling into the room in which his mother, her husband and I were sitting and screamed at her, 'Come away, come away from here, I want you, I want you!' He kicked furniture, lay on the floor and screamed.

The man, Richard, has emphysema and cannot easily move quickly enough to help and so I found myself on my knees beside Ross talking to him soothingly; he calmed down and took my hand after a while; when he had gone out again to the television room his mother showed me the mark on her arm where he had bitten her that morning.

Newspaper of record again: some more facts of what happened at their reunion. When we left the room where Ann and her son wept to and with each other, Desmond Hickey, Father and I walked in the garden and then found a sunny spot where we sat for some time. We did not quite know what to do and we spoke little. After about an hour Father suggested one of us approach them, see if their grief had overwhelmed them.

I volunteered and knocked on the door; no answer; I opened the door gingerly and Ann opened her eyes; Ross lay asleep, his head on her shoulder. I whispered, 'Are you all right?' and 'Food?'; she half-smiled a thank-you and indicated the sleeping boy. I left them alone. About half an hour later she came out to where we sat and asked the question that each of us three men said afterwards we found poignant – she said, 'Is it all right to take him home?'

I fetched the boy's suitcase. We made an arrangement that Father and I would call on her next day, and that was when we met Richard Huttle, the American who is her husband. He said almost nothing; his eyes are sunken deep in his head and his speech is quite difficult to understand. Father had a conversation with Ann, in which he suggested she have the boy checked by her doctor, just as an extra layer of reassurance as he put it. I joined in this conversation and dared to ask her (excitement was tearing at me like a gale at a sail) how she felt about it all, whether she had plans, into what shape did she think this would force her life?

The first problem she identified gave her considerable

difficulty: her father lived with her and he must have known the truth all along.

'How can I look at him again?' she asked.

'Perhaps,' interjected Father, 'he was not the master of his own life.'

'And of course,' she replied enigmatically, 'Mother is not here.'

'Your son is quite like you,' said Father.

She said, 'Now I have another problem. Ross and his own father. I don't know what to do about that. He gains me. But he loses his father.'

I asked, 'Are there other practicalities? What about school?'

Her husband, Richard: 'The kid is smart. He is bright.'

Father: 'You have this lovely, quiet neighbourhood for him to grow up in.'

Ann: 'He hasn't eaten anything yet. He's in front of the television now.'

Me: 'Are there boys his own age around here?'

Ann: 'I will never be able to thank you enough.'

Richard: 'Kids find what they need.'

Father: 'It will perhaps take a little time. And yet all will be settled probably faster than you think.'

Our conversation had pauses. Time after time Ross opened the door and looked in, as if to check his mother's whereabouts.

Ann: 'I find it all very difficult, somehow. To believe.'

Me: 'Did you truly believe he was dead?'

Ross entered: 'Mamma, can you come and watch this with me.'

Father: 'Is it a war film?'

Ann: 'I suppose, well, I can't tell. I would like to be able to say I knew deep inside of me. And it feels as if I did. But I'm now so mixed up.'

She left the room, tugged by Ross.

Richard: 'Any more drinks?'

Father: 'We must go.'

Later Father asked me, 'And you, Christopher? What about you?'

I replied, 'I don't know how to answer that. I suppose seeing her – I mean socially – is sure to bring me great benefit.'

Desmond Hickey telephoned and invited himself for supper, which I cooked; Father and he did not instinctively like each other; that had already become apparent. The conversation, however, as I recall it at this remove, centred on the legal implications and I could see that Father feared the Coroner would use the matter to advance his own reputation.

'But I have to exhume,' said the Coroner.

'What do you think, Christopher?' asked Father.

'What laws have been broken?' I asked.

'Registration of death was false. Entry in a burial register was false.'

'What benefit will prosecution bring?' I queried. 'It seems to me that the whole matter is simply resolved. Blame nobody but the dead mother. For the boy's sake avoid pressurizing the absent husband.'

'Yes,' said Father. 'We must prevent any further distress reaching the boy.'

'But the other family?' pressed Desmond Hickey.

I had not told him of their financial gain. 'They know,' I said.

'Ha! Conspiracy.'

I became a little heated and said, 'They lost a son tragically. Isn't that enough pain?'

'Were they paid money?'

Father intervened, a veteran, I realize, of medical

politics. 'What we need here is a civilized resolution. We shall enhance matters if all pain is allowed to subside.'

'But if the authorities get to know?' Desmond Hickey pressed.

I was proud of the way I clinched it. 'But you're an authority and you have known for some time.' Father complimented me later.

This morning I woke depressed again, a feeling that has not been around for some time, but unlike my habitual past the depression did not endure. Perhaps my roller-coaster has ended its ride and come to a peaceful stop.

58

The rain is pouring straight down. I went out to get some logs for the fire from the shed, I got my hair wet. That is something I hate. It seems to give me unpleasant memories. Rain or no rain, I have found these last few pieces of remembering very painful. But I don't try to stop myself any more if I want to cry. Two pages back there is a blotch on the page where tears fell.

Richard's condition is not good. Ross, thank God, strengthens day by day. Bees buzzed on Ross's first morning in this house. The kitchen at one stage was full of them. Agnes counted them.

'Ann,' she said. 'Seven bees. There must be a swarm somewhere.'

We opened the tops of the windows and they flew away.

Agnes could not stop weeping. Up to then I never thought she had very big tear ducts. I did her an injustice. From moment to moment I listened at the foot of the stairs. I wanted to be there when Ross woke up. There was plenty of time. He did not wake until noon.

'Ann, no heart is big enough not to crack over this.'

Dear Agnes. She had gone out and bought all kinds of cereals and sausages.

I had to tell her everything. That became my policy

– to tell everyone everything. I told her the whole story as I had gleaned it.

'But what about your father?'

He had gone to Goodwood, was due back that night.

'Ann, he knows. At least I'd swear he does. Kevin rang and said the boss was fierce fussed this morning. Somebody must have said something to him.'

I wanted more than anything to tell him myself. Because now I had a means of showing forgiveness.

'Agnes, tonight I want them back here. I don't care how late.'

'Didn't you think? Isn't that why your mother, God rest her, was always in the height of bad humour?'

Agnes can always turn a coin so that you see its other side.

That first day with Ross feels like the most wearing. Others have been worse and I know that. I couldn't wash myself. He waited outside the bathroom door every time I went there during the day. But that was not what I found wearing.

I could not think straight. I could not put together all the bits and pieces over the years. But without a doubt there had been times when I felt that Ross was alive. For instance, why had I not knelt at his 'grave' when Richard took me there? And even if I had no experience of bereavement why had I not felt a more powerful, a more terminal emotion when I thought about Ross?

I sometimes felt my sadness was that of a parent whose child is in exile rather than a parent whose child has died. That is what I think some of the time. But I cannot be sure and that is what I find so exhausting.

Nor can I believe that they kept up that pretence. It is easy enough to accept the explanation Joey gave to Christopher Hunter, that it all got out of control. But wasn't it evil? To do that to anyone, to someone, to me? I simply have to accept that Mother was phenomenally jealous of me, and that I did something to make Joey so hostile. Add greed to that and I can understand anything, but I'm still puzzling it out.

Now I know why Mother never talked about Ross. Now I know why people around here looked at me in a peculiar fashion. I thought all along it was because they didn't want to reactivate my 'madness' or something like that. Now I know why old Greene had been so terrified.

No wonder there was no trace of Ross's clothes or toys – they had all gone with him. Joey's shiftiness – it was greater than I ever expected. My father's repeated attempts to tell me something and my feeling that it had to do with Ross: I wasn't wrong. I remembered Mother's agitation when we had to drive past the little graveyard where Ross was 'buried'. One day soon I am going to put flowers on that little boy's grave.

It's easy enough to understand the other family, the O'Connells. Agnes knows them, says they were always 'a poor and bewildered crowd'. Their sudden wealth was explained by a son in America winning a lot of money on a sweepstake. They probably saw the whole thing as a blessing in compensation for the death of their child.

I'm still not certain how it all worked. Did Mother and Joey stand at the graveside and mourn while the coffin with the other little boy was buried? And did his real family stay at home? I'm sure I'll find it all out one day and get it clear inside my head.

And Richard – he always spoke of 'the little guy gone missing?' Never 'dead'. I asked him did he know and he says he didn't, but that he had heard talk and could find out nothing. If he had told me and then we found it wasn't true, he was afraid I might kill myself.

Kevin brought my father back late that night. I was pottering about near Ross's room so that if he woke he would see me immediately. All day I had been figuring out how to handle it all. I heard Agnes on the phone to Kevin telling him, 'Keep the boss sober.'

I was waiting in the lighted hallway. My father walked towards me as if he expected me to strike him. Instead I gave him the biggest hug the poor man has probably ever had. I wouldn't let him go. He was in a state. I got Agnes to give him his favourite supper, corned beef and potatoes, and I sat while he ate. He never finished it.

'What can you think? What can you think?' he kept saying.

I said, 'I don't know what to think.'

'Do you forgive me?' he asked over and over.

And over and over I said, 'I forgive you completely.' Thank you, Richard.

Then my father became completely overwhelmed with a fit of weeping. I held his hand tight until it finished and asked him what caused it.

He said, 'I have now what I always wanted. I have my only child and my only grandchild near me. But the damage that was done. The damage we did.'

It was one of the few unsentimental things he ever said.

The mind only accepts what it can. The heart has powerful gatekeepers too. I could only think so much. After the practical questions I tried to find answers to a deeper point – Why did this happen to me? My own dishonesty? I like money too. My jealousy? My wish to be better than my family? Oh God, I don't know. No answers come. I still baulk when I ask myself the question, 'How could a mother do that to her daughter?'

But I take the kind view – that they started something reckless and didn't know how to stop it. It snowballed and they got confused. One lie had to cover another, and on and on they went, layers of lies. It is amazing how many people you can get to join you in a lie if the price is right. My head hurts when I consider these things, but I do not like not having answers. They may be supplied by my benefactor, Christopher Hunter. I see him a great deal. As soon as I could I drove out to his house again to thank him and his father.

The English are so strange. Have they no emotions? If I wasn't still so distressed I'd have laughed out loud. When I said to them both that I came to thank them for getting me back my son, they nearly knocked each other down, both saying at the same time, 'I'll make some tea.'

I thought that was only in films and books the English did that.

They are two good-looking men, very alike, each one thin, each jumpy. But they are very nice. They would not let themselves be thanked, it was difficult. They just said, 'Anyone would do the same.'

I was nervous of one thing but I thought I'd better ask. 'Is this all going to appear in your newspaper?'

'Oh, no,' he said a little horrified. 'Not at all.'

I have now taken to inviting Christopher here quite a lot. Ross loves him, feels easier with him than he does with Richard. I think Richard is also a little jealous of Christopher. But Richard is jealous of Santa Claus. My father views Richard with amusement and Richard says American things to him, calls him 'Boss' and 'Big Honcho'.

The English, if the Hunters are anything to go by,

do more thinking than feeling. If I ask Christopher a question he nearly always asks one back and it is often, 'What do you think is the reason for that?'

He doesn't seem like a man who feels any passion. I suppose he has been brought up to believe that passion is undisciplined. He is very quiet, but yet he says a lot.

I had one very good talk with him last week. He is a man I can take into my confidence. I told him that I was the person who had informed on Joey. He knows nothing about the relationship between Joey and me.

'Do you think I did wrong?' I asked him.

He could do with feeding, this Englishman; he is, I think, about twenty years older than me but I don't think he has a clue how to look after himself. I wish I could do something about his clothes.

'Did wrong?' That is something he does. He repeats the key words in a question before he answers it. 'I think wrong is a matter of motive. I think if you did it, say, because you thought people's lives were in danger, that would be no wrong. I think if you did it to gain financially, I think that would be another matter.'

'If I did it for revenge?'

He took a long time to answer. He has a tiny brown mole just below his left nostril. 'I think revenge – or what constitutes revenge – I think that is a matter between you and your God. Who can say that somehow you did not sense that some great good would come about.'

He is kindness itself to me, to Ross, to Richard, to my father when he meets him. I wonder if he is a man who is very troubled inside himself. I often find that to be a characteristic of generous people. His tracking down of an address for Joey in Libya so that Ross could write to his father was a typical example. He has done many such things since.

I get the impression that he has also taken us into his responsibilities. Is this to prevent anything bad happening to us again? He is able to be kind to us without any feeling of the improper. But he'd blush like a beetroot if I said any of this to him and he'd run a mile from us.

His respect for Richard and me as a couple makes me feel married at last. He makes sure we go out of an evening. Not that Richard wants to. And Christopher brings Ross books and things. Last week he gave him a very expensive book about the Book of Kells and talked to him for ages about it.

I have asked people about him. Everybody likes him. They all respect him. He is said to be very good at his job and is often on television. Ross can't wait to see him on the news. One of the Ryans told me his son met someone in England who knew Christopher in school. Apparently he was a champion athlete. Ross asked him and he played it down, changed the subject.

He has no wife and says he never had a wife. But you never know with the English, he might have had four wives. Although I feel he tells the truth. He is not a man who prefers men either. I know that from my own reaction to him. But can you tell that with the English too? He might like both.

I wonder if there are local women interested in him? Mother would have been puzzled by him, might have sneered at his good manners. His manners are such a relief.

Every day, in some way or another, I think about Mother. Yesterday I had an unexpected reminder of her. Lucy O'Connor rang. I thought she might. There was a report in the papers that an agreement had been reached between the Mountgoldens and my father's lawyers.

Basically my father was getting everything back after paying them a hefty whack in compensation.

'The Halpins are rich again,' he said. He can be so crass.

I answered the telephone.

'Oh, ah, Ann, isn't it? Ann, I really meant to ring before now. Poor Moya, we all miss her, but I was away at the time, and indeed I didn't hear for what, a month or so.'

I wanted to say, 'You lying bitch. I saw you in Castlekennedy ten days after the funeral.'

Instead I listened politely. We had some exchanges and I closed the conversation.

'Well, thank you very much for the call. We're a bit tied up here at the moment.'

'So I heard. So I heard – ' and she was about to plunge into the pool for the best gossip she would ever have laid her hands on.

I said, 'And I'm afraid we're not going to be socializing for a long time.'

I am a completely different woman from the Ann Halpin who married Joey Martin and the Ann Martin who bore his son.

59

I have had such pleasure watching Ann and Ross be reunited. At the same time I have been able to observe the social mechanisms of the Irish. They amaze me more and more. Some bizarre parallel exists between the people's inquisitiveness and their secrecy; they wish to know everything possible about their neighbours, yet they accept their neighbours' secrets and guard them. A book could be written about the 'disappearance' of Ross, and yet when he came back to live with Ann, everybody accepted that he had been living in Dublin with his father under some strange arrangement.

Ross has become a pleasant boy; he has his mother's dry sense of humour and is gifted with compassion; he treats Richard Huttle more tenderly than a boy ought to be capable of; and he has as quick a mind as I have known. His return has spread a kind of joy.

Tomorrow is the anniversary and I am planning a party. When I was collecting the groceries in Mooreville today, I had a flashback to that astonishing morning in Desmond Hickey's house (he still asks after my mother). We stood where Ann and Ross could not see us, these three men, and we whispered in wonderment; we knew we were inside a small but momentous event.

Father's authority is such that we all deferred to him, and in those few moments he laid down the pattern for the immediate future, saying Ross must not go to school for that year; there would be time enough for him to catch up on his education, but now the important thing was for mother and son to get to know each other. When I looked, all of us had tears in our eyes; we were embarrassed and we broke up for a moment, then came together again.

What became of the passion I felt all those years? It continues unabated in its force – but the river has gone back underground and to deeper levels, and the surface of my earth is not threatened by it. That evening Father and I went to the hotel for dinner and drank too much; from time to time we lapsed into silence, contemplating what happened.

I think of it all so often and I think of my own difficult pathway – the first days and weeks of desperate feeling, the awful stalking (I shall never tell her), my breakdown, Dr Verne's useless impassiveness, Charles's great force on my behalf, the hard and bloody stories I covered north and south of the Border, the killing of Philip Graves (his parents have left Marlow and gone to live in South Africa), and my coming to terms with Ireland and myself at one and the same time. It is so odd! Three secret burials, first three men, then one man, then one boy – I cannot quite resolve its symbolism. And a boy who never died.

Nothing has fundamentally changed inside me in the matter of what I believe and feel. What is different and more mature is my way of addressing myself. I am less impetuous and less selfish; the long years of undeclared love taught me the value of patience, even though it was forced on me. Now I no longer beg feverishly that Life must make it happen so that Ann lies in my arms as my wife. I am ever content to be her friend; I am as in love with her as before, deeply so. As I have now had the opportunity to love her practically and protectively, I shall continue to do so as long as I live.

They are living here at the moment, she and Ross and Richard. Her father has found someone and Ann wished him to have some privacy, so I suggested that they come and stay here for a while. She and I talk; Ross and I go for walks and we fish; Richard spends most of his time upstairs in bed. Ann and I sit in the living-room, she by the fireside where I had always envisaged her; it had, after all, been prepared for her. When she goes to bed I sit and contemplate my luck; I ask nothing more than what I now have – the fulfilment of being near to a woman I fell in love with a long time ago.

She teases me often. 'Oh, God, you're such an Englishman.' We laugh.

Do I hope one day to marry her? I do not think about that any more. I fear that if I did it would somehow put a pressure on her and I want nothing for her and her son but an untroubled and safe life, and I can help discreetly with that. That she will remain my friend seems a certainty.

'Listen to me,' she said, a phrase she uses very often. 'How can I ever forget the man who gave me back my son? I want you to be part of our lives. But you'll find me very bossy.'

I heard on the car radio this morning – and it felt like the call of a ghost – the statistics for last year. Deaths from the Troubles – 97; bombs and incendiaries planted – 360; explosives discovered – two and a half tons; weapons found – 320. People charged with terrorism – 680. How pleasing that I am no longer a news correspondent; Charles has placed me on a retainer and I have become the paper's 'expert' on all things

Irish. Expert? If the readers only guessed how little I know! I have not yet found a way of conveying that Ireland is best understood through the heart, not the brain.

60

Today I am wearing a red jumper and a black skirt and black patent shoes, not very suitable but it is raining again and I am not going out. The fire is lighting. My father was here this morning. With Nonie. Agnes smiles when Nonie is mentioned.

'You always said, Ann, he'd find a widow.'

I like Nonie. She is not one of the old crowd and my father seems to have shed most of them.

We came to stay here for a while when Nonie appeared on the scene. We never left. Christopher built a tree house, a full, complete tree house in the big beech. Ross and Christopher slept in it the first night it was completed.

Ross grows like a young tree himself. In the last year he has grown four inches. I look at him every day and I marvel. His accent is straightening out. When he came back to me he spoke so flatly. How can I have had such a bonus?

My great fear now is that anything might happen to him, an accident or something. Christopher says life is not like that. That is the other great bonus, the presence of Christopher. He has in many ways held us all together. So quiet, so thoughtful; he never imposes.

I learn so much from him. Ross calls him 'the encyclopaedia', says, 'We'll ask the encyclopaedia.'

Christopher has taught me as much about painters and music as I ever wanted to learn back in the days when I wanted to be the most refined girl in the world. And about Ireland – he knows more about our history and archaeology than I ever did. He speaks four languages and reads two more. You have to quarry him to find out such things about him.

But, God, if You're listening, why do I only know men who can't look after themselves? Joey couldn't wash a cup. Christopher has holes in his shoes. At the risk of being bossy I have to remind him to get them repaired. Look at what happened to Richard who wouldn't let me boss him. I must go upstairs soon and change his pillows.

In the last month Richard has become very weak. The emphysema tightens and tightens and he breathes like an ancient horse. He can speak very little now and I am distressed by my feelings of inevitability. Dr Butler says Richard has poor resistance to illness.

I noticed when he stopped taking part in conversations. The last time we talked at any length he was explaining to me that Desmond Hickey was power-mad.

'Doll, that's why he made you go to his house. That's why he didn't tell you to your face when he came to see you. He wanted to run the situation.' Richard my guru. 'It doesn't matter,' he was saying to me – and he ran out of breath like a train crashing.

If that had happened two years ago I'd have gone crazy with worry. Now I feel the pain of what is going to happen but I am taking it well. I have to; I have to look after Ross.

Christopher reads to Richard at night. He takes a book from these grand, full bookshelves. It may be poetry. It may be history. Ross and I listen too. Sometimes Ross holds Richard's hand.

All this week Christopher has been reading us poems by Samuel Taylor Coleridge. For the last three weeks he read us the biography of Robert Louis Stevenson and before that he had been getting Ross to read *Treasure Island* and *Kidnapped*.

If I didn't have the pain of Richard's condition, this would be like a dream come true. Around us at night is the stillness of the woods and inside this house, once my grandfather's, we are secure. Richard, who used to be so wild, whispers to me how happy he is. Whatever name I give it, this is a family.

Agnes said to me once, 'I bet they're all talking about you.'

'Let them talk,' I said.

But I agree. We must seem unconventional. Outlandish to some. Immoral. Richard and Christopher and me. All under the same roof. With Ross. The parish priest calls to see us. We entertain him well. He never comments. He can't. I know the woman he visits, Mrs English, a widow. He's very friendly with her.

I tease Richard that Father Cregan is going to bless him. Richard uses what little energy he has to make warding-off, Dracula gestures.

My father has begun by taking a leaf out of my book. Nonie lives with him. I asked him were they going to marry.

He grinned. 'Girl, try anything once. After that the odds gets bad.' But he'll marry her. No, she'll marry him, Nonie is no fool.

They go to some race meeting or other every week. He looks so well it makes my heart sing.

Sometimes I wake at night and I can remember just

412

one thing. I can remember feeling the pulse in my neck beat against Ross's face the day he came back to me.

It has been a difficult time for us, no denying that. Ross had to cope with what happened to him. And to me. We did not seek help. We did it ourselves. Although his account of his loneliness and bewilderment nearly broke my heart.

I coped by working out what happened. The idea was that Ross be passed off as Josephine Scannell's son. Joey would marry her, he promised, after the annulment. He did. Oh, well, it is all over now and even scar tissue can disappear in time.

Have I forgiven Joey? Only insofar as I must have regard for him as Ross's father. In fairness Joey writes to Ross and rings him. I have not forgiven Josephine Scannell. I never will.

As for Mother. Mother is dead and I cannot begin to know how the dead get forgiven.

Most of the financial damage has been undone. I am secure for life. Ross is secure forever. My father is in partnership with Nicky Crosbie and they are having a grand time.

I hear Richard coughing again. His coughs have become so weak. I will go upstairs and cradle his head. My poor Richard. He will never go into a hospital. He doesn't want to and I won't let him. I hold him in my arms every night.

We have an oxygen feeder coming for him tomorrow. Christopher says he will learn how it works. When I ask Dr Butler what is the next phase of emphysema he says that nobody can ever say, but I sense that he is being tactful. Christopher knows – but he would never give his opinion. It is so kind of Christopher to have Richard live here.

However, I have spent a lot of time trying to find out what will happen. It is callous of me to think like this. That is what the loss and return of Ross did to me. It made me practical in a callous way. I am like an animal now about my son and his future, therefore I have to know what is going to happen and as I fear the worst I have resolved what I am going to do.

Richard is going to die. When I know his last illness has begun I will climb into bed and lie beside him naked, holding him. Seeing him safely through. Nothing and nobody will stop me doing that. When he dies I will be holding him tight along the length of my body and thanking him for what he gave me. I will be sending him on his way with the warmest love I can find in me.

And then, when the time is right, I will propose marriage to Christopher. He will probably be startled out of his wits, but I don't think he will refuse me, he is too polite. I do not know how he feels about me but I get an odd inkling – especially from his anxiety about me – that he might have feelings for me. It is so hard to tell with people, especially with him. But he would not have us here if he hated me, would he?

I may have a difficult time with him; I don't mind. He is a nervous man and I think I will have to teach him about passion. But I will enjoy that.

And my new name will be the one with which I will live the rest of my life. I will be called 'Hunter', not 'Halpin' nor 'Martin' – I was never known as 'Huttle', Richard didn't want that. And I will be 'Ann', perhaps even 'darling', that is a word the English use well. I will never again have to be called 'Doll' which I always liked but it will ever be Richard's name for me. Above all I will never again be 'Sugar'. No.

Ross tends Richard's pavilion. He cycles there on Saturdays, and reports back to Richard, tells him how everything flourishes – the greengages, the blackberries, the wild flowers, the honeysuckle.

The Amethysts

Frank Delaney

An astonishing psychological thriller
of great force and pace

The Amethysts is a novel of intense power. Frank Delaney uncovers the roots of a great twentieth-century evil through the fractured vision of Nicholas Newman, successful architect and Modern Man. The brutal murder of his lover proves to have a meaning so profound that it dramatically alters Newman's whole life. New values forced upon his consciousness become the central issues in a riveting novel which draws the reader to the disturbing conclusion, 'Sometimes only the unspeakable teaches us how to love.'

'The fusillade of shocks, and the crescendo of menace and confusion are contrived brilliantly. Frank Delaney's new novel cannot fail . . . inescapably gripping and sinisterly erotic . . . the pace rarely flags. *The Amethysts* is taut, tense and full of threatening emotional power.'
Daily Telegraph

'Delaney effortlessly hooks the reader . . . This mix of John Fowles-cum-Ian McEwan turns flammable.'
Guardian

'A compelling novel, written with pace, verve and imagination.'
Mail on Sunday

'A psychological thriller as harrowing as it is absorbing . . . powerful, almost poetic prose style . . . always intense, emotional and uninhibited. This novel may prove unforgettable.'
Sunday Telegraph

'An unusually sophisticated thriller . . . elegantly written and compellingly plotted.'
Sunday Times

'The action pans across Europe with pace and verve, but all the time resonant with dark undertones . . . gripping.'
The Times

ISBN 0 00 649952 X